THIRD IN THE 'HEART OF STONE' SAGA

Legacy *of* Van Diemen's Land

SHELAGH MAZEY

Matador
9 Priory Business Park,
Wistow Road, Kibworth Beauchamp,
Leicestershire. LE8 0RX
Tel: (+44) 116 279 2299
Fax: (+44) 116 279 2277
Email: books@troubador.co.uk
Web: www.troubador.co.uk/matador

ISBN 978 1784623 067

British Library Cataloguing in Publication Data.
A catalogue record for this book is available from the British Library.

Printed and bound in the UK by TJ International, Padstow, Cornwall
Typeset in Baskerville by Troubador Publishing Ltd, Leicester, UK

Matador is an imprint of Troubador Publishing Ltd

Together we kissed the Blarney Stone
For my good friend and mentor
Margaret

TABLE OF CONTENTS

CAST   xi

THE PROLOGUE   xvii
(September 1854)

CHAPTER ONE   1
THE NEW BRIDE AND THE BRIDEWELLS
(September 1854)

CHAPTER TWO   15
ABOARD THE ADELAIDE
(September – December 1854)

CHAPTER THREE   29
THE ANGEL OF HEAVEN'S GATE
(June 1855 – June 1857)

CHAPTER FOUR   42
ANGELS AND DEVILS
(June – December 1855)

CHAPTER FIVE   56
NINESPRINGS AND OFFSPRINGS
(April 1856)

CHAPTER SIX   72
TEA AND STRUMPETS
(June – July 1856)

CHAPTER SEVEN   90
ALMS FOR THE POOR HOUSE
(August 1856)

CHAPTER EIGHT   108
A HINT AT PATERNITY
(November – December 1856)

CHAPTER NINE   119
PADDY AND O'MALLEY
(July 1857)

CHAPTER TEN   132
SOMERSET FLOODS AND
   BENDIGO BUSHFIRES
(November – December 1857)

CHAPTER ELEVEN   150
UP IN ARMS
(January – September 1858)

CHAPTER TWELVE   175
NEW PASTURES
(September 1858 – October 1860)

CHAPTER THIRTEEN   193
CHASING RAINBOWS
(January 1861)

CHAPTER FOURTEEN   205
A CHARABANC SURPRISE
(August 1861)

CHAPTER FIFTEEN   217
EARLY TICKET OF LEAVE
(October – December 1861)

CHAPTER SIXTEEN   232
GONE WALK ABOUT
(September – November 1862)

CHAPTER SEVENTEEN   246
OVER THE BESOM BROOM
(November 1862 – November 1863)

CHAPTER EIGHTEEN   257
THE HOMECOMING
(June 1863 – October 1864)

CHAPTER NINETEEN   275
A MESSAGE FROM MILLIE
(November – December 1864)

CHAPTER TWENTY   288
GHOSTS OF THE PAST
(June – July 1865)

CHAPTER TWENTY-ONE   300
NEW ARRIVALS
(July 1865 – May 1866)

CHAPTER TWENTY-TWO   316
WEDDING BELLS AND MERMAID TAILS
(May 1866)

CHAPTER TWENTY-THREE   334
POETIC JUSTICE
(May 1866)

THE EPILOGUE   353
(June – October 1866)

HISTORICAL FOOTNOTE   357
APOLOGIES   359
ACKNOWLEDGEMENTS   361

LIST OF CHARACTERS

THE DRYER FAMILY
ALVINGTON MANOR
LORD JOSHUA DRYER (1832)
LADY LOUISA DRYER (1833)
AURORA DRYER (1851)
GABRIEL DRYER (1855)

ALVINGTON MANOR STAFF
GARETH WILLIAMS (1798) *Butler/House steward*
MICHAEL PORTER (1800) *Footman*
JOHN MOORE (1827) *Groom*
BILLY RIDDICK (1832) *Stable boy*
PERCY SANDFORD (1810) *Gardener*
THOMAS HAWKINS (1831) *Gardener*
HENRY HODINOTT (1820) *Handyman*
JOHN BOUCHER (1809) *Gamekeeper*
RAYMOND HAWKINS (1832) *Gamekeeper*
MRS ABBOTT (1802) *Housekeeper*
FLORA BOUCHER (1810) *Cook*
ROSA WARREN (1825) *Lady's maid*
LETTIE BOUCHER (1838) *Chambermaid*
EMILY POTTS (1837) *Housemaid*
RUTH PROCTOR (1820) *Assistant cook*
ELSIE HALL (1833) *Kitchen maid*
HARRIETT PROCTOR (1844) *Scullery maid*
CHARLOTTE HODINOTT (1827) *Laundress*
BETH PUDDY (**1835**) *Nanny*
GRACE TWEEDY (1821) *Governess*

THE WARREN FAMILY
HAMLET COTTAGE
MALACHI (1825) & ROSA (1825) WARREN
SIBLINGS: RUBY (1856), ELI (1858) & DAISY (1861)

THE WARREN FAMILY
HOME FARM
GRANNY WARREN (1768)
ISAAC (1792) & ELIZABETH (1795) WARREN
SIBLINGS: JACOB (1830),
LUCY (1836) & BEATRICE (BUNNY) (1844)

PORTLANDERS FEATURED IN BRANDY ROW
MATTHEW STONE (1811) *Joshua's stepfather*
VIOLET STONE (1814) *Joshua's mother*
REBECCA STONE (1838) *Joshua's sister*
BENJAMIN STONE (1832) *Joshua's cousin*
ANNIE STONE ne SHADDICK (1810) *Ben's mother*

CAMP ROAD FAMILIES – ESTATE WORKERS
BERT (1773) & ROSE (1783) SMITH (*Retired*)
MICHAEL (1800) & MAUD (1802) PORTER
HENRY (1820) & CHARLOTTE (1827) HODINOTT
JOHN (1827) & SUSAN (1831) MOORE
SIBLINGS: LUKE (1851) & LILLY (1853)
PERCY (1810) & MARY (1812) SANDFORD
SIBLINGS: ROBERT (1830) & HARRY (1833)
JACK (1805) & MOLLY (1802) HAWKINS
SIBLINGS: FRANK (1823) & THOMAS (1831)

THE BOUCHER FAMILY
KEEPER'S COTTAGE, POUND LANE
JOHN (1809) & FLORA (1810) BOUCHER
SIBLINGS: LETTIE (1838) & TOBY (1846)

THE BONFIELD FAMILY
KNAPP COTTAGE, PRESTON PLUCKNET
ARTHUR (1808) & MARTHA (1813) BONFIELD

THE TOMPKINS FAMILY
MR & MRS TOMPKINS
SIBLINGS: BOBBY (1835) & HARRY (1834)

THE HAWKINS FAMILY
COBB COTTAGE, DRAY ROAD, ODCOMBE
MRS ESTHER (1805) HAWKINS
SIBLINGS: JEAN (1831) & RAYMOND (1832)

THE MEAKINS FAMILY
SUMMERVILLE HOUSE
SIR OLIVER (1793) & LADY ANNABEL (1797) MEAKINS
SIBLINGS: OLIVIA (1813) & NATHAN (1818)
AGNES (1860)

SUMMERVILLE HOUSE STAFF
ALISTAIR MCNAB (1802) *Scottish steward*
MORTON (1813) *Butler*
WADMAN (1818) *First footman*
MRS FAVERSHAM (1799) *Housekeeper*
APSEY (1823) *Olivia Meakins' Lady's maid*
MRS CHUBB (1807) *Cook*

THE BRIDEWELL FAMILY
CLIFTON MAYBANK MANOR
SAMUEL (1791) & EDITH (1795) BRIDEWELL
SIBLINGS: SERENA (1820), KEZIAH (1822)
& ALICIA (1824)

THE PROCTOR FAMILY
RUTH PROCTOR (1820)
SIBLINGS: AMY (1838), EDWIN (1841)
HATTIE (1844) & ELLIE (1848)

RESIDENTS OF SANDHURST
MR & MRS BRUNSVOLD *Emporium*
FREYJA BRUNSVOLD (1837) *Emporium*
JETHRO TULLY *Landlord Eureka Hotel*
RAY CLARK & BRUCE MADDEN *Ranchers*
ZHANG WEI *Chinese headman*
TIAN *Chinaman*

TRANSPORTS
NATHAN MEAKINS (1818)
SAMUEL KELLY (1836)
JOSIAH JONES (1800)
HUGH DAVIES (1808)
BRYN THOMAS (1812)
REG LEWIS (1814)
ANGELICA PITMAN (1834)

THE FAIRWAY FAMILY
CHURCH COTTAGE, STAIRS HILL, YEOVIL
AMBROSE FAIRWAY (1804) *Solicitor's clerk*
DAUGHTER: CLARA (1834)

THE DAVIES FAMILY
HUGH (1808) & SARAH (1811) DAVIES
SIBLINGS: LEWYS (1836) & GWYNETH (1839)

THE THOMAS FAMILY
BRYN (1812) & NELL (1814) THOMAS
SIBLINGS: OWEN (1837) & RHYS (1839)

ABORIGINES
MATARI
PINDARI
KAORA
CAMIRA
AMAROO

SUPPORTING CHARACTERS
SERGEANT GUNDRY
DR GILLINGHAM
DR JESSOP
LORD AND LADY HELYAR *of Coker Court*
COL AND MRS SEYMOUR *of Sutton Bingham Manor*
SIBLINGS: RUPERT (1823) & ASHLEIGH (1827)
MR & MRS WIGGLESWORTH *Coker Poor House*

ALBERT TATTERSHALL *Workhouse inmate*
WILLIAM BELL *Owner of Catkin Mill*
FRED BURNS *Prison warder*
MR & MRS STACE *Angelica's Employers*
AUNTIE SARAH GIBBS *Midwife and herbalist*

MENAGERIE

Hercules, Perseus – *Shire horses (brown)*
Capricorn – *Josh's horse (black stallion)*
Andromeda *(brown),* Cassiopeia *(grey)* & Capella *(bay)*
Honey – *John Boucher's Springer Spaniel*
Paddy and O'Malley – *Irish Wolfhounds*

SKETCH MAP OF VAN DIEMEN'S LAND
CIRCA 1850's
SHOWING THE ROUTE OF THE MAIN ROAD
CONSTRUCTED WITH CONVICT LABOUR

Flinders
Island

BASS STRAIT

Cape Grim

Cape Portland

Banks Strait

Port Dalrymple

George Town

Launceston

Evandale
Perth
Norfolk Plains

Campbell Town

Ross

Anthill Ponds
Oatlands

Oyster
Bay

Macquarie Harbour

INDIAN
OCEAN

Kempton

Pontville

Mt Wellington

Hobart Town

Richmond

Sorrell
Seven Mile
Beach

Maria
Island

Dunalley

Saltwater
River

Pirates Bay
Eaglehawk Neck

The Tasman
Peninsular

Port Arthur

Port Davey

S
t
o
r
m

B
a
y

Derwent
River

PACIFIC
OCEAN

THE PROLOGUE *(September 1854)*

Nathan Meakins is being led up the wooden stairs and onto the platform of the gallows. His hands are tied behind his back and his leg-irons are chafing his ankles. He is halted below the gibbet and feels the material of the black hood placed over his head. He trembles as the darkness enfolds him. The perspiration runs down his face beneath the black cloth. The weight of the coarse thick rope being placed around his neck is numbing. He is petrified. How could his life of leisure and privilege end up like this? A religious man is mumbling text from the Bible and finally he hears the mechanism of the trap opening. Suddenly his stomach turns as he is falling… falling.

He awakes with a jolt. Drenched in perspiration, his heart is leaping wildly. The pungent smell of the bodies packed tightly around him and the lack of fresh air, reminds him that he did in fact escape the noose and he is now lying in the hold of the transportation ship; relief washes over him. His situation is barely an improvement, but at least there is a slim chance he will survive this indignity.

Many of the prisoners are yet to get their sea legs and the lingering smell of vomit is evident and turns his stomach. The regular sound of men snoring and the loud creaking of the fabric of the ship are interrupted by the bugle call at 5.30 a.m. Meakins eases his ankles where the shackles have been rubbing him raw. They were only struck off once they were well out at sea and he is acutely aware that any insubordination will result in them being replaced. He dresses in his raven duck overalls, his jacket and woollen hat.

The warders enter and the men shuffle off to their assignments. Some of them are set to scrubbing and swabbing the decks, some to dry holy-stoning, but Meakins is tasked with his mess group of eight men to picking oakum and they remain below. He hates the smell of the tar-soaked cordage, his fingers become coated in the amber-coloured pitch and increasingly sore from unravelling the fibrous threads. Eventually he hears the eight-bells and joins the men queuing for their breakfast. It is gruel and biscuits and half a pint of cocoa. Beggars can't be choosers and he swallows the unappetising food, rather than go without.

After their meagre meal they are given different assignments and this time Meakins' group is taken above and tasked with polishing ring bolts and dry holy-stoning the more inaccessible areas about the masts and guns. The pensioner guards keep vigil, with the cat-o'-nine-tails handy, lest any gang should take it into their heads to mutiny. They are down on their hands and knees like dogs, using the smaller, flat stones called prayer-books, sliding them about to and fro over the wet and sanded decks.

Not used to any form of manual work he suffers more than most with aches and pains. His back is hurting, his knees are red and inflamed and his fingers are still sore from the oakum. *This is galley-slave work!* A taunting image of the pompous Lord Joshua Dryer sitting in comfort at his mahogany desk, surrounded by his damned legal books, enters his mind. *I swear to God I will make sure that he pays, one way or another, for his dogged persecution of me!*

CHAPTER ONE *(September 1854)*

THE NEW BRIDE AND THE BRIDEWELLS

When Lord Joshua Dryer and his new wife Louisa return from their honeymoon, both looking very stylish in the latest Paris fashion, their employees are assembled outside to welcome them home. Louisa lowers her head slightly as she descends from the carriage, to avoid disturbing the artificial flowers decorating her new bonnet; she smoothes her matching purple gown and adjusts the flounced cape jacket, decorated with a printed border of pale lilac daisies. Joshua takes her arm and she looks up, appreciatively, into his warm, dark eyes. She is very proud of her handsome husband dressed so fashionably in his tall black hat; smart dark-blue, cut-away morning coat; grey trousers, sky-blue necktie and multihued blue waistcoat, that she chose for him herself.

They are greeted warmly by Gareth the head butler, Mrs Abbott the housekeeper, and the remainder of the staff, all lined up in the September sunshine; the male servants bowing and the females dipping their curtseys. Louisa is delighted to see that Mrs Abbott has Aurora held tightly by the hand, but she calls out "Mama!", pulls loose, and rushes forward to hug her, excitedly.

Joshua then picks her up and throws her into the air and she squeals with pleasure. "Again, Papa! Again!"

Mrs Abbott makes a short welcoming speech and

afterwards the members of domestic staff, all smiling happily, disperse back to their chores. Louisa joins her husband, who has Aurora held safely in his arms, as they follow the staff into their home.

There is a huge arrangement of fresh flowers on the round table in the centre of the hall and the room is full of the distinctive, spicy scent of the chrysanthemums. On the side table, Louisa spots a pile of calling cards in the silver salver, but decides to go through them later, after taking tea in the oak with Joshua and Aurora.

That evening, whilst seated in the drawing room, Louisa sifts through the pile of cards. There is one from Serena Bridewell inviting her to attend afternoon tea at Clifton Maybank Manor and she is pleased to see that all the other cards have their top right-hand corner folded over, thankfully meaning that local folk are happy to offer their congratulations on her marriage.

"Look Josh, all these cards are congratulating us. I'm so relieved. I was afraid that being a lowly chambermaid before you proposed to me, I would be shunned. I had convinced myself that I would never be accepted as Lady Louisa Dryer."

"Have no fear, my love; I always knew that because you are modest and genteel they would accept you very quickly. If you were bold and brazen it might have been a different matter."

He laughs at her indignant expression at this notion. "I do know how you feel, for, was I not in the same position when I first came to Alvington? I well remember feeling very uneasy and out of my depth, but I soon got used to it and so shall you. Fate has decreed that we're meant to be together, my darling, and so we shall always be." He kisses her head affectionately.

As he sits down beside her, she looks up from the pile of cards. "Joshua, I have a mind to ask Rosa to be my lady's maid. What do you think?" She watches his expression as he considers for a moment.

"I think that is a very good plan, for you need to have someone with whom you are relaxed and happy to share your most private moments. Shall I ring for her, so that you can ask her immediately?"

"Yes, please do."

Joshua stands up and goes to tug on the bell-pull.

Louisa ponders, "This does mean, though, that if she agrees we'll have to think of someone to replace her as our parlour maid."

"Yes, that's true… perhaps Jean Hawkins would like the position?" says Joshua considering. "I believe that was her post at the Meakins' residence."

She closes her eyes and takes a deep breath, "Please don't remind me of that obnoxious fellow, Josh; besides I had heard that Jean is now working in one of the glove factories."

"I'm sorry, my darling, I didn't mean to upset you." He is at her side in a moment, kissing her gently on her forehead. "I assure you, my dear, you don't have to worry about Meakins anymore, for he is well on his way to the Antipodes by now."

"Thank the Lord."

She is relieved when her husband quickly changes the subject, "Well then, how about Lettie? I think that Toby is now going to school and Lettie would fit in here very well, with her mama being the cook, and her papa the gamekeeper."

She nods in agreement, "That's a good suggestion, my dear."

"In that case I'll go and ask Flora if she thinks Lettie would be interested, while you talk to Rosa." Joshua goes off purposefully towards the kitchen.

Moments later, Rosa knocks and enters. "You

rang, milady." As she dips in a curtsey she is smiling. It is the first time she has called Louisa that.

Louisa smiles back, "I did, Rosa. I have something I would like you to consider. Please, take a seat a moment."

Rosa sits down in the chair indicated. "After working all this time together, Rosa, I feel that you and I have become true friends. I wouldn't wish to do anything that may jeopardise our friendship, but I would like you to consider becoming my lady's maid."

"Oh! Milady, I'd be delighted. Why should it spoil our friendship, it is after all an advancement?"

"Oh! Rosa, I hoped you'd say that. I'm so pleased. It will be less hard work for you and you'll be able to put your artistic talents to good use, when attending to my hair and my costumes. You always appear immaculate and I know that you read well and you can sew beautifully. In addition it will mean a further ten pounds a year, on top of your current salary."

"That will certainly be much appreciated now that I too am a married woman. I will love it, milady. When do I start?"

"Tomorrow morning would be good for me, Rosa. You can come and help me retrieve all my personal possessions from the Dower House."

"Very well, milady."

"Next Wednesday I would like you to accompany me on a visit to Clifton Maybank Manor where I'm to take tea with Serena and Alicia Bridewell. I'm sure you'll enjoy the ride out. John Moore will take us and you'll be able to join their staff downstairs, for they will provide tea for you too."

"Thank you, milady, I'll look forward to that."

"Another thing, Rosa; I thought you might prefer

it if, when we're alone together, you continue to call me Louisa? You only need to say 'milady' when there are others around, to observe the formalities."

"I'm afraid I may get confused if I do that, milady. I believe it would be better for me to think of it as your new name."

"As you wish, my friend, but I don't want you to feel that I'm lording it over you."

"I know you better than that, milady." She smiles affectionately.

"That's settled then."

"May I just say, milady, that I'm very pleased to have you and His Lordship back home again. The house has not been the same without you. We've all missed you very much and Miss Aurora has been quite desolate."

"Well, a month is a long time in the life of a three-year-old, but it hasn't stopped her asking us, 'when will we be going again?' when we gave her the little Paris outfits that we purchased for her at *Le' Bon Marché*!"

They both laugh.

Louisa says, "Right then, Rosa, I'll look forward to seeing you first thing tomorrow when we will sort out the Dower House together."

Rosa gets up to leave. She dips a curtsey, "Very well, milady. Thank you again for my promotion. I can't wait to tell Malachi; he'll be so proud."

The following morning Rosa brings up a breakfast tray for her at eight o'clock. She draws back the curtains and plumps her pillows.

"This looks very tasty, Rosa. Please thank Flora for me."

"I will, milady."

They chat whilst Rosa prepares her mistress's

clothes for the day, and Louisa enjoys her breakfast. "Was Malachi pleased when you told him of your new position?"

"Of course, milady, he was delighted; an extra ten pounds a year will make a big difference to us, and he's glad to know how much I'm appreciated."

"Joshua and I know you both to be hard-working, indispensable members of the estate staff, but to us you are even more valuable as our friends."

Rosa smiles, "Thank you, milady, you're very kind."

"I mean it, Rosa, Malachi is the closest Joshua has to a brother around here, and I would be lost without you."

"We indeed feel very fortunate to have you as our employers, milady. But if you'll excuse me, I'll just go now to fetch some hot water for you to wash."

Her breakfast finished, Louisa lies back and stretches languidly, enjoying her surroundings, revelling in her new luxurious life as mistress of Alvington Manor. The large mahogany four-poster bed is festooned with burgundy drapes and the plump, swansdown mattress is pure indulgence, as it softly moulds to her body. Opposite the bed is the fireplace. The fire that was lit by Emily Potts at seven o'clock, before Joshua arose to go about his business, is flickering cosily. Her hairbrush and French perfume and other personal creams and lotions are set out on the mahogany duchess dressing table, but the commode, washstand and bowl are cleverly concealed behind a Japanese six-leaf, hand-painted silk screen.

Rosa returns with the ewer of hot water and fills the bowl in the washstand for Louisa to wash herself. "Thank you, Rosa. While I wash, would you mind taking away the breakfast things?"

"Of course, milady."

As soon as Rosa has left the room, Louisa is out

of bed and attending to her ablutions. She would prefer to be alone and intends to have her undergarments on before Rosa returns, to save herself, or Rosa, any embarrassment. On Rosa's return she helps Louisa on with her gown and dresses her hair, ready for the day.

It is ten o'clock by the time they are entering the Dower House. So much has happened since she last slept there. Her maid's attire is still hanging in the closet and she turns to Rosa, "Would you like a couple of spare outfits, Rosa?"

"Yes, that would be very useful, milady. Thank you."

They remove the costumes and fold them up on the bed, ready for Rosa to take away with her. Then they collect the rest of Louisa's belongings. Things like her hairbrush, her rouge and hair combs, she had already taken with her when she left for her honeymoon, but there is some underwear and bottom-drawer items and they are soon busy bundling it all together to go back to the house. As they work, Louisa discovers the long white lace gloves and her dancing slippers that Joshua bought for her, for their first ball at Alvington Manor. She smiles, remembering how Becky had joked with her, 'You have the gloves and the dancing shoes, now all you need is a gown to go with them!' *Well, thanks to my generous husband, I now have many wonderful, colourful, gowns to go with these, in silks and satins, decorated with lace and ribbons, all fit for a queen.*

She shows her find to Rosa, "Look at these Rosa, remember how we had to borrow Clara's gowns?" She smiles at her friend, "So much has happened to us since then, we're both married for one thing, and I feel so blessed to have found such happiness."

"Me too, milady. Our lives have certainly changed for the better."

"How are you and Malachi getting along? You've been married for four months now; is it all that you hoped it would be?"

"Oh yes, milady. I truly couldn't want for a better husband. You wouldn't think that such a big, strong, bare-knuckle boxer could be so gentle and thoughtful. We really are very happy, milady."

"I'm so pleased for you, Rosa."

"How about you, milady, was Paris all you hoped it would be?"

"Much more so, Rosa; Joshua too is very gentle and caring, but he has obviously learned a lot from his travels and from the talk of the sailors on the missionary ship, for he has enlightened me with the most ardent loving and I have learnt that there is far more to making love than the missionary position!"

Rosa looks aghast at her friend at this intimacy and then suddenly they are both laughing like in the old days, holding their stomachs, their sides aching and Louisa knows that she has chosen her lady's maid well.

That evening, Joshua is sitting at his desk penning a letter to his mother, when Louisa comes looking for him. "Ah, there you are! What's keeping you? Rosa tells me that supper is served."

"I'm just letting Mama know that we're home safely. I've nearly finished, would you like me to read it to you?"

"Yes, I would." She looks over his shoulder as he puts down his quill.

"Dearest Mama,

We are home at last after our marvellous Paris honeymoon. We had a wonderful time, strolling along wide, tree-lined avenues and admiring the French architecture.

8

We ate superb meals in small, intimate Parisian cafés and meandered along the Seine looking at the work of the artisans. The Louvre and the Tuileries Palace were magnificent to behold and we spent hours looking at Renaissance artwork right up to modern times. We saw there the marble statue of the Venus de Milo and Leonardo da Vinci's, Mona Lisa.

On the third day we took a ride with other sightseers in a horse-drawn charabanc and stood, hand in hand, underneath the Arc de Triomphe. Later, with our tour guide, we admired the beautiful architecture of Notre Dame Cathedral with its amazingly vivid blue, purple and red stained-glass windows.

I took Louisa shopping in the most fashionable part of the city and she has come home with some delightful costumes. I tell you, Mama, I could not be happier. I do believe I am a very fortunate man to have found myself such a wonderful companion in Louisa.

Aurora has been a perfect little darling, according to Mrs Abbott, but she was so pleased to see us on our return, she nearly bowled us over in her haste to greet us.

I hope that all is well with you and Pa, and Ben and Becky.

Your affectionate son,
Joshua."

"That's a very nice letter, darling. We did have a wonderful time, didn't we?" Louisa kisses her husband on the top of his head.

He turns swiftly and pulls her onto his lap. "It was more magical than I imagined in all my wildest dreams, my love," he says, squeezing her affectionately. He wraps her in his arms and kisses her passionately.

She feels her body responding to his ardour and for a moment she is lost in the magic, but now is not the time. With regret, she gently draws away. "I suppose we had better hurry down for our supper, otherwise we will be in trouble with Flora."

"You are, of course, right my dear. Besides, it's not long until I have you all to myself."

Both Rosa and Louisa are excited to be visiting the Bridewells at Clifton Maybank. Louisa is wearing an attractive peacock-blue watered-silk costume that Joshua purchased for her in Paris, which he said at the time looked marvellous with her rich red hair; however, she is a little tense, anxious that she will not do anything to let her husband down.

On their arrival Rosa is taken downstairs with their parlour maid and Louisa is shown into the drawing room. It is a warm, well-lit room with tall transom windows overlooking well-tended gardens, and a stream and meadows beyond. As she enters, Mrs Bridewell is sewing a tapestry in the light from one of the windows, Serena is playing the spinet and Alicia is singing.

Mrs Bridewell quickly casts aside her work. The ladies all stand and curtsey.

"How lovely to see you, Louisa; did you have a wonderful time in Paris?" she asks. Her two daughters join her to sit cosily with Louisa around the lively, flickering fire.

Louisa feels self-conscious, aware of her hands fidgeting in her lap, but she thinks of Joshua and speaks up confidently. "We did, Mrs Bridewell. What a beautiful city it is. There was so much to see and do and Joshua was so generous and attentive. He took me to the Louvre and we saw many amazing paintings. My favourites were the deeply colourful Renaissance paintings by Raphael, Michelangelo and Leonardo da Vinci including *The Virgin and Child with Saint Anne* and the *Mona Lisa*." She smiles at the ladies, reliving the wonderful experience she had shared with her husband. "We went to Notre Dame Cathedral, took a boat trip on the Seine and saw much of Paris from an open-top charabanc."

"It sounds very exciting, Louisa," says Alicia with her usual enthusiasm. "Are the ladies really as fashionable as they say?"

She does not consider herself to be an experienced judge in this matter, but she replies diplomatically, "Well, I believe like everywhere, there are fashionable areas and poorer ones, but they certainly are very stylish."

"Have you caught up with all the news since your return?" asks Serena.

"Probably not, this is my first social engagement so I'm quite ready for your best parlour gossip." She smiles at the three women expectantly.

Alicia then volunteers, "Well, I suppose you know that my ex-fiancé has been transported to Van Diemen's Land for life."

The smile fades. "Yes, Lord Dryer told me on the day after our return."

"Serves him right, the villain! Everyone is glad to see the back of the rogue," says Serena vehemently.

"Apart from his family, of course," says Mrs Bridewell sagely.

Serena's face softens, "That is true. It must have been a dreadful shock for his parents and poor Olivia."

Although aware that she has to be diplomatic in all her social engagements, Louisa cannot suppress her indignation that Serena should be concerned for Olivia, who did nothing to stop her brother committing such a heinous crime. "I don't know about *'poor Olivia'*, she was just as involved as he was! Despite her plea of post-natal insanity," she says, rather indignantly.

"I understand what you're saying, Louisa," says Mrs Bridewell, politely. "Nevertheless, his whole family must be very hurt by his behaviour." She smiles at her, adding, "We tend to live for our children, don't we?"

Louisa feels a wave of nausea and heat coming over her, "Normal folk do, Mrs Bridewell, but unfortunately he is the exception. He was, after all, actually capable of murdering his own baby son!"

Serena interjects diplomatically, "I'm afraid Mama has someone else playing on her mind at present, Louisa, for we have had some disturbing news of Keziah."

Mrs Bridewell looks upset and tearful, "Yes, my dear, we have had the most dreadful tidings, for next month Florence Nightingale is planning to take a number of her nurses, including our dear Keziah, with her to Sebastopol to help nurse the soldiers in the Crimean War. Apparently they are not only dying from their wounds, but also from mortal diseases such as typhus, cholera and dysentery. Miss Nightingale believes that with good nursing practice they will be able to make a difference." Her voice breaks, "Unhappily, we're left behind worrying about Keziah and the terrible danger in which she has placed herself." She takes a handkerchief from her reticule and dabs at her eyes.

Serena attempts to console her, "Please don't distress yourself, Mama, you know it is what she wanted; all we can do is pray for her safety, the same for all of them and, of course, our poor soldiers."

Louisa says gently, "She's a very brave person, Mrs Bridewell, you must be very proud of her?"

Mrs Bridewell appears mollified, "Oh, we are, my dear. If only it wasn't such a worry."

Louisa tries to allay her fears, "I'm quite sure, Mrs Bridewell, that Florence Nightingale will not put her nurses into any military danger. They'll be in a field hospital far away from the battlefields, and as far as these appalling diseases are concerned, I'm quite sure they're all used to caring for the sick at St Thomas' Hospital in London, where these horrible illnesses are quite common."

"That's true, Louisa. Keziah was telling us how the death rate is higher in the towns and cities compared to here, due to the unsanitary conditions and overcrowded slum areas. Apparently Miss Nightingale has been complaining bitterly that the Public Health Act of 1848 is still yet to be acted upon and here we are six years later! There are, apparently, some houses that even have *cesspools* immediately below their wooden floors in London, with ghastly effluent running through open drains in the streets."

Alicia joins in, "Mama is right, the last time we saw her, Keziah was bemoaning to us the fact that there has only been half-hearted talk of sanitary reform, but little has been accomplished. Cholera, dysentery and typhus are common and it's the poorer classes who are suffering the most."

"Sadly, it isn't only in the cities, Alicia. Lord Dryer was asking me only yesterday to stay away from town for a while, as there's been an outbreak of cholera again in Brunswick Street."

"Oh dear, not again! I think that all the disgustingly smelly glove factories have a lot to do with that though," says Alicia. "I heard Papa saying it's something to do with the leather tanning process contaminating the water supplies."

Mrs Bridewell appears thoughtful and then she speaks. "Well, like you say, Louisa, it is true the nurses will be experienced in dealing with those diseases and we must simply pray that our dear Keziah remains in good health during her sojourn there."

She turns to her eldest daughter, "I think we ought to ring now for Parsons to bring in our tea, Serena."

Rosa is supping tea at a large, scrubbed wooden table below stairs in the kitchen when Parsons returns after serving the afternoon refreshments. She glances down at Rosa, before her nose is disdainfully up in the air again. "Your mistress certainly looks the part, all dressed up in her finery. You don't get coloured silks like that in these parts!"

Rosa smiles good-naturedly, "No, Lord Dryer bought her some lovely costumes when they were on their honeymoon in Paris."

One of the other girls then says wistfully, "He came here once, your Lord Dryer. We all thought he was courting Serena, but then we heard he upped and married his chambermaid!"

Their chambermaid scoffs, "Such an 'andsome man 'ee was too and he ends up with someone no better 'un me!"

Rosa replies defensively, "My Lord Dryer is a kind, compassionate, intelligent man and he genuinely fell in love with my mistress. She also has the same attributes and she is a beautiful woman... my friend, as well as my employer. I wouldn't wish to work for anyone else in the whole world."

"Well, I think you'd have to go a long way to find any woman more accomplished and attractive than our three young ladies upstairs, but there is no accounting for taste," says Parsons pointedly.

Rosa sighs and looks at the clock on the wall, wondering how much longer she will be obliged to be entertained by these foolishly prejudiced females.

CHAPTER TWO *(September – December 1854)*

ABOARD THE ADELAIDE

Nathan Meakins, bored with the slowly passing days, enduring monotonous tasks of physical activity, is always looking for something to stimulate his brain. On the Sabbath, whilst half of his fellow convicts are exercising, ironed to one another by bazzels and clanging chains, shuffling dispiritedly round the upper deck, warily supervised by the scarlet-coated warders, the remainder are contained below and allowed to entertain themselves. Meakins is an accomplished card player, who soon finds that his fellow prisoners are willing to gamble their victuals in return for the flutter of excitement at the chance of winning the pot.

He quickly learns to differentiate between the card sharps and the slower country simpletons; thus he is able to ensure that he never goes hungry. The surgeon-superintendent, realising that the addiction to dice, cards, pitch and toss is leading some of the men to gamble away their rations, tries instead to encourage traditional dancing and singing among the prisoners in an effort to distract the men from their temptations, but like most of the convicts Meakins would need to be extremely drunk to join in with that, and the gambling continues regardless.

Lime juice or wine is served daily and every prisoner is mustered to drink their allowance from the ladle at the tub on the quarterdeck. He looks forward to the wine, but the bitter lime juice is not pleasant, although a necessary evil to protect them all from scurvy. The lime juice reflects his mood, as his bitterness is smouldering every time he dwells on Joshua Dryer's dogged pursuit of him and how even his own sister betrayed him. He will never forgive her for abandoning him to the mercy of the courts.

Today the prisoners are all crowded below with the rats, because they are crossing the equator and they can hear the high jinks of the crew on the upper deck, where the 'Shellbacks' are initiating the 'Pollywogs' into the Court of King Neptune. The happy laughter of the families of the pensioner guards, who have never beheld such a spectacle before, wafts down through the ventilation hatch.

An old sailor, Josiah Jones, who is among the prisoners, explains what is going on. "The Shellbacks be all those who be experienced sailors and have crossed the line before, but the Pollywogs be the greenhorns. Sometimes, when there are no genteel folk around, it gets a bit rough 'cause often the Shellbacks beat the Pollywogs with boards and wet ropes and folk get hurt, and those who cannot swim be filled with dread. It's not so bad to be dunked in a pool of water contained in a suspended sail, but the more reckless have been known to throw their victims over the side of the ship, dragging them in the surf from the stern."

Meakins is glad to be below on this occasion, despite his aversion to the rats, as he is unable to tolerate any form of ridicule, but is also terrified of drowning. He remembers long ago, when just a small boy, how he fell into the River Ivell. He relives again the sheer terror of the river swirling up his nose and into his lungs; by madly flapping his arms he was just able to stop himself from sinking below the dirty water; the current was taking him and he was coughing and spluttering, struggling for dear life and screaming for help, when to his great relief his sister, Olivia, came to his rescue with the boat-hook and dragged him back to the riverbank. She had always been his protector. *How could she have betrayed him?* He shakes his head to dispel the memory of his fear and weakness, and of her betrayal.

Turning his attention back to his hand of cards, there is only him and two others left in the game. The other two men are both Welshmen and have become comrades, but he believes them to be working together and so, rather than give them the satisfaction of raising the stakes and being beaten, he folds.

He has made no real companions on this journey, keeping to himself for the most part, marking possible adversaries and successfully avoiding them. He misses the comradeship of his drinking buddies from the Black Panther Club. His mess group of eight are all older than him and, in his eyes, a bunch of yokels. Together they occupy the bunks along one side of the transportation deck, each separated from its neighbour by about a foot of boarding. The four bunks on the upper and lower tiers form their mess and they share a table.

The younger men occupy the mid ship hammocks, slung up each night above the tables. Among these is a chap called Sam Kelly, who is popular amongst the others with his Irish sense of humour and gift of the gab. Being fit and young, Meakins thinks: *this fellow would make a good ally; his stamina may well come in useful during our forthcoming ordeal.* He decides to nurture a friendship with him.

He puts his plan into practice one Sunday when they are becalmed in the tropics. The air has been stifling and oppressive for days, with no draught evident through the barred hatches. The deck above them is scorching hot, causing the pitch to drip from the seams, down onto them, sticking, burning and scarring their flesh. Meakins is fortunate because he has the lower bunk, which is protected by the bunk above him, but the men in the mid ship hammocks are suffering badly and Sam Kelly is one of them. He curses as the blistering pitch burns his shaved head and his bare arms and Meakins uncharacteristically suggests he shares his bunk. "Hey Sam, there is room under here, it will protect you from being burnt by the resin."

"Thank you, my friend; much appreciated." He slips out of his hammock, rubbing his burning skin, and weaves his way through the tables and other prisoners to join him. They both sit cross-legged, facing each other, at each end of the bunk.

"This is insufferable, so it is! Half of us are going down with fever. I'd give anything for a bucket of iced water," says Kelly hoarsely. "It's hard to know how we're going to survive this, with just two pints of blood-warm water a day." He leans back dejectedly against the bulkhead.

"We'll survive, my friend. We're both young enough and I'm determined to get my old life back, one way or another," says Meakins vehemently.

"What was your old life?" asks Kelly.

"I'm the only son of Sir Oliver Meakins, due to inherit my father's estate in Somersetshire one day and I don't intend to let that slip through my fingers! How about you?"

"I am… was… a simple shepherd, so I was. I hailed from Ballyvaughan, a small harbour village in County Clare, on the southern shores of Galway Bay. I worked on an English gentleman's estate. I left nothing of any value behind me. I was, in effect, orphaned during the great hunger, when my poor mother died of starvation and the fever in October 1846 and my baby sister shortly followed her to heaven in December the same year." He sighs disconsolately. "My father was bereft, so he was. In desperation he abandoned me when I was eleven, to work his passage to America to try to make a fresh start, promising to come back for me when he was able. But I've heard nothing from him since the day he departed. I don't know to this day whether he's dead or alive. He left me in the care of his brother, but with the famine, he was unable to feed his own family, let alone another and, I believe reluctantly, he put me into the care of the Holy Fathers, so he did. It's a period of my life I don't wish to dwell upon." He wipes the perspiration from his brow with his sleeve.

"Sorry, my dear chap. I didn't intend for you to dredge up painful memories, Sam."

"It's all in the past now, my friend. Once my sentence is over, I'll be able to make a fresh start on the other side of the world and hopefully it will be a better one than before."

"What was your crime, Sam?"

"Well, times were hard, so they were, and I was near starving. I was in the habit of taking the occasional stillborn lamb, skinning it and cooking it up for myself. I didn't think anyone would know or care, but I was found out and, would you believe, I was done for sheep stealing. I'm sure you know it is, under your English laws, a hanging offence and I must admit to being grateful instead to be transported. How about you?"

Meakins had not planned a response to this question and is pondering. The question hangs in the air like the limp red and white pennant, strung on the ship's mast above them, proclaiming the vessel a convict ship.

Sam Kelly is a handsome young buck. Meakins puts him at around eighteen years old. He looks a charmer, despite his shaved head, with his sparkling blue eyes and ready smile and Meakins is sure that he has had his fair share of giggling, flirtatious admirers. *There may be a way of explaining, that will win his sympathy?*

"I was accused of rape, Sam. But you know what these women are like, they give you the come on and then cry wolf when you respond to their wiles. I was unlucky, for the girl had an influential family and, unfortunately, my fate was sealed."

Sam looks back at him, his face betraying nothing. Meakins wonders if he is comparing crimes. "What was your sentence?" he asks him.

"I got seven years, so I did." Sam has a look of resignation; "How about you?"

Meakins replies with a smile, as he trumps him. "I got life!"

Sam raises his eyebrows. "That's a minimum of twelve years, isn't it?"

Meakins shrugs. "If we survive this indignity, yes!"

"Well, it looks like it might be a long haul!"

Later that afternoon, the prisoners are divided once more. Whilst Sam is up on deck lethargically exercising, Meakins, like many of the other transports, is stripped to the waist, his body glistening with sweat, as he joins another card school. He is pleased that the Welshmen are not involved this time and is looking forward to making a killing. During the games his attention is drawn to a small man, who despite his overalls being stained with sweat, does not disrobe, but appears to be particularly dexterous with the cards and luck always seems to be on his side. He is a cockney called Reg Lewis. When finally the other players have all folded and it is just Meakins and Lewis left in the game, Meakins loses his rag when Lewis lays down a royal flush.

"Where the devil did you lay hands on those cards?" he asks angrily.

"Are you calling me a cheat?"

"Well, let us put it this way, I'm naked above the waist, but you are not."

"What do you mean by that?"

"I mean that *you* always seem to have something up your sleeve!"

Lewis bangs his hand down on the table, "If we weren't stuck down here unarmed, I'd slit your throat for that!"

The shouting attracts the attention of the other prisoners and one of the Welshmen, Hugh Davies, is watching transfixed, as Meakins jumps up and drags the man out from the opposite bunk by his throat, shoving him hard against its wooden supports and banging his head in a frenzy of unfettered fury. Hugh has never witnessed such a look of hatred and evil intention in anyone before this moment and he resolves never to get on the wrong side of that one.

Meakins is grabbed by another prisoner and eventually pulled off Lewis, who collapses on the deck in a state of unconsciousness, blood oozing from the wound to the back of his head. A brawl then breaks out between the supporters of Lewis and Meakins.

In response to the sudden yelling and violence, the hatch of the prison-hold is hastily unlocked and some of the guards arrive to cage the perpetrators. When the warders have their backs to him, Hugh spots Meakins drawing his flattened hand across his throat in a warning to the other prisoners to keep their mouths shut, or else. The six caged men have their shackles replaced and are put on bread and water rations for a week. Meakins is among them, but not one of them offers any explanation to the guards.

Reg Lewis unfortunately dies three days later from his head injuries and Nathan Meakins is always shown his due respect by his fellow prisoners, following this example of his extremely short temper and violent nature. Hugh keeps his own counsel, but he avoids all contact with both Meakins and all the other troublemakers.

Meakins is enormously relieved to finally have the shackles removed and to be released from the cage at the end of their punishment. He exhibits no signs of regret over the death of Lewis. The following day he feels the sensation of a light breeze on his face. *Thank the Lord we're moving again!* He hears the command to the crew to set the sails and feels again the judder of the waves breaking against the bows. It is soon apparent, however, that the calm was the prequel to a violent tropical storm.

Before long everyone is suffering badly from fever and seasickness. The hatches are battened, but the ventilation scuttles also have to be closed, as the sea washes over the ship. Meakins, along with the other prisoners, lies lifeless in the oppressive, stifling atmosphere. Despite being sealed into their quarters the sea somehow manages to seep through the ship's seams; everything is damp and smelling of swirling bilge water and mouldy timber. He cannot stomach the motion of the ship, combined with the fetid stench of vomit and stale body odour. He too succumbs to the fever and mercifully loses several days while the sailors battle with the elements. Sam takes good care of him during this time, wiping the perspiration from his brow, fanning him constantly and gallantly sharing his quota of tepid water. It is thanks to Sam that he survives.

Apart from the death and burial at sea of the unfortunate cockney, Reg Lewis, the remainder of the journey is uncomfortable and tedious, but otherwise uneventful. Finally, as the ship draws near the coast of Van Diemen's Land their shackles are again replaced. The pensioner guards are always wary of mutiny. Most of them plan to settle with their families and they are all excited to see the land mass after their long and weary months on board.

On arrival at the Derwent River estuary harbour they are holed up for about three days before being landed at Hobart Town. Commissariat officials arrange for fresh meat and fruit to be sent aboard daily. During that time they are firstly inspected by the colonial surgeon and thereafter by the port health officer who issues a clean bill of health. The principal superintendent of convicts and some other officials then come aboard. The prisoners and crew are all mustered, in order to check the indent papers with each individual prisoner. They check their names, offences, sentences, date and place of conviction, their trades and any form of personal identification, such as eye and hair colour, scars, et cetera.

Nathan Meakins watches as the official looks him over and then checks on his papers that his description tallies with a thirty-six-year-old English gentleman with grey eyes, 6 feet tall and convicted at Taunton County Assizes on 6th May 1854. He asks him if his hair colouring is usually light brown and wavy with side whiskers and Meakins replies in the affirmative.

Because of the gravity of his crime and because he has no trade, Meakins is designated hard labour with the timber gangs at Port Arthur. He shrugs despondently, but he later overhears that the two card-playing Welshmen are to go to Saltwater Creek coal mine, and he gives a sigh of relief, as he could not bear to have to work underground and he feels he has the better option.

Next is Sam Kelly, described as an eighteen-year-old Irish youth, 5 feet, 11 inches tall, with blue eyes and dark brown wavy hair. Sam confirms his hair colouring, however, there is no trade recorded on Sam's indent paper, neither is the date of his conviction recorded.

He tells them, "I was a shepherd, sir."

"And what was the date of your conviction?"

"It was September last year, sir."

"You're a young, fit man and you'll be placed with the agriculture workers near Saltwater Creek on the Tasman peninsular. Your date of release will be sometime in September 1860, if this is confirmed by the Irish authorities in County Clare."

"Thank you, sir."

"You're dismissed, Kelly." He turns and is marched out by the pensioner guard. "Next!" cries the superintendent.

Once all the prisoners have been inspected and their indent papers have been checked, they are ready to disembark. They are moored alongside whalers and seal boats and the estuary is bustling with seamen, traders and shipbuilders. The town looks lively and interesting. The skyline is dominated by a huge, tree-covered mountain, which Meakins learns later is Mount Wellington, and on the coast to the right and left of the town are many small bays.

He feels unsteady on his sea legs as they are marched down the gangplank into Hobart Town. They are chained together in their groups, according to their final destination. Meakins, Kelly, Josiah Jones and the Welshmen are with a muster of about forty men.

As they are marched through the town they pass the house of correction, known as the Cascades Factory, and Meakins is surprised at the unruly behaviour of the female prisoners who are whooping and hollering down at the men from their dormitory windows.

Someone shouts out, "What ship are you from?" and Sam Kelly replies, "The *Adelaide*. How about you?"

"The *Duchess of Northumberland*. Where are you bound?"

"Port Arthur."

"Good luck. What's your name?"

"Sam Kelly. What's yours?"

"Angelica Pitman."

Meakins, walking immediately behind Sam, can only just make out her words as several other inmates are also shouting out their names and waving madly at the men. They then hear the angry shouts of the warders and the women withdraw from the windows, Angelica Pitman still waving defiantly.

They muster at Franklin's Wharf in Sullivan's Cove where they are put into boats and delivered to Kangaroo Bay on the eastern shore of the Derwent River, opposite Hobart Town. They have a lengthy march ahead of them traversing the coastal track to Port Arthur, which is where they will be based. The prisoners form a long centipede as they traipse alongside the pensioner guards with the wagons conveying their families and supplies, and the soldiers occasionally cursing and cracking their whips if the men should start to dawdle. Uphill and down dale they march along the well-worn dirt track, passing unfamiliar foreign vegetation, such as the blue-tinted eucalyptus trees, the woody liana vines and pepperberry bushes. As they go along, in the main, they are overlooking the sea. The inlets and numerous islands form a superb seascape and when they reach the wide scoop of Seven Mile Beach, Sam tells Meakins how he is sadly reminded of his Ireland home overlooking Galway Bay. Then they are herded in groups onto Dodge's rope ferry for several trips across Pittwater.

Meakins is now limping from blisters as they march on through the scrub, inland to reach the well-worn track east. The sun beats down on them; the temperature must be in the seventies as they pass through Copping, then eventually they turn southwards, back towards the coast. They overnight at Dunally, a small fishing village, situated on the narrow isthmus connecting the mainland with the Forestier peninsula, where they are given bread and water. They sleep fitfully in a barn and then wearily set off again the following day. Today Meakins is chained to Josiah Jones. Unused to walking any distance, having been penned up on the ship for three months; in addition to his blisters, he finds his muscles ache and his ankles are rubbed raw again from the shackles.

Finally they arrive at Eaglehawk Neck, another narrow isthmus connecting the Forestier and the Tasman Peninsulas, overlooking Pirates Bay on the one side and Norfolk Bay on the other. They pass the guards' quarters and a patrol of soldiers guarding the high fence, beyond which is a line of nine hungry, snarling dogs, attached to posts across the neck of land to deter and warn of any convicts attempting to escape. The soldiers unbar the gateway through the fence, and armed with batons, make a great show of removing some of the vicious animals to allow the convoy to pass through unharmed, then they re-chain them.

"This reminds me of the causeway onto Portland," says the old sea dog, as he walks wearily beside Meakins.

"I didn't realise you hail from Dorset, Josiah," says Meakins with surprise.

"Ye', strong in the arm an' thick in the head, that's me!" He chuckles.

"What did you do to deserve this?"

"Well, you see, years ago, as a young man in me twenties, I be caught landing smuggled goods on the beach." He pulls at his beard and takes another long breath. "And because of this I were impressed into the navy, but I were involved more recently in a mutiny and so they sent me here. There be a convict prison on Portland too, the narrow bank of pebbles connecting the island to the mainland makes it easier to patrol and prevent escape. I heard the old ferry house was washed away some time ago and they have a bridge now, but they don't have the dogs back home."

"Do you know where you're headed?" Meakins asks conversationally.

"The farm at Saltwater Creek, apparently; too old for much else, I expect."

"I'm going to Port Arthur to work with the lumberjacks, but I think you'll find Sam Kelly is going to the Saltwater Creek Farm too."

About half an hour later they reach a small settlement called Taranna, which is the point at which the prisoners allocated to the settlement at Port Arthur and those making for Saltwater Creek are divided into their two groups. The chains are struck dividing him from Josiah Jones and Josiah is linked to Sam Kelly.

Meakins is disheartened to be parting from Sam, his only ally, who calls back to him, "Keep your chin up, Nathan, you'll see, the time will fly by and we'll be free men again eventually."

He calls to him, "Don't forget to look me up when you're released, at the end of your sentence, Sam."

"I will pal, I will, to be sure."

"Come on, get in line!" shouts the pensioner guard pushing him forward impatiently.

CHAPTER THREE *(June 1855 – June 1857)*

THE ANGEL OF HEAVEN'S GATE

Angelica Pitman is standing in the cold, with the other probationer pass-holders. They are lined up outside the Cascades Female Factory Prison, where she has spent the last three years of her five-year sentence as a second-class prisoner, after her arrival in Van Diemen's Land in 1852.

She was told the original building was an old rum distillery. Built in an east-west running valley about four miles from Sullivan's Cove, it nestles under Mount Wellington. The Hobart Rivulet runs through the valley next to the site, which has always been damp and bitterly cold in the winter and hot in summer. She looks up at the snow-capped mountain, with its distinctive cliff of columns known as the organ pipes, situated presently just below the snowline, and she shivers as a gust of Antarctic wind blasts up Macquarie Street.

She pulls together the lapels of her serge jacket and turns her head, so that her bonnet takes the worst of the wind, as it whips her chestnut hair into straggly rat-tails. Her shoulders slump in begrudging resignation at the thought of standing in line waiting to be selected by one of the men who are patrolling up and down the row of women to make their choice.

A man approaches, hesitates and then drops his handkerchief in front of her, but the wind takes it and it lands before Esme, the girl stood beside her.

Esme looks him up and down and, when he smiles at her, she makes her decision, bending down and retrieving the handkerchief as a gust of wind threatens to blow it away again. He takes her arm and with a cheery wave she goes off to an unknown destination, to be the bride of a man she has only just met.

Angelica sighs, shuffling her feet dispiritedly; she is desperate to be chosen by someone. Bearing in mind the misery of prison life, she is also eager to escape the gang of unruly, criminal third-class offenders who terrorise the rest of them, known as the Flash Mob. She has finally worked her way up to a first-class probationer pass-holder and earned her ticket of leave, trained in domestic skills and obedience, and is standing on the brink of a new phase in her life, if only she manages to be assigned today.

Eventually her patience is rewarded and a smile lights up her face. She is singled out by Robert Stace, who, she is to discover, is a married rancher who owns 200 acres of land in an isolated spot in the midlands, just outside Anthill Ponds. She is relieved the man is already married, for unlike Esme, she is not ready to pledge her life to some stranger. She is also pleased at last to be embarking on an adventure away from the confines of the prison walls, looking forward to the trip across Van Diemen's Land, even though it is a long, rough journey from Hobart on the farm cart.

They are traversing the only roadway through the midlands, leading ultimately to the north coast, constructed by her fellow convict labourers, and although after her long incarceration she is enjoying the changing scenery, she is tired and weary when finally they reach their destination.

She soon settles into her new routine, even though Mr Stace is a hard taskmaster and doesn't hesitate to use the whip on the three girls who work for him. It is not long, however, before he makes it clear to her that he wants more personal services than purely domestic.

She is helping with the milking early one morning when he pulls her aside and thrusts her down into the loose hay. Despite her kicking and struggling, he forcibly beds her in the barn with the full knowledge of the other workers outside in the yard. Tears sting her eyes at the injustice of this brutality. Her reason for transportation had been theft, *not prostitution* and she feels mortified, but powerless to complain. Not wanting her ticket of leave to be revoked and being totally dependent on him for her survival for the next two years, she resigns herself to put up with this treatment, rather than return to the prison.

When frequently he leaves his wife's side to come into Angelica's attic room at night, his exhausted wife, with four young children under the age of seven, seems oblivious of what is going on under her own roof. He is reckless, not caring if she falls pregnant, for if that should happen he will just blame one of the ranch hands and ship her back to the Cascades.

Jane Thompson, the elder of the other two female servants, befriends her and tells her how to avoid pregnancy by using a strip of pig's intestine. It is some time before she finally manages to persuade Stace of the benefits of this suggestion, but once she is able to put aside her fears of pregnancy, she realises that coupling is not so repugnant to her, when there is no violence or aggression. Nevertheless, she cannot wait to be free from this man and in desperation she comes up with a plan to earn more money, by voluntarily offering her services to the other ranch hands, all of whom are younger and fitter than Mr Stace.

As time goes on, however, she becomes more indignant and angry with the master for the callous way he is treating her. She confides in Jane. "He can be quite sadistic you know, expecting me to perform unpleasant and painful acts for his gratification. I feel like his slave; he clicks his fingers and expects me to come running!"

"The trouble is we don't have too many options, do we? We don't have any power."

One day, after months of putting up with this treatment, Angelica notices how he fawns around his wife and, formulating a plan, she decides to bide her time, waiting for the opportunity to confront him. The next time he attempts to bed her, she plucks up the courage to question him. "You do really love your wife and children, don't you, master?"

He looks down suspiciously at her. "Of course I do. They are everything to me."

"Then why do you need me?"

"I make love to my wife, Pitman, on the rare occasions when she feels generous in that way, but I simply have carnal sex with you, girl."

"How would your wife feel, if she were to find out what we do in the attic and the hay barn on a regular basis?"

He grabs her roughly by her chin, speaking angrily into her face, his spittle landing on her upper lip. "She will not find out girl, for I would kill you first."

From her experience of bullying in the prison, she believes that her master is really a coward, desperately trying to keep the upper hand with his workers by laying down the law, harassing and displaying his short temper and aggression. However, she is *almost* sure that he is no killer. The following day, after much deliberation, she decides to call his bluff. Knowing the master and his wife are together, she enters the main parlour and asks to speak to Mrs Stace. "Excuse me Ma'am, but may I have a moment of your time, please?"

"What is it, Pitman? I'm busy fitting Mary's gown at the moment." Her eldest daughter is standing by her side, whilst she adjusts the fitting of a sleeve. She adds haughtily, "I trust it will wait. I will come and find you later in the kitchen."

Angelica nods and dips a curtsey, "Yes, Ma'am." As she turns to leave the room she looks meaningfully at Robert Stace, whose face is as white as a bed sheet. She fervently hopes he is remembering their conversation of the previous night. She only intends asking Mrs Stace for more candles for the servants' rooms, but her husband doesn't have to know that.

She is not surprised when he comes looking for her shortly afterwards, and braces herself for the confrontation, as he grabs her arm angrily, "What is it that you want from me, Pitman? You returning to your criminal ways and resorting to blackmail now?"

Angelica steals herself; looking down pointedly at his large hand tightly gripping her wrist, and backing down, he lets her go.

"I was just thinking of a fair payment for services rendered, that's all, Mr Stace. I'm sure it's worth preserving your wife's belief in her happy marriage and maintaining the façade of marital bliss for your family, friends and neighbours."

"How dare you speak to me like that?"

She can see that he wants to strike her and is having difficulty holding himself in check. "I'm only asking for what I'm entitled, Mr Stace. The ranchers never quibble, so why should you?"

By the indignant expression on his face he is obviously stunned to learn that he is not the only man to benefit from her generosity. He blusters, "The ranchers?"

"Yes, there are about seven of them who have sampled my wares and I'm sure they would defend me if any serious harm should befall me."

There is a new caution in his eyes and, as he suppresses his anger, she knows her plan is working. He won't be happy sharing her with his men, but he must now realise she's probably earned their loyalty. She believes she has successfully called his bluff and eventually, begrudgingly, he clandestinely passes her two promissory notes for the payment she has requested.

She has only six more months to go before she is given her ticket of leave. By then she'll have earned enough money to leave and move on to pastures new. She knows he'll be glad to be rid of her; he'll simply go back to the Cascades Factory and pick out another poor creature to do his bidding.

She continues to ply her trade on the quiet with the ranchers and saves up enough sterling, plus the few promissory notes for the larger sums from Robert Stace himself, to be able to escape with her ticket of leave and make her way by horse-drawn bus to Port Dalrymple.

Thus, despite gaining her freedom at last, she has graduated from being a convicted petty thief to a lowly prostitute. She leaves the ranch carrying all her worldly goods in a small cloth bag and waits where the coachman changes his horses for her ride. It is nearly eleven o'clock when they are ready to move off again and she climbs gratefully into the carriage with an enormous sigh of relief.

As the coach passes over the Blackman River Bridge at Tunbridge she recognises the postman on his weekly walk, delivering mail along the route and she waves to him from the carriage, but he does not spot her. He is the last person she recognises from her time as an indentured servant. She is embarking on an adventure all alone, leaving behind her recent past, beholden to no one and she is at the same time exhilarated and terrified.

Stopping to change the horses every ten miles, they pass through the garrison town of Ross and then over another convict-built, red-brick bridge over the Elizabeth River in Campbell Town. They have a comfort stop at the Bald Faced Stag in Cleveland, then on via Evandale on the Esk River and through Norfolk Plains. They pass Gibbett Hill just outside Perth and continue through Kings Meadows, the river valley settlement of Launceston, Mowbray with its racecourse, along the Tamar river to George Town and then finally to arrive at Port Dalrymple at nine o'clock that night. Angelica is exhausted and makes her way to the Pier Hotel. She can feel the fresh breeze off the sea and is looking forward to exploring the small port in the morning. She is relieved to be able to book a bed for the night, but she sleeps fitfully, anxious to arrange her crossing to Australia.

Her journey by sea to the Victorian gold fields is with some kindly local fishermen who don't even consider charging her, as they are fishing in the Bass Straits and unloading their catch on the southern coast of Australia. She joins them for the day, cleaning and gutting the fish as they catch them. After a long day's work they finally sail into Australia's Portland Bay at sunset, where she wearily manages to locate a cheap hostelry for two nights.

The next day as she strolls along Bentinck Street, she can still smell the fish and the salty seaweed, as the seabirds screech and wail above her. There are seals swimming in the Strait and lazing on the boat ramps on her right, and koalas up in the trees on her left. The small port is busy with fishermen, sealers and whalers and she is relieved to leave this masculine area to mingle with the local women. She is looking to spend her hard-earned money on some practical and some alluring items of clothing. She finds a general store and enjoys the novel pleasure of being able to buy various pretty things for herself. She purchases a large leather trunk and fills it with her crisp, new, fresh-smelling clothing, a pair of leather buttoned boots and some hair combs, beads and trinkets, that she was advised by the kindly sailors to invest in, if she wants help from the local aborigines.

The following morning she sets off on her trip to Bendigo on the back of the drayman's cart. The journey is spread over three days, hostelling overnight at Hamilton and Ararat en route. There are others on the road using a variety of means of transport, but most are on foot slowly pushing barrows before them in the January heat, containing all their worldly goods, or simply carrying a pick and a shovel.

Unnervingly, they also pass the occasional group of sad and despondent folk, travelling on foot towards them, away from the goldfields, having lost heart and given up the struggle to survive when the red land proves unfruitful.

Undeterred she finally arrives in the dusty township at Bendigo Creek, which to her surprise has grown over the preceding five years, since gold was first discovered there, from a tented shanty town along the river into an established settlement, now known as Sandhurst. She is relieved to discover there are stores built on both sides of the creek; they pass the barracks where she can see the foot and mounted police and then a large block of stables, a log cabin lock-up, the gold receiver's office and the licence tent. The community has even organised street lighting. She feels immediately optimistic, for surely it is prosperity that has encouraged this sense of permanence. Nevertheless, the shanty town she was expecting is still there, but it has spread out and up into the surrounding hills and she believes that it will be up there, where she will best find her fair share of the gold.

She clambers down from the back of the dray, dragging her heavy trunk behind her. The drayman had stopped the oxen outside the general store in order to deliver their supplies and thus it is very convenient for her to enter the stores and make her purchases. She selects a wheelbarrow, a wooden, metal-ringed washtub and a galvanised water pail, inside which she places some kiln-dried biscuits, a jar of golden syrup, some ant-proof, screw-top containers, some more dried foodstuffs, candles and a tinderbox. She then finds some cooking kettles, pannikins and a hurricane lantern, which she places inside the washtub. She puts both the filled tub and bucket into the wheelbarrow. Finally, she chooses a straw mattress and two blankets, a sheet of calico tenting and smaller necessities like soap, a few items of cutlery and scissors for her survival in the bush. The store man adds up all her items and she hands over her cash. She will have to pick up anything else on her future trips into Sandhurst, but this lot will do for now.

It has been a long and tiring journey over several days, across the sea and over rutted tracks and she is stiff and exhausted, so when she spots the small group of aborigines squatting by the creek, she approaches them and somehow makes them understand, with a combination of pointing and miming, that she needs help in return for her coloured beads. The tallest of their number, who only comes up to her shoulder and obviously has a rudimentary understanding of English, takes hold of the wheelbarrow and saying, "Come, follow Matari," he sets off towards the hills, with his three friends following, two of them helping by carrying the mattress, and the only girl helping her with her trunk.

Because she believes there will be fewer women there, Angelica has decided to settle north of the main town, on the high ground at the southern edge of the range of hills known as the Whipstick. Having trudged along between the masses of settlers with her helpers, they finally arrive at a vacant spot she is happy with, overlooking the Bendigo creek and the flats which were once the pasturelands. Beholding the miles of flat lands below her, she is reminded of a place not far from her home town in Wiltshire, known as Heaven's Gate, renowned for its spectacular scenic views and she is very pleased with her choice.

In return for the trinkets she has sensibly brought with her from Portland Bay, the aborigines offer to help her build a bark *gunyah*, which is a small ironbark shack. They go off together, returning later with huge ironbark slabs for the sides and they help her with the construction, finally erecting the calico tented roof. On a whim she has taken up one of the thinner ironbark slabs and carved it with the words: 'Heaven's Gate', which she fixes above the entrance.

Her helpers seem thrilled with their reward of the trinkets and beads, especially the young girl, who she learns is called Camira, which their leader, Matari, explains means 'of the wind'. Matari says to her before leaving, "You need more help, just come find us black fellows." He points to the other two boys, "Pindari and Kaora."

Angelica repeats their names, "Matari, Pindari, Kaora and Camira."

"We good black fellows want to help white fellows."

She smiles and shrugs, "Where will I find you?"

"You want us, we find you."

She laughs, not quite sure how that will work, but she holds out her hand and they all shake hands solemnly.

Now alone again and unpacked and organised, Angelica wanders through the bustling, noisy settlement known as Eaglehawk. She has never before seen so many prospective customers crammed into such a relatively confined area and her passage is accompanied by whistles and lewd suggestions. Unlike most women she takes no offence, recognising that their bawdy comments are in fact endorsing her presence there. She will definitely need help eventually, but in the meantime she certainly intends to make the most of the fact that she is one of very few European women who apply their trade here.

She discovers that, apart from the Chinese who have settled in their own enclave, she is right; there are hardly any families. Much of the scrub has been cut down and used for temporary shelters. There are groups of men of all nationalities felling trees for the ongoing building of Sandhurst and for the sinking of the mines, and Germans and Chinese planting competing vineyards and hewing out wine cellars, others are charcoal burning, horse dealing and setting up shanty grog shops and general stores for provisions for the multitudes; thus, there is a cosmopolitan society speedily developing alongside the gold miners. She learns from her neighbours that it was only two years ago in August that the first land sales were held in Sandhurst and by October all the available allotments in the centre of the town had been taken up and all around was a building boom.

From her vantage point she is able to observe the bustling township below and the vast encampment eventually giving way to pastureland and scrub. She notices the stone slab church, built at Golden Point and as the sun slowly sets she watches the flickering lights of the campfires and the gas lights of Sandhurst, until finally, exhausted after an eventful few days, she crawls into her *gunyah* and falls asleep on her straw mattress.

About a week later, she has just eaten a tasty meal of damper and golden syrup, or 'cocky's joy', as the store man had called it, when she hears a knock on her wooden sign and a man is standing there looking embarrassed.

"What can I be doing for you, mister?"

"I was told by the smithy that I could find a good time here."

"Is that right? Well, what have you got for me in return?"

The man holds out his hand and in his palm is a tiny nugget of gold. Angelica laughs. "You must think I'm desperate. I'm not even prepared to let you cop a feel for that!"

She turns away from him and shuts the makeshift ironbark door in his face. He knocks again and she opens the door a crack. He is holding out a nugget that is at least double the size.

"That is more like it," she says with a welcoming smile, at the same time opening wide the door to Heaven's Gate.

After her punter has left she moves the bucket of pig's intestines soaking in brine to the back of the shack and breathes a sigh of relief. He was a decent enough fellow, simply yearning for the gentle touch of a woman and the happy release resulting from their union. He was quite content to comply with the makeshift protective sheath, which she explained was as much for his benefit as hers. There was no funny business and it proved an easy way to earn her lump of gold. At least she is free now to make her own decisions. Thankfully it is a far cry from the Cascades Factory Prison with its Flash Mob, or Robert Stace, the randy rancher at Anthill Ponds.

CHAPTER FOUR *(June – December 1855)*

ANGELS AND DEVILS

It is not long before Louisa suspects that she may be pregnant. She keeps this to herself until her morning sickness is noticed, firstly by Rosa and then Joshua. Her doting husband insists that she sees Dr Gillingham, who cheerfully confirms her pregnancy and pronounces her to be in excellent physical health.

For Louisa the time seems to pass very slowly, as her belly swells a little more with each passing day. She is due to give birth in July, and her confinement is tedious, but as the days become warmer, she fears the coming ordeal. Memories of her sister Millie's suffering creep into her mind and begin to worry her. Despite this, as her body becomes more cumbersome in the heat, she cannot wait for her baby to be born at last and for it all to be over.

In the meantime Joshua realises that they will need to employ a nanny to care for both the new baby and Aurora, and so he places an advertisement in the *Western Flying Post*. They soon receive a number of applicants for the position and he arranges for Louisa and Mrs Abbott to interview the five most promising women all on the same day.

The first young lady they interview is delivered by her father in a pony and trap, which has a sign on the side advertising their grocery store. Her long brown hair is plaited and tied up in coils at the back of her head and she is dressed in a simple rose-coloured, long-sleeved dress, tied at the waist, with a wine-coloured shawl. She looks very neat and tidy and Mrs Abbott is impressed by her appearance. She takes her through to the oak where they find Louisa sitting comfortably with her hands resting protectively on her baby-bump.

"This is Miss Elizabeth Puddy, milady."

Louisa looks up and gives her a warm smile, "Please come in, Miss Puddy, and take a seat."

Mrs Abbott and the young girl both enter and sit down in separate armchairs.

Louisa has never interviewed any of the staff before, but she has taken the time beforehand to read all the letters of application very carefully and she remembers that Miss Puddy is twenty years old. She picks up her letter from the occasional table beside her. "I am very impressed with your references, Elizabeth. How long did you work at Montacute House?"

"Five years, milady, but the young master is now with a tutor."

"Did you enjoy your time there?"

"Yes, very much, milady. He was a dear little fellow."

"Did you miss your family at that time?"

"No milady, for I was able to visit them when I took Master James out in the perambulator, which we did most days, weather permitting."

Louisa thinks about this for a while and looks again at the girl's letter. Then she looks up and asks her, "What have you been doing in the meantime, since leaving your last post?"

"I've been helping in my parents' grocery shop in the borough in Montacute."

"What especially do you feel you could contribute to caring for a newborn baby and a four-year-old?"

"Well, I can read and write and I'm good at sums and using money, but I have a younger brother and sister who I've always looked after, until they both started school, because my parents were always so busy in the shop."

"How old was the child at Montacute House when you first started looking after him?"

"He was six months old, milady."

"If you're successful and we offer you this position, you do appreciate you will be expected to live in? We will, of course, provide a room for you near to the nursery."

"Of course, milady; I lived in at Montacute House until they no longer needed me."

Mrs Abbott looks at Louisa, "May I have permission to speak, milady?"

"Of course, Mrs Abbott, that is why you are here."

The housekeeper turns to Miss Puddy and asks her, "Do you realise that you will be solely responsible for the welfare of the child, both day and night?"

"Yes, of course, Ma'am." She turns to Louisa, "I'm a light sleeper, milady. You won't find your baby left to cry without attention, even during the night, you have my solemn word."

Mrs Abbott continues with her questions, "Are you confident in bathing the baby and caring for teething and other development problems?"

"I am Ma'am. I think the old wives' idea of hanging a dead mole around a baby's neck for teething pain is ridiculous, but a tiny bit of diluted clove oil, massaged into the painful gum area should do the trick and a teething ring is also soothing for them."

Louisa looks at Mrs Abbott with a smile, "Well, I think that is all for now, Miss Puddy. Mrs Abbott will take you down to the kitchen for some refreshments and we'll call you back later."

Mrs Abbott returns with the next woman, who Louisa can see immediately is far too old to be contending with a newly-born baby, but they repeat the process and she is quickly proved right.

The third girl is only fourteen years old and has walked down alone from Odcombe. She is very nervous and although she explains that she has a large family of brothers and sisters, she has no work experience and Louisa is not prepared to entrust her children into the care of a girl who is little more than a child herself.

Then there is a more mature woman from Ivell who has been working as a nurse in the Ivell Union Workhouse. She is wearing her nurse's uniform and has a rather brusque manner that Louisa finds disconcerting. She cannot imagine this woman having any empathy with Aurora, let alone a tiny baby. In fact she believes the children would be frightened of her, and so they arrive at the last applicant. This is a woman from Bradford Abbas, who arrives in the nick of time, in an exhausted condition having walked all the way. She looks undernourished and her fingernails are dirty and both Louisa and Mrs Abbott dismiss any notion of employing her on first sight.

The women are all given refreshments and sent on their way, apart from Elizabeth Puddy, who is shown around the manor house by Mrs Abbott and introduced to Aurora who seems to be rather taken with her.

Mrs Abbott then takes her back to see Louisa again. "Well, Elizabeth, you are the best of the applicants we have seen today and I'm prepared to offer you the position for a probationary period of three months, commencing 1st July, at one pound a month rising to an annual wage of fifteen pounds, if you prove to be satisfactory. Would you be happy with that?"

She looks relieved and smiles. "I would, milady, very happy."

"There is just one thing I ought to mention; it will be much too far for you to walk with the children all the way to Montacute on your constitutionals in order to visit your family. Will that be a problem for you?"

"I don't think so, milady. I will have some time off to visit them, won't I?"

"Well, we're unusual here in that we do allow our staff a half day off every other week, and on those occasions I will be happy to care for my own children, with the help of Mrs Abbott who has done a sterling job with Aurora."

"That sounds grand, milady."

"Good, then we'll see you back here on 1st July, ready to settle in and get to know Aurora before this little fellow arrives." She taps her baby-bump affectionately.

Joshua is extremely excited at the prospect of properly becoming a father. He has so enjoyed being a father figure to Aurora; he cannot imagine how wonderful it will be to have a child who will have his own, and his ancestors', features and characteristics. Aurora very strongly mirrors the Bonfield family and now he hopes they will also have a child who will resemble his own relatives.

The baby eventually enters the world at 4.15 p.m. on Thursday 26th July 1855. Joshua is frantically pacing the floor on the landing outside the bedchamber, anxiously trying to blot out the agonising moans and groans from the other side of the door, and trying his best to control his desire to rush in to comfort his young wife; when finally he hears his child's first cry and Rosa opens the door to announce they have a son.

He hurries in to hug an exhausted but elated Louisa. "Well done, my darling, what a beautiful child!" He turns to Dr Gillingham, "How is she, Doctor?"

"She has done very well, no problems at all." Dr Gillingham shakes his hand, "Congratulations, my lord. You have a healthy boy."

The midwife places the baby in Louisa's arms and Joshua sits close to her, on the edge of the bed. He fondly puts his arm around his wife, and they both look lovingly down at the little chap. His skin is pink and soft and he has wispy tufts of black hair. His eyes are shut and his tiny hand grips his father's index finger.

Joshua is choked with emotion as he asks Louisa, "What are we going to name him, darling?"

"There's no rush, let's wait and see; he'll let us know, I'm sure," she replies, seemingly loath to make a hasty decision.

He reluctantly gets up. "I'd better leave you both together for a while, to rest and get to know each other, while I show Dr Gillingham out." He leans over them, kissing his wife lovingly and gently touching his lips to the baby's soft black hair. Then he leaves them with the midwife and goes back downstairs with Dr Gillingham. He feels so elated he wants to celebrate, "I think this warrants a toast to my baby son, Doctor. How would you like a cigar and a glass of my finest champagne?"

"That would be most acceptable, my lord. I'm glad, actually, to have this opportunity to talk with you."

"Oh, right, excellent. Well, come on through to the oak and we can make ourselves comfortable."

Joshua serves the champagne and cigars himself and they toast his son: "To my baby boy, may he be loving, healthy and wise and a credit to our family."

Dr Gillingham says: "Here, here!" and they both drink his health.

"Have a seat, Doctor, and relax. Thankfully your work here is done, but what was it you wanted to talk to me about?"

"Well, I was rather hoping that I might enlist your help." He takes another sip of his champagne and continues. "You see, my lord, I'm extremely concerned about the state of the dwellings and the appalling conditions endured by the labouring classes in our town. It may be partly due to overcrowding and the lack of adequate ventilation in the workplace, but many of my patients are suffering and dying from consumption." He draws on his cigar. "Unfortunately, it's more common here than elsewhere in the country and I believe this is partly because so many of the Ivell population work in the gloving industry. The factory workers, and in particular the glove cutters, are suffering the most and looking pale and unhealthy."

Joshua gives a nod of agreement, remembering his gamekeeper, Raymond Hawkins', father who was a beamsman in one of the factories and who died of consumption only last year.

"In addition there still exists the most deplorable and unsanitary conditions of the water supply. Several wells in Belmont Street, where fever is raging, have been contaminated with offal and refuse, and I believe it's time the factory owners took responsibility for this." The doctor looks weary with frustration. "The well at the bottom of Kiddle's Lane is now totally unfit for use and has had to be abandoned. Many folk have contracted cholera and typhus; and unfortunately other infectious diseases resulting from these filthy conditions are rife."

The good doctor takes another drink and continues with his litany of grievances. "Several of my patients live in Deans Court, in Middle Street. There are six cottages there that share one privy and one well, which are so badly designed and maintained, the privy acts as a duct into the well, which is, in consequence, too polluted for use."

Joshua is shocked and disgusted. "I agree with you entirely that something has to be done urgently, Doctor. I've thought myself, for some time now, that we do seem to be getting more than our fair share of these mortal diseases, and I've warned my wife to avoid the town whenever cases of cholera and typhoid are rife, but what can I do to help you, Dr Gillingham?"

"To give them their due, the old town commissioners did push for local self-government by an elected council, and to this end they moved for an Ivell Improvement Bill in parliament. Last year the bill was finally approved. I'm sure you're aware that a Royal Assent was granted for the establishment of a municipal borough and the incorporation of the mayor, aldermen and burgesses of the Borough of Ivell. However, these men of influence are, in the main, the glove-factory owners themselves, and I wondered if I might be so bold as to ask, if you'd join me on the borough council? We need fresh piped water, my lord, and I wish to put pressure on the glove companies, who really should join together to provide some finance towards this."

Joshua, flattered that the good doctor should be approaching him for help in this important matter, considers carefully, before replying: "I can see your problem, Doctor, and I'd certainly be very happy to serve the town as a councillor, if you're able to get enough votes from the committee for me to stand."

Dr Gillingham puts down his glass and jumps up to shake his hand enthusiastically. "That's grand news, my lord. I'll commence diplomatic canvassing at our next meeting and let you know the outcome."

After the good doctor has left, Joshua goes to find Aurora, who is with Miss Puddy. As soon as she sees her father she runs across to him excitedly. "Is the baby here yet, Papa?"

"Yes he is, poppet; would you like to come up with me to see him?"

"Oh! Yes, Papa! Can we go right now?"

"Of course." He turns to Miss Puddy, "Thank you Beth, I'll take her up with me."

Rosa meets them both on the landing.

"How are they, Rosa?" asks Joshua.

"They're both doing well, my lord. Milady is sleeping and baby has been washed, dressed and fed, my lord."

"Thank you Rosa, we'll just creep in to show the little one to Rora."

He puts his finger to his lips to show the child that she must be quiet and then he opens the door to their bedroom. They creep towards the cradle, but Rora is so excited she cannot help whispering, "Can I kiss him?"

Joshua nods his assent and watches her, as she leans over the cradle and kisses the baby gently on his forehead. Then she pulls back and cautiously rocks the cradle, but the creaking motion wakes Louisa immediately.

"Hello you two, what do you think of him? He's been a little angel."

Aurora runs to her mother's bedside. "He's so tiny, Mama. What's his name?"

"Well, I've been thinking about that and because he's been so good, truly like an angel, I wondered if we might call him Gabriel, what do you think?" She looks up at her husband questioningly.

He looks thoughtful and tries out the name, "Gabriel Dryer. I think it has a nice, solid, honest ring to it. I like it. What do you think Rora?"

"I like it too."

"Well that seems to be settled then. Gabriel Dryer it is." He kisses Louisa lovingly. "Well done, my darling. I'm so proud of you."

When Rosa enters the kitchen to make herself a cup of hot chocolate all the women huddle around her. "What's he like Rosa? Is he like his pa, or is he a redhead like his ma?"

Rosa laughs, "He's just like his pa with black hair and a nice temperament."

Flora smiles, "'Ee is Thursday's child. 'Ow does the old rhyme go?"

Elsie and Emily repeat the rhyme in chorus, *"Monday's child is fair of face, Tuesday's child is full of grace, Wednesday's child is full of woe, Thursday's child has far to go, Friday's child is loving and giving, Saturday's child works hard for a living, but the child who is born on the Sabbath Day is bonny and blithe and good and gay."*

Emily says, "That means he has far to go. Perhaps he'll be a traveller like his pa was. Maybe he'll be a soldier or a sailor?"

Flora says sagely, "We shall 'ave to wait and see; time will tell." She appears thoughtful and then she says, "That means young Aurora is *full of grace,* for she were born on a Tuesday."

"No Flora, that was actually when I discovered

her, it could have been Monday when she was born," says Rosa, remembering the excitement in the kitchens that morning.

Flora shrugs, "Well in that case she'd be *fair of face*. It don't make no odds, because she's both of those anyways."

The following morning Joshua sits down to write a letter to his parents conveying the good tidings.

> *Dearest Mama, Papa and Becky,*
>
> *I am very pleased and relieved to announce the safe arrival into our world of Master Gabriel Dryer on Thursday 26th July. Louisa chose this name because he really has behaved like an angel, a strong, healthy little fellow at 8lb 7oz, very contented and much loved by us all at Alvington. Louisa did very well, motherhood obviously suits her and she looks radiant, as always. Aurora adores him.*
>
> *With love and affection,*
>
> *From myself and Louisa; Aurora and little baby Gabriel.*

By early November Nathan Meakins has been in Van Diemen's Land for eleven months. He has become used to the punishing daily grind, from five-thirty in the morning until six at night, digging the sawpits near to where the colossal trees are felled, using the pit-saw, creating the hillside log-slides and hauling the massive cut beams. The worst job is being the 'bottom dog' in the sawpits, when your eyes, ears and mouth become filled with the fine sawdust but, as is his nature, Meakins always makes sure that he is the 'top dog'.

He was the 'bottom dog' only once, for after that

Johnnie Firth, the prisoner who had taken the position at the top edge of the sawpit, had an unfortunate accident. He fell into the log-slide, just as a huge tree trunk was sliding down, hitting him, trapping and pushing him along, breaking his leg in two places. He was lucky to escape with his life. The guards suspected that Meakins was responsible for tripping him, but Firth kept quiet and Meakins was again shown his due respect after this second regrettable incident.

Although the work is demeaning for someone in his previous position, he is finding the labour is developing muscles he never even knew existed and he is proud of his newfound strength and fitness. They are fed adequately to get the most work, or profit, out of them. The trees are enormous, far larger than any he has ever seen in Somerset, and when put with a sixty-man centipede gang, hefting a huge beam up onto their shoulders and carrying it back to the settlement, the bulging muscles in his back, arms and thighs are burning by the time they reach their destination. He wipes the sweat from his brow, just as the gaffer tells them to take a water break.

He sits down wearily alongside the other convicts in the shade of a blue gum tree and he listens to the conversation of the guards nearby, one of whom is quoting from the *Hobarton Mercury Newspaper.* "It says here, '*on 24th October a tumultuous crowd gathered in Hobart to hear that the Tasmanian Constitution Act has been granted Royal Assent from Queen Victoria*'."

His comrade smiles, "This is a historical moment, my friend. It means that we have at last succeeded and we're no longer Vandemonians, we're now Tasmanians."

The guard continues to read from the newspaper, "Well, it says here that '*the colony of*

Tasmania is to be governed according to the principles of the Westminster system, which is to be a form of government based on the same method as in the United Kingdom'."

His comrade frowns and asks him, "Do you think it'll make much difference to us? The Anti-Transportation League has already stopped the penal transportation of British convicts. They'll be recalling the British forces once the prisons are empty."

"I don't think you have anything to fear there. We still have a lot of lifers, so that's at least another twelve years of employment." The guard rolls up his newspaper and turns to the convicts. "Come on then you lot, back to work."

The men stand and stretch, looking like a swarm of hornets in their yellow and black prison clothes. They spend the afternoon working around the larger covered sawpits constructed near the prison dockyard, within the bounds of the settlement. There the timber is cut up into the spars, beams, planks and boards needed for the shipbuilding and for transporting to other parts of the island. All day long whilst he is labouring, Meakins watches the convicts constructing the latest ship in the dockyard and he dreams of the time when he will be able to sail back to England a free man. This thought tantalises him until the end of the long day, when jadedly he is ready for his supper of bread and gruel and his cell in the penitentiary. He wearily joins the line of prisoners as they patiently queue for their victuals.

He is woken during the night by the most spine-chilling screeching he has ever heard; he feels the hairs standing up on his body. His hammock and his two blankets are damp from perspiration. He listens anxiously, as the screeching, howling and growling goes on and on. *Whatever unworldly creature makes a blood-curdling, vicious sound like that?*

The following morning he is having his breakfast and he can hear the other prisoners talking about the noisy fighting during the night; by eavesdropping he learns that the animals were Tasmanian devils.

"Probably two males were fighting over a female," says an old lag, knowledgeably, "or a female was protecting her young imps. Vicious little things they are, no bigger than a small dog, but with the sharpest teeth and strongest jaw."

"Have you ever seen one then, Geordie?"

"Yes, I have, only once because they normally hunt after dark, but this one was scavenging out in the woods. Black as pitch it was, with white splodges. They're much smaller than they sound, but I kept well away, I can tell you. Apparently they carry their little imps, like the kangaroo does, in a belly pouch."

"Well, they certainly sounded extremely vicious last night, but as we all know, females in all species will go to great lengths to protect their young."

CHAPTER FIVE *(April 1856)*

NINESPRINGS AND OFFSPRINGS

Olivia Meakins is lonely and discontented, missing her younger brother dreadfully and heartbroken at the loss of their baby, Helios. It has been a long, dismal winter and she regrets leaving the coven and the activities and comradeship of her fellow witches. She feels that time for her to find love again is surely running out, and her future is looking bleak. Is she doomed to forever be a lonely old spinster who will never have another child of her own?

She decides to cheer herself up by taking a constitutional from Summerville House to Ninesprings with Apsey, her lady's maid. It is an exceptionally warm April afternoon and, after a rather wet winter, it is good to step out and get some fresh air.

She is trying to persuade Apsey to go with her to the next meeting of the coven, but Apsey is adamant. "I'm sorry milady, but after all that happened, I no longer want to be involved. I know they have asked you to take the place of the high priestess, but I'm afraid I would rather leave your employ than go through another trial by water. You cannot imagine how terrifying that mob was."

"Well, in that case I too will have to turn them down, for it wouldn't be sensible for me to venture out late at night alone, and I don't want to lose you Apsey, you're my only confidante. Besides, I suppose you're right, it might be tempting fate and rather foolhardy to involve myself again, after irrationally consenting to sacrifice my poor Helios. I really don't know what came over me, Apsey. Nathan had such a hold over me."

"I know that milady, but I think it's all best forgotten and never spoken of again, for both our sakes."

"I understand how you feel. There's no need to say anymore on the subject."

The footpath through the trees is slippery and steep and they are both glad to reach the top of Summerhouse Hill, above the oak grove and beside the Round House. There is no sign of the old high priestess and they continue along the footpath, with its fine views of Ivell below them on their right. There is lush pastureland on their left, and as Olivia looks southward towards Stoford, she can see the Fish Tower and Jack the Treacle Eater follies. Finally they reach the wooded area of Ninesprings and they stroll along enjoying its attractive pathways, small stone bridges, ferny dells and waterfalls. Ahead of them is the secluded Thatched Cottage Tearoom and Olivia suggests they rest and take refreshments there, before they return home. She finds a seat in dappled shade, beneath the overhanging trees and she watches the sparrows and chaffinches taking crumbs from the other tables, whilst Apsey goes inside to ask for service. She returns with a waitress and Olivia orders tea and scones.

It is very pleasant and relaxing listening to the water trickling through the stones under the small bridge and down the waterfall beyond. Whilst they wait to be served Olivia takes in the scene before them. The cottage is tiny and there is only one other table that is occupied. She recognises the rich red hair of Lord Dryer's new wife, seated with her lady's maid and two small children playing nearby. They must both be around four years old and the little girl has the exact same colour and density of hair as Lady Dryer.

Olivia looks at Apsey and says in a low voice: "Don't you think that that child is the image of Lady Dryer?"

Apsey turns to look back at the children on the bridge. "Yes, she is, and she has the same colouring, but surely they've only just wed, they can't have a child that age… unless it was born out of wedlock." She watches the little girl as she runs back and forth across the bridge with her friend, waiting each time for their twigs to float through to the other side. "You know who she reminds me of?"

"Who?" responds Olivia.

"Our old chambermaid, Millie Bonfield, the girl who drowned herself about four years ago; perhaps she was hers? I believe the new Lady Dryer to be her sister."

Olivia is thoughtful. "Yes, I do remember her."

Apsey then adds, "It wouldn't surprise me if it was hers, for she was definitely one for the men. I can remember how she used to make eyes at your brother."

Olivia cannot take her eyes off the child. "Hmm, that is very interesting!" she says distractedly.

Louisa is dismayed that Olivia Meakins is seated near to them and well aware that she is watching Aurora with interest. It is the first time any of the Meakins' family has seen the child and Louisa is anxious lest she suspects the child's true identity. She doesn't want to be drawn into conversation with the wretched woman and so she suggests to Rosa that they should return to town shortly, to meet Joshua.

"We'd better set off soon Rosa; otherwise His

Lordship will be waiting for us, rather than the other way round. He'll be tired after being in court all day. It was kind of him to collect us during his midday adjournment."

"Of course, milady." Rosa finishes the remains of her cup of tea; then she picks up Aurora's velvet cape and Luke's fustian jacket and calls to them. "Come here children and put your things on, it's time to go."

They obediently run to the table and are soon dressed and ready to go. Louisa inwardly gives a sigh of relief, for she was expecting protests, but the children know there is the duck pond at the bottom of the hill and so they voice no objections. As they pass Olivia's table Louisa gives a brief nod of recognition; her heart pumps with anxiety as she turns quickly away, so as not to engage in dialogue. However, she senses the added interest in the witch's eyes and is convinced that she is suspicious.

They descend along the narrow footpath beside the rivulets of water from the nine springs and Rosa becomes aware of her mistress's troubled silence. "Is something bothering you, milady?" she asks.

"That was Olivia Meakins back there, with Apsey the other witch."

"Do you know, I thought I recognised her from the summer ball," says Rosa.

Louisa drops her voice to a mere whisper, "I'm afraid she might have realised that Aurora is too old to be the product of my marriage to Joshua, and I'm fearful that she may suspect that she's my sister Millie's child."

Rosa looks startled, "Your sister's child?"

"Shush!" She looks at the children to see if they are listening, then reassured they are busily chatting together, she continues, her voice low, "Yes, I'm afraid it's true, she was Millie's child and Olivia is, in reality, her aunt."

"Oh Lou-Lou, why did you never tell me?"

"We could tell no one. We couldn't risk that devil, Nathan Meakins, discovering the truth. But I'm very afraid that his sister may have guessed."

"Oh no, milady! I can see why you look so worried. That would be disastrous!"

"I know Rosa, why did we decide to go to Ninesprings, today of all days?"

They reach the bottom of the hill and the large duck pond, where the children count the different ducks and they excitedly spot a water vole. Then they continue through the town to the courthouse, passing the many glove factories along the way. In Frogg Street the two women and children put perfumed handkerchiefs to their noses, the stench is so bad.

They are all weary by the time they reach the courthouse and Louisa and Rosa are glad to be able to sit in the landau and wait for Joshua to join them.

Louisa fidgets impatiently. "I can't wait to get home to see how Gabriel is; he has been really troubled with his teething this time."

Rosa reassures her, "I'm sure he'll be fine; Beth is very experienced." She pauses and then continues tentatively, "Actually milady I've some good news to tell you myself, but I've been rather worried about it."

"Why would you be worried about good news, Rosa?" asks Louisa confused.

"Malachi and I are expecting our first child."

Louisa hugs her affectionately, noting the emotional tears of joy in her eyes and she offers her a handkerchief. "That's wonderful news, Rosa, you and Malachi must be so excited. When's the baby due?"

"In November, milady, and we're both over the

moon, but I'm concerned lest you'll require me to give notice."

"Of course not, you may stay for as long as you're fit and well and when the time comes that you're feeling tired, we can reduce your hours until the baby is born. Even when the baby is here, I'll be able to manage quite well, until you're quite sure you're able to cope."

"Oh! Lou-Lou! That's such a relief." She puts her hand up to her mouth, "I'm so sorry, I meant milady."

"We'll always be friends, Rosa. Never forget that, whatever our roles in life may be."

"Thank you, milady; Malachi's mother and Lucy have offered to mind the baby, while I'm at work."

"Well, on any occasion when Malachi's mother is unable to care for the child, you can bring the little one with you."

"Thank you, that's so kind; I'm very grateful."

"No Rosa, I'm the one who is grateful. I don't know what I'd do without our friendship; it's very special to me. Please reassure Malachi that your position is secure."

Finally her husband comes out of the courthouse and they set off home. He congratulates Rosa on her and Malachi's good news and although he appears tired, he joins in their conversations cheerfully. "Lord Helyar tells me that Keziah has returned from the Crimea and is visiting her family at Clifton Maybank. It might be a nice gesture to invite the young ladies over for afternoon tea, my dear."

"Did he mention how she fared during her time there?" Louisa asks with concern.

"No he didn't, but by all accounts she is hale and hearty."

"Thank the Lord that war is over. She must have undergone some dreadful experiences though, Joshua. I hope she hasn't been too traumatised."

He nods in agreement, and adds sagely, "She's a very courageous person to have considered such a selfless act and I hope everyone gives her due deference, my dear."

"I think your suggestion of inviting them to a soirée is the best idea and I will send out an invitation this evening."

On reaching their home, having dropped Luke off on the way, Louisa rushes up to the nursery with Aurora to find Gabriel playing happily with some wooden bricks. She gives him a warm hug and a kiss, and then asks Beth, "How has he been?"

"Like a little angel, as always, milady."

"I'm so pleased, thank you for looking after him. I'll take him downstairs now to see his father. Come on, Rora. Let's go and see Papa."

She had noticed a letter in the silver salver when they all came in and now she picks it up and takes it into the oak to read with Joshua later. The children settle together on the rug beside the fireplace. Gabriel has a toy train and Aurora is looking at her favourite story about Hansel and Gretel in her picture book, the *Grimm's Fairy Tales*. Moments later Joshua follows them in.

Louisa shows Joshua the envelope. "Look Joshua, it's a letter from Becky. Shall I read it out to you?"

"Yes, please do." He sits down in his armchair beside the empty fireplace and rests his feet on the fire fender. "Right, I'm ready now for Becky's news."

Louisa opens the seal and removes the letter. Then she slowly reads out his sister's words.

"Dearest Joshua and Louisa,

I am so excited to be able to tell you that Ben and I are now officially engaged to be married. We plan to follow the custom of the island and wait until I am with child before organising the ceremony, but when the time comes, I would very much like Aurora to be my handmaiden and Louisa, would you please consider being my maid of honour? Ben also has requested me to ask you, Joshua, if you will be his best man. I know it may be a while away yet, but we are saving for our bottom drawer at the moment and we want you to be prepared for it when the good Lord sees fit to bless us. Anyway, I thought you would be pleased to hear of our engagement.

Fondest regards,
Becky and Ben"

"Well, that is good news. It's about time Ben made their union official." He picks Aurora up and puts her on his knee. "What do you think Rora? Would you like to be Becky's flower-girl one day, and wear a pretty handmaiden's gown?"

"Yes, I really would, Papa." Joshua plants a tender kiss on his daughter's forehead.

"And you, Louisa, would you like to be her maid of honour?"

"Of course I would, Josh. You'd better reply this evening and let them know how pleased we all are for them."

"I will my dear. In the meantime, would you mind passing me the *Western Flying Post?*"

"Of course." She picks up the newspaper from the small table and passes it to him. "I noticed yesterday there's an advertisement in there for family portraits done by a Mr Brown at his Collodion Portrait Rooms in South Street. I wondered if we might take the children one afternoon?"

"That's a splendid idea Louisa, I'll ask Gareth to arrange an appointment for us.

Later that night, after Louisa has penned her invitation to the Bridewells, both the children are in bed and Joshua has written his letter, she finally tells him of her encounter with Olivia Meakins and confides in him her fears.

He tries to reassure her, persuading her there is little they can do to further conceal the truth. "I'm afraid, my darling, the truth has a way of coming out, but how can she prove anything? Besides, I'm sure her brother will never again set foot in this country and we have legally adopted Aurora, so she should be quite safe."

Louisa wants to believe what he says, but she cannot dispel the gripping fear that one day Nathan Meakins will return to Somerset and wreak havoc in her family.

That evening Olivia Meakins writes a letter to her brother, care of the Prison Service in Van Diemen's Land. She feels a little guilty, as she hasn't written before and she knows it will be months before the letter reaches the other side of the world, but at least by then he will have arrived and be settled somewhere, and it will be something from home to let him know she is missing him.

At the end of the letter she puts a postscript saying: *Mama and Papa both send their best wishes.* She thought she would add the postscript even though it wasn't true. Her parents have still not forgiven her brother for blackening the family name.

In East Coker, the butcher's boy, Bobby Tompkins, is taking his sweetheart, Amy Proctor, to the Easter Sunday morning service, at the church of St Michael and All Angels, in the hope that they will bump into her family among the Coker Poor House folk, because the following day it is her brother Edwin's fifteenth birthday. They are seated about halfway up the nave when the poor house inmates all file in.

Amy feels guilty; she cannot help feeling sorrow and shame to see her family dressed so shabbily in the workhouse uniform. She tries in vain to catch their attention, but they are not expecting to see her and she is unsuccessful. However, she is able to observe her mother between the intervening rows of the congregation and she is saddened further to see that her poor mother looks so despondent. After the service they have a short opportunity to talk. She rushes up enthusiastically to greet her brother. "Many happy returns for tomorrow, Edwin."

He smiles at her, momentarily thrilled to see her there, but his response seems half-hearted. "Thank you, Sis."

She surreptitiously passes him a bag of chocolate eggs. "For your birthday, Eddie, from Bobby and me, but please share a few with Mum, Hattie and Ellie, for Easter."

He kisses his sister and turns to Bobby. "Thanks Bobby, that's a real treat."

The two girls are both thrilled to see their big sister and rush forward for hugs. Then Amy goes to her mother and kisses her warmly, but she still seems sad and distracted. Amy feels pangs of disappointment. "What's wrong, Mama? I thought you'd all be pleased to see us, but you look so forlorn?"

Her mother is holding back her tears, as she whispers to her, "I don't want to upset our Eddie,

Amy, but they're taking him to the Ivell Union Workhouse after Easter, because he'll be fifteen years old and I can't bear the thought of losing him."

Amy cannot hide her horror. "Oh! Ma! I never thought they'd split you up." Bobby hears her exclamation and goes immediately to her side.

Her mother shakes her head in despair. "Neither did I, Amy. Neither did I."

The master's voice then calls out, "Come along folk, get into line, it's time we were leaving."

Amy blinks away her impending tears, before kissing her family in turn, and squeezing her mother's hand she says, "Please don't fret Ma. We'll do what we can to help, won't we Bobby?" She looks at Bobby appealingly, but he returns her look helplessly. His father's butcher business already supports five people, and she realises by his expression that they would not be able to take on any more.

She frowns, turning back to her mother. "Please don't despair, Mama, I'm working in the office of the glove factory now, maybe they'll need someone. Don't you worry, please, just trust me."

"But where would he live, Amy?"

"Please don't fret, Mama; I'm sure I'll think of something."

After Easter, Edwin Proctor is taken by Mr Wigglesworth, the warden of the Coker Poor House, in his pony and trap, into town to deliver him to the Ivell Union Workhouse. He is desperately sad to be leaving his mother and sisters behind and scared of what awaits him in the town. In contrast to his sombre mood it is a bright, sunny April morning, but he can just make out a rainbow in the west over the treetops, heralding some April showers, no doubt.

The pony trots along at a good pace and they are soon travelling down Hendford Hill. Edwin admires the large imposing properties that line the road as they pass through the manor of Hendford. It must be wonderful to live in such beautiful places. They pass through the town and on through the manor of Kingston and then left along the Preston Road. Finally they arrive at the workhouse.

Edwin counts twelve windows along the front of the large, plain, functional two-storey building. He notes the date 1837 carved in the triangle of stonework that forms the roof over the entrance block, outside which Mr Wigglesworth halts the pony. Edwin reluctantly clambers down, dragging his parcel of personal belongings behind him.

The threatened April showers have suddenly materialised and further dampen his spirits. Mr Wigglesworth hands him over to the porter, John Templeman. He shakes his hand and wishes him well, before hastily leaving him to his fate.

Mr Templeman takes him through to meet the master, Mr Bastable. As they walk through the workhouse Edwin can see they must be quite self-sufficient, for he passes a bakery, a laundry, and a cordwainer's, but the place is surrounded by a high hexagonal wall and it immediately feels to him like a prison.

Mr Bastable runs through the rules of the institution and then he relieves him of his package of personal belongings and provides him with a uniform of hard-wearing, coarse cloth. He is then shown by Templeman upstairs to the men's dormitory and allocated a narrow wooden bed, with a straw mattress and a bed covering, also filled with straw. The room still holds the unpleasant, fusty aroma of body odour. Their footsteps resound on the bare wooden floorboards and, as they leave the long room, he notices at the entrance there is a solitary sign hanging on the painted, plastered wall, displaying the workhouse rules. He follows the porter along the corridor, skirting two women on their hands and knees, scrubbing the wooden flooring. They pass the fever ward and Templeman shows him the men's bathroom, where again there is a sign displaying the bathing regulations, which the porter reads out to him.

He is then taken downstairs, past the schoolroom and outside into the men's exercise yard, thence through an exit to a small holding, through another gate, past the allotments to where he joins the men working in the piggery.

"This is Edwin Proctor. I want you to show him the ropes, Tattershall."

"What ropes? We don't have no ropes!"

"I want no lip from you, boy. You just mind your manners and get back to work before I clip you round the ear." The porter suddenly seems angry, but he turns to Edwin and gives him a reassuring smile, adding quietly, "Don't let Tattershall bully you, Proctor. You must stand up for yourself where he's concerned."

Edwin's heart sinks, as he notes the belligerent, sniggering and defiant attitude of the other boy. How he wishes he was back in Coker. It was no picnic back there, but at least he had his loving family with him.

The porter leaves him and returns to his post at the main entrance.

Tattershall passes him his shovel. "All this muck needs to be cleared away in barrows and taken and spread over the allotments. Then we 'ave to swill the sties down with buckets of water, feed the pigs and replace their bedding."

Edwin gives a huge despairing sigh, as he looks down the row of pigsties to the two other inmates at the far end, but he takes up the shovel and sets to work. He is splashed with the filthy manure as he labours, whilst well aware that Tattershall is taking the easier option of feeding the animals. Nonetheless he is resigned to the task, until the miserable boy suddenly trips him from behind and he falls headlong into the slimy, smelly effluent. As he comes up for air and staggers to his feet, Tattershall is laughing his head off. Edwin has never in his life felt such rage and he hurls himself at the boy who overbalances into the mire. The pigs are squealing madly and running around in circles, whilst both boys are scrabbling and fighting in the pig muck, when an overseer is attracted by the noise.

"What is going on here?" he demands.

The boys separate immediately. Edwin is embarrassed at his filthy condition, having only just been supplied with the new uniform and is terrified of the trouble he will get into as a result. He remains mute with fear.

However, Tattershall is quite the opposite; pointing angrily at him he yells, "It were 'im master, he attacked me, saying the work was too dirty for 'im and calling me a workhouse bastard."

The overseer, who has not come across Edwin before, looks at the boy in disbelief. He has muck all over his face, as well as his clothes and he asks him, "Is this true young man?"

Edwin is dumbfounded at the wretched boy's lies. He doesn't know what to say, he doesn't want to be known as a snitch, but it's his first day and he doesn't want to be known as a troublemaker either. "No sir, not entirely. I didn't call him names, sir. Tattershall tripped me from behind deliberately and when I fell in the muck he started laughing at me fit to bust. I must admit, I lost my temper then, but I didn't start it, sir."

"Well, in addition to no meat for a week, you can both continue with your work in that disgusting condition and let that be a lesson to you. You'll not enter the workhouse with those clothes on. At the end of your shift at midday, you'll remove your uniform and wash it out with buckets of water from the well. You'll clean off your boots and enter the building naked, taking the swilled clothing through to the laundry to be washed properly. They'll provide you with a change of uniform. Do you understand me?"

"Yes, sir," they say in unison.

"Now get back to work," he bellows at them and then he stalks off.

The two boys work in sullen silence, exceedingly uncomfortable with the muck caked all over them. Edwin especially resents his situation, as he feels he did nothing to deserve it.

He is even more resentful when, much to the onlooker's amusement, at the end of the morning he and Tattershall are forced to strip naked in front of the men breaking up rocks in the exercise yard. The pig muck has seeped right through to his underwear. He rinses his uniform in a bucket of water he pulls up from the well. Then he rings it all out over the vegetable patch. He repeats the procedure several times, washes his face and hands in another bucket of fresh water, and finally he pours the remainder over his body, but he cannot rid himself of the smell. All the time he tries to ignore Tattershall and the tittering and ribald comments of the other inmates. Eventually he takes the soiled clothes to the laundry where a couple of old women, with hardly any teeth between them, cackle away at the sight of him naked. Finally they control their hilarity and find him another set of clean clothes.

Even though he is not the only one to look a fool,

he is new, he knows no one and so there is no one to console and comfort him in his abject humiliation. He goes to the bathroom to have a proper wash, before they are expected to muster for their meatless dinner. He is careful to clean up the bathroom sink after he has used it and feels much better once he has washed himself with soap and dressed in the clean uniform.

He finally finds the dining area and sits in a space at the end of a long bench. After he has eaten his vegetables an overseer finds him and abruptly demands that he is to follow him to the bathroom, where to his horror he is shown one of the bathroom sinks in a filthy state and smelling of pig muck.

The overseer is irate. "I can't believe you would leave a sink in this condition, Proctor. I'm aware it's your first day here, but you can see clearly the bathing regulations on the sign. What were you thinking of?"

"It wasn't me, sir. I give you my word. I cleaned up my own mess, before dinner, sir. It must have been Tattershall."

"Well, that is strange because he swears it was you! As it has to have been one of you, I've no choice but to punish you *both*, *again*, and so you'll have a week without cheese, following on from this week."

His tummy rumbles with hunger, after having just one meal with no meat; he is surely going to be ravenous after two weeks. How he hates Tattershall for giving him all this trouble and worry and how he dreads putting up with this, day in, day out, for the foreseeable future!

CHAPTER SIX *(June – July 1856)*

TEA AND STRUMPETS

It is a sunny Saturday in June and Rosa is dressing Louisa's hair in readiness for her receiving the Bridewell sisters for afternoon tea. She asks her mistress, "How's your sister-in-law, Becky, milady? I've not heard about her and Ben for some time?"

"We had a letter from Becky back in April, bearing glad tidings, telling us that she and Ben are now officially engaged and, according to Portland tradition, they're trying for a baby, before they fix the wedding date."

"Oh that's wonderful news. It'll be so good for Aurora and Gabriel to have a little cousin."

Louisa says, thoughtfully, "I know… it will be amazing, especially for Becky. I just hope that, after that bad business with Meakins, she has no problems."

"I'm sure she'll be fine, milady." Rosa holds up the hand mirror for her to see the back of her head. "There! How's that?"

"Very pretty, Rosa, you certainly have a talent for hairdressing. I must say I feel more confident now to go downstairs and meet the beautiful Bridewells."

"They're no match for you, milady."

"I wouldn't go that far, Rosa, but thank you."

Later, whilst chatting to the three sisters, Louisa learns, from Keziah herself, a lot more about her experiences at Scutari. Keziah obviously enjoyed her time there, for she becomes elated whenever she speaks of it.

"Florence Nightingale is a tough taskmaster, but she's no less hard on herself. She was always the last person to do the rounds at night, hence her nickname: *The Lady with the Lamp.*" Keziah smiles at her, "I have to admit, I hold her in high regard. She's clever and intelligent and an accomplished writer. She knows a large number of influential people and is great friends with Sidney Herbert, he was our secretary of war at the time, and I think that's why we were eventually permitted to go."

Louisa is very impressed, "I'm filled with admiration for both yourself and Miss Nightingale, Keziah, but I cannot imagine how any woman could be willing to put herself in such jeopardy. Whatever made Miss Nightingale decide to risk her life and yours, by going to the Crimea in the first place?"

"She believes she's been called by God to devote her life to the service of others."

"But surely she was already doing wonderful work at St Thomas', in London?"

"Miss Nightingale had admittedly made her mark by training up the nurses there, but she felt she was needed more by our gallant wounded and dying soldiers."

"Is that how you felt too, Keziah?" asks Louisa.

"In a way, I suppose. I just didn't want to waste a moment longer on social pleasantries and pointless feminine attributes, but have nothing worthwhile to show for it."

"Very laudable, I'm sure," says Alicia, "but we were left behind at home, worried sick!"

Keziah laughs, "Well there really was no need. We were all quite safe, based as we were in a hospital several miles from the front."

Elsie offers around the sandwiches and Keziah takes one, thanks her and then continues with her story. "However, there was a truly fearless woman from Jamaica, called Mary Seacole, who was actually treating her patients on the battlefield."

"I've never heard of that!" says Serena intrigued, replacing her cup and saucer on the occasional table beside her.

"Well, I was told on good authority that although she was an expert at dealing with cholera, her application to join our team was rejected. But, as a successful business woman, she decided to travel to the Crimea at her own expense. She visited us at our hospital in Scutari, but again her offer of help was refused by Miss Nightingale. So she set up a business on her own, selling food and drinks to the British soldiers very close to the battlefront. The soldiers called it *The British Hotel* and in that way she earned the finance necessary to fund the medical treatments she so generously provided for them. On several occasions she was found treating wounded soldiers from both sides while the battle was raging around her."

"My goodness, I wonder why Miss Nightingale has had so much publicity and we've never even heard of this other fearless woman, Mary Seacole?" says Alicia in surprise.

"I think it's more to do with knowing the right people who wield the influence and have the necessary power," says her older sister, sagely.

Alicia then smiles and happily changes the subject, "Talking of knowing the right people; Keziah has met someone over there. Haven't you, Kez?"

Louisa believes Keziah may be blushing. "I have, yes. Last week I became betrothed to Captain James Blakely, of the 11th Hussars." She holds out her hand for Louisa to admire her engagement ring.

"Oh how lovely, Keziah. Congratulations. So you didn't abandon all social pleasantries after all!"

Keziah laughs, "No, I suppose not. He was wounded and I was, in his words, 'his ministering angel' and we fell in love. We plan to be married next year."

"Well, I'm very pleased your Crimean adventure turned out so unexpectedly fortuitous for you." Louisa is genuinely pleased for Keziah and very glad she invited the ladies to Alvington. She had been apprehensive, but the afternoon has been very relaxed and entertaining.

At the same moment that Louisa is listening to tales of the Crimea, Rebecca and Ben are walking hand in hand down the hill from Fortuneswell on Portland. They have chosen the shortcut through Mallams, as they are nearest to it. Rebecca is enjoying having Ben all to herself for a change; loving the feel of his larger, stronger hand holding hers. The soft, refreshing breeze coming off the sea gently lifts her hair and she couldn't be happier. As they go, they are chatting about their future together when, interrupting them, Rebecca hears the high-pitched voice of a woman calling out from an upstairs window, "Hello, Benjamin."

She looks up and is stunned to see a young woman hanging out of the window, waving to Ben, wearing only her underwear! They continue walking. *Whatever does she think she looks like and how dare she! The strumpet! But... how does she know my Ben?* She looks at Ben, who having smiled back at the little trollop, now looks decidedly uncomfortable. Then she hears another voice. Looking back at the window she can see another young girl has joined her friend and she is calling out, "Hey Ben we've missed you." Her hair is tied up in rags and she has large red spots of rouge on her cheeks.

Rebecca's heart sinks and her stomach churns. She feels tight pangs of jealousy and fear, as she realises that these two women know her Ben well. She turns away from them, unable to speak to him, unable to look at him. *When could this have happened? It's like a brothel! I cannot know him at all!* She walks on beside him, her heart and her eyes downcast. *How can I marry him now! Whatever should I do?* She needs to consider this before she blurts out the dreadful thoughts invading her mind. Her heart beating with anxiety she finally manages to put her thoughts into sober words. "How do you know those hussies?"

Ben looks shamefaced. "They're friends of Ma's brothers, Tom and Henry." His eyes will not meet hers.

"But they know *you*, Ben. They said they have *missed you*."

He looks at her beseechingly. "Please don't get upset, Becky. Let's go and sit on the beach and I'll tell you how I came to know them."

They walk on in silence, through Chiswell towards the cove, until they are seated side-by-side on the warm pebbles.

Ben takes a deep breath. "It all started when Uncle Henry started getting himself dolled up for someone and he wouldn't tell us who it was, so I followed him and, unknowingly, he led me to that bawdy house. I watched outside and saw, through a gap in the curtains, Henry with one of the women behaving saucily." He pauses, looking softly down at her. "I was a foolish lad back then, Becky, and I decided to tease him, but my seventeenth birthday was coming up and he got the better of me, by arranging a birthday surprise. He booked me a session with one of the girls."

She feels her tummy sinking. "You've been with one of those trollops?"

"Becky, it was years ago, I was only just seventeen. I'd such a lot to learn about women and they taught me."

"*They?*" She feels sick. "You went with more than one?"

"I admit I went with all of them over time, but I have *you* now. I don't go there any more. That's why they said they've missed me, Becky. Now that I have you, I don't need them anymore."

Her voice is trembling, "But… while I was in Somerset with my brother, did you need them then?"

"No!" he denies too quickly.

She looks at him, as if she can see into his very soul, and reluctantly he admits: "Sometimes… but surely it's better that I should go with one of them and simply pay them, rather than betray you with another loving beau. I don't love them, Becky. I love *you* and I want to marry *you*. I wouldn't *marry* one of them."

Tears run down her cheeks and fall into her lap. *How can I forgive him for this? He's behaving just like Meakins, unable to control his sexual urges. While I was being roughly and heartlessly defiled, he was carousing with whores!*

She gets up and walks away from him. She cannot think straight. She needs to be on her own. He tries to grab her arm, but she pulls away from him, angrily.

Ben is left feeling guilty, afraid more than anything that he will lose his sweetheart. *We are supposed to be engaged to be married. What if she breaks off our engagement? Whatever will Matthew and Violet think of me? Have I ruined all our future plans? How can I ever make amends?* In frustration he picks up a large pebble and throws it as far as he can into the white surf and then another and another, until eventually he tires and makes his way despondently towards the Cove House Inn to drown his sorrows.

Rebecca arrives home, her happy day with Ben spoilt; maybe her whole future in jeopardy. She sits in the window and stares out to sea. The sunshine sparkling on the water is making a spangled footpath to the shore, the seagulls are soaring overhead on the thermals and everyone is carrying on as normal, but Rebecca feels as if it is the end of her world.

She has no one to confide in. How can she besmirch Ben's name by telling her parents what he has done? He has always been her rock, her confidant, the one she has always turned to in times of trouble. *How can I live without him? I love him with all my heart, but he has betrayed me.*

Several days later, unaware of the tension between her daughter and Ben, Violet asks Rebecca to drop off her father's packed lunch at the boatyard.

Rebecca picks up the lunchbox wondering in exasperation, *why did Pa have to forget his lunch today of all days!* Unable to explain her reluctance to her mother, she sets off on her errand.

She marches straight into the building where Ben and her father are busy working on a new lerret. "Pa! Ma asked me to drop this off for you." She puts the package on the work bench and makes haste to leave, avoiding all eye contact with Ben.

Her father looks up from his work, just in time to see Rebecca's rear as she exits the building. He realises immediately that something is wrong between his daughter and her beau, but he keeps his own counsel.

Later that evening when they are sitting alone together he broaches the subject cautiously. "How come you didn't stop and have a chat with us this morning, Becky?"

"I had to go on some more errands for Ma."

"But you didn't even say 'hello' to Ben."

"Well, that may be because I'm rather cross with him, Pa."

Matthew looks surprised. "That's not like you Becky, you're never cross."

"Well, I'm really cross this time, Pa." She plonks down her sewing, angrily.

Matthew suppresses a smile. "Whatever has he done?"

Rebecca crumbles and goes to sit beside her father on the sofa. "Oh Pa, I didn't want to tell you, but he's been to that bawdy house in Mallams."

"Oh, I see," he responds, gravely.

"The harlots were calling out to him as we passed by there the other day, saying they were missing him. It was too discomforting for words, Pa. They were so wanton and common, they hardly had anything on."

"When was this, Becky?"

"It's been going on for years, Pa, even when I was in Somerset with Josh."

Unshed tears brim her eyes and he tries to reassure her. "But Ben has asked you to marry him. Surely he's not still seeing them now."

"Well, he says not, Pa, but how can I believe a word he says, after he's been deceiving me all this time?"

"Look Becky, you're still young and have a lot to

learn about men, but you're no longer a little girl and you need to understand that men are very different from women. Most men experience several relationships before they settle down with one woman, even though they don't like their women to be so promiscuous."

"But Pa, that's just not fair."

"Look my sweetheart, you love Ben, you always have done and he's a good man; a hard-working man, and he's asked you to marry him. He wouldn't have done so if he didn't love you. You'd be unwise to let his past misdemeanours come between you, when he assures you it's all ancient history. If he gives you his word he no longer consorts with those women, then I think you should believe him. I promise you, my darling, that what he's done in the past is no different to any other red-blooded male around here."

"Even you, Pa?"

"Well, I'm a bit different for I fell for your mother when we were very young."

"Well there you are, Pa. I want someone who loves me in a special way, just like you love Ma."

"Look Becky, we've never talked about this, but I was betrothed to your mother before Joshua's father, Richard Dryer, came on the scene and stole her from me."

Becky looks shocked, "Stole her! No Pa, how could she? I had no idea... that's dreadful!"

Even now after all these years the memory is still painful. "I admit I was left heartbroken, but during that period I never once looked at another woman. Then, after he was killed, I welcomed your mother back, because I simply adore her and I took care of Josh and loved him too, because he's her son. You could never understand the pain I went through when she cast me aside for Joshua's father, but I'll love your mother forever, and so I had to find it in my heart to forgive her. For me there was no other choice."

"Even though she'd betrayed you?"

"Even so." He puts his arm around her lovingly. "My darling, you must remember that you're quite a bit younger than Ben. He was bound to have flirted a few times before he realised what a beautiful woman you were turning into. You really can't blame him for that."

"If only he was just like you, Pa."

"He's not so different. Don't be too hard on him, love. He's a good catch you know. I always planned to train him up and leave my business in his safe hands, with a view to ensuring that with him, your future is secure." She still looks unhappy and unconvinced and so he decides to try a different tack. "If I were you, Becky, I wouldn't want to give Ben any excuse to return to see those wanton women. I think you should use your feminine wiles and fight for him, make sure *they* are the losers and not you."

Violet then enters the room. Rebecca surreptitiously wipes away her tears and Matthew quickly removes his arm and tactfully changes the subject.

At Alvington Manor one morning in early July, Joshua is engrossed in his estate accounts when Gareth knocks on his study door and enters.

"My lord, I thought you should know that Rose Smith has come down from Camp Road and she's in the kitchen with Flora, in a dreadful state. Apparently she woke up this morning to find her husband, Bert, dead in bed beside her."

"My goodness! The poor woman! Would you kindly see she gets a shot of brandy, and then bring her up to see me, please Gareth?"

"Of course, my lord." The butler turns to leave.

"Oh, and Gareth?" He halts in the doorway. "You'd better send John Moore to fetch Dr Gillingham."

"Yes, my lord." Joshua looks at the family collodion portrait, hanging in pride of place on his study wall. Aurora looks like a mini Louisa, both with their wonderful abundant curls and Gabriel a tiny dark-haired version of him. He cannot imagine the pain of losing Louisa, or any member of his family and his heart goes out to poor Rose.

About fifteen minutes later Gareth returns with Rose dabbing frantically at her red and puffy eyes. "I'm so sorry to bother you, my lord; I didn't know what to do with myself and I thought that Flora might know what I should do."

"Please take a seat, Rose. My sincere condolences at your sad loss, it must have been a frightful shock for you."

"It was my lord, he hadn't even been ill!"

"Well, perhaps that is merciful for both of you. Anyway, Rose, my dear, I want to help you with the funeral arrangements and discuss any future plans you may have."

"To be honest, my lord, I can't collect my thoughts at the moment. I've always been so happy here with my Bert, but now that I'm going to be all on my own, I wish to God I was nearer to my son, Howard." Fresh floods of tears run down her cheeks and she blows her nose, noisily.

"Where is your son, Rose?"

"He's working as a clerk for a solicitor in Bath."

"Well, I think you should take a little time to think about whether, or not, you wish to uproot yourself after all these years. You're still welcome to see out your days in our estate cottage if you so wish."

She sniffs, unhappily. "Thank you, my lord; that's a load off my mind. I don't think I'm ready to make any rash decisions just now."

"I quite understand. John Moore has gone to fetch Dr Gillingham and I'll come back with you, to see that Bert has all the necessary checks and certifications. If you'd like to write a letter to your son, I'll see that it's posted for you."

"Thank you, my lord, I'm sorry to bother you, I know you're busy, but I didn't know what to do." She starts weeping again and Joshua pours her another brandy before going with her back up the hill.

He helps her with Dr Gillingham and promises to deal with Mr Montague, the funeral director. When the doctor has completed the formalities and left, and she has written the note to her son, Charlotte Hodinott knocks on her door and asks her if she would like to stay with them overnight.

Joshua can see she is quite overcome with emotion and speaks on her behalf, "I think that's a brilliant idea, Lottie, and most kind of you." He turns back to Rose. "Come on Rose, go and put some things together. You'll be better off with company and Lottie will look after you tonight."

Ten days later, after the funeral has taken place at the Alvington Manor church and Rose has had a chance to discuss things with her son, she decides she wants to go and live nearer to him in Bath and Joshua arranges lodgings for her in a terraced house on Brooklyn Road, near to her son's workplace. All the staff and her neighbours at Camp Road are very sorrowful to see her go. Flora lays on a special farewell spread in the kitchen and after such a warm-hearted gathering, Rose sets off with Billy more cheerfully, leaving behind her many happy memories.

Back on Portland, over the past few weeks, Rebecca has thought a lot about her father's comments. She has been rather distant with her mother, still annoyed at the way she had thoughtlessly treated her father all those years ago. Her mother in turn has noticed the change in Rebecca's manner towards her and one morning, after she has been particularly distant, she asks her, "Have I done something to upset you, Becky?"

Wrong footed, Rebecca hesitates – it was all such a long time ago, but she wouldn't have treated her father like her mother had done. "I didn't know until recently that you and Pa were betrothed, before Josh's pa came on the scene and came between you."

Her mother looks surprised and uncomfortable. "Who told you that?"

"Pa did."

"Well, it was a very long time ago, darling, and your father forgave me, so I hope that you can too."

Rebecca's shoulders slump. "I just want to try to understand how you could do that to Pa, who is so kind and gentle and wouldn't hurt a fly."

Violet puts her arm around her daughter. "It was complicated Becky, but I loved them both in very different ways. You're right about your father, he is loving and loyal and no one could have been a better husband or father. But your pa and I were young then and, in comparison, Richard was mature, handsome and elegant. He was passionate and mysterious and he made my heart race and my body tingle whenever he touched me and more than that, I knew he fervently loved me."

"But Pa loved you, too!"

"I know he did, darling, and it was the hardest decision of my life, but I was finally swayed by the fact that I needed protection, and Richard was able to provide it for me."

"What do you mean, protection?" she asks, confused.

"Come and sit down and I'll tell you how it all happened." Rebecca sits down impatiently beside her mother on the sofa.

"You see, he rescued me when I was attacked one dreadful night by two drunken sailors. As they came at me, I stumbled and fell to the ground and my lantern smashed. I thought that they were both going to ravage me. One of them was suddenly on top of me and, panicking, I grabbed a sliver of glass from the smashed lantern and plunged it into his chest. It was done out of terror and in my defence, but it turned out that he died."

Rebecca is horrified, tears fill her eyes at her mother's words. "I had no idea! All my life you've never mentioned it."

"Let me finish; now I've started, darling. I was in a terrible state of fear and alarm and Richard, who was patrolling that night, heard my screams and came running to the rescue. The following day he came to see me, to tell me that the sailor had died and he promised to give me an alibi, if I would only marry him. He said that the alibi wouldn't be taken seriously if we hadn't been walking out together."

"But that's blackmail!" She blinks away her tears. "How could you love someone who was capable of such a mean trick?"

"I know, and I mistrusted him at the time for manipulating me, but he had a point and I knew, even then, that he did it because he loved me so much and it was the only way he could see of protecting me."

"Where was my pa when all this was going on?"

"They were all abroad on a fishing trip, your uncles and your grandpa too, and your grandma was sick, which was why I was out after dark that night to fetch a potion for her from Auntie Sarah. Richard was the only one I could turn to and he was there for me."

Rebecca looks sorrowfully down at her hands, understanding the fear her mother felt because of how she felt when Nathan Meakins raped her; recognising the symptoms of true love, for that is the very same effect that Ben has on her. Her mind dwells on her sweetheart for a moment. Despite her distrust, there's no denying she still loves Ben and she cannot bear the thought of seeing him with anyone else, let alone those wanton whores.

"I can see that you must have been terrified, Ma. I'm sorry for misjudging you, without all the facts. I do understand how you were able to love both of them. I believe you were very lucky to have found true love twice."

"I know and I thank God for it every day. I wouldn't have two gorgeous children like you and Josh otherwise. I'm a very fortunate woman."

"Ben and I have had a quarrel and we haven't spoken to each other since."

"Is that what has been making you so miserable?"

"Yes… I suppose so."

"Well, I think you ought to go and see him and have a chat and try to sort it out."

"Maybe… I'll have a think about it."

"I think that's advisable; life is far too short for disagreements." Her mother kisses her on her forehead and Rebecca gives her a warm hug in return. "I hope you can resolve things with Ben, but I have to go now, darling, or Mollie will wonder what has happened to me." She goes to find her bonnet before going off to work at Fortune's Corner.

Since delivering her father's lunch several weeks ago Rebecca has successfully managed to avoid bumping into Ben, but maybe her parents are right and she should at least give him a chance to prove himself. She resolves to go to the boathouse and ask him to take a stroll with her to try to sort things out.

She puts on her favourite floral-print summer gown and pins up her hair; she wants to make a good impression now that she has decided to go and see him. Then a rogue thought sneaks into her head: *It would be so awfully embarrassing if in the last few weeks he's decided he is better off without me.* Her tummy turns over at that thought, but she pushes it aside.

It is a warm and balmy summer day, as she makes her way down to the boatyard at lunchtime. Her heart is thumping in anticipation of the reception she might receive, but when she walks in and she sees Ben, with his loose shirtsleeves rolled up and his tanned, muscular arms working on the hull of a large lerret, she wants the pain to go away forever and for him to take her in his strong arms and never let her go.

Her father is working over in the far corner and he gives her a reassuring smile. The building smells of the sweet scent of sawdust, which Becky always associates with both Ben and her father.

Ben looks up from his work and sees her and for a second they seem frozen in the moment. She steps towards him shyly, "Will you take a walk with me, Ben?" she asks him.

His face remains unreadable as he looks across at her father, "All right with you, boss?"

"Take all the time you need, Ben."

She fears she has left it too late to mend the rift, but reminds herself that she is, after all, the injured party. He follows her out into the sunshine and they walk, side-by-side, along the compressed silt towards the beach. A couple of passing villagers nod to them as they go. Although aware it is really up to her to speak first, she cannot find the right words.

The awkward silence is eventually broken by Ben. "Am I at last forgiven then, Becky?"

Rebecca bristles at the words 'at last', as if she has made him wait deliberately to punish him. This is not going as she had hoped.

She sighs, "I don't think you realise how much you hurt me, Ben," she says defensively, observing him carefully.

He raises his eyebrows and gives a derisive snort, "I think you've made that quite obvious, Becky."

She can detect no feelings of remorse and her heart sinks, but she perseveres, "I wanted our love to be so strong that *no one* could come between us. I've always felt that you're the only one for me and I wanted *you* to feel that way too."

He answers her impatiently, "Becky, I gave you my word that I would no longer visit that house in Mallams. I asked you to *marry me*, for Christ's sake! Isn't that enough evidence of my feelings for you?"

He still doesn't want to admit the damage he's done! He's acting as if it can all be brushed under the rug! "But don't you realise that every time I look at you now, I see you up to things with one of those hussies and, try as I may, I can't get that out of my head!"

His whole body appears to sag, "Then it would appear there is no hope for us, Becky. For I cannot undo what's done!" He turns away from her impatiently, and despondently retraces his steps back towards the boatyard.

She hears him mumble, "At least with them I didn't have to put up with all this crappy nagging!"

Rebecca feels sick to her stomach! *There really is no way back. He's not even trying to make amends.* She stands rooted to the spot and watches, as her last chance to rectify matters slips away.

CHAPTER SEVEN *(August 1856)*

ALMS FOR THE POOR HOUSE

Joshua has been working all day in his study, the late August sunlight is fading and he has just put down his dipping pen when Gareth informs him he has visitors.

"Who is it, Gareth?"

"It's Amy Proctor, my lord, and her beau, Bobby Tompkins."

"Please show them in, Gareth. Then could you also light the lamps. I think a storm is threatening."

Gareth stands aside for them to enter. The poor girl looks terrified.

"Hello Amy, Bobby, how nice to see you again. How can I help you?"

There is an uncomfortable silence as Gareth attends to the lamps, and then Bobby speaks up, "Amy is worried about her family, my lord."

Joshua smiles at the young girl, "Don't be shy Amy, say your piece."

She steps forward. "I'm sorry to disturb you, my lord, but I'm at my wit's end. I'm so worried about my ma. She was bad enough when our pa died, when I had to go into service with the Meakins family, and Ma and my brother and sisters had to go into the Coker Poor House. But now they've taken our Edwin away, she's beside herself with worry and grief all over again and I'm afraid she'll make herself ill, my lord."

"Why have they taken Edwin away?"

She looks down at the carpet, blinking away her tears. "Because he's turned fifteen and so he has to go with the men into the Ivell Workhouse to do harder work and make room for more women and younger children at the Coker Poor House." She looks at him pleadingly, "Please sir, can you help us? Ma is so low in her spirits."

"I'll look into it for you, Amy. I suppose as long as your family are all together you'll be happier."

"Yes, my lord."

"Are you still residing with Bobby's family?"

"Yes I am, my lord, but I'm now employed in the office of the Clothier glove factory in Frogg Street. Jean Hawkins told me about the vacancy, as she also works there now, in the sewing room, sir."

"Are you happy there, Amy?"

"Yes, my lord. Apart from the fact that parts of it are really smelly, the people are nice, but more importantly it means I can pay for my keep at Bobby's house and we're saving up to be wed one day."

"I'm very pleased for both of you. I'll give the matter of your concern some thought and I promise I'll do my best to resolve the problems for your mother and Edwin."

"Thank you, my lord. Thank you so much!" Amy is quite overcome and Bobby puts his arm around her comfortingly. Then he looks up at Joshua. "We greatly appreciate your looking into it for us, my lord."

"You are welcome."

Joshua asks Gareth, who has been standing quietly in attendance at the door, to see them both out.

Later, Joshua discusses the matter with Louisa. "I can see why Amy's mother is concerned; there are all manner of men in that workhouse and Edwin is barely more than a child with no family to turn to if things should not go well for him."

Louisa looks lovingly at him. "I know… but I can't help thinking that if it hadn't been for your kind, soft heart, my darling, allowing for Aurora to be cared for here, it might have been our dear little cherished daughter's fate. It doesn't bear thinking about."

"You know I could never have let her go there… especially after all you girls were so besotted by her."

They both sit quietly remembering the event and Louisa resolves to find a solution to help the Proctor family. "Do you think we might be able to find work for Edwin on the estate, Josh?" she suggests, cautiously.

"Well, it might be an idea to have a sort of man Friday about the place."

"Man Friday?"

"Yes, Louisa. It means a man of all work. It comes from the novel *Robinson Crusoe* by Daniel Defoe. In the story Crusoe rescues a native man from a cannibal tribe and earns his gratitude and loyalty. He becomes his servant and man of all work on the island and he calls him 'Friday' which is the day they first met."

She considers this idea. "Well, I think a man of all work would be very useful. But if we do employ him, where will he stay?"

"I would think there's enough room for him above the stables with Billy, and he could learn from him and the gardeners, perhaps help Michael Porter with his tasks and maybe help with the hedging and ditching if anyone is sick."

Louisa suddenly has an exciting idea, "What about number seven Camp Road? We could house the whole family and take them out of the poor house system altogether, if they were to live in Rose and Bert's old cottage."

Joshua considers this. "Well, I suppose we could find work for the mother and sister too, if they are willing and able." Later he is to wonder why he didn't think of it himself.

"Oh Joshua! That would be wonderful for them and Amy would be so relieved."

"Well, let's not throw caution to the wind. I think you ought to go and meet the mother and see if you think they'll be suitable, without disclosing our possible solution to their problem."

"I could go with Billy when he takes the harvest alms."

"That is a good idea, Louisa. You'll be able to see exactly what they're up against at the same time."

After the harvest supper, Louisa goes with Billy and Rosa to the Coker Poor House. She is eager to see for herself the conditions they have to endure, there and in the candle factory, where many of the inmates are employed. Billy has loaded the carriage with the hamper and other alms that Flora has prepared and is waiting for them outside on the gravel. There is a gentle drizzle falling, but it is not far to Burton Lane in East Coker and once the ladies are both settled inside the carriage, the horses set off at a brisk trot and they are soon on their way. They go up the hill, past Keeper's Cottage and turn left, along Camp Road.

Louisa glances sadly into Bert and Rose's empty estate cottage as they pass by and wonders how Rose is settling into her new home in Bath; hopefully she is feeling better now that her husband's funeral is over and she is so much closer to her son. *That place will make a nice little family home if I can work out an effective plan.*

She turns to Rosa. "Rosa, while we're at the poor house, I want you to look out for Amy Proctor's family. Do you remember the young girl who was working with Jean Hawkins for the Meakins family and they ran away in the night because they were afraid for Amy's safety?

"Yes I do, she attested against Meakins in support of Becky's court case."

"That's right. Well, Amy has spoken to Joshua and she's very concerned about her mother. Apparently they've taken away her son, Edwin, and placed him in the Ivell Workhouse and she's beside herself with worry. Amy has asked if there's anything that Joshua can do to help them."

"That is so sad! I hope His Lordship will be able to help them."

"Yes, so do I."

They cross the main Ivell to Exeter road and then not long afterwards they turn left towards North Coker. The road is narrow and they have to ease slowly past another carriage, before finally turning left again into Burton Lane. Clucking chickens scatter as the carriage wends its way past Burton Farmhouse and down the little lane. Finally they reach the high gates of the poor house and Billy jumps down to open them in order to drive the carriage inside. One of the paupers closes the gates behind them. Louisa immediately notices how thin the majority of the adult inmates are. *Their diet must surely be inadequate.*

The warden comes rushing out to welcome them with a large umbrella and instructs some of the younger inmates to assist Billy. He immediately ushers Louisa and Rosa out of the rain and into his office. Louisa however, is gratified to see through the office window how eager the youngsters are to help Billy unload their alms.

"Good morning ladies, I'm Mr Wigglesworth

and this is my wife who's the matron here." Louisa turns away from the window and the women dip their curtseys and both reply, "Good morning."

He asks his wife, "May we have some tea, please, my dear?"

Mrs Wigglesworth says, "Of course, Cuthbert," and she leaves the office.

"Please ladies, take a seat."

They both sit down on wooden, ladder-back chairs beside his desk. The office is a well-appointed room, housing an enormous bookshelf covered in dusty old books, a cabinet, presumably for inmate's records, and a side table.

"Would it be possible for us to have a look around later, Mr Wigglesworth?" As Louisa speaks his name she notices Rosa holding back her mirth.

"Of course, my dear lady, it will be my pleasure to give you a guided tour."

"Thank you. We'll look forward to that, won't we, Rosa?"

"Yes, I'm sure it will be very illuminating. How many people are housed here, sir?" asks Rosa composing herself.

"There are eighteen women and twenty-four children."

"My goodness, how are they all occupied?" asks Louisa.

"The able-bodied women and older children are employed in the candle factory and the simpler women are employed with cleaning and supervising the younger children."

Mrs Wigglesworth returns with a tea tray and places it on the side table. She pours the tea and serves Louisa, Rosa and then her husband.

Louisa thoughtfully stirs some sugar into the strong tea. "What is the inmate's usual diet, sir?" asks Louisa boldly.

"They all have a breakfast of gruel, their dinner is meat of one sort or another and vegetables, potatoes and dumplings, followed by rice, or suet pudding, and then later they're given bread and cheese, or broth for their supper." He pulls up his braces which tighten over the abundant flesh of his belly. "I assure you they should have no complaints."

Louisa smiles politely and replaces her teacup in the saucer. "Well, I hope that they enjoy the wonderful meat pies and fruit tarts made by our cook and the root vegetables from the farm."

"I'm sure we will, milady," says Mr Wigglesworth, licking his lips at the thought.

She asks him, "Do the children have any schooling, or are they too busy working?"

"They're instructed in reading, writing, arithmetic and Christian principles for two hours a day, after their manual work."

She stands up and places her empty teacup on the tea tray. "May we have a look around now, Mr Wigglesworth?"

"Of course, my dear, please come this way."

Rosa downs the remainder of her tea and jumps up to trail behind them, her advancing pregnancy slowing her somewhat.

They follow him to the dormitory where the cots are divided by wooden panelling and some of the youngest children are on straw mattresses with nothing to stimulate them, being watched by the oldest of the inmates, who at the same time are picking oakum. Louisa feels very sorry for them. *Poor little mites! How dreadful it would have been if Aurora had ended up here in this dismal, hopeless place.* He shows them the ablution block where two younger women are lethargically scrubbing the floors, their hands red raw, and then on to the workplace. He holds the umbrella aloft for the ladies, as they cross the yard.

The candle factory is a large barn-like structure and on their approach, Louisa becomes aware of a rather unpleasant odour emanating from the place. As they enter, Mr Wigglesworth stows the umbrella, and the ladies are forced to take their handkerchiefs from their reticules to hold against their noses. The stench is coming from the rows of troughs containing the hot tallow and the workroom is dirty, humid and airless. Louisa is concerned for Rosa; in her pregnant state the smell must be turning her stomach. She whispers to her, "Do you need to step outside, Rosa?"

She smiles at her mistress's consideration, "No milady, I've a strong constitution."

Mr Wigglesworth is apologetic, "I'm sorry about the smell, my dear. It could be worse. We do use the best sheep and cow tallow and lately we've been mixing it with paraffin wax to give the candles a better light and to reduce the odour." Louisa is aware of him observing her and then he adds defensively, "It would be even more intolerable if we were to use pig fat."

Louisa, still with the handkerchief held under her nose, turns to watch as the four, red-faced women operating the dipping rods are lowering them into the tallow and then raising them out to cool. From each broach there are upwards of one hundred lengths of hemp wick hanging, gradually increasing in size with the tallow mixture to form the candles. The chandler is overseeing their work and when he sees Mr Wigglesworth he beckons to him.

Louisa and Rosa take this opportunity to talk to one of the women. She is dressed the same as the other poor house women, in a blue ankle-length, shapeless shift frock and a smock, covered by a coarse canvas apron. Protruding from underneath her mob cap, there hangs limp tendrils of hair in the steamy atmosphere. Louisa lowers her handkerchief as she speaks to her.

"I wonder if you might help me. We're looking for a member of the Proctor family. Could you tell me if anyone in here is from that family?"

"Yes ma'am, there is: Ruth and Hattie... little Ellie is still in the dormitory."

"Can you please point the mother out to me?"

"Yes ma'am. That would be Ruth." She points out one of the women. "She is over there, ma'am."

"Thank you."

Whilst Mr Wigglesworth is distracted with the chandler, they hastily make their way past the hot troughs to talk to Ruth Proctor. She is wiping the perspiration from her brow, as she labours over the trough of hot tallow.

"Hello, Mrs Proctor, I realise you don't know me, but I'm a friend of your daughter, Amy. She has lately spoken to my husband about your fears for your son Edwin, who's recently been sent to the Ivell workhouse."

Ruth Proctor looks cagey, "I'm sorry ma'am, but who exactly are you?"

"I'm Louisa Dryer, the wife of Lord Joshua Dryer. Do not fear, I'm not here to cause trouble for you, I'm here to try to help you."

"I don't see what can be done, milady," she replies despondently. "He's fifteen now and they say he must be with the men-folk and work to contribute to his living costs."

"Well, I believe I have an attractive proposition for you. There is a recently vacated tied cottage on my husband's estate and if we could provide employment for yourself, your daughter Hattie and Edwin, would you consider coming to work for us and living together in the cottage?"

Ruth Proctor's eyes fill with tears. "You really mean it, milady? There's a cottage where we could all be safe and together again?"

"Yes, Ruth, I really mean it. Would you like that? There's work for Hattie in the kitchens and Edwin could help on the farm, in the gardens, or with the horses. Your youngest daughter… is it Ellie?"

"Yes, milady."

"Well, she'd be able to go to school with Toby Boucher, our gamekeeper's son. Perhaps you would like to help his mother, who's our cook, while Ellie is in school?"

"Oh! Milady!" She draws the back of her hand across her eyes to wipe away her tears. "I don't know how to thank you. Of course we'd like it! When can we start?"

"Well, I'll have to speak to Mr Wigglesworth, but I'm sure the sooner he has three fewer mouths to feed, the better for him."

"Can we come with you now, milady?"

"Well, just leave it with me a moment. If you don't have too much to take with you, and you don't mind Ellie sitting on your lap, I think we could all squeeze into the carriage."

Louisa asks Ruth Proctor to enlighten her older daughter, Hattie, while she explains the situation to Mr Wigglesworth.

Mr Wigglesworth is surprised at this request. "Well, milady, it's not as simple as that, you know. I usually get about three hours' notice in which to prepare and complete all the forms before they can be discharged, and there are three of them."

"I understand that, Mr Wigglesworth, but surely the sooner we take them off your hands the better. The Poor Law commissioners should be grateful they are able to support themselves now."

"Of course, ma'am, I'll do my best to expedite the process while they prepare themselves; I'll enlist the help of my good lady wife."

He strolls over to talk to Ruth and Hattie and he

looks down quite kindly at them, saying, "Go and get changed into your personal things. Matron will find your parcels for you and then she'll help me in the office. I'm pleased for you Ruth, my dear. You and your children have been no trouble at all for us, model inmates, if I might say so."

"Thank you, master." She puts her arm around Hattie and hugs her excitedly, as they walk back towards the poor house to go and find Ellie.

Mr Wigglesworth has a word with the chandler and has soon replaced Ruth with another woman dipping the candles and another young girl takes over Hattie's job packing them into boxes. Then he hurriedly rushes back to his office.

Louisa and Rosa are pleased to leave the smelly factory behind them. It has stopped raining and they go to find Billy and explain to him what is happening next. Then they go to the office and sit patiently waiting, until the official matters are concluded. After about half an hour the matron enters the office to say the women are ready and she joins her husband with the paperwork. Louisa and Rosa go outside into the autumn sunshine.

Ruth Proctor then emerges from the poor house looking quite elegant; she is dressed in a smart rust-coloured, ankle-length skirt and jacket with a matching hat, and eight-year-old Ellie is wearing her older sister's Sunday best frock that now fits her perfectly, but poor Hattie, who at twelve years old has obviously grown out of her original outfits, looks a little embarrassed, as she has had to borrow another of her mother's gowns.

Ruth smiles happily and puts her arm around her discomfited daughter, "I'm afraid Hattie looks rather a Polly-long-frock, but we'll soon remedy that once we get settled."

Ruth and Hattie Proctor climb up into the

carriage and sit down on one side with little Ellie squeezed in between them. Their faces are full of the excitement and anticipation of seeing their new home for the first time. Rosa sits opposite them and they wait patiently for the master and matron to conclude the paperwork. Mr Wigglesworth eventually emerges with the discharge papers. Louisa shakes hands with him. "Thank you for showing us around, Mr Wigglesworth."

"It was my pleasure, Lady Dryer. I'm much obliged to both you and your husband for donating the splendid food hampers, and for your benevolence in accommodating the Proctors."

Billy has loaded up their meagre belongings and he helps Louisa on board; then he climbs into the driver's seat, clicks his tongue and the horses set off.

Mr Wigglesworth waves as he closes the gates of the poor house behind them.

On reaching the last of the Camp Road cottages, Billy pulls the horses to a standstill and applies the brake to the carriage. He jumps down to help the ladies disembark.

"Don't forget the small food parcel for them, Billy," whispers Rosa.

Billy gets the food parcel from the carriage, whilst Louisa fumbles in her reticule for the key and then they follow her along the short path to the front door.

Ruth Proctor is staring with wonder at the long garden. "Oh! Milady, it's perfect. It even has a garden. You don't know how much I've missed my garden at Stoford. I can't wait to see what's growing there."

"Well, Mr Smith was a keen gardener and I'm sure at the end of your plot there will be a very productive vegetable patch. However, to supplement it for now we have a small food parcel for you. We didn't want you to miss out on the harvest festival alms." Billy hands Ruth the food parcel.

"How marvellous! I can't believe how our fortunes have changed. I'm so grateful to you and your kind husband, milady."

"It is our pleasure. Your Amy was very plucky, standing up for herself against a very cruel man and my husband felt such courage should be rewarded."

The door is opened and Louisa stands aside for Ruth and the two girls to go inside their new home. Hattie and Ellie both rush in ahead of their mother, eager to see everything and they are soon racing up the stairs to check out the bedrooms. The rooms are a little dusty, having been shut up for a while, but the basic furniture is all there and, apart from some washing of curtains and bedding, the family have a ready-made home.

Ruth thoughtfully puts the food parcel down on the kitchen table. "When do you think we could have Edwin back, milady?"

"Well, we had to make sure you were happy with the arrangement before we could approach the Ivell Workhouse, but I'm sure my husband will be able to fetch him for you, perhaps even by tomorrow."

Louisa can see the relief in the poor woman's eyes.

"Thank you so much for this. We'll forever be in your debt."

"Well, in return we'll be expecting you all to report at the manor at seven each morning for your duties. To find the manor, you just go along this road towards Odcombe and take the next right down Pound Lane. You'll pass Keeper's Cottage, where our cook and gamekeeper live with their daughter, Lettie, and son, Toby, and then at the bottom of the lane you'll come to Alvington.

"Is it Toby who'll be going to school with Ellie?"

"Yes, Ruth. I'll ask him to wait for her at the top of the lane and then they can walk together to the village school in Odcombe. I look forward to seeing you and Hattie tomorrow morning. Goodbye Mrs Proctor." She calls up the stairs to the girls, "Goodbye Hattie and Ellie."

She hears two shy voices, "Goodbye ma'am," from the bedrooms above her.

Billy assists Louisa and Rosa in getting back into the carriage and they leave the happy family, blissfully exploring their new home.

Rosa looks at her mistress. "You must feel so pleased to be able to do something like that for Amy's unfortunate family. It's been a good day today, hasn't it?"

"It really has, Rosa. This has been so gratifying for me. I'd no idea how wonderful it would feel to be in a position where it was in my power to solve all of someone's problems and bring so much relief and pleasure to them. I can't wait to tell Joshua that he can go ahead with collecting Edwin from the workhouse. Hopefully, he too will have an equally rewarding experience tomorrow."

The following day Joshua sets off to the Ivell Union Workhouse situated on the north side of the Preston Road. He pulls up the gig outside the two-storey entrance block and makes for the porter's room. As one of the guardians, he has visited the boardroom upstairs many times. The porter, John Templeman, greets him through the hatch. "Good day, Lord Dryer, how can I help you?"

"Can you please tell me the whereabouts of a young fellow called Edwin Proctor?"

The porter looks down his list of inmates. "He's

helping in the piggery this morning, milord. Would you care to follow me and I'll take you to him?"

"Well, I'd better have a word with Mr Bastable first please, John?"

"I'm not sure the master is available, milord, but please follow me and I'll take you to his office."

As they approach the hub in the centre of the hexagonal-planned courtyard Joshua can see Mr Bastable in his quarters above the kitchens overlooking the segregated exercise yards. The man smiles in greeting and waves him up.

John Templeman directs him through the kitchens to the stairs up to the master's quarters. Joshua is aware of the female paupers staring at him with curiosity. At the top of the stairs he is shown into the warden's office.

The warden bows his head respectfully. "Good day to you, my lord. This is a most pleasant surprise. How can I help you?"

"Well, you've recently taken into your care a young man of fifteen years, by the name of Edwin Proctor. He is of a good family who, due to the death of the father, have fallen on hard times and I'm of a mind to house them and employ them all on my estate. I know it'll take time to sort out his discharge papers, but I'm happy to return in three hours' time to collect him, once everything is in order."

"Of course, my lord, I'll see to it immediately."

"I should like to go and see him, in the meantime, to tell him of his change in fortunes personally."

"Of course, my lord, allow me." He holds out his hand for Joshua to go back down the stairs and they exit the kitchens via the back door and into the male exercise yard where some of the able-bodied male inmates are breaking up more rocks. Through an exit on the right, they leave the yard and enter the area of a small holding; ducks and chickens hurriedly disperse as they pass through another gate and into an allotment area, where the pigsties are at the far end. Joshua can see two men shovelling manure. The master walks up to the youngest, who must be Edwin. "This gentleman would like a word with you, lad."

"Hello Edwin. I've come to see you, I hope the bearer of glad tidings. I'm here to tell you that your mother and sisters have moved into one of my estate cottages. I have employment for them in my kitchen, and in addition to this, if you can give me your word that you'll work diligently and honestly, and you would care to join them, I'd also like to offer you a home and employment with them on the Alvington estate."

The boy's face lights up. "Indeed I would, sir. You'll not find a more loyal servant, my lord. You have my solemn word."

"I can offer you work, helping the gardeners, in the stables, or on the farm. We'll try you out and see where you're best suited. Mr Bastable is going to sort out the paperwork and I'll return in about three hours to collect you and take you back to Alvington with me, where you'll be reunited with your mother and sisters. In the meantime you'd better go and get yourself cleaned up and changed out of the workhouse clothes."

Edwin passes his muckrake to the other inmate, taking great satisfaction in the expression on his tormentor's face and he says in a low voice, "I'm going on to new pastures, Tattershall. I don't have to put up with your bullying anymore." He is gratified to see the resentful look on Tattershall's face, as he happily follows the two men back through to the exercise yard.

Joshua leaves them to complete the formalities

whilst he goes about his business in town. He is looking forward to witnessing the family reunion later that afternoon.

Edwin's first glimpse of Alvington Manor takes his breath away. *Can it be possible that I will be working here in this magnificent place?* He cannot wait to be reunited with his mother and sisters. They pull up outside the front door at around midday. A young man runs out to lead the horse and gig back to the stable yard. Lord Dryer introduces them.

"Billy, I'd like you to meet Edwin who's starting work here today." Billy looks surprised, but holds out his hand in welcome, "How do you do?"

Edwin shakes hands with him amiably, "I'm pleased to meet you, Billy."

Lord Dryer then continues, "I'm firstly taking Edwin down to the kitchens to find his mother and sister, Billy, but after they've been reunited and had their luncheon, I want both you and John Moore to instruct him in the valuable art of caring for my horses and keeping the stables in good order."

He turns to Edwin, "We'll see how you get on, Edwin, and then perhaps try you with the gardeners next."

"Very well, my lord."

"Thank you, Billy. Come along lad, let's go and find your mother."

As they enter the kitchen, all the staff are seated around a large, scrubbed wooden table enjoying their luncheon. They all stand immediately at the sight of Lord Dryer.

Ruth Proctor's mouth drops open at the sight of him, tears spring into her eyes and he cannot stop himself from running into her arms. Moments later Hattie is hugging them both and he is swallowing hard to try to dispel the huge lump in his throat.

Lord Dryer smiles, "I'll leave you together to catch up, Edwin." He looks at Gareth standing at the head of the table, "Edwin is going to be our man Friday for a while to see where he is best suited."

"Very well, my lord."

Then Lord Dryer turns to Cook, "Perhaps you could find him a plate of food, Flora. He is then to go out to the stables with Billy and John Moore."

Edwin untangles himself from his kin, "Thank you, my lord. You don't know how much this means to me."

"I think I've some idea, young man. All I ask is that you serve me well and you'll be treated kindly in return."

Edwin notices that His Lordship is smiling warmly as he leaves the kitchen, whilst the staff resume their seats and the enjoyment of their meal. Hattie is instructed to serve her brother with some freshly baked bread, cheese and pickle. It is the best he has ever tasted.

CHAPTER EIGHT *(November – December 1856)*

A HINT AT PATERNITY

Rosa gives birth to a little girl on the 5th November 1856 and they call her Ruby. Malachi is overwhelmed with love for the tiny bundle he holds in his arms and for his Rosa, who even after all her pain and effort with the birth, still looks radiant. Outside they can hear the bonfire night celebrations going ahead at Home Farm, but inside their cosy cottage, all is peaceful and they could not be happier.

However, Rosa knows in her heart that all men want sons and, although little Ruby is perfect in every way, she is hopeful that her next child will be a boy. They both would like a large family and Rosa is happy to keep going until they have their son.

Nathan Meakins has been labouring as a lumberjack at Port Arthur for two years when, during breakfast one morning, he realises the prisoners are buzzing with the news that one of their number has escaped. He doesn't know the man, and no one seems to know how the escapee managed it, but he cannot help thinking himself, how good it would be to be a free man again.

His common sense soon gets the better of him as he considers the dubious consequences. Even if he somehow managed to evade capture, how then would he be able to survive in this foreign land? He would never be able to get beyond the peninsular. If he was still back at home on English soil he might actually consider risking it, but here he wouldn't stand a chance.

The sea surrounding the Tasman peninsular is, according to the guards, shark infested and contact with any of the seamen who land at Port Arthur is barred. Besides, all ships have to check in their sails and oars upon landing, as another precaution to prevent the prisoners from escaping. Thus, escape by boat is impossible; besides he hates the water and cannot properly swim. He shrugs disconsolately, reluctantly resigned to completing his sentence; *only ten more years to go!*

One Sunday, about three weeks later, the prisoners have finished their breakfast, and before they are due to attend church, those of their number who have behaved themselves that week are allowed to receive their mail. Meakins is amazed when he is called forward and given a letter. He has not heard from anyone back home since his transportation.

He takes the letter to a quiet spot where he can read it in peace. He recognises the handwriting. It is from his conniving sister and was written eight months earlier. He is annoyed by the delay in receiving it, for it only took him three months to get here, so why should his letter have taken so long, unless the screws were deliberately keeping it from him? He is still so furious with her he is tempted to tear the letter up, but he is eager for news of home and so he suppresses his anger and frustration and concentrates on his sister's words.

April 1856
  Dear Nathan,
  I hope this letter finds you in relatively good spirits,

that your journey was not too horrendous and your situation is bearable now that you have arrived at your destination. I feel guilty for not writing before, knowing it will be months before the letter reaches you on the other side of the world, but I had no contact address. However, I have decided to write care of the Prison Service in Van Diemen's Land, because I want to tell you something rather curious.

I encountered Lord Dryer's wife and lady's maid with two young children in Ninesprings this afternoon. One of the children was a little girl with a mass of red hair, curled in ringlets, about four years old. She is the image of Lady Dryer and yet she is too old to be the product of their recent marriage. However, Apsey reminded me of the chambermaid who you were sweet on and who drowned herself. She says that she was Lady Louisa Dryer's sister, Millie, and it occurred to me that it is possible that she is your child, Nathan. Anyway, I will be keeping a close eye on her whenever I am able and keep you informed, but let me know if you think it is at all feasible.

Mama is well, but Papa is not so good these days, suffering badly with his gout and indigestion and generally grumpy. Please let me know, as soon as you can, the address where you are stationed so that I can continue to write and keep you updated on our lives back home. Eagerly awaiting your first communication, we are missing you so sorely.

Your loving sister, Olivia.
PS Mama and Papa both send their best wishes.

He sits under the shade of the blue gum with his mouth open in amazement. *Could it be possible that the little minx actually ignored my instructions and gave birth after all? I thought that matter was resolved when the silly girl drowned herself!* He folds up the letter and puts it in his pocket feeling frustrated and annoyed. *What does she expect me to do about it, on the other side of the world? What the hell has it got to do with bloody Olivia anyway? I don't want her poking her meddling nose into my business.*

However, if it really is true, the child must have been adopted by that bastard, Dryer. They must know that I'm her father and they have damn well kept it a secret from me all this time. He smiles to himself, deviously. *Dryer and that wife of his must have grown to love the child in the intervening years. I have vowed to get revenge on Joshua Dryer. What better way than to return to Somerset and claim paternity of the little darling! This may be easier said than done, but not impossible. I must make sure my conduct is exemplary, to hopefully gain an early release, for the longer they care for the child, the harder it will be for them, when I show up out of the blue and entice her away.*

The church bell is ringing to summon them to Sunday service when he hears voices, as someone approaches from behind him. "I hear Pratt has been captured at last!"

As the two men pass by, Meakins can see they're both pensioner guards. One man is chuckling and his colleague cannot hide his mirth as he replies. "Yes, the poor blighter must have got hell of a shock, because he actually jumped out of his skin." The two men laugh heartily.

"I hope he took care not to pick a female hide, otherwise he could have got more than he bargained for." There is more ribald laughter and Meakins listens as their amusement continues.

"You know those contrary critters are pretty good at kick-boxing. That match would have been worth a punt."

"I know which one I'd have put my money on."

"Me too," he says, sniggering. "But seriously, I think that Pratt was well named, his plan was doomed from the start." Their hilarity fades away as the two men walk towards the church.

Another louder voice then takes over, as the duty

guard shouts, "Come on men, get in line; time for confession and prayers!" Meakins obediently joins the queue.

After the service the men are given the opportunity to reply to their letters and Meakins now sits in his ground-floor cell, looking out through the bars at the tranquil estuary and attempting to compile a conciliatory note, despite his feelings of resentment towards his sister.

> *12th December 1856*
>> *Dear Olivia,*
>> *Thank you for your letter only received this morning. What you tell me is very interesting. I knew that Millie Bonfield was pregnant, but of course I told her the child could have been anyone's and I wanted nothing to do with it. I suppose it is possible that the child could be mine, if she ignored my advice and it was, after all, born before she died. I should, therefore, like you to keep account of her, whenever you are able, without alerting the Dryers.*
>> *It is a godforsaken place here and I miss my old life. Please assure Mama and Papa that, if it is at all in my power, I do intend to return to Somerset at the end of my sentence, and I promise you, Olivia, that one way or another I intend to repay Joshua Dryer for my current sufferings.*
>> *I trust you are all in good health back home and all is well with Summerville. Please pass on my kindest regards to our parents.*
>> *With best wishes,*
>> *Nathan.*

Later in the day, the puzzling conversation he overheard earlier makes complete sense. He has just handed over his letter to the guard and joined the prisoners for their supper, when he learns from the grapevine a bit more about the convict who had managed to escape capture for the last three weeks. A fellow prisoner tells him, between mouthfuls of gruel, that the courageous escapee was mistaken for a kangaroo and unfortunately shot in the rump by a bushranger.

Another is laughing, "On receiving the wound poor Pratt threw off his disguise and surrendered."

Meakins raises his eyebrows; "Whatever made him think of that as an escape plan?" he asks, grinning.

"Well, you see, he was employed as a cordwainer, day in, day out, handling the skins, when the ill-fated plan came to him of concealing himself within the full-sized kangaroo hide that was in the leather store," says the old man seated opposite to him.

Meakins manages a wry smile when he pictures the scene described earlier by the pensioner guards and he thinks of the audacity of the hapless man. But this latest incident, along with all the other cautionary tales of escape by boat, leading in every case to imprudent prisoners drowning, only demonstrates the foolhardiness of any escape attempt. *I'll bide my time, I don't want to end up buried with the other poor sods on the Isle of the Dead.*

Rebecca is dreading a lonely Christmas spent without the company of Ben. She tries to cheer herself up by going with Violet on the paddler *Prince*, from the new steamer pier at Castletown, across to Weymouth harbour where they disembark to do some Christmas shopping. However, all the time they are perusing the stores she is looking out for ideas for gifts for Ben and wishing they were back together again.

The town is busy with shoppers and festooned with Christmas fare and everyone, even her mother, seems so merry. She must brighten up or it will ruin their day out.

In the milliners she spots a very stylish hat, decorated with pheasant feathers, that matches her brown and gold costume and her mother buys it for her Christmas box. While her mother is distracted looking for something for Aurora and Louisa, she surreptitiously purchases a pretty, beaded reticule as a surprise for her. She finds smart cravats for her father and Joshua; a silver and topaz hatpin for Louisa; a silk-lined fur muff for Aurora and a wooden jigsaw puzzle of some kittens chasing a ball of string, for Gabriel. She is very pleased with her morning's shopping and her mother suggests they stop for refreshments.

They find a little tearoom in St Alban Street and whilst her mother is ordering their food and drink, she realises that she has been abstractedly fiddling with the dainty marcasite ribbon, pinned to the neck of her blouse. Ben had given it to her five years ago when they had spent their first Christmas at Alvington.

Her mother tries in vain to cheer her up, but she is well aware of the problem. "You need to make it up with him, Becky; it breaks my heart to see you so unhappy."

"I know Mama, but he no longer feels the same about me and so there's nothing I can do."

"Rubbish, he just wants to draw a line under it and not feel he's going to have to pay the price for the rest of his life. You know what men are like; the slightest complaint and they say you're nagging."

"The thing is I've forgiven him for the past, Mama, but I'm afraid of the temptations of the future."

"You must talk to him again, darling. I'm sure he has learned his mistake, but the longer you leave it, the more difficult it will be to make up and the more likely he'll resort to the same behaviour. Why don't you buy him a Christmas present and take it around to his house, as a peace offering?"

"Do you think I should? Only I've had loads of ideas for presents for him and I really feel bad about leaving him and his mother out this year."

"Well, I think it'll be a good opportunity to go to him bearing an olive branch, don't you?"

She smiles, "Yes, I do."

"Right then, after our luncheon we'll go back to the emporium and we can both buy something for Ben and his mother. I'm sure your father won't want to leave him out, any more than you do."

She eventually buys him a warm, woollen fisherman's guernsey and her mother chooses a rosewood and brass spirit level, which she thinks Matthew would have chosen for him. "We can make some mince pies for Annie nearer the time; I think we ought to go home now, we've enough parcels to carry as it is!"

The trip back on the paddler is quite uncomfortable, as it is crowded and the sea is choppy, but thankfully, it does not take long and an hour later they are back at Cove Cottage feeling weary, but content to have made good progress with their Christmas preparations.

On Christmas Eve Rebecca makes her way to Annie's cottage with butterflies in her stomach. Still unsure whether or not she is doing the right thing, she takes a deep breath before knocking on the door.

Ben answers her knock and she can tell immediately by his amazed expression that he is

thrilled to see her. "Hello Becky, Merry Christmas."
He bends to kiss her on her cheek, then stands back
to welcome her inside, "Come on in, Ma will be
pleased to see you."

"I've bought some sweet meats and mince pies
for her for Christmas that my ma and I made
yesterday."

"That's very thoughtful."

"I wanted to see if we might make friends again.
I've been so lost without you, Ben."

"I must admit I've been miserable too, Becky."

"Miserable! That's an understatement,"
interjects his mother. "You're a real sight for sore
eyes, Becky. He's been like a bear with a sore head.
Thank the Lord you've put a smile on his face at long
last!"

Rebecca gives a sigh of relief. "These are for you,
Mrs Stone." She passes the confectionery to Ben's
mother. "I've brought some presents for you too,
Ben. This is from Ma and Pa and this one's from
me."

"Thank you, Becky. Well, actually I've a present
for you too. I'd already ordered it for you when we
fell out. I'll wrap it for you and bring it round
tomorrow morning, if that's all right with your
parents."

"I'm sure it will be."

He turns to his mother, "Ma, would you mind
making us a cup of tea, please."

"Of course not." She goes off into the scullery
leaving them alone together.

He looks down at her, appealingly, "Does this
mean that I'm forgiven and we're betrothed again?"

She smiles up at him, but she is still reluctant to
give in too easily, it is far too important. "I just need
to know that you'll never deceive me again, Ben. I
was fearful of living in the shadow of lies and deceit,

but if you give me your word that I can trust you completely and forever, it's my dearest wish."

Ben then takes her hands in his and says earnestly, "I've learnt a lot about myself in the last five months, and I promise you that you're the love of my life, that no one compares with you and I want us to be together forever."

Then he smiles and she smiles too, and he bends his head to kiss her. Relief washes over her, all past discord and conflict ebbs away, as he puts his arm around her and squeezes her affectionately. She is enormously glad that she took her mother's advice and that she and Ben are friends again.

Rebecca's previous pretence at looking forward to the Christmas festivities is now genuine enthusiasm. She awakes on Christmas morning excitedly anticipating Ben's visit and optimistic for their renewed future together.

He turns up, struggling with his gifts, at around ten o'clock and is greeted by the whole family as a special guest. He places his gifts beside the others and is immediately handed a cup of mead and a mince pie by Violet.

Rebecca's curiosity is aroused when she sees the size of her present. "Whatever is it, Ben?"

He smiles, "Open it and see."

Matthew and Violet sit together on the sofa to witness the unveiling.

Rebecca tears off a corner of the paper, revealing a French-polished wooden box standing on turned legs. She looks at him in amazement. "It's beautiful!" She rips off the remainder of the paper and opens the lid revealing the upper layer of padded, satin-lined compartments.

Ben grins at her happily. "*I* made the sewing box

for you, but I gave it to a friend of your Auntie Hannah's who lives in Weymouth to do the linings for me, before you and I fell out. It was supposed to be for your birthday, back in July. Do you like it?"

"Of course I do, it's perfect!"

"Well, I must be honest it was your pa's idea. Apparently he bought one for your ma many years ago and she was so pleased with it, he was sure you'd like one too."

"I do, Ben, and it's even more precious because you made it for me."

Matthew puts his arm around Violet's slender shoulders and draws her close, kissing her on her cheek and then he says, "It's rather ironic, but I was forced to delay giving your mother her gift, as we split up before I had the opportunity too!"

Violet looks up at him regretfully as her daughter says, "Well, we both have our sewing boxes now and so there'll be no need to tempt fate in the future."

CHAPTER NINE *(July 1857)*

PADDY AND O'MALLEY

Gabriel is now two years old. It is the day after his birthday picnic, which everyone enjoyed in the summer sunshine, set out on the lawn, but Aurora cannot help feeling a little peeved at all the attention he was paid.

She knows he is a dear little chap and she should love her brother, but why does everyone keep kissing him and calling him an angel? *He isn't an angel, for they live in heaven. They call her a princess, but she isn't a princess either. Perhaps they like him better than her? He did have a lot of presents and she has never had a picnic for her birthday.*

She is sitting in the small schoolroom attached to the nursery upstairs with Nanny Beth, practising her writing on the chalk board. Gabriel is having his morning nap and so she is getting the undivided attention of their nanny. Beth is kind and clever and always has plenty of time for her.

"That is lovely writing, Miss Aurora. You are a good girl. Now we had better do some sums."

"Oh, I hate doing sums, Nanny Beth. Can't we do some drawing today?"

"I'm afraid we did drawing yesterday, Miss Aurora, and your papa will want you to be able to do your sums."

"But I'm no good at sums; it is too hard for me."

"You can do anything you set your mind to, Miss Aurora, but you do have to listen carefully and concentrate, until it all makes sense. Now go and fetch your abacus, please dear."

Aurora puts down her chalk and runs to fetch her abacus. She returns to Beth and they sit together whilst Beth uses the coloured beads to explain subtraction and division. They are both engrossed in their work, when the door to the schoolroom opens and amazingly her mother walks in. Her nanny stands up immediately.

"Mama!" She jumps up and runs to her for a cuddle and her mother scoops her up into her arms and gives her a big kiss. *Perhaps she does love her too, after all.*

"Sorry to interrupt Beth, but it's such a lovely morning, I wondered if you'd like to come to Montacute market with me and the children." She looks directly at Aurora still held in her arms, "I still want to get your papa an extra surprise birthday present. I know it was last month and we all gave him our presents then, but I have something special in mind that we might be able to collect today. What do you think?"

"Oh, yes please, Mama. That would be splendid."

Her mother continues, "Well, I think it's time we woke Gabriel from his nap, so if you could get them prepared, Beth, I'll instruct John to bring around the carriage."

"Of course, milady. I'll bring them straight downstairs, when we're ready."

Her mother puts her back down, kisses the top of her head and saying, "See you in a moment," she leaves them to get organised.

Montacute market square is overflowing with stalls and people and carriages. Aurora looks out excitedly at all the colourful stands, whilst seated beside her Gabriel squeals with pleasure at the sight of all the animals. John drives the horses through the archway and into the yard behind the Phelips Arms and then he helps the ladies and children to disembark.

"Please would you accompany us through the market, John?" asks her mother.

"Of course, milady. Would you like me to carry young master Gabriel for you?"

"Yes please. That would be very helpful. He's very heavy for me now and I don't want him falling over in the animal muck. Beth, if you could take my shopping basket. Come Aurora, hold my hand; I don't want to lose you in the crowds."

They follow John through the archway and out into the market square. Some of the villagers recognise Nanny Beth and smile and wave to her. They seem to cause a bit of a stir as the village folk are staring at them all with interest and curiosity. Maybe because they make a pretty picture, with John in his smart livery, carefully carrying her brother in his strong arms, pretty Nanny Beth wearing her best bonnet and carrying the basket, and her mother, dressed in her favourite duck-egg blue costume and proudly holding up her pretty, lacy Parisian parasol in one hand, with she herself held tightly in the other. She screws up her nose at all the different animal smells.

They stroll past the cooper, the smithy's stall, and the basket maker and her mother stops at a stall selling preserves and buys some honey and some damson jam, which she places in the basket. They bump into Edwin who is waiting for some knives that are being sharpened for Flora. He doffs his cap.

"Hello Edwin, I didn't expect to see you here," says her mother.

Aurora looks up at the lad, noticing his twinkling

eyes and warm smile. "I come on some errands for cook with Billy, milady."

Her mother returns his smile. "Good lad, I hope you're getting some bargains."

"Oh yes, milady. Billy already agreed it were a good price."

"Well done."

They walk on past vegetables, meat and fruit pies, and fish stands, someone selling milking stools and butter churns and someone else selling pots and pans and kitchen utensils, until they come to a small pen containing kittens and puppies. Aurora watches her mother as she speaks to the woman in charge and they go towards two gorgeous puppies.

"These are the Irish Wolfhound puppies you asked about last month, milady. They're weaned now and ready to go to a new home, if you do decide you'd like them."

She cannot believe her eyes – *two puppies!* She looks up at her mother with disbelief. "Are we going to buy these for Papa?"

"What do you think, darling? Will he be pleased?"

"Oh yes, Mama, so pleased! It will be so splendid! Look Gabriel, aren't they beautiful? Can we have them, Mama? Please can we?"

"Well, this was what I was thinking would be a wonderful surprise for your papa."

Her brother is struggling to get down from John's arms.

"That's all right John, let him pet them." John puts her brother down beside her and he puts his small hands through the cage to pet some kittens, not realising that it is the puppies that his mother is interested in.

"We'll take both of them. You said a guinea for the two, is that right, Mrs Brown?" She hands over the coin to the woman.

"Yes, milady, thank you."

"I think we'll need a large basket to carry these back home with us. Beth, you stay here with the children and I'll go back with John to the basket maker. We won't be a minute."

While her mother and the groom are gone, she and her brother happily stroke the kittens and puppies, laughing at their strange antics and their cute expressions. Billy turns up with Edwin and they chat happily with Nanny Beth, after she has shown them the pups that her mother has purchased for her papa. One of the puppies stands up rather wonkily on lanky legs and licks Aurora's hand with his rough tongue. She is immediately besotted.

A lady comes to the stand and asks the stallholder, "How much for the puppies?"

Aurora immediately panics, "You can't have them, they're for my papa!" she cries. "Mama has just gone to get them a basket; she'll be back very soon."

The stallholder steps forward. "The child is right, I've just sold them to her mother, but the kittens are still available."

The lady smiles, "Never mind, it was puppies I was after." She looks down and addresses Aurora. "I can see why your mother wanted them, they're so delightful." She bends down to pat the one nearest to Aurora. "You know these breeds grow very tall, very quickly, you'll have to be careful they don't knock you over when they are playful."

She decides that she likes this lady who is so friendly and who has taken the time to talk to her. "They won't knock me over; I'm a big girl, I'm almost six years old."

"Then you'll have to look after your brother, because he's much smaller."

Aurora puts her arm around her brother protectively, "I will."

Louisa and John go back to the basket maker's stall and after inspecting nearly all his stock she eventually chooses a large rectangular basket that will be a perfect bed for both the puppies while they are young and large enough for one of them once they are full grown, and she pays the stallholder and orders a duplicate to be made, which will be collected from the market in six months' time.

They wend their way back to the waiting children, but as they approach, Louisa is dismayed to see Olivia Meakins talking to them. She feels sick with anxiety as she rushes up to her, with John following behind with the basket. She speaks boldly, "Is there something I can help you with, Miss Meakins?"

"Unfortunately no, Lady Dryer, I was interested in purchasing the puppies, but I'm told by the pretty young lady here that I'm too late."

"Indeed you are. I've already bought them for my husband."

"In that case, I hope they bring you much joy. Good day to you, Lady Dryer." She turns to Aurora, "Goodbye, my dear." She holds out her hand for the child to shake and Aurora looks very grown up as she responds prettily.

"Goodbye," she says dipping in a dainty curtsey.

Mrs Brown puts the blanket the young hounds are familiar with into the basket. Then she lifts the two puppies and places them gently, side by side, in their new bed.

Feeling flushed and agitated Louisa enlists the help of Billy and Edwin to convey their new pets back to the carriage, then she bends down and kisses Aurora lovingly, taking her shakily by the hand. She is trembling with fear and anger as she turns to Beth, "I'm very disappointed in you, Beth. You should never allow the children to talk to strangers. You never know who you can trust these days. I especially do not want Aurora to have any contact with that particular woman, do you understand?"

Beth looks as if she might burst into tears, "Yes milady, I'm very sorry to have let you down, ma'am."

Aurora kindly puts out her other hand for Beth to hold, but Louisa can see that the child looks puzzled and upset. Louisa is aware that Aurora has never seen her mother being cross with anyone before, but the sight of the puppies quickly restores her good spirits and Louisa is relieved that the moment is soon forgotten.

The children amuse themselves happily with their new pets for the rest of the day, eagerly awaiting the return of their father. As soon as they hear the carriage wheels on the gravel, Louisa and the children rush into the main hall to greet him.

He bends down to kiss Aurora on her cheek and her words burst forth, "Guess what our secret surprise is, that we have for you, Papa?"

Joshua looks wearily at Louisa, but he is amused by their pleasure and enthusiasm.

"I really have no idea, sweetheart. Whatever could it be?"

"It is puppies!" cries Gabriel, unable to contain himself any longer.

They all laugh to see Joshua's expression of amazement.

"Puppies?"

Louisa takes his arm, "Yes, my darling, come and see what we've found for you at Montacute market."

Joshua follows, as the children run wildly ahead into the oak, and there in the chimney corner in their large wicker basket, huddled together, fearful of being left alone in their new surroundings, are two young Irish Wolfhounds.

Joshua bends down and picks one up, cuddling it to him and tickling it behind his ear, its lanky legs dangling.

"They're brothers," says Louisa. "Aren't they beautiful?" She picks up the other one and he licks her face submissively. "We haven't thought up names yet. We thought you should choose, for they're a late birthday present. Flora suggested Romulus and Remus, but it's a bit of a mouthful, besides they were Italian and these two lovely little fellows are Irish. Aren't you boys?" She returns the puppy to the basket and strokes him and he stands there wagging his tail happily.

"Well, the only Irish names that stand out to me, are those belonging to one of the Holy Fathers who sailed with me on the missionary ship. He was called Father Patrick O'Malley and I remember him as a very happy-go-lucky Irishman who was kind and generous and an example to us all. We called him Father Paddy O'Malley. How about calling one Paddy and the other one O'Malley?"

"Which one is O'Malley, Papa?"

"Well, I think that the paler, misty-grey-coloured one should be O'Malley and the darker one, we'll call Paddy."

"O'Malley is my favourite, because he licked my hand and I think he likes me," says Aurora.

"My one's Paddy," says Gabriel stoutly.

"Don't forget they're both your father's dogs, to keep him company when he's out riding, but you can of course play with them while they are puppies. We want them to be our family pets. They'll grow very big very quickly; taller than your pa if they stand up on their back legs, and if anyone should wish us harm they'll protect us and be our guardians. That's their nature. Mrs Brown says they're docile and gentle when stroked, but powerful and fierce if provoked."

"What does proked mean?" asks Gabriel, having difficulty pronouncing the word.

"It means if someone were to make them angry, by being nasty to them, or to us," explains Joshua patiently.

Louisa draws her husband away from the children. "Come, I've something to tell you." He follows her into the drawing room and she shuts the door. "Something happened today which causes me great consternation."

Joshua sits down on the sofa and pats the cushion beside him. "Come, my dear, and unburden your fears."

She sits down wearily beside him. "I'm so worried Josh, because I know in my heart that evil witch, Olivia Meakins, has guessed Aurora's true identity. I caught her making friends with the child in the market today. I don't trust her, Josh, her feigned interest is unhealthy and I fear a threat to our daughter's safety."

"Well, I must admit that these encounters seem more than simply coincidence. All I can suggest is that we must keep Aurora close at all times, especially when away from home. But, you mustn't fret too much, my darling, she's perfectly safe here, not one person on our staff would let anyone harm a hair on her head."

"That's true, but maybe we should warn them to be vigilant?"

"It cannot do any harm. I'll inform Gareth and Mrs Abbott so they can pass on our concerns."

The following morning Joshua decides to enlighten the staff below stairs himself and he asks Gareth and Mrs Abbott to gather them all together at ten, while

Louisa is upstairs with the children. They all stand to attention as he enters the kitchen; Elsie straightening her cap nervously.

"I have asked Mrs Abbott and Mr Williams to gather you all here this morning to warn you of a perceived threat to the family security. We have no firm evidence that Olivia Meakins means any harm to Aurora, but Louisa has observed her on two occasions exhibiting an unhealthy interest in the child. She believes that the woman has guessed the truth of Aurora's true identity. We have decided to inform you all of the unpalatable fact that Louisa's poor sister, Millie, was the child's birth mother and Olivia Meakins' obnoxious brother, Nathan, is Aurora's father, which would make Olivia the child's aunt."

Joshua observes their different reactions. Ruth, Hattie and Edwin look puzzled, not being aware of past events, but the rest of the staff are truly shocked and react in a variety of ways. Having been taken into Louisa's confidence, Rosa feigns surprise. Elsie, Emily and Flora go pale with anxiety. Joshua remembers their excitement at discovering the baby, loving their little waif so much. Previously unaware of the child's origin, but well aware of the depths to which that woman and her brother will stoop, he can understand their obvious distress.

Flora brushes away a tear and with a voice broken with emotion she says, "Don't you worry, my lord, if she do come anywhere near our 'Rora she'll get short shrift from us."

The men are angry and indignant. "Hasn't she learned her lesson? She were lucky not to 'ave been transported with 'er brother," says Billy.

Beth Puddy bursts into tears, "I'm so sorry, my lord. I didn't know who she was. I would never have let her come near, if I'd known."

"Don't distress yourself, Beth. Louisa and I both

realise this and that is why we've decided to make you all aware of the situation and the danger."

Mrs Abbott comforts the young girl by surreptitiously taking her hand in hers.

Joshua, realising that their gossiping might be overheard by Aurora in the future, warns them, "Mrs Abbott, you'd better explain the situation fully to Beth, Ruth, Hattie and Edwin, but *please all of you remember* that Aurora knows nothing of the circumstances of her birth, or the true nature of the man who fathered her and so I expect you all to protect her from this unpalatable fact, please. We're simply asking you to be vigilant; we don't know what is going on in that woman's unstable mind."

Mrs Abbott says stoically, "I will, my lord; we'll all put a loving circle of protection around her. She'll come to no harm while we're responsible for her."

"Thank you for your discretion and loyalty. That will be all, please return to your duties." Joshua leaves Mrs Abbott explaining everything to the new members of staff.

Half an hour later, however, on going to find Louisa, he finds himself climbing the stairs with Beth following dejectedly behind him. He turns to her, "Come on, Beth, don't be downhearted; we don't hold any bitterness against you. You weren't to know the woman has designs on the child."

"But milady was so cross with me, my lord."

"It was her fear and anxiety that caused her to take it out on you. She knows you're a good and efficient nanny who the children adore. You'll see, she'll hold no ill will towards you, I promise."

When they reach the top of the stairs, the sweet melody of Louisa and Aurora singing nursery rhymes to Gabriel is wafting along the passageway. Joshua holds the door open for Beth to enter and then stops in the doorway to enjoy the scene before him. Louisa and Aurora are seated on the window seat with Gabriel on his mother's lap and a picture book held between her and Aurora. The sun is streaming through the window and glowing with red and golden lights in their matching twin heads of copper-coloured hair. He has never seen anything so magical.

Louisa looks up and smiles at him and he gives her a reassuring wink. "I thought you might like to join me for morning coffee."

"Of course." She passes Gabriel to Beth, "It must be time for Gabriel's nap and Aurora's lessons and so I'll leave them with you, Beth."

"Yes milady." Beth is still looking sad and without Joshua prompting her, he is pleased when his wife smiles at the nanny, saying, "I'm sorry I snapped at you yesterday, Beth. You didn't deserve it, I was just worried. I hope you understand?"

Beth looks up at her and this time she is actually smiling, "Of course milady, Lord Dryer has explained to us your reasons and I promise you it will never happen again."

Joshua takes his wife's arm, "Right, my dear, let us go and take some refreshments."

Olivia is sitting in one of the padded green and cream striped, wooden folding chairs outside in the warm summer sunshine, writing to her brother. The birds are singing in the shrubbery and the bees humming among the herbaceous border. It is a very pleasant afternoon and she is happy to be sending her brother some positive news.

28th July 1857
Dearest Nathan,
I am writing to let you know that I encountered the child again at Montacute market and was able to

conduct a short conversation with her before her mother returned and gave me short shrift. The mother was behaving decidedly defensive of the child, which only goes to reinforce our suspicions. During the conversation the child also mentioned that she is nearly six years old, which also fits in with our conjectures. She was with her younger brother who I believe is about two years old and they were purchasing a pair of Irish Wolfhounds.

She is a delightful little girl, perfectly charming and you would be very proud of her I am sure.

I have no further news of note. Mama and Papa are both feeling better and in good health, whilst we are enjoying a spell of warm, gentle English sunshine.

I will keep you informed of any further developments.

Kindest regards,
Olivia

She places the letter in a cream envelope and rings for the maid to take it inside to be sealed with wax, ready for posting.

CHAPTER TEN *(November – December 1857)*

SOMERSET FLOODS AND BENDIGO BUSHFIRES

Olivia is fearful, following successive weeks of rainstorms, hail, thunder and howling gales. The ground is sopping wet and the River Ivell has broken its banks. Several huge trees have been blown down in the grounds around the house. She is waiting anxiously in the hope that Wadman will be able to return with the doctor through the floods to attend to her elderly father, who she believes is showing signs of suffering from the cholera.

She looks out, through the small rivulets of rain running down the panes of glass in the oriel window, at the extensive lake making a virtual island of her home and infiltrating two of the medieval carp ponds. Days ago she had advised her obstinate father not to worry about rescuing the carp from the swamped ponds, but he was determined to save what he could and now she is convinced he has caught the disease from the polluted water, seeping into the river from the town, where the epidemic is raging. Her mother is sitting by his bedside, holding her husband's shrivelled hand and mopping his brow, whilst Olivia paces the room in agitation.

Suddenly her father cries, "The bowl," and he vomits violently into the porcelain basin her mother holds out stoically before him.

Olivia's stomach heaves at the smell of the clear fluid and she hastily leaves the room to go and look out for the doctor. She descends the stairs and stands despondently in the light of the drawing-room window, until finally she is rewarded with the sight of the carriage returning down their windswept driveway. As Wadman ushers the doctor through the front door, closing the large black umbrella and placing it in the porch, Olivia is there waiting ready to greet the old man. "Dr Jessop, I'm so sorry to have to call you out in this dreadful weather, but my father is really very unwell indeed."

Wadman then helps the doctor as he removes his knee-length overcoat and tall-crowned top hat and gloves.

"Please follow me, Doctor." Olivia leads him up the stairs to the master bedroom and as she goes he asks her, "What are your father's current symptoms, Olivia, my dear?"

"Well, he's been suffering firstly from the diarrhoea, but then the sickness too." She turns back as she speaks to him, "He's very lethargic, with laboured breathing and, as you'll see, he has sunken eyes and his skin is a strange bluish-grey colour."

They enter the bedroom and the doctor carefully examines the patient. "Hmm, his pulse is rapid and rather thready and he feels clammy to the touch." He looks up at the two women. "He's very dehydrated and looking at him, I'm afraid I do think it's quite likely he has contracted the cholera."

Olivia sighs, her worse fears confirmed. "He's been complaining of muscle cramps, weakness and a dry mouth and so we've been giving him plenty of water, but he seems unable to keep it down."

"I'll leave you with some opium for his muscle cramps and I'll treat him with my medicinal leeches now." The doctor removes his jar of leeches from his Gladstone bag and places a few of the creatures into a curved glass leech tube. Then he places the tube strategically against her father's skin.

Annabel Meakins watches the leeches distastefully as they attach themselves and suck away at her husband's blood and then she turns to the doctor with an expression of concern on her face. "Is it contagious, Dr Jessop?"

Dr Jessop scratches his head solicitously. "There is a school of thought among us medical men that the disease is a local infection of the alimentary canal which is transmitted through sewage-contaminated water, and thus it spreads very quickly in places where drainage is poorly maintained. In that way it's contagious, but you should all be safeguarded if you make sure everything is washed properly after contact with the patient. I'm sure it has gone through Ivell so quickly because of the parlous state of our wells. Your husband possibly contracted it from the contaminated flood water, Lady Annabel."

Olivia nods in agreement, "We think he may have caught it by eating carp from our ponds that have been infected from the River Ivell."

"I'm sure you're right, my dear. Ivell is suffering from a cholera epidemic the likes of which I have never before witnessed."

Olivia cannot keep the fear from her voice as she asks him, "Will he be all right, Dr Jessop?"

"It's hard to say; some folk do recover. Just keep on giving him plenty of fluids and the opium should ease his pain and calm him. I'll call again tomorrow."

That night they take turns to keep vigil and Sir Oliver dips in and out of consciousness.

The following morning Olivia is dressing, with the help of Apsey, when her mother rushes into her bedchamber, shouting in alarm, "Come quickly!

Please come quickly! Help me, Olivia! Your father is having a seizure and I don't know what to do."

Olivia turns to her maid, "Apsey, please ask Wadman to fetch Dr Jessop."

"Yes, milady."

Olivia swiftly follows her mother to the master bedroom. She is surprised to find the seizure must have passed, for her father is now appearing to be sleeping peacefully. Fearful they may have already lost him, she grabs his frail wrist. She can detect a weak pulse.

The two women pace the floor anxiously waiting for the doctor to come, but when he finally arrives, he is unable to revive Sir Oliver and he confirms that he has fallen into a coma and that there is nothing more they can do for him.

Annabel sits with him during that day and Olivia agrees to take over and sit in attendance throughout the night. She does not relish the eerie, fearful silence of her night-time vigil and in the event she keeps nodding off and jerking awake for the greater part of her nocturne. Finally, exhaustion takes over and she succumbs, falling into a deep sleep in the chair, waking in a panic at dawn, and discovering to her utter dismay that her father has died in those last moments of darkness.

She sends Apsey to inform her mother and the two of them sit in tears at his bedside, thinking their own personal memories of the man who had run their lives for as long as they both could remember. Eventually Wadman returns with Dr Jessop who certifies Sir Oliver Meakins' death from cholera.

Several weeks later, after the funeral, Olivia, dressed in her black parramatta silk mourning costume, anxiously fingers her jet beads, as she sits down to write to her brother to let him know what has transpired. She knows their father's death will be a dreadful shock for him and thus she needs to choose her words carefully.

My dear Nathan,

I am afraid this epistle carries with it some dreadful tidings. I am terribly sad to have to inform you of the death of our father from cholera on Tuesday 14th November 1857. Thankfully, he did not suffer long, it was all over in a matter of days and Mama and I are free from the disease, as is the rest of the household.

We had been suffering at Summerville from numerous storms and constant rain over the last two months and the Ivell had flooded our land, swamping the carp ponds, which as you know were very dear to our father's heart. Anyway, foolishly he busied himself rescuing the carp from the flooded ponds and placing them in those nearer to the house that had not been affected, but in the process he fatally kept one for cook to prepare for his supper.

Dr Jessop believes, as we do, that the fish was infected and was the cause of our father's untimely demise. He was dreadfully sick with diarrhoea and vomiting and could not keep even water down. He became seriously dehydrated and seemed to shrivel, turning a horrid blue/grey colour. The doctor gave him some opium for his muscle spasms and did a bloodletting to no avail. He was floating in and out of consciousness and then he had a seizure and fell into a coma. Dr Jessop said there was nothing we could do after that.

Mama is inconsolable and in constant tears. We kept a lock of Papa's hair and I have had a locket made for her. We are both relying heavily upon Alistair in all legal and financial matters. He has organised the servants' armbands and is overseeing the remainder of the staff who are running the household like clockwork, as before. I don't know what we would have done without him.

Of course, my dear brother, you are the heir to Summerville and Mama and I will see to it that the estate remains in good order until such time as you are able to return and take up the reins once more. I am so sorry to be the bearer of such sad tidings, Nathan, when you are so far away from us and unable to share with us our troubled days of mourning.

Let us hope that this is the last of our ill fortune.
Fondest wishes from your sister,
Olivia

She places the letter in a matching envelope marked with a black band and heats the wax for the seal. There is a knock on the door and Alistair McNab enters, full of smiles, "Olivia my dear. How are you?" He walks towards her confidently, placing his hand lightly on her shoulder. She accepts this small intimacy and looks up at him, relief in her eyes as she hands him the letter.

"I've finally informed Nathan. I must say it is a weight off my mind, for I was dreading putting the most upsetting event into words." She stamps the wax with the family seal, and then adds, "Although knowing Nathan, the sad news will be sweetened with the knowledge that he is now the proud owner of the Summerville estate."

"Not an easy task, my dear, but it is a further incentive for him to return to us as soon as he is able. Would you like me to take the letter to the post office? I have to go into town this morning."

"Thank you, I'd be most grateful, Alistair."

He gives a courtly bow, "You know, my lady, your wish is my command."

As she hands him the letter, their hands touch and Olivia shivers with unexpected desire.

Whilst the south of England is enduring the wettest autumn for decades, the south of Australia is baking in a heatwave. Angelica sponges herself with cold water: despite wearing her thinnest, lightest clothes she is finding the dust, the flies and the oppressive heat unbearable. The Bendigo creek is reduced to a mere trickle and the sheep wash is dry. The nearest water is miles away at either Bullock Creek, or Emu Creek. The alluvial miners and the puddlers, who need water to operate, have resorted to wood splitting for fuel for the quartz miners' steam engines.

Angelica looks disconsolately at the never-ending queues beside the water carriers and she decides to go down into the town instead to find some shade amongst the buildings there. Her neighbour has told her of a new family who have arrived recently and opened up a haberdashery and clothing store and she is curious to know what they are selling.

She is tired and thirsty by the time she reaches the town and before she makes her way to the new clothes shop, she purchases a bottle of milk from the general store, crossing to the other side of the road to avoid the drunken men congregated outside the sly grog shop with their whistles and lewd comments. She observes a man nudging his friend and hears him saying, "That's her?"

"Who?" asks his companion.

"The Angel of Heaven's Gate, I was telling you about," he says impatiently.

Angelica ignores them all today, with their bad language and innuendo, walking on determinedly. She finds the new 'Brunsvold's Emporium' freshly painted and standing out among the other slightly shabby premises. On entering she is surprised to see how well-stocked the wooden shelves are, with a rainbow of colourful bolts of different fabrics lining one entire wall, fancy bonnets and tall hats displayed on stands covering the tops of the cabinets, drawers of multihued threads and buttons, gloves, reticules, fans and parasols and a whole section of pattern and order books available to choose from. At last they have a store catering for women as well as men in Bendigo.

She browses through one of the books and finds an astonishing selection of whale boned basques, corsets and seductive bustiers in wonderful designs and colourful glossy fabrics. She smiles to herself; *my clients, I'm sure, would love these and they might possibly encourage even more to come. It would after all be a business investment and I already have enough gold stashed.*

A young woman comes to her assistance. "Good morning, madame. My name is Freyja. How may I help you?" she asks with a charming foreign accent, which Angelica can only narrow down to European.

"I really like this purple bustier. How long would it take to get here, if I was to order one?"

"We order direct from Paris from this catalogue. Will take about three months. I have another catalogue, for order from Stockholm, but stockist in Melbourne and we could get supplies from them within couple weeks, depending when next delivery due."

"May I, please, look through your Stockholm catalogue?"

"Of course, madame, I help you." Freyja pulls out the heavy tome and turns to the correct section.

Angelica slowly turns the pages, "Oh! I love that scarlet basque! How much is it?"

Freyja goes behind the counter to find the price list and tells her it will cost her one and a half guineas, which includes a fitting and any alterations.

"And how much is the purple one?"

"That one: two guineas, because of handmade lace and hand-stitched jewels."

Angelica wipes her brow with her handkerchief whilst she considers, "Would there be a discount if I should order both of them?"

Freyja looks very pleased to have such a good sale in the offing, but she hesitates, "I have to ask Father, please excuse me for moment."

Whilst Freyja is discussing the discount with her father, Angelica is looking at the parasols. She chooses a pretty pale blue one that has a ruffled edge and takes it to the counter.

Freyja turns to her, "My father says I can give discount on multiple orders."

"Well, I should also like this parasol please, what would the total cost be for all three items?"

Mr Brunsvold has finished with his customer and joins them. "For you, I throw in parasol for nothing, dear lady," he says, smiling congenially down at her. "Please leave us good faith deposit of four shillings."

"That's a very fair deal, sir. Thank you."

He goes off to serve another customer as she passes her money to Freyja. "Please order the two basques for me, Freyja. Can you give me an idea when the scarlet one from Melbourne will get here?"

She calls to her father again, speaking in their foreign language and then turns back to her. "If all well, it be here week on Friday. If you come on Saturday I fit for you."

"Thank you. I'll look forward to that." She turns to leave and then turning back she asks her, "What is that language you were speaking to your father?"

"Norwegian, we from Stavanger."

"I like the accent, it's very musical. See you Saturday week. Bye."

"Goodbye, madame."

Outside the shop the heat hits her. She is very glad of her new parasol, but as she leaves the shelter of the buildings and sets off up the track to her home at Eaglehawk, she can detect the faint, acrid smell of wood smoke. Ahead of her in the hills beyond Eaglehawk, yonder in the Whipstick, she can see smoke curling above the blue gum forest the other side of the scrubland. Her throat constricts in fear. "Fire!" she cries, as she runs up the hill, as fast as she can in the oppressive heat, to join the others in their rush and panic to extend the firebreak around the settlement.

As she passes her *gunyah* she flings down her new parasol. She can see Matari and Kaora ahead of her helping the prospectors to back-burn a wide strip of land between the settlement and the distant forest fire, in order to make the land barren before the flames reach it. Not too far away she spots Pindari and Camira also using branches to beat at the burning scrub, while other men are moving some felled trees, or shovelling away the undergrowth. Luckily there is no wind to fan the fire, but the scrub is tinder dry and the fire, if not halted, will be threatening the makeshift homes of their township.

Angelica decides to help her aborigine friends and soon she is covered in black charcoal dust, her mouth dry from the heat and her exertions. As they work around the perimeter of the settlement she comes across two men working alongside her, shouting to one another in their lyrical Welsh accents, desperate to protect their nearby mineshaft and log cabin. One she recognises as having used her services and she pauses in her labours to wipe her hair out of her face and smile at him.

Eventually, after about three hours of hard beating and burning has passed, Angelica breathes a sigh of relief, for there is a long charcoal pathway, approximately 25-feet wide, of burnt land circling and protecting the settlement. Matari assures her that, as long as there is no wind, they will be safe.

When he says this, he points at Camira and smiles.

She grins back at him, "Very amusing, Matari."

They are all relieved that, thanks to everyone's hard work and co-operation, the emergency has been diverted. Many of the folk involved in the controlled burning congregate around the grog shop and Angelica joins the men there, along with her native friends.

Bryn Thomas offers to buy her a drink and she smiles sweetly, asking him, "How about my friends? They've worked really hard too."

The other Welshman replies, "Of course, we'll bring out enough grog for all of you."

Angelica sits down on a wooden bench cautiously facing the fire, which is still burning through the tall eucalyptus trees in the distant hills. The smell of the eucalyptus wood is not unpleasant, but she can see the danger in the oil spitting, crackling and igniting. However, the trail of smoke is now wafting slowly northwards. Camira joins her on the bench as the Welshmen return with the diluted rum and they all in turn have a long swig from the jug.

Bryn Thomas introduces his friend. "This here is my old mate, Hugh Davies. We were transported together to Van Diemen's Land three year ago."

"You got off lightly!"

Hugh scowls, "Not really; we'd both served three years in a hulk in Cardiff Bay, before being finally shipped out on the *Adelaide*."

Angelica recognises the name, "The *Adelaide*, did you say?"

"Yes. Why?" responds Bryn.

"I remember a load of convicts being marched through Hobart off the *Adelaide*, when I was in the Cascades; one nice-looking young fellow was called Sam something… "

Bryn smiles, "I can remember that. We were there, weren't we Hugh?"

"We were, and I think you must mean the young Irish lad, Sam Kelly; we know him. He went to Saltwater Creek with us, but we had to go down the mine and he was to work the land. We told him, when we were released, that we were off to the Victorian goldfields and he's planning to join us if he can." Hugh grins, "He won't be going down the mine though. It's a life in the open air he wants. I expect he'll be looking for a job on the sheep station and maybe he'll do a bit of panning along the creek in his spare time. The ranchers are paying good money now to get ranch hands after most of them have run off to prospect for gold. The thing is we're both experienced miners, it's what we're best at, so we're working hard trying to strike a rich seam so that we can afford to buy the mining licence; until then we're vulnerable to the digger-hunters."

"Who are the digger-hunters?" she asks them.

Hugh explains, "They're the troopers, constables and inspectors who've been commissioned by the Crown to prevent the illegal mining."

"Oh dear, I wish you good luck," says Angelica.

"That's what we all need here, isn't it? … A bit of good fortune for a change." Bryn nods in agreement.

Matari suddenly beckons to Camira and says, "We go now."

Angelica says, "Bye all of you, and thank you for helping us." She waves and they wave back, as he and his friends wander off, but as Angelica watches them go she notices Camira being singled out and led away by one of the miners. Angelica is immediately concerned; the girl is far too young to be used and abused by grown men, but she knows instinctively that Camira will not be burdened by any inhibitions, such as those imposed by civilised society. She'll be easily bought for a few trinkets. She's powerless to intervene, but she decides to educate the girl the next time she has the opportunity.

The following day Angelica discovers a poor little koala hiding in the bushes outside her *gunyah*. His fur is singed from the fire and his feet and hands have been scorched. She offers him some water from a ladle and he drinks gratefully.

Bryn Thomas happens to walk by as she is feeding him and he comments, "The poor animals always suffer in the bushfires. I found a lyre-bird hiding down the mineshaft after the fire."

"Was it unscathed?"

"Yes it was. It was saved by its clever instincts for survival."

"I must say the brushfire really frightened me, Bryn, and I'm thinking of taking a room in Sandhurst, as soon as I can find a suitable place. I'll also feel happier if I'm able to lock my door at night." She lowers her voice to a whisper, "The folk living all around here must be aware that I'm making money from my punters now. Most of them are ex-convicts and hustlers and it was fine when they thought I had nothing, but now they must realise that I have a bit of gold stashed, I feel more vulnerable at night-times."

"You ought to set up in one of the saloons, Angel. You'd be safer there than up here."

"Yes, I'll look into it. You'll still come and visit me though, won't you, Bryn?"

"Of course I will, *cariad*, although Hugh and I have decided to send for our families back home to come out to join us on the Government Immigration Scheme. I'm afraid once my wife arrives here, I'll no longer be able to see you. It would be grossly unfair of me to do so once we are reunited, but it'll be a long time before it's all organised."

"I understand, Bryn. Of course I do. You must be looking forward to seeing them again, after all that's happened to you."

"We both are and we've already completed the application forms. We only had to confirm that our family members are mentally and physically fit, that they're of good moral character, sober and industrious and in the habit of working for wages for the occupations described on the forms. We've both paid fifteen pounds to the sub treasurer and sent off the certificates for our families' passages to Melbourne. The ladies all travel for slightly less money and each ticket is according to the person's age. My two sons are twenty and eighteen years old and they'll be able to help us with the mine. Hugh's son is fifteen and his daughter is eighteen. It's very exciting, but it'll take some time for them to sort out everything back home and arrange their passage. In the meantime, we've bought a large enough piece of land on the outskirts of Sandhurst, where we plan to build two nice family homes."

"Well, Bryn," she looks at him askance with a wicked grin, "We must make hay while the sun shines, as they say."

He smiles at her and winks, "I'll pop and see you tonight, after dark." And he goes off about his business.

The koala stays in the area for a few days and Angelica leaves a dish of water out for him each morning.

On Saturday she goes down to the emporium to have her fitting and, as she passes the junction with Happy Valley Road, she wonders if they have any rooms available at the Golden Exchange Saloon. She decides to pop along to see. As she reaches the wooden veranda of the single-storey building, she is not surprised that the place appears to be quiet; it is early in the day and most of the men will be working. She steps onto the veranda and looks through the saloon's double doors. A man is behind the bar and so she goes inside.

"Good day, can I help you, miss?"

"I was wondering if you have any rooms available to rent?"

"Well, that depends, see. What do you intend doing in them rooms?"

"I'm looking for a place to stay. Why, what else would I be doing?"

"I don't know you, miss. You might be considering doing a bit of business."

"How would you feel if I was considering doing a bit of business?"

"Then I'd suggest you look elsewhere, miss. We already have a Sheila here who wouldn't be wanting the competition, if you get my drift."

Angelica turns away; she'll call in at the Eureka and see what's available there, after she's had her fitting at the emporium.

On entering the shop, Freyja immediately greets her, "Good day, madame, please come through into fitting room." Angelica follows her into the back of the shop. She gasps with pleasure when Freyja hands her the new garment for inspection. "Oh Freyja, it's beautiful! This is such good quality satin and what wonderful workmanship."

On trying it on for the first time she is pleased that no alterations are required as, once the laces are tightened, the smooth red satin material with its black lace ruffling enhances the rounded shape of her bosoms, cutting away into her tiny waist and easing over her curvy hips perfectly. She happily pays Freyja one guinea, the remainder to be paid on receipt of the purple bustier.

Freyja asks her, "How you fare with bushfire last week?"

"Oh not too bad, thank you Freyja, we managed

to back-burn a firebreak and the only casualty that I know of was a poor little koala, but even he has gone on his way again now."

"It is harsh country, I am finding heat hard to tolerate coming from Stavanger, beside sea, where always fresh and cool, even in summertime."

"It does take some getting used to, but I like the heat. Not too keen on the bushfires though. In fact, I'm thinking of finding a room in Sandhurst, so if you hear of anywhere perhaps you'd let me know."

"Of course, I will be attentive on your behalf, madame."

"Please Freyja, call me Angelica."

"My pleasure, madame, it be Angelica from now. I let you know when next order arrives."

"Thank you, Freyja. Goodbye."

"Goodbye and good luck." Freyja turns towards her next customer and Angelica steps out into the sunshine.

The Eureka saloon is not far from the emporium and on the main street, which would also be good for business if she is successful. As she approaches, there are a few men idly congregated outside on the stoep. She walks in confidently and approaches the elderly man behind the bar. He has a slight cast in his eye as he squints at her rather contemptuously and her confidence wanes somewhat.

"What can I get you, missy?" he rasps.

"Thank you. I'd like a glass of water, please."

His manner improves slightly, "I'll get you a drink, missy, but Sheilas aren't welcomed in the bar."

He returns with a glass of water.

She takes a long drink and then looks up at him, smiling sweetly. "I'm actually looking for lodgings and possibly some bar work. Are you the landlord?"

"I am as it happens." He runs a hand over his whiskers.

"Do you have a room for rent?"

He then smiles. "I do as it happens, missy, vacated only yesterday."

"How much?"

"Four shillings a week."

"May I see it please?"

"Of course, follow me." She drinks some more of the water and follows him towards the back of the bar. He explains as he goes, "Most of the rooms, and I have twelve, are outside in the annex, but the one that is available is upstairs in the main building."

She follows him up the stairs and is pleased to see that the place is light and airy and there are wall lanterns for the night-time.

He shows her into the room which has a 4-foot-wide, proper bed with a headboard, thick mattress and bedding, a washstand, a closet and a chest of drawers. The large window overlooks the main street and she walks across and lifts the lace curtains. She can see the emporium, the butchers, the general store and the grog shop from there. She feels excited. "This would do very well, sir." Then she thinks about how she will be able to get her punters up there without him knowing. "However, I'm a bit concerned about the noise from the bar below. Do you have anything that might be a bit quieter?"

The old man looks disappointed. "I do, but it would mean them taking this room and you swapping with one at the back, in the annex. This is the better room and more suited to a lady."

"Could I please see the annex rooms?"

"Well, I could check if anyone is in, who might let you take a quick look and then I could ask if any of my tenants would like the upstairs room."

"I'd appreciate it, sir."

"Jethro; my name is Jethro Tully, miss." He holds out his hand and she shakes hands with him.

"Angelica. Angelica Pitman."

On seeing the annex she is pleased to note there is a back entrance to the block. Jethro is only able to show her the accommodation through one of the windows, as no one is around, but it looks quite adequate.

"If you're able to move someone into the main building, I'd be very happy to take an annex room, which I'm sure will be quieter for me. I'll return tomorrow, but either way, I'd like to take one of the rooms, please."

"Very well, missy, I'll see what I can do in the meantime."

"How about some bar work, Mr Tully?"

"Jethro, everyone calls me Jethro."

"Sorry… Jethro."

"Well, I do have trouble covering sometimes and I could do with a spare person who'd be happy to help out occasionally."

"That would be ideal for me, if you'd consider it, Jethro?"

"Sure. I'll let you know when I need you and we'll give you a trial."

"Thank you. I'm very grateful."

"See you tomorra' mornin' then, missy."

"Will do… Bye."

Angelica sets off back up the hill to Eaglehawk to pack up all her belongings, hoping she has made the right decision. *He seems a nice enough old fellow, even though it isn't always clear if he is looking at you, or not, because of his squint.* She smiles to herself. A room of her own will be a real treat, especially with a proper comfy bed. Perhaps Camira would like to take on her gunyah? After all she did help to construct it.

CHAPTER ELEVEN *(January – September 1858)*

UP IN ARMS

In Ivell the number of cholera victims has risen to epidemic proportions. The Christmas celebrations have only served to exacerbate the crisis: with people congregating together in the churches, or for social engagements, the disease has spread quickly among the local residents.

Folk are angry and, with the support of the local doctors, blame the parlous state of the water supply and thus the town commissioners have decided to hold an emergency meeting to discuss these problems. Unfortunately, an irate mob of around 500 people have gathered outside the town hall to put pressure on their representatives. The constables try to calm the crowd and keep the peace, but folk have lost their loved ones to the disease and they are frustrated, upset and frightened.

Colonel Seymour is in the chair talking to the commissioners when the noise of the crowd permeates the building and there is a crash against one of the windowpanes. The room falls silent.

Joshua speaks first, "Someone has to go outside and talk to them. Try to calm their fears."

"Be my guest, Lord Dryer. I'll warrant it'll not be an easy task," replies the colonel, sagely.

"I'm sure I recall Ambrose telling me how you Ivell folk are a spirited lot, with the town having a history of rioting. Some of you must remember how armed troops had to be called out to quell the troubles back in 1831."

Colonel Seymour is nodding his head, "Yes, Joshua I remember it well, it was when parliament refused to pass the Great Reform Act."

"Well, I'm very concerned that someone may get hurt. Perhaps a few of you would care to step outside with me. I should feel a tad more confident if we all stand together in this."

"I'll come," says Dr Gillingham.

"You can rely on me," says Lord Helyar.

"This needs to be sorted once and for all," says Thomas Pickford to his friend Robert Gilson, both glove manufacturers.

Soon there is a small contingent of commissioners who all step outside together. They are greeted by angry jeering and a cacophony of noise that resembles wassailing. Joshua attempts to address the crowd several times, before they finally quieten down enough for him to uneasily speak to them.

"Good townsfolk of Ivell, please, we entreat you to remain calm." He takes a deep breath, "We *are aware* of the seriousness of the community's problems, but we ask you to be patient and to put your trust in your town commissioners to take the necessary urgent steps to rectify our present parlous predicament."

A large man shouts from the crowd, "We don't want to be patronised by you landed gentry. What do you know of our living conditions, sat up in your ivory towers?"

"Hear! hear!" shouts the crowd, warming up to express their demands, as a rotten tomato splatters against the oak door behind Lord Helyar.

Joshua can only reason with them, "Look, there's no need for that! We're here trying our best to solve this crisis for everyone. This disease doesn't discriminate, for as you well know, Sir Oliver Meakins sadly succumbed to it back in November. We all need to put aside our politics and work together for a solution to the town's sanitation problems. The committee are very conscious of the need for piped water and a decent sewerage system, but this will take a great deal of money. It means we need to organise fund-raising events and possibly raise the local business taxes to be able to organise this."

"Oh yes! That would be right, raise the taxes of us poor folk to set right something that's caused by you rich buggers."

"No, sir. Not the poorer folk, the rich businesses will have to pay. I assure you your town commissioners are committed to working towards this, as our priority, but we'll need your help too."

"What can we do? We've no power or resources," calls out one of the older female factory workers.

Joshua responds encouragingly, "You can help to keep our local environment clean, free of litter and free of pests. You can also help by fund-raising, holding handicraft sales for example, in the same way as the churches do."

There is a rumble of mutterings within the crowd, but Joshua continues resolutely, "All glove factory workers can make sure that the waste products no longer contaminate the wells and water systems in the town."

"Only with the bosses' agreement," says another disillusioned Ivellian.

Tom Pickford steps forward, "I speak for the Ivell Glovers Association and this has previously been discussed among us. We're all ready to help in any way we can."

Dr Gillingham then affirms, "Everyone has to play their part for, if we truly intend to eradicate these dreadful diseases, we must improve our hygiene."

Joshua continues, "Florence Nightingale has set us a good example: look how she has enhanced the survival rates for the poor soldiers in the Crimea, simply by improving cleanliness and hygiene. She has proved the only way we'll beat diseases such as typhoid and cholera is if we work together, for that's the only way forward. We must all co-operate, not fight or blame each other, for only united will we triumph."

A lone person, at the back of the crowd, starts to clap their hands and soon the rest join in.

Then the man who spoke first calls out, "Fair enough, my lord, you have our blessing, but we want to be able to see this happen in our lifetime. We all want to see our little ones grow up healthy and strong."

"Believe me, we want that for us all too. Now please let us get back to business." Joshua turns away with a huge sigh of relief and the commissioners follow him back into the town hall.

Sergeant Gundry then speaks to the crowd, "Come along now folks, time to go back to your homes," and his men usher the gathering away from the town hall.

Inside the building the men thoughtfully resume their seats.

"Well, Dryer my friend, now we have to live up to your fine promises," says Colonel Seymour, wryly.

When Joshua arrives home, later that evening, he is delighted to find Louisa still up and waiting for him. "This is a nice surprise, my dearest."

She kisses him gently, adding anxiously, "Rosa has gone into labour. The midwife is with her at Hamlet Cottage, but I wanted to tell you straight away. The baby should be here by tomorrow if all goes well. I'm rather on edge for I couldn't bear to lose her."

"She'll be fine, sweetheart. She is young and in good health. Please don't worry."

Louisa pours her husband a glass of brandy and sets a candle underneath to warm it. She then pours herself a glass of Madeira wine. He is telling her about how he had to calm the mob outside the town hall, and she is listening apprehensively, when there is a loud knock on their front door that makes them both jump.

Moments later Gareth is showing Malachi into the oak. "I had to come and tell you straight away, my lord. We have a son, Eli! Rosa is very well and I've left her feeding the little mite. Well, not so little actually, he's quite a bruiser, weighing 9lb, 12oz."

"Wow, he's going to take after his father, I don't doubt." Joshua gets up to embrace his friend. "Congratulations, Malachi, we're both very pleased for you."

Louisa also gives him a warm hug. "That's wonderful news, Malachi. I'm so relieved that all went well."

"Pour him a brandy, Louisa. We must wet the baby's head."

Louisa sets another brandy to warm and they all raise a toast to young Eli Warren.

Malachi then turns to Joshua, "Will you join me and Jacob tomorrow evening? We plan to celebrate in style at the Mason's Arms."

"Of course, count me in."

Louisa then suggests, "Perhaps I should go and sit with Rosa and the children, to keep her company while you men make merry?"

"That'll be very kind, milady."

"My pleasure, Malachi."

The following, bitterly cold January evening, after Joshua has escorted Louisa to Hamlet Cottage, their party is joined by Thomas and Raymond Hawkins and Billy Riddick as they walk along the frosty country lanes to the village pub.

On entering the busy bar, Joshua is overwhelmed by the familiar smells of fresh and stale, ale and spirits, wood smoke from the fire, pipe tobacco and male body odour, but the atmosphere is animated. Because everyone knows Malachi and his small group well, they are all eager to add their congratulations, and so there follows much patting on the back, shaking of hands and buying of beer. Thus they have been partaking of much ale during the past hour and they are all enjoying a game of arrows, when Joshua steps outside to relieve himself.

In his absence Malachi is talking to Jacob, whilst Thomas is carefully throwing his darts, when Malachi is approached by one of the customers. "I know you, don't I?" he asks, "Am I right in thinking you're Malachi Warren, the local bare-knuckle boxing champion?"

Jacob grins as Malachi subconsciously puffs out his chest a little, "That I am, sir. Whom do I have the pleasure of addressing?"

"I thought so. I've a little proposition for you. I'm William Bell, owner of Catkin Mill and I'm prepared to give you three guineas to take part in the next prize-fight at the Black Panther Club Tournament; you also have a good chance of taking the purse for the last man standing."

Malachi looks at his brother persuasively, saying:

"It'd be a good opportunity to earn some extra cash for my growing family."

Jacob shrugs, "I have no argument with it Mal, but what will Rosa think about it?"

"I won't tell her, until I go home with the hard cash, then she won't have to worry herself about me."

"Then if you're sure you want to risk her wrath, I'll be your second, as before," says Jacob.

Malachi turns to William Bell. "You have a deal, sir. What's the date and time of the contest?"

"The battle commences at noon, on Saturday 17th March."

"St Patrick's Day… we'll be there, you can bet your life on it," says Malachi excitedly.

On Joshua's return, Malachi tells him the good news, but Joshua is unimpressed and very concerned. Aware of the reputation of that club, he does not like the idea at all. He whispers to his friend, "Are you sure this is a good idea, Mal? There are a lot of undesirables frequenting that establishment."

"I think it's an offer too good to be sniffed at, Josh."

"In that case I'd better come along too, to make sure all is above board," replies Joshua, anxiously.

"You worry too much, Josh," says Malachi. "You're too young to have all the cares of the world on your shoulders. Let yourself go and let's both get a bit drunk, for a change."

Joshua laughs, "Go on then, I'll have another pint of ale. Though actually I don't think I worry enough sometimes, Mal."

"What do you mean by that?"

"Well, I keep telling Louisa not to worry about Meakins and that's fine at the moment, for he's still on the other side of the world, but in 1866 he'll have done twelve years and he'll be freed. Aurora will be fifteen years old and by the time he's back here, because I'm certain he will do his utmost to return, she'll be just the age he likes them. I tell you Mal, if he comes near her or any of my family, Justice of the Peace or no, I'll kill him."

"Don't you worry about that my friend; there'll be all of us behind you. Besides, we have a few years yet to plan our defences."

A February summer storm is brewing in Van Diemen's Land and Meakins is glad to be in the cooler calm of the small prison chapel. The Sabbath is always a welcome relief from the hard labour of the other six days in the week and the prisoners are usually more congenial on Sundays. Meakins quite likes to sing the hymns, believing he has a good baritone voice and can well hold a melody, although the true meaning of the prayers and the belief in an almighty God means nothing to him. Despite being callously locked into one of the pews with a row of his fellow prisoners, he still likes to watch the warders' wives and the other younger females, all dressed up in their finery; occasionally exchanging glances with a pretty young chorister and boosting his ego.

Today, however, he notices Fred Burns, one of the warders, catching the eye of the governor's young daughter and the significant look that passes between them. He notes the flushed cheeks of the naïve girl and the slightest of winks from Burns. *There is something going on between those two, or my name isn't Nathan Meakins.*

At the end of the service, as the families exit the chapel and pass the rows of prisoners with their guards standing at the end of each pew, he observes a note being passed clandestinely from Burns to the young girl. *Aha… this might be useful,* thinks Meakins with a sly smile. *Though I cannot see what the pretty maid sees in the weedy figure of Burns, unless he has the same gift with romantic words as his famous Scottish namesake.*

Outside, the bubbling cumulous clouds overhead are edged with gold from the rays of the sun beyond them. The atmosphere is oppressive, thunder rumbles in the distance and he feels a headache coming on. Hopefully it will be better when the storm finally breaks.

"Come on… get into line. There's mail to be handed out," calls out one of the guards and Meakins despondently falls into place with the other lumberjacks. There is never any mail for him.

Today however, he is pleasantly surprised when his name is called out and he goes forward eagerly to collect his letter. He is immediately shocked to see the black band on the envelope. *Good grief!* S*omeone must have died?* He feels sick with shock, but he really needs to open this in private. Once they are dismissed he hurriedly returns to his cell to tear open the envelope and discover the dreadful contents.

Oh my God, it's the old man, and I wasn't there for him in his hour of need, to say farewell. He slumps down onto his bed, saddened by the thought he will never set eyes on his father again. Then anger takes over. *Damn Joshua Dryer! If it wasn't for him, I'd now be the proud owner of the Summerville estate, which is alas left rudderless in the hands of incompetent women. As it is, Alistair McNab will be there instead, sniffing around my sister and taking control of my inheritance!*

There is then an almighty crash of thunder, which makes him jump. The storm must be raging right overhead, as the lightning flashes almost simultaneously. He sits there listening to the downpour of rain; he ought to be writing back to his sister, but he is too incensed.

Whilst Malachi is busy working on the farm he has constantly, in the back of his mind, the eager anticipation of the Catkin Mill Boxing Match on St Patrick's Day. He has been pickling his hands regularly and training hard since January, when William Bell first enlisted him to fight.

He and Jacob are sparring in the barn early one morning when they are interrupted by a screaming Lucy. Assuming her brothers have had an argument she is most distressed and rushes to come between them, the scream however, momentarily distracts Jacob, who ends up with a throbbing black eye as a result. Thus Lucy is brought in on the secret. They buy her silence by reluctantly promising that she can come with them to the event.

However, it is more difficult to explain the black eye away to their mother and Rosa, without revealing the truth. Jacob makes up a story that he stumbled on the stairs after supping a few ales and hit his head on the newel post. Unfortunately, a few weeks later he is injured again. This time it is a sprained wrist and he brushes that away by explaining how he was tired, after birthing twin lambs late one night, and had tripped over a tree root on his way home, bruising his hand as he fell. The brothers are relieved when both women seem to believe their explanations.

Nevertheless, the time flies by too quickly and despite Malachi worrying he is not yet match fit, he soon finds himself stripped to the waist, on a relatively warm, breezy spring afternoon, and seated among the other contestants awaiting his first bout.

The owner of the mill has arranged for his Black Panther Club bouncers to surround the 24-foot-square roped area that forms the ring, and there is a further outer ring, decorated in fluttering red, white and blue bunting. There are five other pugilists hailing from Chard, Evershot, Langport, Sherborne and Wincanton. The Wincanton man is known as *The Big Fellow*. The others are all about the same height as Malachi, somewhere between 5 feet 11 inches and 6 feet 2 inches and he comments quietly to Jacob, "That fellow from Wincanton is a huge chap! He must be at least 6 feet 7 inches tall, and I reckon he weighs nigh on 250 pounds."

The pugilists are all seated within the outer ring with their supporters, including Malachi's sister, Lucy; the club bouncers; the local doctor and any local nobility. Joshua acknowledges Colonel Seymour and his two sons seated opposite them.

A sizeable crowd of local people has congregated about them in the meadow adjoining the mill and beside the lake. Malachi points out to Lucy their small group of friends and Lucy catches the eye of Billy Riddick and waves merrily. Billy acknowledges them and nudges Thomas and Raymond who both wave back to Lucy and signal thumbs up to Malachi. The crowd, mostly male but not entirely, for some of the wenches from the club are among them, is scattered, gossiping and gambling, until William Bell strikes the gong to announce the start of the contest, then they all surge forward. William Bell clears his throat and speaks through a bull-horn.

"This contest is to take place according to the London Prize Ring rules. Hitting or grabbing below the belt, head-butting, biting, gouging and kicking are fouls. Any fighter knocked down has to come to his feet under his own power, not be carried back to his corner by his seconds. It's not allowed to strike your opponent, or inflict damage once he is down, apart from falling on him. A round ends only when a man is down, and there will be a thirty second break before the next round, which will be signalled by the timekeeper's gong." William Bell strikes the gong to emphasise this. "We have as contenders, *The Big Fellow* from Wincanton, *The Iron Bender* from Langport, *Magnificent Malachi* from Ivell, *Jumbo Jones* from Chard, *The Pit Bull Terror* from Sherborne and *The Melbury Monster* from Evershot! Right my good men, let the battle commence."

The men then draw lots. The first bout is between *The Melbury Monster* and *The Big Fellow.* The two fighters occupy diagonal corners, each with their seconds. These supporters are ready to administer water and sal volatile if necessary between bouts. A line has been scratched across the centre of the boxing ring, dividing it into two halves. From the time the two men toe the line, the bout lasts about half an hour before the smaller man is knocked senseless and the backers of the Wincanton man go amongst the crowd with a hat, collecting the nobbings.

The next bout is between the two contenders from Chard and Sherborne. This match lasts for three rounds and goes on for nearer an hour. Malachi hopes that he doesn't have to fight this fellow *Jumbo Jones* from Chard, because he is a dirty fighter, whom the crowd enjoy jeering. Unfortunately this unpopular man beats *The Pit Bull Terror* hands down.

Finally it is Malachi's turn and he is to fight the rather muscle-bound blacksmith from Langport known as *The Iron Bender.* He has a lucky horseshoe tied to the stake in his corner, along with his purse for his stake money, and there appears to be heavy betting on this match, Malachi being the most local man.

Jacob and Joshua are both ready in his corner with water and sponge and smelling salts. Should he be quickly knocked out, then Jacob will be his second. The timekeeper strikes the gong and

Malachi energetically springs forward to toe the line. His heart is pumping with adrenaline, but he soon realises that the blacksmith is slower on his feet than he is, which means the pugilist prefers the wrestling holds and Malachi unfortunately finds himself fighting in hold for most of the match. As much as he can, Malachi breaks free and dances around his opponent, hitting home a few good right jabs, followed by some well-aimed left hooks. But the man is determined to bring him down and Malachi is astonished to find himself being picked up bodily by his waist and thrown to the ground. He has not been picked up by anyone since he was a small child. He is slightly winded, but jumps up instantly, luckily unhurt, apart from a bruised ego. He immediately returns to his corner, but his opponent seems to have hurt himself whilst lifting him and he now moves as if in great pain, back to his supporters.

When the gong sounds, Malachi is quickly back at the line, but *The Iron Bender* is counted out, before he can toe the line within the mandatory eight seconds, and he is forced to retire from the contest, due to debilitating back pain, where he can hardly walk. Whilst the doctor is attending to *The Iron Bender*, there is jubilation amongst the gamblers, who it seems mostly had their money on Malachi. Billy and Raymond are going around collecting the nobbings for him.

The three remaining bout winners are now matched for the final contest. Malachi is pitted against the Chard man, known as *Jumbo Jones,* and the winner is to fight the Wincanton *Big Fellow.* There is a longer break to give everyone time to place their bets before the contest resumes again. Malachi drinks a load of water and Jacob massages his brother's neck and shoulders.

Joshua takes the opportunity to wander over to

speak to Colonel Seymour and Lucy goes with him. They interrupt him having a quick swig from his hip flask. "Good day to you, Colonel. What a good day for the event and an excellent turn out," says Joshua, smiling.

The elderly colonel quickly pockets his flask and struggles to his feet. "That it is, my lord, and very nice to get a bit of spring sunshine." They both shake hands.

"Allow me to present to you, Miss Lucy Warren, Malachi's sister."

"Charming to meet you, my dear." She curtseys and he kisses her hand, gallantly. "Your brother is doing very well."

"Yes, sir. I'm very proud of him."

Then turning to the two young men seated beside him, he says, "Have you met my sons: Rupert and Ashleigh?"

"No sir, I have not had that pleasure," Lucy curtseys.

"Boys, this is Lord Dryer of Alvington Manor and Miss Lucy Warren, sister to the *Magnificent Malachi*."

"Pleased to make your acquaintance." Joshua leans forward holding out his hand and both the young men respond amiably. Joshua can see by his animated expression that Ashleigh is rather taken with Lucy. "Are you enjoying the tournament?" he asks them.

"We are, my lord. Our money is on *The Big Fellow*, how about you?" asks Rupert.

"Oh! Malachi is my man. Not only is he a good fighter, he's a good friend."

Ashleigh smiles at Lucy, "No need to ask who you're backing, Miss Warren."

She smiles back at him, "I'd be backing Malachi, even if he wasn't my big brother."

William Bell then announces the imminent recommencement of the competition.

Ashleigh Seymour says, "Why not stay here with us, Miss Warren, while your brother is fighting, rather than sit over there all alone?"

"Thank you, Mr Seymour, I'd be most grateful."

Joshua excuses himself to return to support Malachi, who is skipping, ducking and weaving and punching the air, warming up for the next bout. He leaves Lucy behind, seated between the two young men, both dancing attendance on her.

At the sound of the gong Malachi springs forward to meet *Jumbo Jones*. This man is the second tallest in the competition, with a long reach and therefore he has a slight advantage over Malachi, but Malachi loves his sport and enjoys the challenge.

He has learnt a lot more about the wrestling moves whilst fighting the more stocky *Iron Bender* and he puts a few of these into practice on *Jumbo Jones* in an attempt to prevent the low body blows he witnessed against *The Pit Bull Terror* in his previous fight, but the man still catches him out on three painful occasions. Malachi doubles up each time, finally losing his temper: *You dirty bastard; I'll get you back for those illegal blows.* Joshua and Jacob both protest vociferously and the crowd all boo and jeer loudly, but the fight is not halted.

Malachi steels himself to be the victor come what may. The battle seems to go on and on, with move and countermove not exposing any weakness, or advantage. However, just as Malachi suspects his opponent is finally tiring, the Chard man gets him in a choke hold. It takes all of Malachi's strength and determination to bend forward, taking his opponent across his back and crash the man down to the ground; he then falls heavily on top of him, pinning him down until the gong is heard.

Most of Malachi's punches have been to the head of his opponent and *Jumbo Jones* is looking very battered and bruised, but his stamina is incredible. There is, however, a cut over his right eye and that side of his face is slowly swelling. Malachi resolves to keep aiming to his blind side and maybe he will get in a good punch.

During the next round his opponent's eye gradually closes and Malachi is able to put his plan into practice, aiming an excellent right hook and suddenly the man is out for the count. Malachi is standing in the ring shattered, his arms hanging limp at his sides; he is desperately willing the man to stay down, when finally his arm is lifted high as the victor of the bout.

William Bell takes up his bull-horn, "The final of this tournament will be between the two victors *The Magnificent Malachi* and *The Big Fellow*." The crowd go wild with excitement, shouting and applause. Then William Bell continues, "Let's have a big hand for the losing semi-finalist *Jumbo Jones* of Chard." There is a mixture of weak applause and loud jeers.

Moments later Jacob is attending to an exhausted Malachi, when Joshua notices Rupert Seymour sneaking off towards a small copse in the corner of the field with one of the Black Panther Club harlots. *I doubt his father would be very impressed with that*, he thinks to himself. *Maybe I shouldn't have encouraged Lucy to sit with the Seymours?*

Billy is over the moon that Malachi has won again, especially as he has made himself a few bob which he is planning to spend on Lucy. He is wandering among the crowd with Raymond, again collecting the nobbings, when he notices her standing beside Ashleigh Seymour. They are laughing together and he watches the man fawning all over her. Jealousy surges through him and his happy holiday is ruined.

He has loved her for years but she still treats him like a kid brother, and here she is blushing and flirting coquettishly with a man she must have only just met. The Seymour family own the Sutton Bingham Manor and the land around it and he is just a humble assistant groom, with nothing to offer her, apart from a loving and loyal heart. *It is just not fair! How can I compete against that toff?*

Then the gong is struck again and Malachi is back in the ring once more, but this time he is matched with *The Big Fellow*. Joshua hopes that it won't be a long contest, because his friend surely cannot take much more of this, especially having to fight again so close to his last two challenges.

The Big Fellow comes to the match quite rested, but he is not rippling with lean muscles like Malachi; he is carrying a fair bit of bulky flab. Malachi is more nimble, but he would be extremely lucky to get in a head punch, without encountering his opponent's huge fists in the process, being more than a head shorter than him. The first round is mostly Malachi ducking and dancing around the ring, but he manages to get in a lucky blow, by leaping off the ground as he delivers it and the man is knocked off balance. Malachi falls on top of him for the count and is rewarded with the short, thirty-second break.

Jacob advises his brother, "I think you should change tactics, Mal. Try aiming for the man's ribs, just below his heart and keep thumping him in the same spot, until you weaken him."

"Will do, Jake," he replies breathlessly. "That's good advice."

The next round he puts the plan into practise with left and right punches, one after the other below his opponent's heart. It is easier for him to aim a bit lower than the chap's chin, but he is concentrating so hard on this task, he is caught out several times. The other man must be ambidextrous because, whether left or right, each blow Malachi receives is delivered with the same awesome power.

Jacob comments to Joshua, "I'm afraid my brother's good looks will be marred by this constant barrage."

"I agree, Jacob. His weathered features certainly look puffy and swollen."

Then a devastating left hook knocks Malachi flying through the ropes and into the onlookers, not far from where Lucy is sitting. He hears his sister's cry of fear, and as he staggers to his feet he turns and grins at her reassuringly. Then, apologising to the person he landed upon, he climbs hastily back into the ring. His head is throbbing, but he is determined to continue. *How can he go back home to Rosa, beaten black and blue and defeated?*

Lucy is now tearful and anxiously wringing her hands to the extent that Ashleigh Seymour takes her hands in his to calm her. This does not go unnoticed by a vigilant Billy.

In this round, Malachi manages to keep up his assault on the man's lower ribs until finally his last left-right attack hits home, followed by a ruinous upper cut and *The Big Fellow* drops to his knees. Malachi is stunned. He is victorious and Joshua, Jacob and his other supporters run into the ring to hold up his hands triumphantly.

William Bell announces, "*The Magnificent Malachi* is the popular local winner of our St Patrick's Day tournament at Catkin Mill today," and he hands over the winner's purse. Malachi is lifted onto the shoulders of Jacob and Joshua and together they parade him around the ring.

Lucy is now crying with happiness, and jumping up and down excitedly she turns to Ashleigh and gives him an affectionate hug. Billy watches as they chat together intimately and he thinks his heart will break, but he steels himself to go to the ropes to encourage her into the ring with the rest of them, particularly enjoying being the one who comes between the two lovebirds, *but have they made further plans?*

On reaching Home Farm, Malachi, Jacob and Lucy all enter the farmhouse warily. Their father is still outside doing the evening milking, but their mother is in the kitchen preparing supper. She turns around sharply as they all walk in, "You've all been in town a long time; I was getting worried." Then she stares in absolute horror at the state of her eldest son, exclaiming, "Oh my God, Malachi, whatever has happened?"

Malachi, noting the trembling of his mother's lower lip, tries to make light of his injuries; he holds up his hand to calm her down. "Don't worry, Ma. I haven't been assaulted in town. I've been in a boxing tournament and look… " He holds up the purse, triumphantly. "I won the whole damn contest."

"I don't care about the prize money!" she cries, her face etched with worry, "Just look at the state of you!"

"You should see the other fellows, Ma," says Jacob, trying unsuccessfully to make light of the situation. Their mother scowls at Jacob and then turns back to his brother.

"I'm sorry, Malachi, but I'm that mad with you I could kill you myself! Have you no sense of responsibility? You've *two* young nippers to care for now, not to mention a beautiful wife, who has no wish to become a young widow, I'm sure! What if one of them boxers had hit you senseless, so you never got up again, like that poor chap in the *Western Flying Post* last year? What then, I'd like to know?"

"It wouldn't happen, Ma, I'm far too quick for them."

"Don't you kid yourself, son. You never know what's waiting for us around the corner."

Malachi puts his arm around his mother's shoulders and pulls her towards him affectionately. "But if we're all too scared to have a go at anything, how do we know what we can achieve? Look what I've won, Ma." He tips out the coins on the kitchen table.

His mother refuses to be mollified and continues to harangue him. "I don't care! What would we all do without *you*? Your brother couldn't manage alone. Besides, your poor pa and I wouldn't have the energy to provide for our own family *and* yours, that's for sure." She shakes her head in frustration, "Blooming boxing! Haven't I enough to worry about, with your grandmother lying upstairs at death's door?"

"Is she no better, Ma?" asks Lucy solicitously.

"No, if anything she is getting worse daily."

"I'll go up and see her." Lucy leaves the room to go and check on her grandmother; relieved to escape from the atmosphere in the kitchen.

Malachi feels repentant, "I'm sorry to deceive you Ma, but it was too good an opportunity to miss and I didn't want you, or my Rosa, worrying all day about me. I just hope you'll forgive me when I tell you that I won the twenty-guinea purse, plus the three guineas for taking part *and* I more than *doubled* that with the nobbings!" He proudly spreads the gold coins out on the scrubbed wooden table.

At that moment his father enters the room, "What's all the shouting about? I could hear your mother outside in the yard!"

Malachi feels quite crestfallen. "She's angry with me for taking part in a boxing tournament, but look how much I have won, Pa. There's enough here for us to put some away for a rainy day. I intend saving up for our Eli to get a proper education and this is a grand start!"

His father walks over to the table in his stocking feet to see the spoils. His eyes open wide with shock and pleasure, "How many blokes did you have to defeat to win that much, Mal?"

"He fought and defeated *The Iron Bender* from Langport, *Jumbo Jones* from Chard and *The Big Fellow* from Wincanton, Pa... he was amazing!"

"Well done, my boy. I'm very proud of you!" He turns to Malachi's mother. "Don't dampen his enthusiasm, Beth. You know he's a good boy. He works damned hard and he only wants the very best for his family."

His mother's tone softens then, "I know you mean well, son, but your folks at home should always be uppermost on your mind now." She glares at her husband for his lack of support, and then turns back to Malachi, "Come here and sit down and let me apply some balm to those cuts and bruises."

"Looks like I'm getting my own supper then," mumbles his father.

Malachi catches the sly wink he throws him and he winks back, grateful to his father for once more restoring calm to the household. Jacob helps with the supper.

"Thanks, Ma." Malachi gratefully slumps wearily into the armchair. It has been a long and exhausting day and he has Rosa yet to contend with! He heartily hopes the glint of the gold earned in barely a few hours of exertion will somehow smooth the threatened troubled waters. His mother has fetched her first aid basket and she begins to apply some balm.

"When you've finished covering me in goose grease, I'll pop up and see Grandma, before I go home to Rosa."

"No you will not!" says his mother sternly, "You'll frighten the life out of her and finish the poor old dear off, if you go up there looking like that. Anyway, it's not goose grease, its Flora's arnica cream."

Over at Summerville, Olivia is wondering around the house in a dreamlike trance. Alistair has been courting her and she feels like a young girl again. He respects her opinion, advises and consults her on all decisions regarding the running of the estate and she is the happiest she has been in years. He sneaks into her room at night and he is the most marvellous lover, initially gentle, intuitive and considerate, and then, once she is fully aroused, wonderfully passionate covering her body with ardent kisses and loving her long into the night.

Last night, when the lovemaking was over and she lay with her head on his broad chest, her warm naked body wrapped within his strong arms, he had asked her to marry him and she was completely overcome with emotion, weeping tears of joy, before emotionally accepting his proposal.

The wedding must be organised well before Nathan is likely to return from the Antipodes, so that it is a fait accompli. She decides not to inform him. She does not want him interfering and preventing her happiness, now that she can see a good and happy life for herself at long last.

Together they inform Lady Annabel who, since the death of her husband, has been drifting on a fragile cloud, on the edge of senility. She accepts all they say, whether estate business or social gossip, with mild indifference and their proposed nuptials are no exception.

The wedding is planned as a quiet affair to take place on 6th August in the church of St Mary Magdalene in Barwick. Olivia and Apsey will have their work cut out getting it all organised by then and she is so excited that she cannot think straight.

Although she has not yet gone through the change, the likelihood of her having a child at the late age of forty-five is extremely slim, but it would fulfil all her wildest dreams. She believes Alistair is also keen on the idea, which might mean he sires a possible heir to Summerville, in the absence of her brother, or his progeny.

The thought of Aurora, possibly being her young niece, creeps again into her mind. She resolves to tell Alistair of her suspicions.

It is a mellow, misty morning in late September. Aurora has just turned seven and Nanny Beth is taking both her and Gabriel out into the dairy meadows to gather mushrooms. They are in the kitchen selecting their baskets. Nanny Beth has found a trug for herself and a colander for Gabriel, whilst Aurora is climbing on a stool to reach her mother's basket, which is stored up on a high shelf and not often used.

Ruth Proctor holds her steady as she wobbles bringing it down and then Flora gives them all clean white cloths to line their containers and they are ready to set off. Outside the kitchen door in the boot room, Gabriel is struggling to put on his rubber wellington boots and Nanny Beth bends down to help him, whilst Aurora waits patiently holding his colander for him. The kitchen door is ajar and she can just make out some of the conversation between the kitchen maids. Her attention is alerted when she hears a reference to herself, "She's such a pretty child and so like her mother."

That sounded like Hattie's voice and Aurora smiles at the compliment. Then curiously she catches another voice, perhaps it was Elsie's, saying, "Don't it just take you back seeing Aurora carrying the old basket that she was found in."

She knows that people say babies are delivered by the stork, but she has never seen a stork and it is all very confusing for an innocent seven-year-old. *Gabriel wasn't delivered by the stork, because he came out of her mother's tummy. Besides, how would it have managed carrying a heavy basket?*

They set off across the first field, with cattle grazing at the far end, and Aurora is glad that the large animals do not notice them. Then they come to a field where the cattle had grazed during June, but is now empty. Nanny Beth finds the first clump of mushrooms and she shows them how the grass is thicker and greener, indicating the right conditions for the mushrooms to grow. "Look out for patches of longer greener grass, because that is where you'll find the mushrooms, because it's the site of an old cow-pat."

"Err!" says Aurora, pulling a face and making her brother laugh, but she is thrilled when she spots a large clump and gathers them up quite happily, thinking to herself, *these will be lovely for Pa's breakfast.*

The dew is glistening in the hazy sunlight and the grass is covered with cobwebs that shimmer in the light breeze, but all the time they are gathering their mushrooms, Aurora is musing over her overheard conversation and imagining herself, tucked up in her mother's wicker basket and flying through the air with the stork.

Once they have exhausted the area and they have a nice crop of mushrooms, they return through the more recently occupied fields to Home Farm, but en route Gabriel slips over landing in a smelly, runny cow-pat. His indignant howling is so funny that it banishes all thought of the stork and after Nanny Beth has pacified him, they return home triumphantly.

Everyone in the kitchen makes faces at her smelly brother, until he also can see the funny side of it. He is stripped of his clothing and taken upstairs to find a clean outfit.

CHAPTER TWELVE *(September 1858 – October 1860)*

NEW PASTURES

Lucy Warren has been seeing Ashleigh Seymour for some months now and she looks forward to their regular jaunty outings in their carriage. For the sake of convention, her mother suggested that Clara Fairway might like to join them. The two boys are tall, charming and good looking and Clara and Rupert are also now involved romantically, the four of them spending many hours together, boating on Bingham Lake and picnicking on the shore, or socialising with all the Seymours' friends.

The brothers are regular visitors to the Black Panther Club and, unbeknown to her parents, Lucy has become quite a celebrity there. One night she was cajoled into playing the piano and everyone enjoyed the sing-song so much, that whenever they walk in the door now, there are requests for her to play for them. The music sheets are far more fun than those she plays at home on her spinet, and Lucy finds her new life with Ashleigh filled with merriment and pleasure.

Clara is more reticent about their visits to Catkin Mill, but she doesn't want to do anything to unsettle her relationship with the others and so she goes along with it. Although great fun, she feels the two men drink rather too much and she finds it difficult to handle Rupert at such times.

Whilst Lucy and Clara have been entertained in new pastures, the days turn rapidly from autumn into winter. Lucy's grandmother, who has been virtually bedridden all year, suddenly worsens and the doctor tells them she has pneumonia. Her mother has been run ragged caring for her, running up and down the stairs, but when finally she succumbs to the disease in the New Year, the whole family are devastated. The funeral takes place in the small church at Alvington Manor and the family go into mourning. Lucy finds it difficult, dressed in her sombre black bombazine mourning weeds, having to restrict herself to more moderate pastimes, whilst still going out with Ashleigh. She has to curtail their relatively riotous visits to Catkin Mill and a cloak of sadness falls on them all. She is fearful that she will lose Ashleigh's love during this period.

In the meantime her little sister Beatrice turns fifteen and it is soon apparent that she has fallen for young Edwin Proctor. Lately he has been exercising the horses with Billy and they invariably ride past Home Farm. Lucy notices Bunny hovering outside, feeding the chickens, or collecting the eggs at the likely time when the two lads will be passing by and she observes her waving happily on these occasions. Eventually her sister's patience is rewarded when Billy and Edwin halt the horses in the farmyard and Edwin invites her to go with him to the half-yearly St Bartholomew's Fair on the last Friday in June. Lucy happens to be standing nearby at the time and she is very aware of Billy staring sadly down at her, knowing that her heart belongs to another.

The two lads continue on their ride and Bunny looks at her with concern. "Do you think I might be allowed to cast off my mourning, Lucy? It's only a matter of days until the six-month mourning period for Granny is over. Do you think Ma and Pa will mind? I really don't want to have to be draped in black for the fair."

Lucy smiles at her sister, understanding completely how she feels about the dismal mourning costumes and how important this opportunity is to her. "I'm sure Ma and Pa won't mind. Ashleigh and I will be going to the fair too and so I'll come with you and we can explain, and ask Mama if it can apply to both of us."

"What if she says no? Surely he won't want to be seen with me looking so sombre."

"Well, he asked you, didn't he, and you're dressed in black now?"

"True."

"I thought the same, Bunny, but Ashleigh has been so understanding. If anything it has brought us closer together, so I shouldn't worry."

Beth Warren cannot see what difference a few days will make and she agrees that the girls may leave off their mourning. Bunny is able to go to the fair, dressed in a pretty new blue and purple gown, made for her by her mother with the help of Mrs Abbott's sewing machine. She has a wonderful time and it is the start of a budding romance with Edwin, her first love.

On Christmas day 1859 both Lucy and Clara become engaged to be married to the two brothers. The Seymours hold an engagement party for them at Sutton Bingham Manor and Clara's father and the whole Warren family are all invited. It is a rare celebration and after losing Granny Warren last January, even her parents feel they are now ready to lighten their mourning and enjoy themselves at this splendid news. Beth Warren decides to wear mauve, but in deference to her mother-in-law she still wears her jet beads. Malachi and Jacob are befriended by Rupert and Ashleigh and future family relations look promising. It is a wonderful, jubilant event and draws a line under the past painful two years for the Warren family.

However, this happy union could not be more distressing for Billy, as he sees all his hopes and dreams shattered.

In the Alvington Manor kitchen, Flora comments to Mrs Abbott, "'ee is never a bad-tempered lad, but 'is ready smile 'as disappeared since that announcement."

Flora's daughter, Lettie, overhears the remark and knows they are talking about Billy; she has been friends with him ever since he first came to Alvington and she decides to do something to cheer him up. In her spare time at Keeper's Cottage she sets to work with paper and scissors and pieces of material.

This year she will make two valentine cards, one for her Raymond and one for Billy, then at least he will be thinking there is someone else who wants to be his sweetheart and maybe then he will look around him and notice the other young, available women working at Alvington.

On Valentine's Day she happily takes her own card from Raymond into the kitchens to show the girls. Everyone is pleased for her, but of course Elsie, Emily, Hattie and Beth are all without lovers and even the older Ruth and Mrs Abbott become pensive and Lettie is sure Mrs Abbott is remembering her poor, dear husband who died in London in a cholera epidemic in 1832, well before his time and before they had had a chance to have any children. Ruth was also widowed and ended up in the poor house and Lettie realises in that moment that matters of the heart can be sublimely spine-tingling, but also sadly devastating and she feels a little guilty at being so thoughtless; she had only been thinking of Billy and trying to cheer him up, but maybe she has disheartened her other companions.

The women are having their lunch break when Edwin and Billy join them. Lettie decides to keep quiet about her card, not wishing to brag, or to rub further salt in their wounds. However, Elsie decides to show them instead.

"Look at Lettie's valentine card from Raymond." The card is covered in red roses and bluebirds and is cleverly folded so that a red heart pops out when it is opened. She demonstrates and both the lads seem to be suitably impressed.

Emily asks them, "Have you had any cards?"

Edwin says, "Not yet," optimistically.

Billy goes bright red and Lettie is sure she can detect a smug smile, but he does not reply. However, Lettie is convinced her plan has worked.

On the other side of the world in Sandhurst, Angelica has settled well into one of the annex rooms at the back of the Eureka Hotel. Most of her punters have continued to visit her, but she suspects that those others, who don't come into the town regularly, are now happy to take advantage of Camira.

She smiles as she remembers how she had shown Camira how to make use of the animal intestines as protection, how they had ended up giggling hysterically at her miming what she should do with them. The young aborigine seemed to understand that it was for her own good and also for the good of her punters, and she is confident that Camira will now be protected from the pox.

Jethro has turned out to be a kindly old man. She usually has a shift behind the bar most days, either afternoons or evenings, and she manages her other affairs around her shifts. She does not miss the swarms of black flies around the settlement at Eaglehawk, nor the ants after the cocky's joy, but she does miss seeing her aborigine friends and the camaraderie of the prospectors up on the hills there.

One warm spring morning in October she is standing in front of the emporium talking to Freyja, who is placing some advertising material outside on the boardwalk, when the horse-drawn omnibus arrives and stops outside the general store. Four people disembark and Angelica's attention is immediately drawn to one of the young men. Surely that is the young Irish chap, Sam Kelly, from Van Diemen's Land?

"What is it?" asks Freyja, looking at her curiously.

"Nothing, Freyja, it's just someone I recognise from the past." She is pleased to see him, but fearing her flushed cheeks might betray her interest, she turns hastily away from the travellers. She does not want to make a fool of herself. She will be seeing Bryn later and can tell him then of his friend's arrival.

Sam Kelly is relieved to finally disembark in Sandhurst. He has had a long and arduous journey from Tasmania. Having looked up and down the main thoroughfare, he decides, possibly because of its Irish name, to book into the Shamrock Hotel, before going on to the local sheep station to find employment. He drops his duffel bag beside his feet, whilst he checks in. He is then shown a serviceable room overlooking the main street. On plonking his bag down on the thinly-covered bed, he looks out of the window, noting with disappointment that the two young women, who were there when he arrived, have now gone. Being a young man only recently released from incarceration, he is eager to acquire for himself a comely woman. *Never mind, it is early days.*

He spends the first day hiring an elderly horse from the pound. The horse-keeper explains, "It's Hobson's choice I'm afraid; all the young fit animals are employed on the goldfields." Then, following the instructions given him by the landlord, he travels out to the Ravenswood Sheep Run to see if they are prepared to give him work.

He sets off following the directions, but the stubborn old nag seems to have other ideas and in the end Sam gives in and lets her have her own way. After all, he does need to have a look around the area and get to know the lie of the land. The horse must have been used regularly at Kangaroo Flats, for that is where the animal is heading.

As he leaves the main town of Sandhurst behind him, the scenery changes from regular slab buildings to a shanty town of canvas and disordered shacks. This area seems to be predominantly Chinese. There are Asian men fossicking for gold everywhere, paring off the surface soil from the reefs and washing it in the nearest pool, or sinking holes in the gullies. The land is pockmarked with holes and heaps from the diggings. Horses are circling round and round within their puddling machines. *This poor old nag was probably employed in one of those machines in the past.* It grieves him to see good pastureland laid to waste for the sake of man's greed.

As they near the creek, the horse begins to struggle in the mud and Sam steers her back onto a rough track. They take a wide arc around the settlement to see if they can cross the creek further along and he finds a shallow area through which the horse is happy to venture, busy with men panning for gold with sluicing rockers, tubs and cradles, but they pass through unhindered.

He believes the Ravenswood Homestead to be between Golden Gully and Spring Gully and as he wanders east, the odd prospector is happy to give him directions. The hot sun beats down on him and he is grateful for his canister of water and Californian-style sombrero. Finally they leave the prospectors behind to travel across a large area of saltbush over which a noon-heat haze shimmers; eventually it gives way to rich pastureland. Kangaroos and wallabies scatter as they go and they encounter a huge flock of merino sheep. There is a lake on their right and in the distance Sam can see the silhouette of a wind-pump and a group of buildings that must make up the ranch and homestead he is seeking. There are tall blue gum trees behind the ranch and Spring Gully is running beside the property to the east and into the lake on his right.

As he approaches, he can make out the stable and shearing shed and what sounds like a sawmill and smithy. Behind a barn there is a small wattle and daub building, outside which two elderly, native women are squatting in the dirt with three small children, playing with a mangy dog. The dog spots him and begins to bark. The sawing stops and a man appears in the doorway of the sawmill. The dog slinks back into the shade and lies down with its head on its paws. "You're a bit off the beaten track mate, what can I do for you?"

"Good day to you, sir. My name is Sam Kelly. I'm a shepherd and I'm looking for work." He notices that the man is using this interruption as an opportunity to massage his gnarled hands.

The man squints at him in the bright sunshine, "Have you done any shearing, son?"

"Yes sir, and lambing."

"Well, you'll need to speak to the gaffer, but I

expect he'll be able to find you something, so many of our men have scarpered off to the goldfields. He's in the shearing shed. I'll take you over."

"Thanks mate." Sam dismounts, ties up the horse on a hitching ring set in the stable wall, and follows the man to the shearing shed. It is almost empty, apart from a couple of men working together at the far end, crutching a small pen of sheep.

"Hey Gaffer!" the ranch-hand calls out, "There's a man here asking for work."

The larger of the two men puts down his shears and strolls over to take a look at him. His fustian sleeves are rolled up above his elbows, exposing powerful, tanned, muscular arms and massive hands. Sam feels rather inadequate being smaller than this huge, fit-looking fellow.

"So you want to be a jackaroo, mate?"

"Yes sir, I'm an experienced shepherd and it's the only way I know to earn myself a crust."

"Where was your last position?"

"On the Tasman Peninsular, sir." He knows he need say no more, for the man will put two and two together and come up with 'ex-convict'.

"I see," he says, thoughtfully tugging his beard. "Well, we're desperate for work-hands at the moment and so I'm prepared to give you a trial, but I don't want any trouble. First sign of problems and you're out on your ear."

"I understand, sir. You won't have any bother with me; I give you my word, so I do."

"Right then, my name is Ray Clark."

He holds out his huge hand and Sam shakes hands with him. "Sam Kelly, sir."

"Well Sam, you'll find yourself a vacant bunk in the barn, and I'll pay you three pounds, ten shillings a month, tucker and board all in."

"Thank you, sir. I'm very pleased to be working

for you." Sam hesitates, "Err… I'm afraid I need to return the horse to Sandhurst. Do you have one I can use for my return tomorrow morning?"

"Yes, you can take Socks, show him will you, Bruce?"

"I'm much obliged, sir, so I am. I'll stay overnight at my current digs and be back early on Monday morning ready to start work, if that will be all right?"

"I suggest you take one of the young abos with you and they can show you the shortest route. You'll find them in their area, behind the barn."

"Thank you, sir."

The ranch-hand tells them, "I'll fetch Kaiya; he is a good buck and will be back before nightfall." The man returns with the young aborigine, telling the boy, "This here is Sam Kelly, we want you, take him, quick way back to town."

"Yis Boss."

He turns to Sam, "My name is Bruce Madden. Looking forward to working with you, Sam. See you tomorrow."

The young buck leads the way on Socks and the journey takes a fraction of the time he took getting there. Sam muses as they go along; *thank the good Lord in heaven I have found myself a position so quickly and with the ranch not being too far away from Sandhurst, maybe I will be allowed to spend the odd Sabbath day in town.*

On reaching the town he sends the young aborigine back to the ranch and returns the old nag to the horse-keeper, paying the man to look after Socks for the night. Then he returns to his digs intending to wash and change out of his dusty clothes. However, as he approaches the general store a young, well-dressed woman steps outside and crosses the road. There is immediately a chorus of whistles and vulgar comments from the idle men lounging outside the grog shop. The girl ignores the men, but one drunken fool lunges after her, grabbing her arm and causing her to drop her packages.

Sam rushes to her aid. "Let the lady be," he says firmly, pulling the man away and forcing him to release his grip.

"Hey!" shouts his comrade, "What's it to you? All them doxies be fair game."

The other man comes staggering over to support his drunken friend. Sam is shocked and disappointed; *surely this eye-catching girl is not a prostitute?* He watches as the girl picks up her parcels and she is about to say something to him, when the second layabout grabs him from behind, but the idiot loses his balance and pulls Sam down with him into the dust and dirt of the roadway. Sam indignantly pushes the man away from him and gets up, brushing himself down, causing billowing clouds of dust and looking sheepishly at the girl. "That didn't go quite as I planned," he says, laughing, his face reddening by the second, whilst the first man staggers off muttering to himself and the other one is left struggling to drag himself up from the ground.

The girl smiles at him gratefully as he walks with her to the other side of the carriageway. "Do I recognise you?" she asks him.

"I doubt it. I've only just arrived here from Tasmania."

"I recognise your accent. You're the Irishman, Kelly, aren't you?"

He stops in his tracks, removes his hat and runs his fingers through his hair, then he looks at her askance, "I am," he says, quite amazed. "But how do you know?"

She laughs at his astonishment. "Don't worry, I'm not a witch. I was in the Cascades Factory when you passed by with a couple of my friends, Bryn Thomas and Hugh Davies."

"Well, I'll be damned! What a stroke of luck, bumping into you." He pauses, thinking about his two colleagues and turning his hat in his hands. Then he looks up at her, "I don't have much time, but I'd really like to catch up with those two old Welsh reprobates… this evening if possible, because I have to be back off to Ravenswood early on Monday."

"Well, I can take you to their claim now if you like," she says happily.

"Do you mind if beforehand, I just go back to my digs and change. It's been a long day and I'm absolutely filthy, as you can see."

The girl ponders for a moment, "Perhaps you'd like to call for me at the Eureka Hotel in half an hour." She points to one of the larger buildings with that name blazoned across its front.

"Of course," he says, realising she would not want to be waiting outside on the boardwalk, with all the drunks about. "That would be dandy. See you then."

They both turn away and then she calls to him over her shoulder, "Just ask for Angelica."

Having washed and changed into a fresh serge shirt and clean hose, he hastily throws on a colourful waistcoat and matching sombrero and goes off to meet Angelica. She is waiting for him, whilst talking to the old man behind the bar of the Eureka Hotel. She seems pleased to see him. She has changed her bonnet and he suspects she has applied some rouge to her cheeks. *Is this for my benefit or for someone else,* he wonders.

They set off up the track towards the Whipstick and the Eaglehawk settlement.

"How long ago is it since you last saw Bryn and Hugh?" she asks him, chattily.

"It must be near on three years now," he says, remembering how they had sought him out to say goodbye.

"They've done well; I think you'll be surprised. They have their official mining licence now and have formed a proper company called the Brecon Valley Mining Company. They've sunk two mineshafts already, the Maerdy and the Taliaris."

"Wow! That's great news. I'm pleased for them. They didn't deserve to be transported, no more than I did; we were only trying to survive in dreadful hard times."

"What did you do, Sam?"

"Well, I was done for sheep stealing, but it wasn't like that at all. I was that hungry that if a lamb was stillborn, rather than bury or burn it, I used to cook it up and eat it. I swear to you, I always did my utmost to revive them first, but they were sometimes born dead and I was starving, so I was. I was caught in the act of cooking one and they accused me of killing it myself. I had no one to speak up for me, no witnesses, for I was all alone up on the hills of County Clare. How could I prove my innocence against those toffee-nosed buggers? I couldn't." He looks at her to see her reaction, but her eyes give nothing away. "How about you?" he asks her.

She looks sad, as she recollects what happened to her, "I was caught stealing bread for my mother." She sighs, "Our pa was sick and there were five kids for her to feed; I was only trying to help her, for we were all so hungry. She'd begged me to be careful, and when I was caught, she felt so guilty for asking me to do it… it was dreadful to see how she blamed herself." She stares up ahead; shielding her eyes from the bright sunlight and then continues. "While I was in prison my pa died, and they put my family in the workhouse." She blinks away threatening tears.

Sam tries to console her, "Times were hard for everyone back then. Bryn told me that both he and Hugh were done for nicking coal in the wintertime. They were only trying to protect their families from the cold."

Angelica nods, "I know, Bryn told me. The trouble is the British laws are so harsh, people who have done small crimes end up having to do time with hardened criminals. I've found there are a lot of folk here who're the salt of the earth, but you have to be wary, for some are real villains who'd slit your throat as soon as look at you."

Sam agrees with her, "You realise that, as soon as you step foot on the transport ships. It's important for the decent folk to stick together, for we'll only survive in life down here, against the rogues, with the help and support of each other."

"Bryn especially has been a good friend to me, but I've also got to know some of the aborigines and I've found them to be very helpful and always happy and cheerful, but some folk around here treat them like dirt."

Sam grins ironically, "I know what you mean; a lot of the English treat the Irish that way too."

She smiles at him, "Well, I promise you, I won't," and in a gesture of friendship, she takes his hand. He feels a wonderful stirring sensation run through his body, like he has goose bumps and he looks down at her tenderly.

They reach the community of Eaglehawk and Angelica points out her old *gunyah*. "That was where I first settled. My aborigine friends helped me construct it." However, there is no sign of Camira, or her friends.

She is explaining to him about the bushfire and her decision to leave, when a voice calls out, "Angel, what are you doing up here?" and Sam spots his old mate walking towards them. Angelica drops his hand and runs to give Bryn an enormous hug. Her pleasure at seeing him is obvious and Sam suspects that Bryn is the reason for her adding the rouge.

Then Sam removes his sombrero and Bryn recognises him. "Sam, my friend you've made it at last. What took you so long, boyo?"

He holds out his arms in greeting and gives him a manly bear hug, as Sam explains. "I only arrived yesterday and luckily I bumped into Angelica, who said she'd bring me up here to find you."

Bryn puts his arm around Angelica, "Thanks Angel." Then he looks back at him, "Come and join us. Hugh is preparing a supper of mutton stew and we can show you our quartz mine."

They follow Bryn back through the encampment, passing folk still working at their shaft-heads; a few homeward bound, carrying their picks or shovels and some outside their tents preparing their meals, or drinking their sundowners beside the sly grog shop.

Hugh welcomes him, as they all arrive at their log cabin, "How are thee, my friend?" He thrusts out his arm and they shake hands.

"I'm good, Hugh, and glad to see you both looking so fit and well."

Hugh and Bryn are still dressed in their working clothes, with their trousers tied with a lace below the knees and the sleeves on their woollen shirts rolled up above the elbows. The two men look almost like brothers, although he believes Hugh to be slightly older. Both of them have bushy eyebrows, sideburns and unkempt beards, but Bryn is darker than Hugh, who has a reddish tone to his hair and he has greenish eyes, whereas Bryn's are blue.

"Excuse the state of me; I wasn't expecting guests." He moves away from the cooking kettle on the fire and brushes himself down. "Would you like a pannikin of tea?"

"Yes please." Sam and Angelica both speak at once. Hugh pours them all some tea and they sit on roughly-hewn wooden benches around the fire, while the mutton stew is cooking.

Bryn lights his pipe and puffs away happily while they all chat. "Tell us about the blokes we left behind at Saltwater Creek. How is old Josiah and is that guard still after all the younger blokes?"

Sam swallows his tea before answering, "Josiah's a free man now and he's found himself a good position on a dairy farm near Sorrell Creek. The old haricot bean is still there bullying and pestering the young lads, but he did get himself beaten up, not long before I left, so maybe he's not quite so keen these days."

"A bit of rough justice, eh? Good for them," says Hugh.

"What about your old mate Meakins?" asks Bryn.

"He's not due out for another six years yet, but I did go and see him before I left and I think he'll be coming over here, as soon as he can."

Hugh sighs, "I was never too sure about him, lad. He has a vicious streak. I saw him lose it once and attack a fellow prisoner. The man later died from his injuries. It all blew up over a game of poker. He accused the chap of cheating, but I believe it was him who always kept his cards close to his chest. I always felt he had something to hide."

Sam laughs, "How can you say that, the way you two used to team up and play cards, no one stood a chance against you two."

"Nevertheless, I think he's a sly one and if I were thee, I wouldn't trust him," warns Hugh sagely.

"Well, he's never done me any harm and it was

because he was generous when we were on board the *Adelaide* that I befriended him," says Sam, good naturedly.

"He befriended thee, thy mean," replies Hugh. "I remember him asking thee to share his bunk that time, when the hot pitch was falling on us. He was the one who initiated thy friendship and thee looked after him like a brother when he had the fever."

"Well, I can only speak as I find."

"That's true my lad, but just thee be a bit wary. There's something machiavellian about him, I can't put my finger on it, but please take my advice and don't be too trusting where he is concerned." Hugh chucks away the dregs of his tea.

"Who is this?" asks Angelica curiously.

"Nathan Meakins, he's someone I befriended on our voyage to Van Diemen's Land. He's a wealthy Englishman, but he didn't act condescending to me, like most do." Disregarding Hugh's advice he adds, "I think you'd like him, Angel." He uses the shortened version of her name, adopted by Bryn, wanting to be accepted as a close friend, like he is.

"What was his crime?" she asks him.

"He was done for raping a local toff's sister, but honest, Angel, he'd never have done anything like that, he's really nice… "

"That's *exactly* what I mean," says Hugh. "None of us here ever hurt a soul, but I tell thee, he's vicious. As well as causing the death of the prisoner on board the *Adelaide*, he was done for *rape and* I heard he also murdered his infant son, so however much he might protest his innocence, he was tried in a court of law and found guilty… just tread carefully is my advice." Abruptly, he gets up to see to the stew.

"I never heard anything about any murder, honest, Angel. He told me the girl he was accused of raping was more than willing; however, her family had it in for him… I believe he's basically a good fellow. Anyway, if he ever makes it here, you'll all be able to judge for yourself when the time comes."

Hugh dishes up the mutton stew, which Sam discovers is extremely flavoursome and everyone compliments Hugh on his tasty tucker, which eases the hint of tension over Meakins.

After they have eaten, Sam explains he has an early start the next morning and they are soon saying their farewells and arranging to meet again the following Saturday night. Sam walks Angelica back to the Eureka and shyly says goodbye, but Angelica has other ideas and steps towards him going up on tiptoe to kiss him on the lips. *She didn't kiss either Bryn or Hugh on the lips. What could this mean?*

CHAPTER THIRTEEN *(January 1861)*

CHASING RAINBOWS

Three months later Sam Kelly is with the group of friends up on the hills again looking south out over the view. Angelica has persuaded Freyja to join them. The sun has been shining all morning, but there are rain clouds threatening too. Soon they can see the sheets of rain falling in the west of the valley and the watery light is split in two by a large complete rainbow. On one side of the rainbow, above Bendigo Creek, there is a warm, sunny golden glow, but on the western side is a dark, indigo sky that appears stormy and mysterious. Sam thinks the scene is amazingly beautiful.

Angelica says, "Look Sam, one end of the rainbow is right over to the east on Ravenswood pastureland. That's where you should find your gold."

"And the other is up here to the west of the Whipstick," says Hugh. "'Tis a good omen for all of us."

Sam points towards the far end of the rainbow. "Can you see that tall wind-pump, north-east of where the rainbow dips down?"

The two girls both look to where he is pointing and say in unison, "Yes."

"Well, that's the Ravenswood Homestead and I'd say that the rainbow's end is quite near to Golden Gully. I'll definitely keep my eyes open when in that vicinity in the future," he says, grinning at them.

Hugh is pleased with the good omen, "We think we're quite close to a profitable seam in the Taliaris mine, don't we Bryn?"

Bryn looks up from his thoughtful whittling. "We do, but we've had problems keeping up with pumping out the water; given a good, dry spell we could strike it lucky."

Angelica is curious to know what task is engrossing him. "What are you making, Bryn?"

He looks up abashed, "A few clothes pegs, ready for when my wife arrives."

Angelica looks dismayed. "You mean you've heard, Bryn? When are they coming?"

"Yes I have, I'm setting off for Melbourne tomorrow, to meet them there on Wednesday."

"So soon! Why didn't you tell me?"

Sam can see that she feels hurt.

"I didn't know myself, Angel, until two days ago; Nell's letter took so long to get here. It only arrived at the Bendigo post office last week and I didn't go in there until Friday. It's lucky I did, or they might be waiting on the quay for me, and me not even aware they were here."

"Oh dear! Is your house on Myrtle Street ready?"

"It's been ready for some while, but it's been the furnishings that have taken the time getting here. It's been a labour of love over the last three years."

"What about *your* family, Hugh?" asks Freyja.

"I'm afraid they've been delayed. My wife's mother has been at death's door ever since they received the papers and she naturally wants to stay close to her mother until her time comes. The old lady is hanging on for dear life and who can blame her, but I know they'll all come as soon as they possibly can."

Sam looks at Bryn, intently. "You must be very

excited at the prospect of seeing them all, after such a long time."

"That I am lad, but maybe a little anxious too. I know I've aged, in our time apart, and I fear we may feel like strangers after such a lengthy separation."

Sam reassures him, "I'm sure, as soon as you see her again, all your old feelings of love will come flooding back."

"I hope so, lad."

Sam gives a sidelong glance at Angelica who is looking very down in the mouth.

That night, after Sam has escorted the two women back into town, he is in his room preparing for an early night, ready for a dawn start on the Monday, when he notices from the hotel window a shadowy figure sneaking around the back of the Eureka Hotel opposite. He is absolutely sure it is Bryn when he catches his features in the lamplight. *How could he, when his family is arriving in Melbourne this week!* He thought the chapel-going Welshmen were more moral than that, but obviously not.

The next morning he sets off back to Ravenswood feeling a bit out of sorts. He is irked by the behaviour of both Bryn and Angel. He might leave it a few weeks before he next comes back into the town to see them. He had held them both in high esteem, but now he realises they are both willing victims of their sexual desires and Angel, in particular in his eyes, has fallen from her pedestal.

Bryn finally arrives in Melbourne after a tiring journey overland on the horse-drawn coach. He feels dirty and dusty again, despite going to the bath house in Sandhurst before his trip. He finds himself a cheap lodging house and has soon washed off all the travel grime, changed into a clean set of clothes and applied some cologne. However, conscious of his more aged appearance since he and Nell were last together, he decides to go to the barber in Melbourne to have his hair, beard and sideburns trimmed and a hot-towel razor shave. He feels a different fellow as he exits the barber's. For the first time since being in Australia he is totally clean shaven. He wonders what Angel would think of him now and then chastises himself, for surely his first thought should be for Nell and his family.

He sets off towards the port at Hobsons Bay with a feeling of butterflies fluttering in his stomach. *It has been such a long time. What if they don't hit it off?*

The docks are full of whalers and seal boats, hawkers and fishermen and he is wary of pickpockets. He can make out the rigging of a tall ship anchored in the harbour and small boats travelling to and fro conveying the passengers to the jetty. He sees a group of two young men and a woman. *Is that them?* He rushes towards them as the woman looks in his direction. It is his Nell! Now she is running towards him, leaving his sons standing with their luggage. She flies into his arms and they embrace each other warmly, "Oh *cariad*, how I've missed you!"

"Dearest Bryn, I've been on tenterhooks waiting for this moment." She kisses him lovingly. "We've been living in limbo all the time you've been gone."

"I know, *cariad*, but now we must make the best of the time left to us, in our new life together in Australia." He breathes a deep sigh of relief. *It's all going to be fine after all.* He reluctantly draws away from her and putting his arms around her slender shoulders he says, "Come, let me say hello to Owen and Rhys." He walks her back to their two sons who greet him equally warmly.

"Wow Pa, it's so good to see you and to be on firm land after such a horrendous journey," says his youngest, Rhys, who although younger, is a head taller than his older brother.

His father is immediately concerned, "Was it terrible?"

"Don't worry your father with that, Rhys. It wasn't so bad, but we really had no idea of the huge distance we were committed to travel."

"It was dreadful, Pa. Everyone was so sick, the stench was appalling. It's an enormous relief to arrive here in one piece," says Owen. "And we had such tremendous storms; even Ma thought we might sink."

"Well, you're all here safely at last and what a joy it is to see you all. Owen, go and fetch that porter and we'll find ourselves a growler to take us to the post house, where we can catch the horse-drawn omnibus to Sandhurst."

The young aborigine porter comes and loads up their trunks onto his trolley. He follows them along the dockside to the nearest hackney carriage and transfers their luggage. Bryn tips the porter and instructs the driver to convey them all to the post house where they are able to board the next omnibus.

Sitting with his family in the carriage he is able to study them. His sons have changed the most, of course, because over the last ten years they have become young men, both of an age to shave, but his sweet wife looks just the same, perhaps a little thinner in the face, but still with that calm equanimity and poise that makes him admire her above all others. He vows that he has had his last night with the beautiful Angel of Heaven's Gate, for he could never hurt his gentle, loving Nell. He knows only too well that if she ever found out, it would break her heart.

The conversation is animated throughout the journey. There is so much to convey from both sides. They compare notes about both voyages from Britain. Bryn points out that they were lucky *they* did not have to put up with the shackles. He informs them of his time spent down the mine on Tasman Island and they tell him about the hardships they have suffered back home without him. Nell passes on the latest gossip about their neighbours, their extended family and the mine workers. Then he gets really enthusiastic telling them all about their quartz mine and how successful he and Hugh have become.

They stop to change horses at a post house in Kyneton, just after crossing the Campaspe River, and with the other passengers they take some refreshments there and then set off again. They are halfway along the second leg of their trip, passing through a wooded area, when Bryn notices some riders cantering out from the trees towards them. They have black triangular scarves tied across their faces and are brandishing rifles and muskets.

"Bushrangers!" Bryn warns. Then he sighs despondently, *why did this have to happen today of all days?* The driver pulls the shires to a standstill and the bushrangers demand that everyone steps out of the carriage. The outlaws are unruly, swearing and shouting and pushing the folk around as the other three male passengers disembark.

Bryn says quietly to his wife, "Come on, Nell, follow me and don't be afraid. They only want to rob us, not hurt us."

Nell whispers back to him, "But I have everything I own in my trunk on this carriage!"

He replies softly, "They don't know that. Have no fear and betray nothing. I'll give them my purse and they'll want the jewellery you're wearing, my dear, but I'll replace it." He turns to his sons, saying calmly, "Come boys, follow us and don't try anything, we're outnumbered and they're unpredictable and dangerous."

His dear Nell has blanched in fear, but they clamber down after the other travellers and stand huddled together beside the carriage. The men go from one to the next and take what they want. The smell of their unwashed bodies and alcohol is overwhelming. He hands over his purse.

They strip Nell of her jewellery and she looks up at him with tears in her eyes, as they roughly remove her wedding band. He puts his arm around her protectively, whispering, "Don't fret, Nell. I'll make another for you, this time out of our own gold."

Unfortunately, his sons have nothing to offer them and one of the bushrangers angrily hits Owen in the belly with the butt of his Brown Bess. The boy doubles over in pain, holding his stomach defensively.

Nell cries out in horror, "Please don't hurt him!"

There is a fearful silence as they all contemplate the danger they are in. Bryn can see the anger and frustration of the leader who is obviously disappointed in the haul. He watches in horror as the outlaw, losing his temper, suddenly thrusts his pistol to the back of Rhys' head, shouting, "Hand over your valuables, or I shoot the lad where he stands!"

His son's eyes are open wide in panic and terror and a wet patch seeps into his breeches. Bryn immediately steps forward, angrily holding himself in check; his heart is thumping with anxiety. "There's no need for violence! My sons have nothing to offer you… but I forgot… I have this." He draws out from the inside pocket of his waistcoat his great-grandfather's ancient gold Hunter timepiece. "Here, take my gold pocket watch. It's a family heirloom and very valuable, but I beg you to please leave my boys alone."

The gang leader lowers the pistol and snatches the watch from him. For a split second Bryn's heart races as he contemplates disarming him, but the gang is too many to risk it. The bushranger inspects the timepiece and seems satisfied. Then, at the sound of horses approaching, one of them shouts, "Let's make tracks!" and they all mount up and take off back into the woods, leaving everyone traumatised and shaking fearfully.

Rhys looks at his father gratefully and says in a tremulous voice, "Thanks for that, Pa. I'm sorry you had to give up your watch."

Bryn holds his son tightly across his shoulders, "Think nothing of it, my boy. You're all worth far more to me than any old timepiece."

"Damn the bastards!" says one of the other travellers in annoyance.

"At least no one was killed," says Bryn, looking compassionately at his youngest son.

The driver says, "Come on folks, let's all get back into the carriage and make haste, in case they come back for more."

Once back inside the vehicle, Bryn cuddles his trembling wife close to him, but he notices Owen is still clutching his stomach. "Are you all right, lad?" he asks him.

"I'll live, Pa." But then he adds despondently, "It doesn't bode well for our new life in Australia though, does it?"

It is dark by the time they reach Myrtle Street and they are all so travel-weary and disturbed by their experience that Bryn shows them straight up to their bedrooms and they settle down to try and sleep. He spends the whole night with his Nell nestled in his arms.

The following morning Bryn proudly shows off

the rest of their new home, before they sit down together for breakfast. He leaves Nell unpacking their things and settling in and takes his sons with him to the mine to see Hugh.

The boys take in all the unfamiliar scenes as they go. When they pass the barracks, where some troopers are lounging about outside, chewing tobacco, Rhys comments to his father, "Where were they when we needed them?"

Bryn thinks back to last night's events, "I suppose we ought to go in and report what happened."

"I think so, Pa. I dread to think what might have happened if you hadn't had Great-Grandpa's watch," says Owen.

They enter the building and Bryn speaks to the duty officer, who records the details in a log book. "It sounds like the Hanging Rock Gang. If we ever get our hands on them, would you be prepared to bear witness against them?"

"Yes, we all will," says Bryn decisively. "If they hadn't been so well-armed, we might have stood up to them last night, but we were absolutely defenceless." In that moment Bryn vows to purchase pistols for himself and his boys. In future journeys they will carry arms.

They leave the barracks and continue up the high street, passing the stable block, the lock-up, the gold receiver's office, the licence tent, the bath house and finally the stores. As they pass the emporium he explains they can get almost anything they need there, and on impulse he says, "Come on; let's see if they stock any guns."

Inside, Mr Brunsvold approaches them.

"Can I be of assistance, sir?"

"Do you stock any firearms, Mr Brunsvold?"

"I do have some I keep locked in stockroom. What you looking for?"

"Well, we were robbed at gunpoint last night by a well-armed gang of bushrangers and I'll be happier if my two sons and I have a decent pistol each, for self-defence."

They follow him to the back of the shop. "Please wait here. I'll see what's in stock." He disappears into the storeroom and returns with a wooden box. "These brought in about month ago. Take look at them and I see if I have anything else."

Bryn draws from the box one of a pair of 35-calibre, smoothbore, flintlock discreet pocket pistols. It feels nice and smooth in his hands and he passes it to Owen. Then he hands the other one to Rhys. They have screw-off, steel, smoothbore cannon barrels, about two and a half inches long. They are both engraved on the left-hand side of the lock with the name 'Twigg' and on the right-hand side, 'Strand, London' and stamped under the breech with London proof marks.

Mr Brunsvold returns with a smaller case, and smiles at the two boys. "Those very best workmanship. The gunsmith, John Twigg of Strand, London, England." He passes the second box to Bryn. "This one very nice, sir, just feel weight." Bryn removes the gun carefully from its velvet nest in the box.

"It made by Robert Wogdon of London, but, according to lady who brought it in, has been converted from flintlock to percussion by Clough and Sons of Bath. It is 37-calibre, muzzle-loading pistol, with stub twist barrel and flat top. See London proof marks."

"I like the way the stock extends into the longer muzzle." He looks up at Mr Brunsvold. "How much for all three?"

"I would like five pounds for pair and three pounds for this one."

"If you throw in some ammunition you have a deal?" Bryn holds out his hand to shake on the bargain.

Mr Brunsvold shakes hands with him. "You have deal, sir."

Bryn hands over the money. "Would you mind holding them for me, for now, and we'll pick up the packages on our way back home?"

"Of course, sir."

"Thank you for your help, Mr Brunsvold."

Owen and Rhys are both excited and, as they leave the shop, Owen is looking back and talking to his brother when he nearly bumps into Freyja, who is carrying a large pile of material before her. "I do beg pardon, sir," she says to him, smiling sweetly.

"My fault entirely," he bows to her and moves to one side to let her pass.

Bryn then recognising her, says, "Ah Freyja, this is Owen and Rhys, my two sons."

"Oh! Hello Bryn." She turns to the boys and says in her Norwegian accent, "Pleased to see you." She dips a small curtsey. "Please excuse, I have customer." She turns away and hurries off.

Bryn notices with a smile that Owen looks mesmerized, as his eyes follow her trim figure appreciatively.

They step outside into the sunlight.

"We'll have to have some lessons, Pa. We've never fired a pistol before," says Rhys.

"You're not alone there, boys. We'll have to have some target practice, but I don't think we should worry your mother with this just yet."

They continue on their route through the town and up to Eaglehawk. When they reach the shaft-head they are stopped in their tracks by the sound of laughter. Hugh appears in the doorway of their cabin office, "Whatever has happened to you, boyo? You look like a young pup!"

Bryn suddenly realises he is referring to his new, clean-shaven appearance.

Owen is curious, "What's so funny, Pa?"

Bryn chuckles along with his friend. "He's laughing because, before I came to meet you, I was as hairy and unkempt as he is." He gives Hugh a friendly shove, "I've brought my two sons to meet you and you ridicule me! This is Owen and Rhys." He turns to his sons, "Boys, this is my old mucker, Hugh."

CHAPTER FOURTEEN *(August 1861)*

A CHARABANC SURPRISE

There are not many highlights in a pastoral lifestyle but, for the estate children at Alvington Manor, 14th August 1861 is a memorable day for them all, when Lord Dryer organises a day trip to Weymouth for the younger folk on the estate.

Early in the morning Aurora excitedly jumps out of her bed and runs barefoot to the window to see what the weather is like. Her papa is already rowing on the lake with Paddy and O'Malley languishing lazily on the jetty, patiently waiting for him to finish his morning exercises. However, it is disappointingly misty, but at least it isn't raining. She quickly washes and dresses herself and then rushes into the nursery to wake Gabriel, but finds Nanny Beth is already dressing him ready for their outing. Whilst Nanny Beth is tidying herself and the nursery, Aurora and Gabriel eagerly run down the stairs to have breakfast with their mother.

Elsie is clearing away the breakfast things when Gareth comes to tell her mother that the charabanc has arrived. "We must go and say goodbye to Papa, Mama," she cries, feeling sorry for her father who is being left behind.

They go with their mother to kiss their papa, before setting off. He has stowed the rowing boat and is striding up the lawn as the two children excitedly greet him, "The charabanc is here, Papa. We have to go now!"

Her father kisses them goodbye. "I hope you all have a lovely day at the seaside, while I'm stuck in the town hall with the commissioners!"

Her mother smiles lovingly at her pa, "We will darling, and thank you for organising it for us all. I hope your day is not too tedious. I look forward to seeing you tonight and telling you all about it."

There is then a chorus of goodbyes and her father strides back into the house with Paddy and O'Malley trailing him.

The driver of the charabanc, she discovers, is called Amos. Luke's papa, who is her father's groom, is going along too, as back-up, because all the Moore family are included on the trip, which means Billy is able to enjoy his day off with his friends. In addition to the young family groups, Raymond, Lettie, Elsie, Emily, Toby, Bunny and Nanny Beth have all been invited to join them for the excursion.

There is much excitement as they all clamber on board in the early hours, seated in their rows. Luke insists on sitting beside her, thus with her mother and Gabriel, they take up the first row. Rosa, who is again heavily pregnant, hauls herself up into the next seat and Billy passes up Ruby and Eli to sit beside their mother. Nanny Beth perches on the end of that row; to take care that none of the little ones are seated on the outside, followed by Ruth Proctor with Hattie and Ellie in the third row.

Luke's mother, Susan, has become close friends with her neighbour, Ruth, and she helps her daughter Lilly to climb up next to Ellie and then clambers up beside them. This leaves Edwin, Bunny, Emily and Elsie, sitting together in the next row and finally Raymond, wearing his familiar wide-awake hat, climbs up beside his sweetheart, Lettie, and her brother Toby and Billy join them in the back row.

Everyone is dressed in their Sunday best and

Aurora thinks it makes a pretty picture with the ladies all in their colourful costumes, decorated bonnets, gloves, furled parasols and reticules, and the men with their Sunday suits and a variety of smart headwear. As soon as they were all told about the excursion, Emily had set about making and decorating straw bonnets especially for the occasion, for Hattie, Elsie and Lettie.

John Moore helps Michael Porter load the towels and picnic hampers at the rear; then he climbs up beside the driver and, with a flick of the reins, the four horses all toss their heads and set off. All on board shout their goodbyes and wave frantically to those left standing on the front steps, Mrs Abbott, Michael Porter, and of course, Flora, who had filled the hampers for them and offered to stay behind to feed her father and the remaining staff.

Aurora is glad of her cape for the air is crisp and fresh and the morning dew is still on the ground as they leave, but the warm sunshine soon evaporates the early haze, and scattered white fluffy clouds eventually disperse leaving a clear blue sky.

The journey seems interminable with several comfort stops, but her mother focuses their minds by saying, "The first one who spots the sea can have tuppence." Luke is the lucky lad with the presence of mind to shout out, as soon as the carriage surmounts the top of Ridgeway Hill, "The sea, I see the sea," he screams excitedly. Her mother takes up her reticule and finding her purse she rewards him with his prize. There is a chorus of disappointment from the other children. "Never mind, when we get there I'll buy you all a toffee apple each," she says laughing.

She knows her papa has given her mama enough money to hire deckchairs for the adults, and to buy some buckets and spades and pay for donkey rides and treats for the children, and just thinking about it makes her heart race in anticipation.

There is a light sea breeze as they descend Ridgeway Hill and the carriage finally wends its way alongside the Radipole Lake. Aurora is anxiously searching among the many waders for a stork, "Is that a stork, Mama?"

"No darling, it's a cormorant; storks are white."

She keeps searching until she spots another large bird, "Is that a stork, Mama?"

"No, darling, that's a heron. What is all this interest in storks?"

"I wanted to see how big they are, 'cause they would have to be very strong to be able to carry your wicker basket."

Louisa has no idea what her daughter is talking about and so she just agrees with her, "Yes they would, but I don't think we have any storks around here, Rora." However, her daughter is so eager to learn, the seed is sown that maybe it is time they employed a governess for her and she resolves to speak to Joshua at the earliest opportunity.

The carriage turns south towards the seafront and they continue through the town, until they reach the back of the Prince Regent Hotel where Joshua has arranged for the charabanc to be stabled for the duration of the day. Amos, their coach driver, John, Billy, Edwin and Raymond all help the ladies and children to disembark. After which, they form their family groups and process in an orderly fashion towards the beach. The men convey the hampers between them.

On the esplanade Louisa locates the deckchair attendant and with his help they set up their picnic area on the sandy shore. She sends Billy and Edwin off to purchase seven sets of buckets and spades, and Elsie and Emily to find the confectionary vendors, and they soon return with their purchases. A large rug is spread out in the centre of their adopted area and the small children sit down on it happily to eat their toffee apples.

The young couples are sitting slightly apart in the deckchairs, Edwin and Bunny chatting merrily, Raymond and Lettie holding hands companionably and, Louisa notices, Billy is staring dreamily at Beth as she talks to him. She smiles to herself: *That would not be a bad match! He must have finally given up all hope of Lucy, now that she is betrothed to Ashleigh Seymour.*

Once they are all quietly eating, they can hear the strange, squawky voices of the Punch and Judy show some distance away and Aurora spots the gaudy booth with a crowd of children all shouting and laughing at the strange antics of the glove puppets. "Can we watch the Punch and Judy Show later, Mama?"

Louisa looks in the direction of the booth and she can see there is a tearoom close by, which would be the perfect place to keep an eye on the children while enjoying some refreshments. "Of course you can, we'll go over there, after you've all finished eating."

She looks at Rosa, "I'm dying for a cup of tea, aren't you?"

Rosa looks rather pale, but she says enthusiastically, "Yes, milady. I am rather thirsty."

"Me too," says Susan.

"Are you all right, Rosa?" asks Louisa, with concern.

"Yes, thank you, milady. Just a bit shaken up after the journey, that's all."

The older ones have decided to play ball and have gone nearer to the shore, so as not to disturb the day-trippers. Louisa watches as a horse tows one of the bathing machines into the water, with the stout female attendant standing ready to help its occupant into the sea. "What a palaver, having to remove most of one's clothing, simply with a view to getting wet. I cannot see the point of that, can you?"

The other ladies all laugh. "It wouldn't be so bad if we could swim, I suppose," says Ruth. "I think I'd quite like the liberty of it, if it was after dark and no one could see you anyway."

"Well, according to Joshua, it's apparently all the rage since King George liked to visit Weymouth to enjoy it." Louisa points in the direction of the monument, standing majestically in the centre of the road. "As you can see over there, they even erected a statue to commemorate his Golden Jubilee, he was such a popular man here."

John Moore then asks, "Isn't he also the chalk figure on the white horse, carved in the hillside above Osmington?"

"Yes, I'm sure you're right, John. I believe Joshua mentioned that, but I don't think you can see it from here."

She watches the children as they enjoy their toffee apples and, as some of them have finished and are licking their fingers, she says, "Right children, once you've all finished eating, who wants to go and have a paddle and wash their sticky hands?"

There is a chorus of 'me's' and half the children stand up, ready to run off. "Just a minute, children," says Nanny Beth, "the little ones haven't finished yet; besides we need to remove your shoes and hitch up your clothing first, so you don't get too wet."

The ladies attend to their clothing and then follow them down to the water's edge. The boys immediately start to kick and splash each other, until their mothers intervene. Aurora gets her own back on Luke first though, and they are both soaked. "Never mind, you'll dry out eventually," says Nanny Beth, patiently.

Then they all set off to watch the Punch and Judy Show. The adults enjoy tea and cakes whilst the children are occupied, but during that time Louisa notices Rosa occasionally wincing in pain. She does not draw attention to this, but resolves to take her to one side later to find out what is ailing her.

After the show Aurora and Luke ask if they can ride on the donkeys and of course all the little ones want to have a go too. This means someone having to support the smaller ones and the young men volunteer for this job, which is the safer option, because of the long dresses of the ladies.

Thus Eli, Ruby and Gabriel are supported by Edwin, Raymond and Billy. Aurora, Luke, Lilly and Ellie insist on going unattended and the others are all too mature to be interested. The youngsters have a nice long ride along the beach and come back happily cuddling and stroking their donkeys.

While they are gone, Louisa again asks Rosa if she is feeling unwell.

"I have to admit I'm having regular pains Lou-Lou, and I'm fearful it's the baby, but surely it's too soon."

"I thought your baby wasn't due until the end of next month."

"I know! I'd never have come if I thought there was any risk! But the children were looking forward to it so much and I wanted to enjoy seeing them having fun."

"Don't worry, Rosa. I'm sure it is just practise spasms."

"I'm not so sure now, I've been having them for two hours and they're getting stronger."

"Well, I think you should come back with me

and sit down in the deckchair and remain calm and we'll monitor them." She turns to the others. "Beth, would you, Ruth and Susan please look out for the children for me. I'm going back with Rosa because she's feeling unwell."

"Yes, of course, milady."

On their way back to the deckchairs, Rosa's waters break and she is horrified. "Whatever shall we do, Lou-Lou? I can't have the baby here on the beach, in front of all the children and everyone else!"

"Just stay calm; we have some time to plan."

There is a look of horror on her friend's face, "With the greatest respect, milady, I don't think we have much time at all. This is my third child and they get quicker coming each time. I'll never make it back home. I know that much."

Louisa looks all around her and suddenly makes her decision, "I'll hire a bathing machine; at least that will afford some privacy for you."

Rosa doubles over in pain, "It'll not be long, milady. It feels very low now."

"Come Rosa, we must make haste. You'll feel much better if you can lie down."

The spasm easing, Louisa takes her by the arm and they march as quickly as they can over the soft sand towards the row of bathing machines. Louisa explains the situation to the person in charge and he leads them to the nearest available machine. Rosa goes up the steps and lies down on the wooden flooring. Louisa stays protectively in attendance.

Elsie notices Louisa heading away from them all with Rosa leaning heavily against her and points them out to Emily, just as they are entering the bathing machine. "Something is wrong with Rosa, Em. I think she may have gone into labour!"

"Oh my Lord! It's far too soon! We'd better go and see if there's anything we can do to help."

The two girls anxiously make their way over the sand in their bare feet. Elsie taps on the door of the bathing machine, "Is everything all right, milady?"

After a moment Louisa opens the door a crack. "I'm afraid Rosa's little one can't wait until we get home to be born. Please would you keep the children occupied and away from here, especially Ruby and Eli, and could you also bring us some of the bathing towels and some drinking water from the tearoom." She is thinking back to Aurora's birth and how she managed on that frightening occasion. "Also, Elsie, could you ask if they can spare us a pair of sterile scissors?"

"Of course, milady."

Louisa closes the door on them and goes back to attending to Rosa.

Elsie says, "You go and tell Susan, Ruth and Beth and get the towels and I'll go to the tearoom for the scissors and the water."

After the donkey ride, Aurora and Gabriel immediately look around for their mother. Nanny Beth explains that she is busy with Rosa and will be back soon; but not long after, Aurora spots Elsie going to the bathing machine with an armful of towels and assumes they are going to be towed down the beach by the horse and go into the water. She is immediately worried for her mother, who she believes is unable to swim; she has never seen her swim in their lake.

Luke has gone off with his own mother to buy a kite with his tuppence and whilst Nanny is preoccupied with Gabriel, busy making sandcastles with Ruby and Eli, she slips away unnoticed and runs across the sand. When she arrives at the bathing machine, she suddenly has doubts. What if she is mistaken and someone else is inside there? She sits down on the steps outside. All around her there is a cacophony of noise, from the rumbling of the passing carriages along the seafront, the seagulls mournfully wailing overhead, the vendors shouting their wares, the Punch and Judy puppets, and the excited shouts and screams of the children, but she can just make out whispering and moaning and groaning from inside the bathing machine. *Something is very wrong in there!*

She cannot hear enough to be able to recognise her mother's voice and so she sits outside worrying for what seems like ages. Then she hears a baby crying! She is sure it is from inside the bathing machine and she is rooted to the spot. Eventually the door opens and her mother steps outside with a newborn baby, wrapped in a towel.

Her mother looks shocked to find her sitting there. "Hello, darling; what are you doing here? I thought you were with Nanny Beth."

"I was worried for you, Mama."

Her mother sits down on the top step beside her. "Well, there was no need to worry, for both Rosa and your mama are fine, but Rosa would like you to meet her dear little daughter, Daisy!"

Aurora is flabbergasted, "Oh my! She's tiny." *But how can this be? Where is the stork?*

"Would you please run and fetch Nanny Beth for us darling, and ask her to bring Ruby and Eli with her, but leave the other children with Susan and Ruth? You can tell her the good news if you like."

"You're not going into the sea then, Mama?"

"No darling, I think we have to look after this little sweetheart and after our picnic we'll be setting off for home."

She runs off happily with the news, feeling excited and important to be the bearer of such glad tidings.

A week later, Louisa and Joshua are entertaining a prospective governess who has been recommended to Joshua by Lord Helyar. Her name is Grace Tweedy; she is recently widowed and wishes to move into the locality from Longbridge Deverill, near Warminster, Wiltshire, to be nearer to her married sister who lives in Sherborne. Her family is well known to Lord Helyar and much respected.

Louisa thinks she looks rather gaunt, but this is probably due to the recent death of her husband. She is well dressed, has an attractive smile and a friendly, confident manner. She has listed her accomplishments in her reply to Joshua's letter.

They are seated in the drawing room and he asks her, "Please tell me a little about your background, Mrs Tweedy?"

"Well, my lord, prior to my marriage, I was the governess to the Garrett family at Crockerton. They owned the silk mill there and had a daughter of nine years."

Louisa says encouragingly, "That's the same age as Aurora is now."

Grace Tweedy smiles, reflectively, "It's a lovely age when children are most eager to learn."

Joshua continues, "How long were you employed by the Garrett family?"

"Until Miss Lucy was eighteen, my lord."

Louisa then asks her, "Were you employed anywhere else beforehand?"

"Yes, milady, before that my first situation was governess to another young lady, for a family in East Monkton, from the age of ten until she too was eighteen. That seems a long time ago. She's an accomplished pianist now."

"Well, Grace, could you give me some idea of what your lessons will cover?"

"Of course, my lord: they will include English reading and writing; basic arithmetic; geography and history; sewing and embroidery; drawing and painting and studying nature; singing, dancing and playing the piano."

"Well, I must say that sounds very satisfactory, don't you think, Louisa?"

"Yes, my dear, I do."

Joshua stands up, "Well, we'd like to employ you on a six-month trial basis, but I see no foreseeable problems. I'm happy to start you on an annual salary of thirty pounds, rising to thirty-five once you have completed a satisfactory year. Perhaps you'd like to take some tea with Louisa while you think about it and then she can show you around and you can decide whether or not you want to accept."

"Thank you, my lord."

Joshua pulls the bell rope, "I'll leave you to enjoy Flora's delicious baking together. It has been a pleasure to meet you, Grace, and I hope you do decide to join our happy household."

CHAPTER FIFTEEN *(October – December 1861)*

EARLY TICKET OF LEAVE

Meakins keeps constant vigil with regard to Fred Burns and the governor's daughter, for by monitoring the warder's every move, he hopes he will be able to compile sufficient ammunition to encourage the man to support him, when it comes to the next parole board. He finds Burns to be an irritating little Scotsman who constantly reminds him of his shrewd steward Alistair McNab and his own frustrating conviction that he will be making a play for his stupid sister in his absence.

One Sunday he is seated in the shade of the tallest blue gum with a group of prisoners who are reading their mail. He has no post and is lounging and relaxing when he catches sight of Fred Burns and Mary strolling together in the governor's gardens. These are formal gardens tended by the older prisoners, but as he watches them, he sees him leading her apparently willingly by the hand, out of the garden and around behind the church.

Curiously, he decides to investigate. He gets up nonchalantly and wanders in the same direction, trying to appear inconspicuous. He sidles along the side of the stone building, glances around the buttressing and spots them. He has her pinned against the wall, but she appears to be trying to hold him at bay. Meakins is only too familiar with this reaction and is feeling aroused just watching.

The girl, although reluctant to make a scene, is

beginning to struggle more. As Burns is frantically tugging up her skirts, she is desperately trying to pin them down. Then he puts his left hand across her mouth to ensure her silence. This only makes her panic and struggle further, but still he is pressing his upper body hard against her, whilst yanking up her petticoats.

Meakins has to decide whether to do nothing and enjoy the spectacle; use this scene in his armoury of persuasion, but keep *Burns* on his side; or rescue the girl, alienate Burns, but hopefully get *her* undying gratitude. It is a huge risk, because she may be too ashamed to speak up; but if she does tell her father, the governor might be willing to give him his early ticket of leave.

Fred Burns' breeches are already unbuttoned and he is fumbling there with his right hand, trying to release his equipment to do the business. She is clawing at the hand covering her mouth, trying to prize away its grip in order that she can cry out.

Meakins has seen enough and in a snap decision he rushes forward, grabbing Burns and roughly pulling him off her. Holding the furious man tightly within his strong muscular arms, he looks down at the distressed girl and smiles reassuringly. He needs her trust and belief in him. "Be off with you, miss, but please remember who it was who rescued you."

She immediately rushes away in tears.

Fred Burns says angrily, "Get your filthy hands off me, you interfering bastard. How dare you!"

"*How dare you?* Is more the question, Sergeant Burns. That girl is traumatised enough to tell her parents of your attempted rape and believe me, I know the trouble that can cause!"

"That was no rape; she's been giving me the eye for months now. She was well up for it!"

"Not according to her struggling she wasn't, nor

by her expression of gratitude, as she ran off to her mama."

"It's just your word against mine Meakins. Who's going to believe a convict against a respectable prison guard?"

"You may be right Sergeant Burns, but if she speaks up it will be two against one, and I'm sure the governor will believe his own daughter." Meakins releases the man, carelessly shoving him aside and walks back the way he had come.

The next Sunday in church, Mary is staring straight at him. There is gratitude in her eyes and something akin to adoration. *Oh no! This is not the plan at all!* The last thing he wants is her transferring her affections to him! But at least he knows that she has recognised him. Moments later he catches her whispering in her father's ear and the governor looking in his direction.

The following morning the prisoners are all mustered, after breakfast, to form a line outside in the exercise yard. Meakins registers the unusual presence of the governor; his bald pate, bushy beard and sideburns are easily recognisable and his smart dress quite distinctive. Meakins is singled out, whilst the remainder are dismissed and sent off on their work details. Eventually, Meakins is frogmarched into the governor's office to find the most important man in the prison seated behind his cluttered desk, peering at him over the top of his reading spectacles.

He tells him, "You may stand easy, Meakins," and so he relaxes his posture, but keeps his eyes straight ahead. "I understand from my daughter that you stepped in and saved her from being assaulted by one of the prison guards last Sunday. Is that correct?"

"Yes, sir; she was about to be violated by Sergeant Burns and I was in a position to prevent it."

"Well, thanks to your brave intervention, you have earned my daughter's undying gratitude and my own and her mother's grateful thanks. Needless to say, the man in question has been taken from here and is under arrest."

He leans back in his chair and removes his spectacles. "I've been checking your records and I find it rather ironic that you've been serving a life sentence in part for the same crime attempted by Burns, in addition to a shockingly deplorable charge of infanticide. Can you tell me more about that, Meakins?"

He glances slyly at the man to try to gauge his disposition and then hangs his head, "I'm ashamed to admit it was the laudanum had me in its thrall and through that, the devil had me by the nose, sir. My sister didn't want the birth of the child and thus her shame to be discovered by our parents and friends, because she was still unmarried." He lifts his head and looks at the governor. "She begged me to spare her the disgrace and humiliation… and so I did it for her, sir."

The governor abruptly closes the file before him, a serious expression on his face and then he vocalises his reasoning, "You have already served eight years hard labour with no major black marks against you and what you did for my daughter illustrates that perhaps you *have* learned the error of your ways." He looks Meakins straight in the eye. "Do you feel guilt and remorse for your past misdemeanours?"

Humbly, he looks down at the floor again, "I do, sir. I realise I was on the wrong path before, but I've turned to Christ since being at Port Arthur." He then holds his head up and returns the governor's penetrating stare, resolutely, "I only wish to spread the word of the Lord now, sir, and follow in the steps of Jesus."

The governor looks searchingly into his face, trying to measure his sincerity and Meakins holds his breath when the man slowly says, "It is in my power to grant you a free pardon." Hoping for an early ticket of leave he is stunned when the governor appears to be considering a free pardon. *This would mean I could leave Tasmania whenever I want.* The governor then continues, "Do you believe and attest you have learnt your lesson, during your time here at Port Arthur?"

Everything depends on this man believing me. "I have, sir. I assure you, Governor, I'm now a reformed man."

"Well, in that case, I consider your act of bravery and gallantry towards my daughter sufficient grounds to convey upon you a free pardon and I'll arrange to have your discharge papers prepared. Do you have any questions?"

"No sir. Thank you, sir… Oh I'm sorry, sir, there is just one thing; I'd like to be able to travel to the goldfields in Victoria, to try to make enough money to return to England. Will I be able to pay for my voyage there? I don't recall what monies I had on my person when I was first detained."

"Your possessions will be returned to you and in addition I'll personally arrange your passage, man. I owe you that for my daughter's sake. You're a free man, Mr Meakins. Good luck and God go with you."

"I'm much obliged to you, sir. Please pass on my kindest regards to your daughter." He cannot believe it – *free at long last!*

Nathan Meakins arrives in the Bendigo Valley on horseback at the beginning of November 1861. He passes the barracks and the lock-up and rejoices in his freedom. However, he must find some form of employment, or another way to make some quick money in order to return to England as soon as he possibly can. Perhaps he could apply for the position of trooper, guarding the consignments of gold, as they are conveyed to the City Bank in Melbourne. *That might offer up a lucrative opportunity.*

He ties his mount up outside the grog shop and enters; eager to quench his thirst with a mug of porter. Opposite is the Eureka Hotel and he is considering whether or not to book in there for a few days. He asks the keeper of the grog shop, "Can you recommend a respectable hostelry where a traveller might expect clean sheets and a decent meal?"

"You won't go far wrong with the Eureka, the Shamrock, or the Golden Nugget, mister. You may as well try the one over the road first. They also have other services to offer a fellow there, if you get my drift."

Hmm! That would be most acceptable, I've been playing my own solo tune on my trumpet for long enough. He downs his porter and wanders over to the Eureka. The stooped old man behind the bar looks up at him, boss-eyed. "Good day, sir. What can I get you?"

"Do you have a decent room to let, landlord?" Meakins scans the bar area and finds it clean and tidy.

"I expect I can accommodate you, sir. For how long will you be requiring the room?"

"Shall we say a month, for starters?"

"Please follow me and I'll show you what we have to offer."

He follows the landlord around the back of the bar and is about to go up the stairs behind the old fellow, when a young woman enters from the back door. She dips a curtsey as she passes him and he is struck by her low-cut gown, exposing handsome, rounded breasts and her enticing, smiling eyes. Although merely a barmaid, the wench has her thick chestnut curls pinned up high on her head in a fancy comb and she smells of a floral scent. *I wonder if this is the one who provides the extras? If so, things are looking up already.*

Angelica is musing about the handsome stranger, when they both come back down the stairs and Jethro introduces her to him. "This is Angelica, my very capable barmaid." He turns to her, "Angel this is Nathan Meakins, who's taking one of the rooms upstairs for the next month."

She dips a curtsey, "Welcome to Bendigo Creek, sir." *So this is the infamous Nathan Meakins. I won't let on I have heard of him just yet.*

He takes up her hand and kisses the back of it, oozing with charm, and she smiles at his English county manners.

Jethro says, "Have a tot of whisky with me to seal the deal, sir?"

"I'd be delighted, Mr Tully."

"What brings you to this neck of the woods, sir?" she asks him, as she places two small glasses on the bar and pours the two tots out for them.

"I'm planning to make my fortune here, like everyone else, but I chose this particular gold fossicking area because I'm also hoping to meet up with a colleague of mine, Sam Kelly." He downs the whisky in one hit.

Angelica says, smiling to herself, "I know him, sir. He hasn't been into town for a while, but he may well show up on the next Sabbath. He works out on the Ravenswood run. It's a fair trot from here."

"I'm happy to wait until Sunday; I've a lot to organise, myself." He turns to Jethro, "Do you have stabling for my nag?"

"Yes sir. You'll need to bring her round the back way and into the barn."

"Right you are. Thank you for the toddy, Mr Tully. I'll settle the animal and be back later."

Meakins spends the following week learning the lie of the land. He manages to sign on with the Bendigo Volunteer Rifle Corps, the mounted police ranger unit, to commence work the following Monday. He had a little money returned to him that was confiscated when he was arrested and a little more that he won from playing cards with his fellow prisoners, but he is well aware that it will not last him long. In the meantime he seeks out the Chinese communities, and not far from where they are constructing the red brick Joss House Temple, he discovers an opium den, known by the Asian squatters as The Lotus Pond.

The area is squalid, with a number of short, stocky Chinese men guarding the place, where gambling, prostitution and grog can be obtained at any time of day or night. He shudders with distaste as he spots a rat among the rubbish in the alleyway, recalling once more the prison hold and his voyage to Van Diemen's Land. The rat slinks off and he relaxes once more. He is looking for the person in charge of this enclave, but these men all seem to be at the same level of subservience. "Do any of you speak English?" he asks them.

One of the younger men, sporting a tasselled skullcap and a long, single plaited pigtail steps forward. "I speak little."

"In that case I'd be much obliged if you'd take me to your boss?"

"Why?"

"That's my business."

Pigtail turns away, "Then it stay that way," he says, stubbornly.

"He'll not be happy if I take my opportunity and offer it to someone else."

Pigtail considers for a moment, "Stay here, I see if he see you," and he wanders off down the alleyway, leaving Meakins standing outside the den with the other Asians staring sullenly at him.

Shortly Pigtail returns, "Come… Zhang Wei will see you; follow me."

He trails the man through the shanty town, until they reach a small stone-built building. On either side of the doorway stand impressive stone-carved, lion-headed dragons. The man beckons him to follow inside. He enters a room smelling of incense and festooned with red and gold silken wall-hangings. Two massive golden Satsuma urns have been placed on either side of a low couch, upon which is seated a large, rotund Chinaman. The man is wearing a predominantly jade-green patterned robe with jade toggles and he has a straggly beard growing from beneath his chin, with two long strands of hair growing from either side of his upper lip. He too is wearing a skullcap and sporting a long, plaited pigtail. Two heavyweight, Oriental henchmen stand either side of him.

The man looks up impatiently. "I hope this important. I am busy man." He idly twirls his mandarin-style moustache.

Meakins bows, displaying the deference he assumes the plump Chinaman will be expecting. "I'm new to the area and I wish to find employment that is lucrative, but does not involve getting my hands dirty, sir."

He halts fiddling with his strands of hair. "I see; well, what do you have to offer me?"

"I've recently joined the Bendigo Volunteer

Mounted Rifle Corps, but of course the position is part-time and unpaid. However, in due course we'll be guarding the gold shipments into Melbourne and I'm wondering if anyone might be willing to pay for information with regard to this?"

"I see. You mean me to be go-between?"

"If necessary; in return for a finder's fee, of course... do you know of anyone?"

"I might. Come back with useful information and I'll see what I do." Zhang Wei dismisses him with a wave of his chubby hand, and he bows once more, before the henchmen usher him out ceremoniously.

Meakins returns the way he came, back through the alleyway, wary and on the lookout for rats, until he is once again outside the den. The distinctive smell of the green ash is enticing him. After eight years of abstinence, he believes he is able to control his drug habit, thus he decides to exercise his freedom of choice by quenching his hunger. A shiver of anticipation runs through him as he enters the den.

In that first week he visits the den every night, his yearning for it, if anything, stronger than ever before. He manages to make a few pounds some nights by gambling with the dice or cards, they favour a game called 'two-up', but unfortunately he is not likely to win enough to fund his extravagantly debauched lifestyle.

On his first day with the troopers he is issued with a smart, dark-green uniform, similar to that worn by the 13th Light Dragoon regiment: a pair of leather half-wellington boots; leather gaiters; a shoulder belt and pouch and a rather jaunty slouch hat. He is armed with an Enfield musket and supplied with some musket balls, a powder horn, form and sealing wax. He believes the uniform suits him well and he is pleased to be armed for the first time in his life. His training is quite rudimentary, repeatedly making the paper cartridges and moulding the musket balls, polishing his boots, drilling, fencing, grooming and equipping his horse, and target and bayonet practice. He is surprised to find that some of the men in the company are aborigines and he is expected to be on an equal footing with them. *Well, we will see about that!*

On Saturday night Sam Kelly rides into Sandhurst after a busy day, having separated, mustered and corralled the wether lambs ready to drive them into market on Monday. He has not been into town for over a month and wonders if he will have been missed. He walks into the Eureka Hotel to look for Angelica, accompanied on this occasion by Bruce Madden and although he is gratified to see the look of surprise and pleasure on Angel's face, he is absolutely amazed to see his old buddy, Nathan Meakins, standing before him at the bar.

"Nathan! I can't believe it! How the devil did you get here *so soon?*"

They shake hands, simultaneously patting each other on the back.

Meakins grins mischievously. "I escaped by stowing away in one of the vessels moored by the docks at Port Arthur."

"Oh my God! You're one of the very few then! They'll be doing their utmost to track you down and recapture you, you know."

"I know. I was hoping you'd hide me for a few months."

Sam looks uncomfortably at Bruce Madden. *The boss isn't going to like this.* "I …"

"Don't listen to him, Sam, he's been given a free

pardon!" interjects Angelica, laughing heartily at his discomfiture.

"You rotten bastard! I really fell for that one, so I did. Well, that's a relief, but how come?"

"It's a long story mate; let me tell you over a pint of beer."

During the course of the evening they are joined by Hugh, Bryn, Owen and Rhys and there is much recalling of their past years spent at Port Arthur. Sam has missed the camaraderie of his friends over the preceding weeks and, aware that Bryn is eager to cement the friendly relationship developing between Angelica and Nell, they arrange to meet the following morning after church. Somehow Hugh manages to keep his own counsel with regard to his distrust of this machiavellian friend of Sam's.

Angelica has felt the loss of the regular visits of Bryn and so, when there is a knock on her door one night, and she finds Meakins standing there, she happily welcomes him in. He is after all a handsome, well-groomed fellow and she has no reason to deny him. He is still in his prime at forty-three and is fit and athletic.

The first time they couple together, he adamantly refuses to use the pig sheaths. It may be because Angelica is quite attracted to him that she reluctantly allows this. Despite his stubborn refusal he is gentle, considerate and in remarkably good humour. Angelica realises he has been celibate for the last eight years and she shows him a good enough time for him to want to return again and again. She teases him with her tongue until he is rampant with desire, then she wraps her legs around him to ensure that every last inch of his tool is buried deep inside her soft, sensitive warmth, enjoying being held for a change in lean, muscular arms.

She is pleased when he returns the following night, but then he doesn't come for several days. She wonders what, or who among her competitors, is enticing him elsewhere. It isn't long before she realises that he likes to chase the dragon. Meakins admits to her that Zhang Wei is allowing him to 'use now and pay later' for his facilities, which means he is quickly building up a sizeable debt. She suggests that he should seek some kind of paid employment with Bryn and Hugh, and so a month after his first arrival he goes with Sam and Angel up to the Whipstick to discuss this with them.

They find Hugh seated outside his shack reading the *Melbourne Argus* newspaper. He looks up at them. "The news is very sad folks. His Royal Highness, Prince Albert, has finally succumbed to the typhoid fever. He died on 14th December."

"Oh no! He's been ill for so long with this and that, but I never thought he'd die so young, he must be only in his early forties," says Angelica, sadly. "Our poor Queen, she loves him so and all those little children."

"He's a year younger than me," says Meakins.

"According to this, the Queen is at Osborne House on the Isle of Wight. It says that because of the infectious nature of the illness the Queen and other members of the Royal Family were not permitted to attend upon the patient."

"They must all be heartbroken," says Angelica, "How very sad."

"There's an extract copied from a correspondent's letter from the *Mauritius Commercial Gazette,*" Hugh reads out loud. "It says: *Amidst the pomp of heraldry, a memento of domestic love was laid upon the prince's coffin; a messenger brought from Osborne to Windsor, three little wreaths and a bouquet; the wreaths were simple chaplets of moss and violets, wreathed by the three elder princesses, the bouquet of violets, with a white camellia in the centre, was sent by the widowed Queen."*

They are all affected by the melancholy of this news and Hugh goes off to the sly grog shop to get some rum to cheer them all up.

Expecting some resistance from Hugh, Sam takes this opportunity to bring up the subject of Nathan needing work, whilst he is absent. "Bryn, Nathan urgently needs to find himself a proper paid position. He's unfortunately, at present, running up debts and we thought you might be willing to consider him for any work that doesn't involve him going down the mine?"

"Well, to be honest with you Sam, there's only paperwork at the moment and I tend to be in charge of that myself, but… I could do with more time to spend with my family."

"Well, there you are, Bryn. If you show Nathan the ropes, you won't need to be up here working so late every night," says Sam, supportively.

"I'm sure Nell would appreciate seeing more of you, Bryn," says Angelica, kindly.

"It's true that I'd like to be able to work alongside my two lads a bit more, to help with their training. It would mean that Hugh could supervise one of them in the Taliaris and I could supervise the other one down the Maerdy."

Hugh returns in the middle of this conversation and soon puts two and two together. Angelica can tell by his deep frown and black expression that he is not happy to allow Nathan access to their accounts. "What's this?" he asks them, indignantly.

Bryn responds, "I think it might be time to consider employing an accountant, Hugh?"

Hugh looks at Meakins suspiciously, "Well, what doest thee know of accounts, boyo?"

Meakins isn't going to beg. He looks at him

arrogantly, "I was responsible for the running of my father's estate in Somerset, Hugh. I'm sure I could handle the accounts of your two mines without any problems. Why don't you give me a trial?"

It comes across as a challenge and Bryn, Sam and Angel are all looking at Hugh expectantly. He feels outnumbered and reluctantly backs down. He looks at Bryn, then spitting out his chewing tobacco he says begrudgingly, "Well 'tis thy job he's after, Bryn, what doest *thee* say?"

Bryn, ever the peacemaker, replies, "I say we should give him a month's trial."

"Looks like you're one of the team then, mate," says Sam, happily slapping his friend on his back.

Angel, Sam and Bryn all seem to have welcomed him into their lives with open arms, but Hugh knows him to be devious and conniving. Later, after the others have gone back down the hill and, as Bryn is leaving to go home to Nell, he tells him of his fears. "Thy man is manipulative, Bryn, and not to be trusted. I think thee will rue the day we give him access to our financial information."

CHAPTER SIXTEEN *(September – November 1862)*

GONE WALK ABOUT

Meakins enjoys dealing with the accounts and the gold receiver's office for Bryn and Hugh, but he finds Hugh's constant suspicion wearing. He is employed regularly with the troopers, but it is some months before he is able to offer Zhang Wei any information. Then one morning he overhears the arrangements for the next gold shipment taking place the following day, Tuesday 15th September. He goes immediately after his shift to report to Zhang Wei to tell him of the decision.

Pigtail, or Tian, which he discovers is his proper name, escorts him to see his boss. He finds him smoking a long clay pipe of tobacco, whilst a young concubine kneels beside him, massaging his fleshy feet. He clicks his fingers to dismiss the girl, who immediately leaves them alone.

Meakins tells him the details and explains that, "Rather than alerting the bushrangers to a large convoy, a small contingent of armed troopers will be concealed within the regular mail coach. I myself will be one of the troopers who'll be protecting the shipment and I want your assurance that I'll be spared any danger."

Zhang Wei agrees and promises to pay him for the information, once the raid is successful.

On the Tuesday morning the mail coach with its escort sets out as usual from Bendigo. In charge of the escort is Sergeant Cridge, who sits by the driver's side, the other police being Senior-Constable Henry Graves, Constable William Horsey, an aborigine trooper called Amaroo, and Meakins himself. These all ride inside the vehicle. The consignment carried in the coach comprises of 3,700 pounds in cash, and boxes of gold for the Oriental Bank, the Bank of New South Wales and the Commercial Banking Company. The total value is a sizeable sum of around 14,000 pounds. In addition to this treasure there are several mailbags, in which there are letters and packets containing various sums of money.

The mail coach rattles briskly along the road towards Melbourne with the troopers unaware of impending disaster. They have been on the road for around three and a half hours and it is nearly noon when they encounter two abandoned drays, drawn by bullocks, standing in their path. Without due alarm the mail coach turns sharply into a narrow passage between the drays and the massive rocks bordering the road at this point. Owing to the limited space and the curve of the roadway the driver reins in the horses to a walk.

Meakins can feel his heart beating in anticipation. *This must be their trap!* Suddenly from behind the boulders appear the black-masked faces of the bushrangers, whooping and hollering and firing their carbines into the mail coach, wounding the sergeant and Constable Horsey and blowing off the driver's broad-brimmed, cabbage-tree hat. Meakins shoots back at the men, aiming wide of his target on each occasion. This, however, causes the horses to take fright and bolt, with the carriage bumping and lurching and finally capsizing onto its side. The driver is thrown off into the bushes on the other side of the track and the troopers, feeling trapped in the carriage and too exposed in the open, also seek cover in the brush. From this vantage point they endeavour to hold off the villains, but they are so outnumbered by the bushrangers they decide it advisable to beat a retreat and seek assistance, abandoning the loot to the jubilant plundering of the outlaws.

Amaroo and the driver assist the two wounded soldiers, as they make their way to the nearest sheep station, with Meakins and Henry Graves alert for trouble, and covering their withdrawal. The squatter at once despatches a messenger to Bendigo. The officer there promptly organises a party of troopers and aborigine trackers and by nightfall they are on the scene of the ambush. The trail of the bushrangers is picked up and followed, the troopers eventually coming upon the remains of a fire, where they find some torn-open mailbags, empty boxes and a litter of torn paper and letters. From the direction of the hoof marks, the trackers conclude that it is the Hanging Rock Gang, but they soon lose their trail when they disappear back into their haunt in the mountains.

Bendigo Creek is aghast with the news of the bushrangers' successful haul and the town's losses. Meakins lets a few days pass before he goes to Zhang Wei for his reward, then he goes to the den to pay off his gambling and opium debts. He is left with a smaller sum, which is not going to last him long, considering his huge appetite for the green ash.

He is on a high when that night he goes to find Angelica. He taps on her door, only to find her busy with another punter and he is asked to return in an hour. He goes into the bar and sinks a few glasses of absinthe, but he is annoyed to be kept waiting and his mood darkens.

When eventually he returns to her room, she is ready to receive him and she smiles happily once she realises who it was whom she had knocked back earlier. But he is tight-lipped and not in the mood for her cheeriness. He soon wipes the smile from her face by grabbing her roughly by her hair, thrusting her face down on her bed and taking her aggressively from behind.

Angelica is shocked and frightened by this angry, aggressive side to him. Her face is buried in the bedding and she can hardly breathe. She is too frightened to fight him off, for he is too violent and strong to defy. When he has finished using her and he slumps exhaustedly over to one side, she is stiff and sore from his forceful treatment. She wipes away her tears of humiliation and drags herself away from him, standing up shakily and adjusting her clothing. Looking down on him lying nonchalantly, with his smug, triumphant expression, indignation takes over and she decides *he cannot get away with this* and she stoically holds out her hand, saying, "I charge double for that type of behaviour."

He gets off the bed with slow deliberation and stalks around to her side, standing over her angrily, "You've never said anything about double, you dirty, swindling tart. What makes you think you're worthy of that kind of money?" Then he strikes her around the face. His slap knocks her off her feet and she lands vulnerably back on the bed. She is relieved when he turns away to leave. Then resentment burns inside her and she calls out to him, "I expect payment for my services, Nathan, and if you don't pay me now I'll get help from Sam, Bryn and Hugh to extract it from you, one way or the other."

He looks down at her distastefully, takes out his purse and, throwing the money into her lap, he casually opens her door to leave.

She picks up the coins, "I may be just a tart, Nathan, but I don't deserve to be treated with such disrespect and I want you to understand this, for I'll not change my mind. That is the last time you take your pleasure from using me. I won't be available to you in the future. Goodbye, Nathan."

He stalks off saying, "It's no skin off my nose. After all, variety is the spice of life."

So Sam was wrong and Hugh was right, he is a bastard!

Nathan Meakins is annoyed with himself for losing his temper last night. Angelica is a temptress all right, but obviously in great demand and he doesn't appreciate playing second fiddle to some squatter. It might even have been a native, the way she panders to them! *Who the hell does she think she is, banning me? I could teach her a lesson she'll never forget for that. She's very fond of that little abo lubra and I know where to find her when I'm of a mind.*

About a week later Camira's brothers and Matari have painted and decorated their bodies and gone off to Ballarat to take part in a *corroboree*, where they will dance and perform for the gold-diggers to their native music and hopefully earn themselves some money. Camira has opted to stay behind, as she believes she can earn more lying with her usual punters.

Thus, late that night she is all alone, lying on Angelica's old straw mattress and sleeping soundly when a drunken man bursts in. She is used to being disturbed, but usually her punters knock gently, or quietly call out her name, so that she has the choice whether or not to answer them, but this man pushes open her ironbark door and stands silhouetted in the entrance to her *gunyah*. He awakens her from a deep sleep; her heart is thumping wildly as he frightens the life out of her. The smell of alcohol fills her shelter. The door bangs shut behind him, as he staggers towards her, ripping away her possum-skin cloak, leaving her naked and vulnerable on the straw mattress.

In the dim light of the moon she can see his huge shadow towering over her and she can hear him fumbling with the buttons of his breeches. She tries to reach out for her bucket of sheaths, but he swears at her, kicking over the pail. The brine splashes her skin and she realises immediately there is no arguing with this man.

He drops down, his knees placed on either side of her. She can smell his erect member as he pushes it towards her mouth. In horror she turns her head away; this is not a service she has offered before, but he punches her full in the face. Leaning over her, supported with one hand above her head, he holds her nose painfully, until she has no choice but to open her mouth to breathe; he quickly uses this opportunity. Once she submits to receive him, he finally releases her tender, throbbing nose. Her instincts are to bite down on him, but she is too terrified of what he will do to her. As he pushes back and forth inside her, she is choking and urging by the time he reaches his climax. She vomits on the floor beside her mattress once he withdraws.

She keeps her eyes on him warily. He sits at the base of her mattress and takes a swig from a hip flask. She is too frightened to move and so she stays still, hoping he will leave; but he is not yet ready to go. Suddenly he grips her legs, bruising them as he forces them apart. She feels something cold and hard inside her. The pain is excruciating and she cries out, begging him to stop, but he hits her again, in the stomach this time.

She weeps silently as he eventually withdraws whatever implement he had been using and then once more aroused he leaps upon her, wanting to climax again. She endures the repeated rape and beatings throughout the night, time after time, until finally he leaves just before daylight and she slides into unconsciousness.

Several weeks pass and Meakins does not cross Angelica's path, then one morning Bryn comes down to the Eureka to find her. "You'd better come up to Eaglehawk, Angel. Camira's in a bad way."

Angelica is immediately concerned, "What do you mean, Bryn?"

"Well, it seems she's been badly beaten by one of her punters."

"I'll come straight away. Thanks for letting me know."

"Actually, Nell is with her at the moment, but she's asking for you, Angel."

Angel walks briskly with Bryn back up the hill, "How are you keeping, Bryn?"

"I'm very well, thank you, Angel. How about you?"

"Not so bad." She looks down at her feet as she goes. "I'm missing you actually, Bryn; and Sam, since he has been too busy with the shearing to come into town. I have to say, Bryn... between you and me... Hugh was right about Nathan Meakins. He's a wolf in sheep's clothing. He was loathsome to me the last time I saw him and I've refused to deal with him anymore."

"Why, what happened?"

"He got violent, Bryn. I think he was in a bad mood because I'd kept him waiting, but he was horrible and he struck me when I asked for my money."

"Did he now? Perhaps Hugh and I ought to make *him* wait for *his* money, in that case, Angel. Leave it to me, sweetheart, he won't go unpunished."

"I think Hugh was right all along. He's a dangerous man, so be careful how you handle him, Bryn."

They reach her old *gunyah* and there is poor Camira with Nell doing her best to apply balm to her bruises. Bryn says, "I'll leave you ladies to deal with this," and he continues on his way. The young girl looks up at Angelica with her huge, trusting, sad black eyes and Angelica goes down on her knees to hug her. Although her skin is dark there are bruises evident on her arms and legs and her mouth and eyes are puffy and swollen. There is a scab forming between her nose and her mouth where it has been bleeding.

"What happened, Camira?"

"Sam's friend, he beat me and did it many times, forcing me. He nasty fellow… not use pigskin. I cry out, but no one help Camira."

"I'm so sorry, Camira. When was this?"

She spreads out the fingers of both her hands and flashes them at Angelica twice.

"Twenty moons ago?"

She nods.

"Do you have pain?"

"Here it hurt." She holds her stomach. "Still blood!" She points between her legs. She looks hot and sweaty and Angelica holds her hand against the girl's forehead. She looks at Nell, "She has a fever."

Camira lies back on her straw mattress, "I not stay here. I go bush, to my people. I wait for Matari… he come."

Angelica sits down beside her. "I'll stay with you." She turns again to Nell. "Thank you, Nell, for helping her. There's no need for you to stay. I'll wait until Matari gets here."

"If you're sure, Angelica? I do have a lot of chores and I don't think there's anything else I can do to help her now." She replaces the lid on her balm pot and steps outside the *gunyah*.

Angelica gets up then, deciding to follow Nell to speak to her confidentially. Out of earshot, she asks her, "Do you know who found her?"

Nell lowers her voice, "Bryn discovered her this morning not far from here. She'd collapsed and everyone else was just walking by unconcerned."

Angelica frowns, "It's because she's a native; many Europeans treat them like animals. It makes me so mad!"

"It's shameful, but I'm glad she has a friend in you, Angelica. I fear she's suffered more serious emotional and internal harm than the cuts and bruises that are so evident. Anyway, I'll leave her now in your capable hands. I expect I'll see you in church on Sunday."

"Yes, I'm sure I'll be there. Bye, Nell, and thanks again for helping her."

It is not long before Matari arrives with Pindari and Kaora, and Angelica asks them to take Camira back to her people and keep her safe. Together they help Camira to her feet, gather her belongings, her monies and her valuable possum-skin cloak, then they disappear off into the Whipstick forest.

Four days later Matari seeks her out, "I come to tell you of 'sorry business'."

Angelica immediately recognises the aboriginal expression for death. Poor little Camira has died of her injuries. Angelica is desolate. *Sam's so-called friend did this to her. He shouldn't get away with it!*

She asks Matari if she can attend the funeral ceremony with him, but she is too late.

"I take you to Jaara people's burial ground, if you wish to see where her spirit lives."

"I should like that, Matari."

"We no longer speak her name now. It is custom."

Angelica nods her head slowly and sadly, understanding their beliefs, but worried she may speak out accidentally.

They set off up the hill in the hot sunshine towards Eaglehawk in complete silence until they reach the Whipstick. The scrub has completely recovered from the bushfire five years ago. On the edge of the forest she notices the large red blooms of the waratah bush and she asks Matari if it will be all right to take some with them. He smiles and agrees and so she breaks off some of the branches. They enter the cool of the forest and the huge blue gums tower over them, with the sunlight filtering through and making patterns on the red earth and among the liana vines. She can hear the tinkling sound of bell chimes and wonders if they are near to the aborigine encampment. But the sound seems to be travelling along with them. In the end she asks Matari, "What is that tinkling sound?"

"It is bellbirds." He points up into the woodland canopy and she can just make out a small but sturdy olive-green miner-bird with orange eye patches and a bright-yellow bill looking down at them. In seconds it flits away and several follow, making their characteristic tinkling sound. It is very melodic.

"They help us black fellows by leading us to honey."

"Mmm, I love honey."

"You'll like black-fellow's sugar, Angel? I show you." He searches as they go along the well-worn aborigine trail, disturbing a large possum from the shrubby undergrowth as they go, until they are

241

standing below a white gum tree and there on the ground is the manna he is looking for.

She tries some. "Mmm, it tastes just like marzipan. Thank you, Matari."

They set off again with Matari leading the way until finally they come to a clearing in the forest. There is a large rock formation to one side and the remains of a funeral pyre in the centre.

Angelica places the flowers beside the pyre. Then she drops to her knees to say a silent prayer for her friend, whose spirit is now literally once more 'of the wind'.

Bryn and Hugh are incensed when they hear of Camira's death and when Meakins turns up for work, Hugh tells him angrily, "Go home Meakins, thee no longer works here. Thy despicable behaviour towards both Angel and Camira is not to be tolerated. I cannot even bear to look at thee. Thee's fired."

"What do you mean, for Christ's sake? They're whores, aren't they? What do they expect?"

Hugh grabs hold of him by his lapels and chucks him out of his office. "I don't want to set eyes on thee ever again, thy miserable bastard. Thee have betrayed Sam's faith in thee and confirmed all my suspicions about thy true nature. That poor, trusting native girl is dead, thanks to thee."

A flicker of surprise crosses Meakins previously contemptuous face. *So the abo girl snuffed it did she? Well good riddance, she was a crap ride anyway.* However, he knows when he is not welcome and he strolls off back down the hill to drown his sorrows.

As the weeks go by Meakins is getting deeper and deeper into debt at The Lotus Pond. Finally, he once more overhears the plans for the next shipment. As a result of public condemnation over the last daring ambush by the Hanging Rock Gang, this time there will be a contingent of six mounted troopers in advance and to the rear of the consignment. Meakins is one of them.

The convoy sets off early on a Wednesday morning in November. They are well on their way, about three hours into the journey, when they are caught up in a volley of fire exploding from the cover of dense woodland either side of the roadway. Several troopers are shot dead in the first surprise attack and the driver is wounded in the shoulder. Meakins observes there are rocks strewn across the path ahead, which would undoubtedly overturn the carriage if they continued; however, he believes with the extra troopers, the odds this time are more even.

Sergeant Cridge orders two of the advance party to go ahead and remove the obstacles then he instructs the remaining troopers to encircle the carriage and keep moving, while the two troopers inside the carriage are to reload and replace the muskets for the mounted guard outside. As the battle continues, Meakins personally shoots two of the bushrangers himself, whilst his horse is prancing edgily from side to side. Beside him Constable Horsey wounds one. The outlaws are well concealed behind the huge trunks of the ironbark and eucalyptus trees, whereas the troopers are rather more exposed. The driver is finding it difficult to steady the horses with his painfully wounded shoulder.

On the other side of the carriage from Meakins, Amaroo manages to kill four of the robbers and William Horsey shoots the gun out of the hands of one of them, effectively disarming the man. Meakins then catches a fellow running between the trees and shoots to kill. Thus eight thieves have been either killed or disabled. Meakins estimates there must be around four men on either side left to fight on.

Then tragically William Horsey is shot in the head, dying instantly. Sergeant Cridge is brought down when his horse is shot from under him. He runs for shelter under the carriage, recharges his musket and continues to shoot from there. Then the bushrangers manage to shoot the two troopers inside the carriage and they break cover, moving slowly out of the forest on foot, towards the remaining men of the escort. Besides himself, Meakins can see only Amaroo and the driver left and seeing an opportunity, he gallops to the front of the harnessed horses yelling to the driver to move forward. The driver whips the horses into action and the robbers are left standing in the road, surrounded by the dead troopers. Forgetting that Sergeant Cridge is still pinned under the carriage they inadvertently roll over him, leaving him injured and vulnerable in the middle of the roadway.

Riding like the devil, Meakins hears shots and looks back, as the robbers swiftly and callously dispatch Sergeant Cridge and the other wounded and dying men, before running back into the forest to mount up and follow them.

He is the senior trooper now and he orders the carriage off the roadway. The driver shouts at him, "What's going on mate? It's against regulations for the Royal Mail to leave the road."

Meakins replies, "We need to outwit the robbers."

They have travelled about a mile into the bush when Meakins rides to the front of the carriage and cold-bloodedly shoots the driver dead. Amaroo is shocked and taken off guard, when his fellow trooper immediately produces a pistol and he too is shot in the centre of his forehead.

Meakins wastes no time in plundering the mail coach. He shoots the padlock off the large iron box that is too large for him to carry and fills his saddle bags with as much gold and cash as he can. He quickly removes his uniform and dresses in the driver's jacket and breeches, swapping his regulation slouch for the driver's cabbage-tree hat.

With no time to waste, he leaves behind the mail packages to keep the robbers occupied should they come across the wagon, and gallops away through the scrub, keeping off the beaten track and travelling with speed in a southerly direction.

He grins to himself... *so far so good. If I pull this off, I've managed to outwit the troopers, the bushrangers, the miners and Zhang Wei!*

CHAPTER SEVENTEEN *(November 1862 – 1863)*

OVER THE BESOM BROOM

The folk in Sandhurst are dismayed to hear that the Hanging Rock Gang have massacred their brave troopers and again stolen their gold. The aborigine trackers follow the hoof prints up into the mountains, where, as before, they lose their trail. Meakins is the only guard unaccounted for but no one official seems to connect him with the dastardly deed. When he does not show up, Angelica and her friends discuss the possibilities that he might have been taken by the gang, or have actually joined the gang, but all are united in thinking *good riddance!*

The dead bushrangers are identified from their wanted posters and buried in un-consecrated ground on the outskirts of the town. Many of the townsfolk attend the funerals of the troopers, Angelica, Bryn, Nell and Hugh among them. Constable Horsey's widow stands desolate beside her three small children and Angelica is moved when her eldest boy, about seven years old, protectively takes his mother's hand in his. Sergeant Cridge and Tom Curtis, the coach driver, are buried that afternoon. Their families are older, but their grief is painful to witness and after their consecration Angelica turns away and does not attend any more of the ceremonies conducted for the other troopers; it is too upsetting.

The takings from the Taliaris and the Maerdy were among those stolen and Hugh and Bryn are devastated that all their hard work over the last few months amounts to nothing. Hugh is the only person who suspects that Meakins has outwitted them all. They had refused to pay him and gave him instant dismissal, but ironically, perhaps he has had the last laugh by making off with all their gold! This thought niggles away at him, as the rest of the town comes to terms with their losses.

Several weeks pass and Angelica has not been feeling her usual self for some time. Then one Sunday she is with Sam and they are strolling along the creek together after church when she suddenly feels faint. He grabs hold of her, lest she falls into the stream, and he helps her to a boulder where she sits with her head between her knees until she recovers her composure.

"What's wrong, Angel? Are you unwell?" Sam's genuine concern is touching and it would be easy to imagine that he truly cares for her.

The summer breeze wafts her hair and she brushes it out of her eyes. "I've not been feeling well for the last week or so, Sam. Maybe I'll go to see the doctor tomorrow."

"I think you should. You look very pale." He appears to be worried and so she reassures him.

"I feel quite recovered again now, Sam." She stands up gingerly. "Come on, let's go and find Freyja."

Sam glances down at Angelica as they make their way along the creek and back into town. He has never seen her looking so pale and he is concerned it is something serious. He still feels guilty for introducing her to Nathan Meakins. *If only I could stop her from selling herself, it's far too dangerous and she's worth so much more than that. Who knows who she might pick up next; she could be killed like poor Camira.*

He wonders if she has got over her infatuation with Bryn. He believes he hasn't visited her room since Nell and the boys arrived. *I'd give anything to see that look of love in her eyes for me.*

"You're very quiet, Sam. What are you thinking?"

Should he put into words what's on his mind? He hesitates and then takes the plunge, "I was thinking how I wish you'd give up whoring, Angel, and find yourself a nice job, perhaps working with Nell, or Freyja."

"I must admit, Sam, lately I've been thinking on those terms myself. I was hoping that I could save enough gold to one day open my own saloon, but really all I want to do is find myself a nice home, like Bryn has, and settle down and have children of my own."

At the mention of Bryn, jealousy stabs mercilessly at his heart. He likes the man himself. He has been a good friend to him and he can understand her attraction to him; a hard-working man, with his soft, melodic Welsh accent and his strong and reliable, kind and gentle nature, but it is a hopeless cause, for he's a married man. He gives a sigh of exasperation. *Compared to me, Bryn's an old man and here am I, single and available, and she doesn't give me a second thought!*

They reach the emporium and Angel uses the knocker on the side door. Freyja answers her knock and invites them to join her family for afternoon tea.

Seated in the parlour of the Brunsvolds' home, Angelica looks at Sam and wonders why he has never come to her for his comforts. Surely he has some feelings for her? He rides into town most Saturday nights to spend his Sundays with her and they get on so well together, but unlike Bryn, or Meakins, he has never asked for more than her friendship. *Maybe it's because I'm a whore that he finds me distasteful. Perhaps, if I give it up, he'll look at me in a more favourable light?*

Freyja and her mother pass around tea plates and cups of hot tea and they enjoy cheese sandwiches and some small, treacly cakes. About half an hour later Angelica hastily leaves the room to be sick outside their back door. She confides to Freyja that she fears she may be pregnant.

That night she is unable to sleep. *What if I really am pregnant? How will I be able to support myself then?* She tosses and turns, mulling over her situation. *Jethro will not want a pregnant barmaid and my punters are not likely to pay for my services in that condition. I'll be forced to live off my savings and forget my dreams, for soon I'll be destitute with a child to care for into the bargain.* She weeps silently, until eventually slumber mercifully overtakes her.

Freyja goes with Angelica to the doctor's rooms on Monday where he confirms her worst fears; she is about four months pregnant. Angelica is mortified! *The only punter who refused to use the pigskins was Nathan Meakins and so it stands to reason that, in all probability, he is the father!* She bursts into tears of despair, wailing to Freyja, "How will I ever find a husband and have a proper family of my own now? I'm a fallen woman in more ways than one."

Freyja puts her arm around her friend, "It be all right, Angel… your friends… we look after you."

"I cannot rely on my friends, Freyja. I don't want their charity. I always take care of myself."

"It not be for long, I sure. There are many men look for companions in goldfields."

Angelica looks at her friend sadly, remembering standing beside Esme outside the Cascades before she was whisked off to wed a stranger. *If that had been me, I'd have my own family by now and not be in this position, and at the time I'd been relieved it had been Esme instead!*

When Sam rides into town the following Saturday night, Bryn waylays him outside the Shamrock Hotel and tells him of Angelica's predicament. Angelica has assured Bryn that he is not responsible.

"She believes Meakins to be the father, Sam."

Sam sighs, guiltily, "Why did I ever recommend him to you all?"

"You can't blame yourself for his actions, Sam. But there is a way you could make amends. I know you have feelings for her, Sam, and I know she's enormously fond of you. Have you never thought that you two would make a perfect couple?"

"To be honest, Bryn, I've always believed that she's in love with you, mate."

"Don't be daft; what would she want with an old fellow like me? It's you she is interested in, boyo. Why, she remembered you well from her first, fleeting image, when she set eyes on you marching past the Cascades in Hobart. You must know she's hankered for you ever since then."

"Then why hasn't she said anything?"

"She's a tart, Sam. She feels she's not good enough for you."

Sam is dumbfounded. "Are you serious?" *Bryn knows Angel better than anyone, perhaps there is hope after all.*

"Go to her, Sam. Let her know how you feel about her. She really needs you now."

"Thanks, Bryn."

Bryn slaps him on the back, "Good luck, boyo."

Sam walks around to the back of the Eureka Hotel and knocks on Angelica's door. The door opens and a sad and blotchy face peers out at him. She has been crying and his heart goes out to her.

"Can I come in?" he asks her.

She opens the door wide to let him enter.

He removes his hat and stands before her, plucking up his courage to speak, then he admits, "Bryn has told me that you're expecting Meakins' child."

She looks even more crestfallen. "I am, but I would not have it so, if I could change things, Sam."

He tries to encourage her to look on the bright side, "But you told me you wanted to have a family, Angel."

"Not like this though, Sam. Not like this." Tears spring into her eyes again and she blinks them away.

He desperately wants to give her some hope of a future. Suddenly he blurts out, "What if we were to wed, Angel? Would that make it all better?"

It is hardly a conventional marriage proposal. She looks at him in astonishment. "You'd marry me, even though I'm carrying another man's child?"

He looks into her sad eyes and is overwhelmed with love for her. "I have to be honest with you, Angel. I love you. I've loved you for ages now, but I thought you favoured Bryn."

"Oh Sam, you silly! Bryn has always been a good friend to me, but in that way he's been the same as all my other customers." She sighs, despondently. "I thought Meakins was a friend, just like Bryn, but he was nasty, Sam, and now I'm a fallen woman in every way."

"Don't talk like that, Angel. Would you look at

yourself? You're gorgeous and in my eyes you're still perfect."

She looks at him in disbelief, "If that's really true, why didn't you come to me for comfort, like the rest of them?"

"I didn't want to use you like that, Angel. You're worth far more than that. I want you to give up the whoring, because I want to keep you safe from harm. I adore you and I want you to marry me. Together we can use our savings to buy a small plot and eventually we'll be able to build ourselves a nice little home alongside the other squatters."

"It sounds wonderful, Sam, but I cannot accept."

"Yes you can, Angel. All I've ever wanted, since I lost my own family in Ireland, is another family of my own."

"No Sam, I can't expect you to take on another man's child."

"Yes, Angel, you can! You must accept it is true, I'll love and care for Nathan's child. It's not the child's fault his father's a bastard. You'll soon be able to give me my own children, darling. Believe me; you'll fulfil all my happiest dreams if you consent to be my wife."

He holds his breath as she looks at him lovingly and then she smiles, "In that case, I say… if you truly mean it… my answer is… yes, please." She throws her arms around his neck and kisses him passionately and moments later they are making love on the bed, tenderly entwined in each other's arms. It has been a long, emotional journey, but finally they are both able to express their previously suppressed feelings of love for each other.

Sam and Angel cannot afford a church wedding, so they decide to pledge their allegiance over the brush.

They do this on St Valentine's Day, in the consecrated grounds of the church at Golden Point. Bryn and Hugh, standing beside a yew tree, hold the besom broom whilst Sam and Angel jump over it, hand in hand, dressed in their wedding costumes, loaned by Freyja's parents for the occasion. Then the wedding party all set off to Myrtle Street for a wedding breakfast, contributed by all their friends.

It is a rare event on the goldfields and everyone lets their hair down and enjoys themselves. Owen is lavishing all his attention on Freyja. Nell notices his devotion and smiles as she points this out to his father. Bryn turns to her, "He couldn't do any better, for she's a fine catch for our son and will be a wonderful companion for him."

Angelica is pleased for Freyja, and when she spots them together she throws her bouquet of wild flowers in her direction after the reception. She is thrilled when her friend enthusiastically catches it.

There are some abandoned squats around Angelica's old *gunyah* where the prospectors have moved away to Elysian Flats for more promising yields and she and Sam increase the size of their plot, purchasing the larger area officially through the land registry.

"There's such a splendid view from up here, Angel. We'll be able to build ourselves a wonderful home in time."

"I never imagined when I first came up here with Matari and Camira and the others and we were constructing my *gunyah* that I'd end up having my family up here. I'm the happiest I've ever been in my whole life, Sam."

He kisses her, contentedly.

"I've been thinking, Sam. If we have a little girl I'd like to call her 'Camira'. It's a pretty name and I think it goes well with my new wedded name of Kelly."

"Hmm, I agree and I think it very fitting you honour your friend. Besides, I also think it would annoy her real father, if he knew."

"*You* will be her *real* father, Sam. But yes, I think he would be furious!" They laugh at this small act of rebellion.

Angelica finds employment assisting Nell teaching the schoolchildren. She comes up against opposition at first, some of the mothers not happy for their children to be in the company of a whore, but Nell intercedes, saying, "This is a new country of second chances for folk. Who among you have never been forced to do something you later regret?" The women mutter disparagingly among themselves, but Nell is adamant, "I'm giving Angelica her second chance and I'd like to think that you will support her with me, but you have a choice. You don't have to bring your children to us if you prefer not to." No one turns away and it is not long before Angelica is as much loved as Nell, by the children and their parents.

She finds she enjoys the satisfaction gained from helping them to read and write and she nurtures a true friendship with Nell. Each month, as they bring home their earnings, they manage to purchase some more building materials and during this time Angelica still lives behind the Eureka and Sam works away all week at Ravenswood. The groundwork and first phase is completed by the time their baby girl, Camira, is born on 15th June 1863 and then they decide to move into the first phase of their home. Sam has orchestrated the delivery of their essential furnishings, many purchased through the emporium, and Angelica soon settles them all into their new home.

One Wednesday evening, when she returns home with Camira after school, Angelica is surprised to find Sam already waiting for her. "What are you doing back in town so soon?"

"I've something to tell you, sweetheart. I think you'd better sit down."

She sits down anxiously in a small armchair and places Camira on the rag rug beside her to play with her home-made wooden toys. *It must be bad news! Why else would he be here midweek? Perhaps he's lost his job? But he doesn't look very worried.*

Sam sits in the rocking chair. "Do you remember that time when we were up on the hill, looking at the rainbow that ended in Golden Gully and you said to me that that was where I should look for gold?"

"Yes." Her heart begins to race.

"Well, I always keep my eyes peeled around there and on Tuesday, after a short rainstorm, I saw something glinting in the sunlight. I pulled Socks to a standstill, dismounted and picked up this large lump of quartz that's dappled with gold and just lying there on the surface of the ground." She looks at him wide-eyed. "It's a sizeable piece and so I took it to Ray, the gaffer. He was surprised I was so honest, Angel, and he said for me to bring it into town on Wednesday to the receiver's office to see how much it's worth and we'll split the proceeds."

"Oh! Sam. How marvellous! Well, what did they say?" she asks him excitedly.

He takes a deep breath, dramatically. "It weighs 380 ounces and is worth around 5,000 pounds!" They both burst out laughing in disbelief.

She jumps up and hugs him warmly, "Oh Sam,

it's a fortune! That means we'll get around 2,500 pounds. We can finish the building and buy the remaining furnishings with that amount." Her delight is exhilarating as Sam looks down at her and kisses her tenderly. She is kissing him back and she can feel his body melding into hers and she knows he is responding with real and genuine ardour.

Baby Camira gurgles away happily at their feet.

CHAPTER EIGHTEEN *(June 1863 – October 1864)*

THE HOMECOMING

It is a warm, sunny afternoon in June; the birds are busy feeding their fledglings and a dainty damselfly dazzles, glowing in ultraviolet light and flitting from plant to plant in the bright sunshine. Olivia is playing hide-and-seek in the shrubbery with little Agnes when she hears horse's hooves on their carriageway. She pokes her head out from behind a sweet-scented choisya bush to see who is approaching and Agnes leaps on her with delight. "Found you!" she cries, happily.

Olivia holds her daughter in her arms, but is staring right past her to the rider. "Oh! My God!" she cries, "You're back!"

Agnes looks up at the man on horseback, "Who is this, Mama?"

"It's your Uncle Nathan, child."

Her brother stares down at them malevolently. "I see things have moved on somewhat in my absence," he says sarcastically, "Am I to assume there is a husband?"

Olivia addresses her daughter, "Senga, go inside and find Nanny." Then she turns back to her brother, "I think you ought to stable your mount first, Nathan, and then come inside and Alistair and I will happily update you in comfort." Then she rushes inside to warn her husband of her brother's return.

About ten minutes later, her brother marches in through the front door, agitatedly tapping his leather riding crop against his thigh. The study door is ajar and he can see Alistair McNab sitting in his father's study looking very at home. Alistair jumps up and comes out to greet him, "Good afternoon, Nathan, good to have you back." He holds out his hand, affably.

"Let's get one thing straight, McNab, you are now once again my steward and you will address me appropriately."

Alistair immediately reverts to his former subservience, "I beg your pardon, sir, but as your brother-in-law, I assumed we would now be on friendly, first name terms."

"Well, you can think again, you bloody usurper." He bangs his whip on the desk, making McNab jump. "There is nothing friendly about stepping into my shoes as soon as my back is turned!"

Olivia enters the study and quickly closes the door behind her. She speaks sharply, "Nathan, there is no need to take that tone with Alistair, he has done nothing wrong. He kept the estate going in your absence, before our father died, and he's worked hard for his rightful place by my side."

"Rightful place! He's an opportunist, Olivia, but I'm back now and things are going to change."

She smiles calmly, as she says, "I'm afraid things may be changing for *you*, Nathan, but not for us. You see our father did not believe you'd ever return from the Antipodes and he was so disillusioned when you brought such shame on the family name, that he changed his will, leaving everything to me. Summerville is now *mine* and so you *will* be civil to my husband, as long as you wish to remain living here."

Meakins is dumbfounded, the wind completely taken from his sails. He is absolutely speechless!

Disinherited! We'll see about that! I'll contest the will. How could my father do this to me? It's against all English tradition and custom. He is pacing back and forth across the study. Then without a word he stalks out of the room to go upstairs to his old bedchamber, subconsciously reverting to his deep-rooted behaviour, after being chastised by his parents as a child.

On the stairs he encounters an elderly woman, who screams as soon as she sets eyes on him, madly waving her walking stick in his direction and yelling in a highly-pitched voice for his sister. "Olivia! Olivia! Come quickly! We have an intruder!"

To his relief, his sister is soon on the scene calming the old bag.

"It's all right mother, it's only Nathan."

Mother! This frail old hag is his mother! He swallows back his astonishment, "Mother, I am come home at last." He attempts to embrace her.

She struggles free, screaming hysterically, "Get your hands off me! You're not my Nathan. Get out of my house!"

Feeling totally dejected he continues up the stairs to his old bedroom. *This is definitely not the homecoming I expected!*

At suppertime Nathan can smell the aroma of hot food permeating the building and his hunger gnaws at him. *I cannot sulk forever. I have to be practical and get them all on side. I'll play the game until I work out how I can get my hands on my rightful inheritance once more.*

He goes back downstairs and seeks out his new brother-in-law. "Look Alistair, I'm sorry about earlier, but I was a bit cranky, having been on an old rust bucket for three months at sea, in addition to a long journey on horseback from Southampton. Can we let bygones be bygones and bury the hatchet?"

Alistair looks at him warily, perhaps wondering where the hatchet is likely to be buried, but the old master/servant habit is hard to break. "Of course, Nathan. I hope that, now I'm part of the family, and we've cleared the air, we can be colleagues." His brother-in-law holds out his hand once more and this time Nathan shakes hands with him.

"Of course." But he is at the same time thinking: *Over my dead body!*

"I believe Mrs Chubb is about to serve supper. Will you join us?"

"I will, thank you, I'm ravenous." *And I cannot wait to see this little family charade!*

They walk into the dining room and Olivia is already seated at the dining table with Agnes beside her.

It galls him to see Wadman pulling out the oak carver chair at the head of the table for Alistair McNab to be seated, but he bites his lip and sits down opposite his sister. He smiles at the footman, "Good evening, Wadman."

Wadman replies, civilly, "Good evening, sir." But he betrays no hint of surprise, pleasure, or displeasure at seeing his old master back home.

Nathan studies the child seated next to his sister. She must be about three years old. *They didn't waste any time after his father died.* The young wench serving the food asks the child, "Would you like some broccoli, Miss Agnes?"

He looks at his sister in confusion. "I thought you called her Senga earlier?"

"She was christened Agnes, because she is English, but in deference to Alistair's ancestry, he and I call her Senga, which is the Scottish version of Agnes. You see the name is reversed."

Typical of the backward Scottish barbarians, "I see, well at least she has been christened in the English traditions."

The child then asks her mother, "May I have some of Mrs Chubb's fruit pie and custard after this, Mama?"

"I'm sure Mrs Chubb has made some especially for you, dear. She knows it's your favourite."

The child has a very appealing accent, quintessentially English but with a slight Scottish lyrical lilt. He recognises his own and his sister's icy grey eyes in her, but she has darker brown, curly hair, which hangs prettily in ringlets. Seeing her seated at his dining table his thoughts turn to the question of his own daughter's existence. *It should be my family seated around this table, not Olivia's!*

He takes a deep breath. *I must calm down and play the game.* "Where's Mama, Olivia?"

"She often takes her meals in her room, and after the upset this afternoon, I thought it best."

"Is she demented?"

"I wouldn't say demented exactly, but she does get a little confused."

"She seemed stark staring bonkers to me!"

"Really Nathan, you're so heartless, she's an elderly widowed lady now and obviously she was unsettled, seeing a strange man on the stairs. It's not her fault you have been in the Antipodes for the past decade and she was unable to recognise her only son!"

On the other side of the world, up on the hill at Eaglehawk, Hugh is heartily tired of waiting in vain for his family to join him. He is feeling extremely dejected one damp morning in July, when Bryn thoughtlessly says to him, "Cheer up boyo, it may never happen!"

He snaps back at him in exasperation, "That's exactly what's bothering me, Bryn; my wife may never be brave enough to make the voyage out here with my children. It's all right for thee, mate, but I'm lonely; even more so now that thee have *thy* family here. I feel rather left out in the cold."

Bryn immediately looks guilty, "I'm sorry, Hugh; that was thoughtless of me. You must miss them dreadfully."

"I do and I've been ruminating for some time now over doing something about it." He takes a deep breath, and then blurts out, "How would thee feel about me returning to England and tracking down that devil Meakins and the money he stole from us?"

He watches Bryn closely as he considers his question. "Well, the boys are making good progress and are now earning their keep, so I can rely on them. I do believe we could manage; but you will come back, won't you Hugh?"

Hugh grins, he knew he could rely on his friend, "If thee will allow me to take some funds from the business to pay for my travel costs, of course I'll come back and hopefully return the miners' money as well."

Bryn holds out his hand to him, "If that's what you want to do, Hugh, I'll not stand in your way. You've worked hard; and I know your home is already prepared, but sadly standing empty, waiting for Sarah, Gwyneth and Lewys; if you can persuade them to travel back with you, all the better."

They shake hands warmly, "That's a relief, mate. I really want to see them so badly and it means I could possibly track Meakins down, before I bring them back with me. I know he has a family estate in Somerset; it's not much to go on, but I'll talk to Sam and see if he can give me some more information before I leave."

"Well, I'm not sure you'll have much luck with that slippery character, but at least you'll have more chance of persuading your family to endure the voyage here, if you're travelling with them."

"Thank thee Bryn. I have to tell thee, mate; I don't know how I'd have survived transportation without thy constant support and companionship. Make no mistake I'll do my utmost to return with my family and with the missing gold, if it kills me."

"Don't say that, Hugh. We don't want any more victims of that sneaky villain."

It takes Hugh some time to contact his family and inform them of his intentions. It would be disastrous if he was to set sail for Britain and in the meantime they were already on a ship bound for Australia. Finally his family confirm they are staying put in the Rhondda Valley until such time as he should return to them. He is then able to organise his travel documents and his passage.

Hugh finally arrives home at his terraced cottage in Bute Street, in the small village of Treherbert just before Christmas 1863. His wife throws her arms around him. The joy in her face is not lessened by the fact there are tears streaming down her cheeks. She is so pleased to have him home after such a long time; he cannot bear to tell her he will be leaving them shortly to go on his detective work in Somerset. He will just have to wait until the novelty of her having him near, wears off.

He immediately sees for himself how very poorly Sarah's mother is, when he spots her bed downstairs in the corner of their parlour and he completely understands why his wife could not leave her. The poor woman is crippled with arthritis and is now bedridden, having also suffered a severe stroke five years previously. The parlour is warm and cosy with a fire flickering merrily in the hearth. His mother-in-law seems pleased to see him, although it is hard to tell, with her features rendered lopsided by the stroke. He bends down and kisses her on her cheek. Tapping her hand gently, he says, "It is good to be home," and she manages to nod her head to show she understands.

He turns back to Sarah, "Where are Gwyneth and Lewys?"

"Gwyneth is still working in the kitchens up at the big house for the Chrichton-Stuart family. Their son is only fifteen, but he succeeded to the marquisate when he was only six months old and so he's the 3rd Marquess of Bute." She appears proud that their daughter is working for this wealthy family, but then her expression changes, "I'm afraid Lewys has recently started working down the mine; he's at the Tynewydd Colliery now, as thee was."

His heart soars, as he realises his son is following in his own footsteps. Thus, when they do eventually manage to sail back to Australia, he will be able to work in the Taliaris and the Maerdy with him, Bryn and his boys. However, he can see that she worries about their son, as much as she always worried about him going underground, but there is no other work in the Rhondda Valleys and so the men have no real option.

"While I'm preparing supper later, if thee goes to the shaft-head before dark, thee'll be able to meet him returning from work and surprise him."

"When shall I be able to see Gwyneth?"

"She'll be home this evening, hopefully in time for supper. We live so near the big house, she doesn't have to live in, and prefers to come home, but she does find it hard getting to work on time, at six in the mornings."

"I'm sure she does. She always was a fusspot where her appearance was concerned."

His wife puts her hand up to tidy her hair, self-consciously. "I'm afraid I've been busy in the kitchen all day, I must look a dreadful sight!"

"No sight has ever been dearer to my heart, Sarah. How about thee take me upstairs so I can prove it to thee?"

He is surprised and overjoyed when she takes his hand and leads him upstairs. He soon realises just what he has been missing all these years. All his uncertainty dissipates and he knows he made the right decision to come home to his family.

Later, he wanders through the village, checking the progress on the two coal mines where he was previously employed. It is bitterly cold and he buttons up his overcoat gratefully. He is drawing close to the pit head at the Lady Margaret Colliery, when the steam whistle blows and the men shortly come pouring away from the shaft. He is greeted cheerily by those who remember him, but there are many new, young faces he doesn't recall. He makes haste to the Tynewydd Colliery and, as he walks against the flow of workers leaving for home, it begins to snow lightly; then he hears someone shouting, "Pa!"

Moments later his son is nearly bowling him off balance with an enthusiastic hug. "Wow! Pa, it's so good to see thee. Thee looks so fit and well!"

He turns back towards their cottage and they walk on, shoulder to shoulder, happily chatting to each other and greeting friends as they go, everyone's breath wafting white and misty before them. As they draw nearer to their cottage, the snow falls more heavily and Hugh is reminded of all the Welsh white Christmases he has enjoyed in the past. Gwyneth, who has been looking out of the window in anticipation, rushes out and flies into her father's arms, "Pa! Oh Pa! I've missed thee so much."

"I've missed thee all very much too, even more so when my mate Bryn's family all arrived safely. I've built a new house and it's all prepared for thee, when thee are ready to return with me. It's so different to here, *cariad*, and such an adventure for thee. The plains are so vast and the animals so strange, I'm quite sure thee will love it there."

They enter the cottage together and his dear Sarah has set out their supper things in readiness. Hugh feels a hugely contented glow in the pit of his stomach, as he enjoys the heart-warming company of his loving family and his first home-cooked meal in fifteen years. It even looks like they will be having a white Christmas. It couldn't be more fitting.

At dawn the valley is strangely silent and Hugh looks out from the bedroom window to find them snowed in. The fine white icy flakes fall heavily for several days and the valley is cut off from the rest of the world, the snow waist-high down the main street. The men-folk dig the drifts away from their cottages to form two pathways on either side of the carriageway, and Hugh realises that, even if he wanted to, he wouldn't be able to go anywhere for a few weeks. When the ice thaws the River Rhondda will come flooding down from the hills through their community and homes will be in jeopardy. Hopefully not his, because they are not that close to the river, but those situated near to the river bank will more than likely be flooded, unless the thaw comes very slowly. He will be needed to help his community and resigns himself to another long wait, probably until the spring.

It is the day after the Easter egg rolling competition and Aurora is pleased that Luke has chosen her to go with him to fly his kite. He told her he had discovered it in the cupboard under the stairs, where it has been hiding for the last three years, since their charabanc trip to Weymouth. They had played with it many times that summer and then it had been stored away over the winter and he had forgotten all about it.

It is a pleasant, breezy Saturday in March. Her governess, Grace Tweedy, has gone to visit her sister in Sherborne for Easter and luckily her brother is playing with Eli and so she is able to enjoy some quality time with her closest friend. As Luke had to do his chores in the morning, he had suggested that she should call for him, so that they'd both be high up on the hill to catch the breeze. Thus she sets off in the spring sunshine after her luncheon.

She is dressed in her buttoned boots for running across the field, and a blue, lightweight cotton frock with a crisp white pinafore over the top and a dark-blue shawl tied in place around her shoulders against the breeze. Her hair has been braided into ringlets by Nanny Beth and she feels like a young woman now, rather than a little girl. She wonders if Luke will notice the change in her appearance, and if he will approve.

They have always been treated like brother and sister, but lately Aurora has found herself wondering what it might be like if he were to kiss her. She has seen Edwin and Bunny kissing and she is curious to experience this for herself. He is a good head taller than her and he has twinkling, mischievous hazel eyes and lovely clear olive skin and wavy hair.

As she reaches the top of Pound Lane she spots Luke lingering there, clutching the brightly-coloured kite, which is wafting in the breeze. She rushes forward to meet him, but as she gets closer, she is disappointed to see that his sister, Lilly, is there too. *There will obviously be no opportunity for kissing today!*

They take it in turns to run with the kite. Luke is

quite expert, releasing the string until it is flying high in the sky and he can relax and enjoy the spectacle. The two girls watch him, eagerly awaiting their turn. Aurora goes next and the kite flops around her until suddenly it is taken by the breeze and she too is thrilled to see how high it will go. Finally it is Lilly's go and Luke and Aurora watch and wait for her, standing together underneath a huge beech tree, just across the road from Luke and Lilly's cottage.

Their casual chatter is interrupted by the sound of a rider on horseback and they both turn their heads to see who is approaching. The man reins in his horse on seeing them and Aurora is rather disconcerted, as he has a strangely smug smile on his face. "Good morning, that's an excellent kite you have there," he says conversationally.

"Thank you, sir," replies Aurora, uneasily. For some reason she feels glad that she has Luke and Lilly with her and she's not alone with this man.

He continues to chat in a friendly manner. "It's good kite-flying weather, with this fine spring breeze."

"That it is, sir," agrees Luke.

However, the stranger is staring intently at Aurora, "I recognise you, young lady." He pauses as if trying to recall and then exclaims, "I know what it is; you're the image of Millie Bonfield, who used to work for me, a decade ago."

Aurora is taken aback, but she manages to reply, "She was my mother's sister, sir, but she died before I was born."

He continues to stare, "A sad business that, but you look so like her, it's uncanny."

"I'm told she was very like my mother, sir."

"She must have been, for I could swear you could be Millie's child."

Aurora thinks about her rag dolly that she has had since she was a baby and wonders for the first time why the doll had been named Millie. The horse flicks its tail and side steps and the man lifts his hat, says, "Good day to you," and rides on, leaving her feeling unsettled.

She glances at Luke and he asks her, "What was that all about?"

She looks thoughtfully back at the diminishing form of the stranger, as he continues towards Hamdon Hill, "I have no idea."

Luke's mother has been keeping an eye on the children, whilst standing in the window doing some ironing and she is immediately vigilant when the stranger on horseback stops to speak to them. Having been warned by her husband, after the other staff members were instructed some time ago to watch out for Aurora, she is concerned that the man in the saddle might be the infamous Nathan Meakins. She is relieved when he passes on his way, but later when her children return home, she asks Luke what had passed between them. When he tells her the stranger was comparing the child to Millie Bonfield, she is convinced that Lord and Lady Dryer should be informed and at the soonest opportunity she resolves to tell them what has occurred.

Meakins feels sure he has successfully sown the seed of doubt in his daughter's mind, but, before he makes any further moves on her, he needs to be in a position of power, to be able to entice her away from her adopted family.

He is frustrated at the lack of progress his inadequate solicitor is making in compiling a case for him to contest his father's will. It is obvious his father was not of sound mind, leaving everything to a mere woman, when he had a perfectly capable son and heir. But his solicitor insists there is no evidence of this and, on the contrary, plenty of evidence to prove his father had been quite sane, when the will was drawn up in 1855.

He continues on his journey towards Taunton to attend another appointment with him, but unfortunately when he finally arrives, it is bad news. "I'm sorry, Nathan. I may have been able to contest the will if we'd applied earlier, before probate, and there'd been something amiss, but not simply because you weren't happy with your father's decision. If you'd been able to prove your sister, Olivia, had intimidated, or coerced your father into changing his original will, or put any pressure on him at the time to influence his decision, you may have had a slim chance, but there's no way we could prove lack of testamentary capacity and in any case it is all irrelevant, because the time limit before probate has passed."

"I know my sister, Mr Johnston, I can just see her dropping hints about her loyalty and affection and dripping away at him about what a bad boy her brother is and how he's brought shame on the family name."

"I'm afraid, even if that was the case, it doesn't constitute grounds for contesting the will. She would have had to threaten physical violence, or used deception for us to have a valid case and I'm sure she didn't resort to that. I'm very sorry, but no matter how unjust it may seem to you, I have to say that you simply don't have a case."

"Well, thanks for nothing, Johnston. I came all this way to Taunton to instruct you, because I was assured you were the best! What a waste of money that was!" He jumps up and storms out of the office. *I will not be defeated. I will simply have to find myself another estate to purchase with my illicit gold. That will show my damned sister and her barbarian husband who they are really dealing with!*

The following morning Louisa is in their woodland area picking a trug-full of daffodils to fill the vases and bring the sunshine into the manor. There are early bees buzzing in the hellebores and she is humming happily to herself when she hears someone approaching. She looks up to see Susan Moore looking tentatively at her.

"Hello, Susan. Were you looking for me?"

"Yes I was, milady. I have something I need to tell you. I don't want to worry you, but I'm sure I saw Nathan Meakins yesterday afternoon speaking to Aurora, when she was kite flying with Luke and Lilly up on Camp Road."

Louisa's carefree moments are over. She puts a hand to her mouth in horror. It's her worst nightmare. *He's back!* Eventually she finds her voice and she asks her shakily, "Do you know what passed between them?"

"I did ask Luke and he told me that Meakins said he thought he recognised Aurora and then he said it was because she's the image of his old employee, Millie Bonfield. Aurora said that Millie was her mother's sister and that she died before she was born, but they were very alike. Then he said something like, 'they must have been, because I could swear you could be Millie's child'."

Louisa's eyes brim with tears as she pictures Susan breastfeeding their little foundling on that very first day after she had been found beneath the clock tower. Her generosity in volunteering to be her wet-nurse had saved the day.

She blinks away her tears, "I know what he's doing, Susan. He is undermining us by making

Aurora question her true parentage. He's an evil, nasty devil and I'll do anything to keep her away from him. Thank you for letting me know, Susan, I'll alert Lord Dryer and all the staff to be more vigilant."

Once the snow thaws, the raging waters of the River Rhondda are calm, and their neighbours have reclaimed their homes from the subsiding floods, Hugh finally explains to his family that after Easter he plans to travel to Somerset to try to track down the man who stole the miners' gold.

He is busy packing a change of clothes into his travel bag when unfortunately his mother-in-law suffers another stroke. His poor wife is panicking, believing her mother's death to be imminent, but when the doctor finally reaches them, he tells her he is unable to predict how long her mother might linger. After the doctor has gone she begs Hugh to stay longer, in order to take charge of everything when the time comes and so his trip to Somerset is again postponed.

The summer is spent with Gwyneth and Lewys continuing to work, Sarah nursing her mother, making gruel, washing her bedding and giving her bed baths, as well as the cooking and washing for the rest of the family and the ironing that she takes in for her neighbours. Hugh keeps busy doing the heavy work, such as scrubbing the floors, cleaning behind the heavy furniture, going up a ladder to clean the windows and the gutters and painting the interior, in readiness for them vacating the cottage when the time finally comes. He also writes regularly to Bryn to inform him of his current situation.

Some evenings he goes with Lewys to sing with the Tynewydd Colliery Male Voice Choir, as they practice the traditional music of the Welsh bards, in preparation for the next Eisteddfodau music festival. He enjoys the camaraderie of their friends and neighbours, but most of all, he looks forward to coming home and spending the nights with his loving wife wrapped securely in his arms.

In October the old lady contracts pneumonia which is, sadly for the family, her final undoing. The disease is known as 'the old folks' friend' and in his mother-in-law's case this is perfectly true, as she finally slips away peacefully in her sleep. Sarah draws the curtains across the windows throughout their cottage, underlining their sombre mood and, according to tradition, showing their sympathy, the neighbours do likewise in the adjoining homes. Hugh arranges the funeral at the Blaen-y-cwm Chapel and in the meantime their friends and neighbours call to offer their condolences.

On the day of the funeral the preacher calls at the house for the first service. Sarah had made black cravats and armbands for the men in readiness for this day and for herself and Gwyneth she had made black bombazine gowns and they both wear matching strings of jet beads. The two women are weeping inconsolably by the time the preacher's oration is over.

Members of the Tynewydd Colliery Choir gather outside the cottage and sing *Guide Me O Thou Great Jehovah*, before Hugh and Lewys lead the male mourners before the hearse, and the funeral procession moves off to the Blaen-y-cwm Chapel. Sarah and Gwyneth remain behind to compose themselves and prepare the refreshments.

As Hugh walks beside Lewys, he cannot deny the feeling of relief that washes over him, knowing that it will soon be over. There is a distinctive smell of mothballs all around them, as the November wind tugs at their black overcoats and threatens to blow off their bowler hats.

Later, at the graveside, Hugh and Lewys stand with their heads bowed, each with their black-gloved hands held clasped before them, and after the commitment the choir members sing *Abide with Me* and the mourners return to the cottage for the food and drink that Sarah and Gwyneth have prepared for them.

On entering their cottage once more, ahead of the other mourners, Hugh feels a great lifting of his spirits, as they pull back their curtains letting the light flood in. At last they are all free now to make their new and exciting plans for the future.

CHAPTER NINETEEN *(November – December 1864)*

A MESSAGE FROM MILLIE

It is not long before Meakins falls back into his old habits of drinking, gambling and chasing the dragon. His sister and brother-in-law have no idea that he has returned from Australia with plenty of gold to invest in their estate, or elsewhere if absolutely necessary. He has instructed the local estate agents to look for a decent manor house with sufficient land for a gentleman and to inform him as soon as one comes onto the market. In the meantime, he is making up for lost time and enjoying himself to the full.

His cronies at the Black Panther Club are pleased to see him back and even more so when he is ostentatious with his wealth. There are many simple souls who hang onto his every word. The old coveners from Stoford are all very obliging, some for money and some out of fear, but his every whim is catered for at the club.

One dark night in November, after much alcohol has been consumed, one of the Stoford witches, known as Moira, suggests they have a séance. She produces a small heart-shaped wooden planchette, or pointer, and a wooden board, on which is painted: the alphabet, numbers up to ten, and the words 'Yes', 'No', 'Hello' and 'Goodbye'. She explains the principle of planchette writing and the spirit board before they begin and says she has used it many times and she will be the medium, if someone would like to have a go with her. Meakins is scathing of any success, but eager to partake to prove his point. Never having done such a thing before and well primed with absinthe, he is soon ready with a small party of curious folk gathering to observe the happenings.

The Seymour twins are among those who are keen to be involved and Lucy and Clara both stay with them to watch. In all, there are about two dozen people in the room. Meakins and the medium are seated opposite each other, with the board placed between them on a small card table. Moira is equipped with a dipping pen and paper and she enlists Lucy to write down any messages. They dowse some of the oil lamps to induce the best ambience and the spiritualist calls for quiet. There is, however, still a lot of giggling and whispering among the women, and derisive mocking amongst the men.

Moira, acting as the medium, instructs Meakins to place his index and middle fingers lightly on the planchette and she does the same. She tells him, "We need to move the indicator lightly around the board for a moment or two to warm it up and not to stop until it feels automatic."

Eventually, the onlookers begin to get impatient, and so Moira, apparently sensing they are losing interest, asks the spirit world, "Is there anybody there?"

Meakins believes he feels a twitch, or a slight pull on the indicator, but he is too tense and nothing happens, so they continue with the warming-up exercise and the medium asks the question again. He doesn't have much faith this is going to work, but in the vain hope that he might contact his father, he lets his mind empty, as Moira suggests, until the circular motion is involuntary and Moira asks her question once more, "Is there anybody there?"

He is certain then that the indicator is moving, as it heads towards the word 'Yes', and there is a murmur of anticipation among the observers. "Do you have a question for us?"

This time the planchette swings to 'No'.

"Do you have a message for us?"

Again the planchette swerves back to 'Yes'.

The candles flicker as a hush falls over the onlookers.

"Please spell out your message."

Everyone quietly speaks the letters as they come and Lucy writes them down: L – E – A – V – E – A – U – R – O – R – A – A – L – O – N – E. Lucy gasps as she realises what the letters are saying. She is about to read out the whole sentence when the wooden board flies off the table and hits Meakins square in the chest. Lucy drops her pen in horror and the other women in the group all scream and run from the room, terrified.

Meakins is left a gibbering wreck. *My God, there can be no mistake about that message! It has to be from Millie!*

Lucy and Clara are both stunned at the communication that could only have come from Aurora's mother, beyond the grave. Lucy asks Ashleigh if he would take them home and the evening is suddenly curtailed.

The following morning after a restless night she confides in her mother. "It's hard to explain to you, Mama, the spooky atmosphere and the apparent supernatural presence of Millie's spirit in the room, but the message was so specific I believe that Louisa should know about it. Don't you?"

"I think you're right, Lucy. She should be

warned. You ought to go and tell her immediately. I think her poor tormented sister may be trying to warn us of the man's ill intentions."

Lucy tidies her appearance and puts her cloak around her to go over to the manor. The wind is whipping her skirts as she avoids the puddles, crossing the farmyard and going along the track past the stables, from where she can hear the horses stamping and snorting in the cold, and on to the front entrance. She lifts the heavy knocker and waits to be admitted. Gareth answers her knock and she asks to speak to Louisa.

"If you would care to take a seat here, Miss Lucy, I will go and find Lady Louisa for you."

"Thank you, Gareth."

Moments later Louisa appears, looking pleased to see her, "Lucy, what a lovely surprise, to what do we owe this pleasure?"

She is so focused on her message she forgets convention and fails to curtsey, "I need to speak to you privately, milady, please."

"Oh! I see; well, let us go into the oak. We'll not be disturbed there this morning."

Lucy follows Louisa through the hallway and into the small, cosy, wood-panelled room they call the oak. There is a welcoming fire crackling and flickering in the grate and the ladies each take a seat in the armchairs beside the fireplace, the warm glow from the flames reflecting in their faces.

Louisa asks gently, "What is troubling you, Lucy?"

"I don't know where to start, milady, but I need to warn you first, that it's to do with Nathan Meakins." She sees the tranquillity immediately erased from Louisa's face.

"What has happened now?"

"Well, to put it simply, there was a séance at the

Black Panther Club last night and I believe the medium made contact with your sister Millie." She thinks Louisa might faint, she looks so blanched. "Are you all right, milady?"

"Yes, Lucy. Please do continue. I need to hear what happened."

"Nathan Meakins was using the spirit board with the medium and there was a message from the spirit world that said, '*Leave Aurora alone*'. Then the spirit board flew from the table and hit him violently in the chest."

"Oh my goodness; it hit him in the chest?"

"Yes, he was in quite a state, I can tell you."

"Good! Maybe Millie is intending to haunt the miserable devil. But it does mean that my poor, dear Millie fears for Aurora and she is warning him off."

"It would appear so, milady, but it also means that your Millie is still looking out for her daughter and that there is life after death. This is the amazing part, milady."

"That is true, Lucy. Thank you so much for coming to tell me."

"Well, I know it all sounds a bit unbelievable, but Clara was there too and she'll vouch for me. We'd all been drinking, but Clara and I hadn't had very much at all."

"I've no reason to doubt your word, Lucy. It all makes complete sense to me and I will inform Joshua. We'll definitely heed the warning and keep an even closer eye on Aurora from now."

Hugh Davies takes the post-chaise through South Wales to Portskewett, where he finally disembarks by the riverside at Black Rock Pier with his overnight bag and is able to stretch his legs and take some refreshments. He then catches the paddle steamer,

Relief, run by the Bristol, South Wales and Southampton Union Railway to cross the River Severn. He stays overnight in the New Passage Hotel on the Somerset side of the estuary. The next morning he is up bright and early to catch the train which will take him through Somerset to Ivell Town. He relaxes, tries to doze a little, but with the train stopping and starting at each station he is too often disturbed and so he gives up and resigns himself to watching the countryside flying by for the remainder of his journey.

On reaching the Ivell Town station, Hugh is extremely tired and he asks one of the porters to direct him to a nearby hostelry. The man points out the adjacent Alexandra Hotel and he wearily makes his way up the steps to see if he can book himself a room. He is relieved to find he is in luck and the hotel porter directs him to a very pleasant room that overlooks the railway station and the green hills dotted with cattle behind it.

Later he is thankful to be sitting down to a dinner of roasted lamb, potatoes and root vegetables and enjoying a pint of ale. He asks the landlord to give him directions to the courthouse, as he plans to have an early night and then go there first thing in the morning to begin his enquiries. He is given directions to the town hall situated in the main borough and opposite the Mermaid Hotel.

The following frosty morning, after breakfast, Hugh feels refreshed as he wanders up the main street through the small market town of Ivell, carrying his leather pouch of paperwork under his arm. At the impressive town hall he asks the clerk to see the court records relating to the year 1854. The man takes him into a back room full of cabinets and locates the relevant section for him to peruse. It takes him all morning to finally locate a trial record of the

Easter Quarter Sessions relating to Nathan Meakins and a charge of smuggling, but on reading the documentation he is disappointed to learn that the charge of rape and infanticide is dealt with at the County Assizes in Taunton. However, the local trial gives him Meakins' address and the names of the arresting officer and magistrate. He doesn't want to alert Meakins to his arrival just yet and so he learns from the clerk the address of Lord Dryer at Alvington Manor and the location of the local lock-up, just around the corner on Wine Street and decides to visit the house of correction first.

Officer Gundry unfortunately is not on duty until the following morning and so he sets off to visit Alvington Manor instead. He is tired, cold and hungry when he finally spies the manor house, standing in the weak winter sunshine, at the end of a long carriageway, and he realises it is mid-afternoon and he has been so focused on his detective work, he has had no luncheon.

He bangs the heavy knocker and stands to one side looking around him, admiring the impressive clock tower with stables behind it and a smaller dower house opposite. The door opens and the butler asks, "Can I help you, sir?"

Hugh is amazed and heartened to recognise the distinctive accent of a fellow Welshman. "I'd be very much obliged if I might speak to Lord Dryer. I've travelled a great distance, from the other side of the world actually, and I believe Lord Dryer would be very interested in what I have to tell him regarding an old adversary of his, Nathan Meakins."

The butler looks immediately interested, "I'm afraid Lord Dryer is not here at present, but he is expected shortly, sir. If you would like to step inside to wait for him, I can offer you some refreshments."

"That would be most welcome and very kind of

thee." Hugh steps over the threshold into a large wainscoted hallway, where there is a huge fire roaring in the fireplace. He manages to hang onto his leather pouch, as the butler takes his outer garments and puts them to one side, then bids him follow, as he takes a door on the right into a long passageway.

The butler then says, "I recognise a fellow Welshman. I hail from Cardiff, from where do you originate, sir?"

"My name is Hugh Davies and I have family in the Rhondda Valley; my wife and I were both born in Tynewydd."

"Beautiful part of the countryside, sir."

"Yes it is, but once I've spoken to Lord Dryer we plan to return to Australia, where I've been mining for gold with a colleague of mine for the last nine years."

The butler pauses at the first door off the passageway, "Well, if you would like to make yourself comfortable in here, sir, I will ask cook to bring you some victuals."

"Thank thee, that is most kind."

Hugh takes a seat in the drawing room beside another log fire that is burning merrily, and it is not long before he is hungrily tucking into some ham sandwiches, some lemon drizzle cake and a nice hot cup of tea.

Gareth is in the kitchen talking to Flora, "He says he has some information for His Lordship, regarding Meakins, so I thought I ought to keep him here until His Lordship returns. I hope he won't be too long, otherwise I don't know what we shall do with him. The mistress is still visiting her parents with Aurora and Gabriel, so I had no one else to ask."

"I'm sure you 'ave made the right decision, Gareth. What else could you do with 'im?"

"He seems a nice enough fellow. He's a gold miner from Australia."

"Well, I 'ave some more tea things prepared for His Lordship when 'ee gets 'ere. 'Ee shouldn't be much longer."

Joshua arrives home at around half past four in the afternoon and is greeted by Gareth, who takes his hat, gloves and overcoat and tells him of the visitor, awaiting his return in the drawing room.

"You say he has information about Meakins, Gareth?"

"Yes, my lord."

"Then I cannot wait to meet him! Did he give you his name?"

"Yes, my lord, it is Hugh Davies."

"Right. Oh! Gareth, please would you ask Elsie to bring in additional refreshments?" Joshua goes immediately into the drawing room. "Good day, Mr Davies. I hope my butler has been looking after you."

Hugh stands up and they shake hands. "He has been most kind, sir."

"Good. I understand you have some information for me regarding Nathan Meakins?"

"Yes, sir. I do."

"Please do sit down."

The two men sit down, just as Elsie enters with the tea tray and more sandwiches and cake. She pours them both their tea and then discreetly leaves.

"Please go ahead with your story."

"Well, my lord, I believe Nathan Meakins has absconded from Australia with a stolen consignment of gold and other valuables that were being conveyed under guard from the Bendigo Valley mines to Melbourne by troopers, when they were attacked by bushrangers."

"What makes you think that Meakins is responsible?"

"Because he was one of the troopers who were guarding the consignment and all the others were killed, along with a number of the outlaws. *I* believe that those, who were not killed by the bushrangers, were finished off by Meakins and *he* has scarpered with as much as he could carry on horseback. Why else would there be no sign of the man? Some folk believed he was taken by the outlaws, but I'm convinced he intended double-crossing everyone and stealing it all for himself all along, before escaping back to England."

"Well, you're certainly right, in that he has returned to England."

"I knew it! He'd never have been able to afford the passage unless he'd stolen some of the gold. His very survival is enough for me to believe he is responsible."

"It's all right, believing he's responsible, but we have to prove it, Mr Davies."

"Well, as I see it, if thee were to check his bank account in England their records would tell thee if a substantial amount was deposited on his return. I can assure thee he was not involved himself in any gold-mining; he's stolen from the hard-working miners of the Victorian goldfields and he's not entitled to a single penny. He spent most of his time whoring and chasing the dragon, which is why he was always broke."

Joshua can see just how angry he is, but he cannot afford to make any mistakes where Meakins is concerned. "I don't want to show my hand too soon. It could be that he got a pay-off from the robbers for information on the gold consignment that was just sufficient to pay for his passage home and this would leave us with no proof. We'd need him to have a large amount deposited in the bank to confirm his duplicity."

Hugh shakes his head in frustration, "I feel it in my gut that the man was vicious enough to kill in cold blood to get what he wanted, but I do understand that thee will need more corroborating evidence, before thee can actually accuse him."

"I'm grateful for you coming all this way to find me, Mr Davies. I promise you that I'll do my utmost to get to the bottom of this."

"My greatest wish is for justice to prevail and for all the money that was stolen from the miners to be returned to them, especially to myself and my partner, who both had a sizeable sum robbed from us that day." He takes a roll of paperwork from his leather pouch. "I have here copies that I can leave in thy charge of the paperwork from the mining companies involved, detailing their bank account withdrawals, totalling a sum of around 14,000 pounds."

Joshua takes the paperwork and looks through it. The industrious miners have lost a considerable sum. Then he goes to his Davenport and takes out a sheet of paper. "Please let me have your post office address in Australia in order that I might keep in touch and inform you of our progress."

"My house is on Myrtle Street, in the town of Sandhurst, and any mail will reach us via the Bendigo post office, Sandhurst, Victoria, South Australia."

"Thank you, Mr Davies. I promise you, I'll do my utmost to nail him. I know from bitter experience what a mean, self-centred, arrogant and violent man he is. I don't want him to prosper at your expense, any more than you do."

"There's something else thee ought to know, my lord. He raped two women in Bendigo; one was an aborigine, who later died from her injuries, and the other girl was a friend of ours who unfortunately was made pregnant by him. She's had a little girl since, who she has named Camira after the young aborigine who died. Meakins is, however, unaware of the birth of his daughter and *I know* Angelica would not want him to know about her."

Joshua is stunned. *So Aurora has a half-sister in Australia!* He sighs despondently, unhappily recalling the trauma suffered by both Louisa's and his own sister. "A leopard doesn't change its spots. I'm not surprised, but all the more reason he must be stopped at all cost. When will you be returning to Australia, Mr Davies?"

"As soon as we can sell up and arrange passage for myself and my family. It's a huge load off my mind, to have passed on to thee the hopeful means of accomplishing Meakins' arrest and conviction, and getting our money returned to us eventually. I can now concentrate on a new and rewarding life with my family in the Antipodes."

They have finished eating and drinking and Joshua asks him, "Where are you staying in Ivell?"

"I've booked into the Alexandra Hotel at the bottom of town."

"I don't suppose you realise that you can actually see his land from there?" Then a wicked thought sneaks into Joshua's mind, "Would you like to come with me to visit your old friend, before you go back to Wales?"

Hugh grins, "It might be amusing to see the look on his face, finding me standing on his doorstep."

Joshua shakes his head, thinking better of it, "I'd like so much to see the smug smile wiped from his face, but maybe it would work better in our favour if he was left unsuspecting of the information you've delivered to me."

"Yes, I think you're right, perhaps that would be the wiser option, although I would have enjoyed witnessing his discomfiture."

Joshua then stands up decisively. "In that case I'll arrange for my groom to return you to your hotel. You can rest assured I'll do all in my power to trap the villain, as soon as I possibly can."

Hugh stands up on his cue to leave. "Thank thee, my lord. I'm very grateful for thy time and trouble."

"I can assure you it is no trouble. Any ammunition I can gather to ultimately bring about Meakins' demise is as valuable to me, as your gold is to you."

Once the Welshman has gone, Joshua goes through the paperwork he left in his care, thinking and planning all the time the best way forward. He knows he will have to play the long game and allow Meakins to show his hand first, for at present the evidence is purely circumstantial. Once he is convinced he has all the money from the robbery, he will need to find out, somehow, which bank Meakins uses and organise a court summons for the bank to produce his statements. It is not going to be straightforward and he needs to bide his time, for now. *Let's get Christmas over and then perhaps I should employ an investigator?* He decides to speak to Ambrose. *After all he was the one who managed to track me down when I was still in the Fiji Islands, to inform me of my inheritance.*

CHAPTER TWENTY *(June – July 1865)*

GHOSTS OF THE PAST

Considering she is in her fourteenth year, Aurora is given very little freedom ever since her outing with Luke and Lilly flying the kite, and as the months pass by she is beginning to fiercely resent being so confined; while the other children on the estate are allowed to wander free and uninhibited, she is under the constant jurisdiction of her governess.

The next occasion she is allowed to enjoy herself is in the town at the St Bartholomew's Fair on the last Friday in June, when she is chaperoned with her mother, Rosa and Nanny Beth. Her brother Gabriel, Rosa's children and many of the other estate children are there, Luke and Lilly among them.

Gabriel wanted to take their dogs with them, but Paddy still has a sore paw where they had to pull out a thorn from his pad, so he stays behind. However, O'Malley happily walks with them, his tail swinging heavily behind him.

It is a pleasant stroll into town and the children are all excited and dressed in their Sunday best clothes. The fair features sideshows, acrobats, jugglers, puppet shows, the town band, Morris dancers, food vendors, caged wild animals and the popular boxing ring. Louisa has seen it all before, but gets pleasure from watching the elated and fascinated little ones. She is aware that Malachi is going to be fighting later and she is conscious that Rosa wants to protect her children from any distress by keeping them away from the pugilists' ring. The women feel like three sheepdogs herding the children hither and thither. It is very tiring and hot in the June sunshine and she wishes that Joshua could have come with her. He may join them later, but he has been in court all week and is overwhelmed with paperwork concerning the piped water and sewage plans for the town, so he is obliged to stay behind and put in some extra hours.

Louisa can see that both Aurora and Gabriel are pleased to be out and about with their young friends and they run from one stall to another, amazed by the skill of the wandering jugglers and agile acrobats, fascinated by the exotic animals and enthralled by the puppet shows.

They are tiring after about two hours and Louisa suggests that the ladies sit down and have a cup of tea, but the children are not ready to sit still.

"Please can we go along to the barrel-organ, Mama?" asks Gabriel.

"He wants to buy some fudge really, Mama," says Aurora knowingly. "The stall is right beside it."

Louisa can see the stall from where they are seated and so she agrees that they should go together to listen to the barrel-organ and, at the same time, purchase some fudge. She gives Aurora some coins from her purse and with Luke and Lilly leading the way, they set off, including Rosa's three little ones, Ruby and Daisy holding hands and Eli following behind Gabriel, who is hanging on to O'Malley with all his might.

The women smile to see how happy they are with this small amount of freedom and they sit back, relaxing and chatting. It is not long before they can hear the town band approaching along the wide, grassy pathway between the stalls.

Aurora goes up to the lady selling the fudge and orders seven small bags, one for each of them and she hands over the coins. Soon they are all happily chewing, hooking the fudge from between their teeth, and the younger ones are even dribbling, while they listen to the barrel-organ. A little mechanical monkey is sitting at the foot of the organ holding up his hat and Aurora gives Gabriel a halfpenny to place in his tin.

Then they hear the town band getting louder and the barrel-organ stops playing for a time. Aurora looks towards the sound of the rousing music, and to one side of the band, approaching them, she spots the man who they encountered last spring, when they were flying Luke's kite. Luke nudges her, as he too remembers him. She is also sure that she recognises the lady who he is with, but she cannot quite recall where she has seen her before. They are with a little girl of around five years old.

They reach the barrel-organ just as the band passes by and the woman smiles and says, "Hello again."

Then it comes to her. She is the lady who wanted to buy the puppies. She finds her voice, "Hello."

Luke is standing beside her protectively and Gabriel is close by, with O'Malley tugging at the lead and growling quietly, his hackles raised. The lady shows no interest in the dog now he is fully grown and apparently bad-tempered.

The man asks her, "Are you enjoying the fair?"

"Yes, thank you. It is most entertaining." She tries to sound grown up, but cannot help feeling curious as to why these people are so interested in her.

The man then introduces her to the little girl, "This is Senga, my niece." Then he lowers his voice, "She would actually be your cousin if it turned out that you are, after all, Millie's child."

She is baffled and wonders if Luke also heard that. "I don't understand?"

"Then you should talk to your parents. It's their job to explain it all to you, my dear. I'm surprised they haven't done so before now!" He sounds so reasonable, but she is instinctively wary of him. Then he says, "Goodbye," and moves forward for them to continue on their way, having completely confused and bewildered her. As he moves closer to O'Malley, the dog bares his teeth and growls loudly and then suddenly he goes for the man, biting his lower arm and hanging onto him, drawing blood. The lady is upset, and her daughter is screaming in terror. Ruby, Daisy and Eli all run back to their mother.

"Get your bloody hound off me," he yells and he kicks out at him furiously, which only makes matters worse, until eventually, after entreaties from Aurora and Gabriel, and frantic tugging from Luke, the dog finally lets him go.

Aurora is mortified, and she says apologetically, "I'm so sorry, sir. He's never done that before."

But Gabriel is cross that the man kicked O'Malley. "It's because he doesn't like you. That's why," he says defensively. The man takes the woman by the arm and he marches off angrily, with the little girl, Senga, dragging behind them, tightly gripping her mother's hand, for fear the dog will go for them again. They disappear into the crowds.

Aurora looks at Luke in her confusion; surely if he heard what was said, he must be as baffled as she is, but she doesn't want to make a big deal of it, with her brother and Lilly listening.

Luke says quietly, "Whatever came over O'Malley? I've never seen him go for anyone before!"

"Me neither," says her brother.

Luke pats the hound affectionately, "People do say that dogs instinctively are good judges of character, and O'Malley obviously didn't like him."

"I don't blame him," mumbles Gabriel.

Aurora is too troubled to comment. She is extremely thankful their mother did not see that disagreeable incident, because the town band was passing between them at the time. She hurries back with the others to see what Ruby, Eli and Daisy have said. They find all three children trying to explain to their mother how O'Malley had bitten a stranger. The unpleasant episode has unnerved them and they are ready to return to the sanctuary of their home.

Aurora, in particular, is very disturbed. *That man obviously believes I'm not my mother's child. Does this mean that I've been living all this time with two people who are not my real parents, or is this man some sort of imbecile? But there's also the woman and this little girl, Senga. Who are those people and why are they seeking me out at every opportunity? Are my parents hiding something from me?*

It is 26th July and the day of Gabriel's tenth birthday. A picnic is arranged down beside the lake for his special day with his sister and his friends: Luke, Lilly, Ruby, Eli, and lastly little Daisy who is now four. Louisa, Rosa and Susan are seated in deckchairs and supervising their children, whilst enjoying chilled glasses of sherry cobbler in the warm July sunshine, with Paddy and O'Malley stretched out and lazily sunbathing at their feet. The women have been watching their children playing garden quoits, but little Daisy is getting frustrated and goes for a cuddle with her mother.

Lilly suggests the rest of them play hide-and-seek. Her brother, Luke, can see an opportunity here, "All right Lilly, as it's your suggestion you can be the first seeker and we'll all go and hide," he says artfully.

Lilly closes her eyes and Luke grabs hold of Aurora's hand and they run off swiftly into the woodland to the east of the garden. Ruby hides in the glasshouse and Gabriel and Eli gingerly conceal themselves among the clumps of colourful plants within the herbaceous borders below the terrace.

Once away from the others and in the shelter of the trees and shrubs, they are far enough away to be able to whisper to each other and Luke plucks up the courage to ask Aurora how she is feeling. He has been concerned about her, having witnessed what occurred on the occasions when the stranger spoke with her and aware both times how she was shaken by the encounters.

He watches her gently as she tries to put into words her utter confusion. "I'm rather perplexed, Luke, for I have this terrible suspicion that my mama and papa are not actually my real parents." She sighs sadly, "That man and woman have been singling me out ever since I was a small child and it is very disconcerting."

He can see tears filling her lovely green eyes and he wants to take away her unhappiness, but what can he say? "I think you ought to talk to your mama about it, Rora. She's the only one who'll be able to answer your worries."

She is looking down at her hands, her rich auburn curls, in ringlets, hanging prettily over her face and hiding her pained expression from him. "But how can I ask her if she's my *real* mother, without hurting her feelings?"

He takes her hand in his, "Don't put it that way, Rora. Ask her instead why she believes the stranger and the woman are interested in you and see what she has to say."

Aurora is looking at him distantly, her mind going over past events. "The man said that the girl may be my cousin, which would mean that the woman would be my aunt. Do you think it at all possible… that the man might be my *real* father?"

"I don't know, Rora. I just know that your parents love you dearly and it's likely that those other folk are quite mad."

She looks up at him with gratitude in her wide, sad eyes and he is no longer able to resist his ever-present urge to kiss her. He draws her close and touches his lips to hers, very gently. He can feel the dampness from the tears trickling down her face, where she is still silently weeping, but she returns his kiss inquisitively. Her sadness is soon cast aside, when he puts his arms around her protectively and lovingly, holding her and kissing her until they are both quite breathless.

Aurora, having worried for so long about the strange man and woman, is relieved to finally be able to confide in Luke. She feels even better knowing that Luke, her childhood companion, now feels romantic tenderness towards her. For all their fourteen years together they have been as close as brother and sister, but she has wondered for some time what it would be like to be kissed by Luke. Now she has discovered that he is so much stronger than her and how comforting it is to be held in such capable arms. Her first kiss gives her goose bumps and she will never forget it. It is a momentous moment and for a short while it banishes all other worries.

Her father has arranged for Luke to be apprenticed with Ambrose Fairway. He commences his training next week and so this is the last opportunity for them to enjoy some freedom together. From now on they will be limited to the

Sabbath and this makes her sad, but nevertheless she is pleased that Luke has made the first move and she hopes that it will not be the last.

Louisa has been sleeping fitfully, having had a busy day with Gabriel's birthday celebrations, when she is awoken by a sound on the landing outside her bedchamber. She eases herself out of the bed, so as not to disturb Joshua's slumbers, and tiptoes through the shafts of moonlight to the door. The door creaks slightly as she opens it and peeps out. Her heart leaps, fearfully; for in the dim light of the passageway, she can just make out the shape of a white figure, standing at the top of the stairs. As she watches, the figure begins to descend the flight of steps. Something in the way it moves makes her realise, with enormous relief, that it is her beloved daughter and not the ghost of her sister Millie!

She quickly and silently follows the child along the passageway to ensure she is not feeling poorly. She catches up with her at the bottom of the stairs and quietly shadows her, as she makes towards the kitchen. However, in the moonlight streaming in from the kitchen window she can see Aurora's glassy, staring eyes which immediately confirms her suspicion that she is sleepwalking. She knows that you are not supposed to shock a sleepwalker awake and so she gently steers her back up to her bedchamber.

Louisa is most concerned because, to her knowledge, Aurora has never done this before and she is convinced the child must be very troubled, to be anxious enough to disturb her sleep pattern. She resolves to speak to her in the morning to see if she can elicit the cause.

After breakfast the following day Louisa asks Aurora to go with her to the library and they sit in the comfortable armchairs for their chat.

"We haven't had a chance to talk, just the two of us, for ages, darling, and I've been wondering how you are progressing with your lessons?"

Aurora fidgets uncomfortably in her chair, wondering if her mother spotted her with Luke on Gabriel's birthday. She blushes at the thought. "I think I'm doing very well, Mama."

"Aurora, I want you to tell me if there's anything at all troubling you at the moment, only you seem to be a little anxious and sad, which isn't like you at all, darling."

At the thought of her mother's genuine concern, Aurora cannot stop herself from bursting into floods of tears. Her mother immediately rushes to comfort her, gently drawing her from her seat, then sitting down herself and taking her grown-up daughter upon her lap for a motherly hug.

"You know you can tell me anything, sweetheart. I don't want you to worry about a thing, especially when your dear papa and I could help."

"That is *just it*, Mama, I'm not sure I truly am your daughter." She blurts it out all of a sudden and feels gratified to see the shock on her mother's face. *Of course she is shocked for it cannot be true!*

"Whatever gave you that idea?"

She dabs at her eyes with a handkerchief, "Well, there's this man who's spoken to me twice… and he's suggesting that the lady who wanted our puppies… is my aunt and her little girl, my cousin. He said that he thought Auntie Millie… might be my real mother."

"I see."

"Then there is the special basket, which ages ago I heard one of the kitchen maids saying… that it was the basket *I was found in*."

"I see."

Aurora shakes her head in frustration, "But *I* don't see, Mama; that's the point. *Please* tell me who I am and who are my *real* parents?"

Louisa feels sick to her stomach, but she has no choice now, she has to tell Aurora the whole story. She takes a deep breath, "Your papa and I are your real parents who have loved and cared for you for the last fourteen years, and we truly want it to stay that way." She kisses her daughter on the top of her head. Then she braces herself to tell her the facts. "However, there is truth in that man's innuendo, Rora. My sister, Millie, was your birth mother and unfortunately that man, whose name is Nathan Meakins, is your real father, but he doesn't know that for certain and Papa and I have been doing our utmost to keep that information a secret, to protect you from him. He's not a nice man, darling."

Her face contorts with the pain of it. "Oh! No! Mama, I didn't want it to be true. Why didn't you tell me before?"

"You were too young to understand and we were desperately trying to hide the truth from Nathan Meakins, so the fewer people who knew, the better."

"But what has my father done that is so wrong?"

"I cannot tell you, darling, you're still too young, but he's arrogant and cruel and you're safer here with us."

She rests her head in the crook of her mother's neck and weeps as if her heart will break.

Louisa will never forget her fear for her sister when she finally confided in her that she was pregnant, and she's been filled with guilt ever since for the decision she made to take the baby and conceal her underneath the clock tower at the big house. Although Aurora has never wanted for anything, believing that she and Josh were her real parents, it led to her poor, dear Millie being overwhelmed with grief and ultimately taking her own life.

When Aurora has calmed somewhat Louisa tells her the rest of the story, of Millie telling Meakins she was carrying his child; of him telling her he didn't want her, or the baby; of her traumatic birth in her parents' home, of abandoning her underneath the clock tower and her discovery; of Luke's mother being her wet-nurse; of her mother Millie's sadness and her dreadful drowning; of Joshua working it all out, his proposal, their marriage and their adoption of her. She does not, however, tell her that she believes her sister Millie killed herself, or all the evil things Nathan Meakins has done, for she believes that it will devastate her to know that she is the child of such a man.

Later, lying in her bedchamber, with red and swollen eyes from her weeping, Aurora mulls over what her mother has finally revealed. She is hurt and angry that it has taken all this time for her to finally be told the truth. She was instinctively wary of Nathan Meakins, but that was because she didn't understand why he was singling her out and she didn't understand what he was trying to tell her, but now, when she thinks about it, he was not unkind to *her* and maybe he has a right to see her and to know who she is? Maybe he regrets his attitude towards her mother all those years ago?

Although she has always been happy with her adopted family, she is devastated to know that it has all been a lie; her little brother Gabriel is really her cousin; her mother is really her aunt and her papa is her adopted father and in truth no blood relation at all!

She resolves secretly to pursue a relationship with her father, the puppy lady and her little cousin Senga, if she ever gets the opportunity to see them again.

CHAPTER TWENTY-ONE *(July 1865 – May 1866)*

NEW ARRIVALS

On 16th July 1865 Hugh's family finally arrive in Hobsons Bay, Australia. Hugh takes them from the docks on the horse-drawn omnibus straight to Sandhurst and their new home on Myrtle Street, next door to Bryn and Nell. He cannot wait to introduce them to all his old friends, but first he must settle them in and purchase some groceries and anything that his wife and daughter desire to console the ladies after their harrowing journey.

He believes they will be dwelling in Sandhurst forever, for he would have an impossible task persuading his ladies to step foot on a sea-going vessel ever again. Their journey on the emigrant ship was constantly beset by violent storms and although they had an upper-deck, family cabin, which was far more comfortable than Hugh's first journey south, they were all terribly sick throughout the voyage.

Their spirits rise somewhat on seeing the kangaroos and wallabies, but as they lurch along the rutted track in the omnibus they still feel queasy and are enormously thankful to be able to disembark in Sandhurst.

As soon as Bryn returns home with his sons from Eaglehawk he realises that his old mate is back at last and he rushes next door with his sons to meet Hugh's family. Their reunion is a joyous event and there is much noisy chatter among them. It is not long before Nell and Freyja join them and Bryn pops back home to fetch a bottle of rum with which to celebrate.

In the exchange of gossip Bryn tells Hugh that Sam and Angel have had another child while he has been away, a little boy they have called Connor, and Freyja and Owen are now betrothed. "Owen took Freyja to the opal mines where he had a ring designed for their engagement, using our very own gold."

"Well done, boyo! I'm very pleased for thee."

"I'm very lucky, Hugh. She's a beautiful lass and I love her very much." He puts his arm around her affectionately.

"Let's have a look then, lass."

Freyja holds out her hand for them all to see her betrothal ring. "I'm so pleased with it. It's wonderful fiery opal and it remind me of aurora borealis, magical fiery lights in northern skies back home where I comes from."

Gwyneth is very impressed, "It's so pretty; it's hard to believe it's dug up from underground in the mines here."

Hugh smiles to see the girls making friends and he happily holds out his glass for some more rum punch.

Nathan Meakins has been looking at a few local properties without much success and then, in the late summer of 1865, he finds exactly what he has been searching for in Ryme Intrinseca. It is an old manor house built of the golden limestone from Hamdon Hill, significantly with lands extending to Summerville and he is keen to purchase it. The small village is little more than a hamlet, situated in the Wriggle Valley, on the edge of the Blackmoor Vale. It is close to the border between Dorset and

Somerset, approximately five miles south of both Ivell and Sherborne and near enough for him to keep an eye on both the Summerville and the Alvington estates.

He visits the Wiltshire and Dorset Bank, in the Borough in Ivell, to discuss the purchase with the bank manager. As he approaches the imposing, double-fronted building, he observes the young lad, who he has noticed on both the occasions he has encountered his daughter, crossing the Borough with some documents under his arm. The lad also spots him and so he raises his hat in a friendly manner, in the hope that this will get back to his daughter, but the impudent lad turns away without reciprocating.

No matter, it's going to take a few months to organise the purchase and furnishings for Merry Meadows. I've plenty of time to entice my daughter away from those charlatans.

On Portland, Rebecca is sitting with her parents around a driftwood fire wondering however she will be able to sleep tonight with the November storm raging outside, the strong wind rattling the shutters and the torrential rain incessantly beating against the windowpanes. She can hear the sea roaring against the beach, with the long, pebbly suck of the groundswell.

"Do you hear that death groan?" asks her father. "There'll be lives lost along the south coast tonight, I'll be bound."

Rebecca shivers at the thought of the ships and their sailors battling at the mercy of this cold, tumultuous, unforgiving sea and takes another sip of her mother's tasty broth.

"Thank heavens all the locals came ashore before the storm hit," says her mother.

For some reason, Rebecca suddenly feels nauseous. "Would you like some more broth, Pa?"

"Why? Can't you finish yours?"

"No, Pa. My tummy's all churned up, thinking about the poor sailors. I think I'll go to bed, but I'm not sure I'll be able to sleep."

She takes up the go-to-bed and uses a taper from the fire to light it. Then she kisses her parents in turn, "Goodnight Ma, goodnight Pa," and she goes upstairs to her bedchamber.

She feels exhausted and in the end sleeps surprisingly well. The following morning the storm has subsided somewhat, but she still feels sick and if anything it is worse. When she finally ventures downstairs, her mother is laying the breakfast table, "Morning Becky. I'm afraid Chiswell is buzzing with the tragic news of yet another shipwreck on Chesil."

"Oh no! Pa said there'd be lives lost."

"The neighbours are saying a French brig named *Emmanuel* was driven ashore in the night and has broken to pieces on the beach. As far as I know there were no survivors."

Rebecca is about to respond when she is overwhelmed with a feeling of nausea and she runs into the back yard to be sick. She re-enters the scullery rather sheepishly. "I'm sorry Mama, I couldn't help it. I feel so rotten." She washes her hands and face at the sink.

"Don't worry, I'll wash it away. Perhaps some fresh air will help?" suggests her mother, with concern.

Rebecca goes to the window. "It certainly looks windy enough out there. Oh my goodness, I can see the wreck from here, the poor souls!"

Her mother comes to stand beside her. "Oh I can't believe it; look, there are some folk scavenging amongst the wreckage."

Rebecca turns away sadly, "Some folk have no respect for the dead."

Her mother adds, "I'm afraid some folk have no shame at all."

When Rebecca's sickness doesn't abate, Violet soon realises that it is a strong sign that her daughter has finally fallen for her long-awaited baby. She observes her pale, wan face and is convinced she is right, but she is fearful of putting her thoughts into words, lest she be mistaken. Rebecca has longed for a child for so long, fearing that it will never happen for her, fearing that she may lose her loving Ben if her greatest wish is not fulfilled.

By the time December arrives, Rebecca is exhibiting all the signs of being eight weeks pregnant, but still she is reluctant to believe that a miracle has truly taken place. She confides in her mother who questions her about all her symptoms and they go together to consult the aged Auntie Sarah who confirms their suspicions. Rebecca is, of course, overjoyed and she goes with her mother to the boatyard to tell Ben and her father the glad tidings.

Ben looks at Matthew, "Now I suppose is the right moment to ask for your daughter's hand in marriage, Matthew?"

Mathew looks from one to the other of them, grinning widely, "I think that is a given, son, don't you?" He grabs his hand and shakes it enthusiastically.

Violet kisses her daughter, "This is wonderful news. I'm so pleased for you both." Then she kisses Ben on his cheek. "I hope you'll all be very happy."

The wedding is then planned for 14th May 1866 at the same church that Violet and Matthew married in. Ben suggests she should include an invitation to their wedding in her brother's Christmas card.

However, during December they have yet another violent storm where the sea overwhelms Chiswell, pouring over and through the beach, flooding and damaging the houses there, flinging its pebbles and other larger missiles at the beachside properties and smashing windows that are not protected by shutters. Rebecca prays to God to keep her family and neighbours safe and fervently hopes they all live high enough to be out of danger from the swirling, destructive sea. Although there is some structural damage there is no loss of life and the Portlanders buckle down and repair their homes and look ahead to the seasonal celebrations.

Joshua and his family are preparing for Christmas at home when he receives the card and letter from his sister. He seeks out Louisa who is helping the children decorate their Christmas tree in the drawing room, where the two hounds are lying stretched out on the hearthrug, in the warmth from the log fire. He is delighted to be able to tell them all her exciting news. "Come listen to this, I have a letter here from Becky; I'll read it to you:

> *"Dearest Joshua and Louisa, Aurora and Gabriel,*
> *I am so excited to be able to tell you that the good Lord has seen fit to bless us, and Ben and I are, at last, going to be parents. The little one is due sometime in August next year. We plan to marry on 14th May 1866. I trust Aurora is still happy to be my handmaiden and Louisa, my maid of honour? Ben is truly looking forward to the celebration and is keen to push the boat out with his best man. It is just as well you decided not to visit us this Christmas, as the weather has been particularly*

305

abominable. The beach road has been cut off several times and many homes have been flooded. Even the brand new railway line, only opened in October, has been undermined where the land was washed away by the surging seawater, leaving the rails suspended in several places. The men are working hard on the lines now to restore them. Anyway, we both wish you all a splendid Christmas and hope you are as pleased as we are with our glad tidings.

> *Fondest regards,*
> *Becky and Ben"*

"Wow! That's amazing news, Josh, I'm so happy for them," says Louisa. "Becky has been longing for this for so long." She looks at Aurora, "We'll have to plan all our costumes in readiness."

Joshua puts down the letter, "I've been thinking about that. I did think it might be a good idea to take you, with Rosa in attendance of course, up to Bath on the steam train to choose the outfits."

"Oh Joshua, that would be wonderful."

He smiles at her enthusiasm, "It would be a nice day out for us. It might even remind you of Paris."

She smiles at his raised eyebrows, but then she asks, "What about the children?"

"Well, I think if we take their measurements, there's no need for them to come too. It would be nice for us to have some exclusive time together for a change."

"Ooh! I want to go on the steam train," complains Gabriel petulantly.

His father looks down at him, patiently, "Well, I tell you what we'll do, Gabriel. We'll all travel together on the train to the wedding instead. I'm sure you'll find that more fun. A day's shopping will be dreadfully boring for you."

Gabriel accepts this compromise happily, and although Aurora feels disappointed, she knows that it will do her mother good to spend some special time with her father for a change and so she raises no objection.

As the New Year of 1866 dawns, Nathan Meakins has finally finished furnishing his new home and presently has a contingent of staff ready to provide his every need. All he wants now is a family to fill the empty rooms. His thoughts turn to his daughter. *There is no denying she is a pretty little filly and the image of that young minx, Millie, whom I remember fondly leading me a merry dance through the corridors of Summerville House. It is regrettable that she would never have lived up to the image of my wife, in the eyes of my parents, or their social equals, for she was definitely the most enthusiastic ride I have ever enjoyed.*

He is ready now to make a move on her, the girl has had plenty of time to mull over his insinuations and hopefully question her adoptive parents. Maybe she will be ready to give him a chance to get to know her properly. His heart races at the thought; *she may well be as tender and loving towards me as her mother had been. But how should I approach her? Maybe I could befriend the young lad who is now working in Ivell and in that way get some information on her movements.*

On each occasion he visits Ivell he spends an hour or so keeping vigil in the Borough where he last spotted the lad, lingering in the market square, until he is rewarded by the sight of him strolling through the town. He approaches him with a friendly smile and asks him, "I recognise you from Camp Road, young fellow, and I'm curious to know the name of the young girl you were with that day?"

He can see the lad is taken aback, but he has given him no option but to answer honestly. He tells him, "Aurora Dryer, sir."

He appeals to him, "Would you mind giving her a message from me, son?"

"Of course, sir."

"My name is Nathan Meakins. Would you please tell her I'd like to meet her? I'll be here, just outside St John's Church tomorrow morning for your answer and for her suggestion as to where and when would be convenient for her."

"I'll tell her, sir."

He smiles again reassuringly, "Thank you, son. By the way, what's your name?"

"It's Luke, sir. Luke Moore."

Luke is unhappy to be the bearer of these tidings for his friend, but he has to let her know what has transpired and so after he has eaten his evening meal with Mr Fairway and Clara, he excuses himself to walk out to Alvington with Meakins' message.

He can see that Aurora is surprised and thrilled to see him midweek and they go outside to walk in the little copse where they had experienced their first kiss. As soon as they are hidden from view by the shrubs and trees and standing in the dappled light from the mellow evening sunshine, he takes her hand in his and gently kisses her, delighting in the tingling sensations running through him.

Luke eventually pulls away, reluctantly. "I've something to tell you, Rora," he whispers. "I'm not sure that I should, but I think that you need to know his intentions."

"Whose intentions?" She looks puzzled, "Who're you talking about, Luke?"

"Nathan Meakins." He watches her, as she catches her breath.

"What has happened; have you seen him?"

"Yes, I have. He approached me today and asked me to give you a message. He wants to meet you, Rora, and I'm not sure it is a good idea, but he'll be waiting for your answer tomorrow morning and I have to tell him something."

"Don't worry, Luke. You did right to tell me. I want to meet him. He is my real father and I need to know more about him, for my own peace of mind."

"I'm not sure you should meet him on your own, though, Rora. It's not seemly for you to be alone with a man you hardly know. You only have his word he's your father."

"No, I don't Luke; my mother has admitted that it's true. So there's nothing unseemly about a father meeting his own daughter."

He looks shocked, "Well, what do you want me to tell him?"

"Tell him I'll meet him this Wednesday." She pushes a stray hair away from her eyes. "Mama and Papa are going up to Bath on the steam locomotive to shop for wedding costumes and so I may be able to slip away unnoticed."

"But where could you meet him that will not alert the staff?"

"I don't know." She gives it some thought, "Perhaps I could walk across the fields, through Broad Leaze Farm and meet him on Watercombe Bridge?"

"What time shall I say?"

"Well, I think it might be easier to get away after my lessons in the afternoon, so say four of the clock on Wednesday, at Watercombe Bridge."

"Very well, if you're sure?"

She looks determined, "I am sure, Luke. I want to meet him and give him a chance to redeem himself." She looks pleased to have finally made this decision and Luke kisses her on her rosy lips and feels her responding and reciprocating lovingly.

When the time comes, Mrs Tweedy and Nanny Beth are luckily enjoying afternoon tea in the nursery, so Aurora tidies her hair and then sneaks down the stairs to escape unnoticed. She does not take into account the distress she is likely to cause the staff, as soon as they discover that she is missing.

It is a breezy, sunny afternoon and she is happy to escape into the fresh spring air after being indoors for most of the day studying geography. She skips through the long grass, disturbing bees and butterflies as they search for nectar in the pale mauve lady's smock and the golden buttercups. She feels as if some of those butterflies are fluttering in her tummy. She is anxious about meeting Nathan Meakins on her own, also lest any of the domestic staff or farmhands should spot her, but she is soon leaning breathlessly against the stonework of the small Watercombe Bridge waiting apprehensively for her rendezvous. She is not sure of the time, but believes she is quite early and so she tries to keep calm by leaning over the wall of the bridge, watching the water trickling by and looking out for water voles and other small creatures.

Finally she hears a horse and carriage approaching. *Could this be my father?* Her heart races with nervous excitement. She is pleased and relieved to recognise the driver of the gig as Nathan Meakins. He smiles to see her standing there and she hitches up her petticoats and clambers up into the gig to sit beside him. Knowing now that she is his daughter, she glances up at him at regular intervals, trying to familiarise herself with his handsome features, without him realising.

Meakins turns the gig and then it rattles on up the hill to the Crewkerne road. They turn left towards Ivell, until they come to a right turn onto the Dorchester road. Aurora is wondering where he is taking her when he says, "I thought you'd like to see my new estate in Ryme Intrinseca."

"Is it very far from here?" she asks him, nervously.

"No, not far at all, we'll be there in a jiffy."

She relaxes and watches the countryside passing by. They pass the Needle Folly and then they go over the railway bridge. Her father does not say very much and she feels too shy to make conversation herself.

Then he suddenly breaks the silence by saying, "Your friend, Luke, seems a nice enough fellow."

"Yes, he is. He's my best friend really."

"Is he your sweetheart?" He grins wickedly at her.

She blushes, "Well, we're very close, but we're still rather young and he's more like a brother to me." She does not think it wise to confide in him too much.

"It was good of him to take my message for you. Did he manage to tell you when you were on your own?"

"Yes, he did. I don't think my parents would allow me to meet you, otherwise."

"No, I thought not."

They turn left off the Dorchester road and Aurora notices the fingerpost pointing in the direction of Ryme Intrinseca and Yetminster.

"I think you'll like Merry Meadows; it's not as big as your present home, but it's a nicely laid out property."

"I'm sure I will." She wonders if she will be alone with him there. "Do you have servants?"

"Yes, I do now. They are all quite new to me, but seem very obliging."

"Where does the lady and the little girl, who you say might be my cousin, live?"

"My sister, Olivia, and my niece, Senga, you mean. They live at my old family home of Summerville, just outside Ivell. My father didn't believe I'd ever return from Australia and so he foolishly left *my* inheritance to Olivia."

They arrive at the entrance to a long driveway through pastureland and her father guides the horse through the entrance. At the end of the drive, the manor house is a charming, two-storey, Hamdon stone, rambling home with a low thatched roof. The mullioned leadlight windows are framed by climbing purple wisteria, white frilly clematis and pale pink roses and there are stables and outbuildings to the left and right of the property.

The combined scent from the roses and wisteria is quite overwhelming, as Meakins hands her down from the carriage and then shows her through the front door and into the interior of his new home. He gives her a guided tour of the downstairs and she is impressed with the well-appointed drawing room, dining room, lounge and parlour. The wood panelling, oak beams and inglenook fireplaces give the property a homely feel and she can imagine what a lovely family home it would make. It is a shame that all this is wasted on a single man.

He does not show her the upstairs, probably thinking it would not be appropriate from the servants' point of view, but he orders afternoon tea for them both and she could almost imagine feeling relaxed in his company, but not quite. There is still something about him that makes her feel uneasy.

"I want to talk to you about your mother, Millie. She was the image of you, Aurora, with the same rich red hair and beautiful, sparkling, liquid green eyes. We had some fun times when she was working for me, but she suddenly left without telling me she was pregnant."

Aurora is sure that this is a lie, because of what her mother had told her, but she doesn't argue with him. There is no point in making him angry.

Meakins continues, "I was so sure when my sister wrote to me and described seeing you many years ago in Ninesprings that you had to be my daughter, that I made a promise to myself to return to England and find you."

Aurora smiles sweetly at him, uncertain exactly how to respond and he continues with his charm offensive. "I'm so pleased that I did, and I can't believe you're sitting here with me, after all this time."

She takes a bite from her sandwich. "This is a lovely, warm and welcoming home you have here."

"Well, my dear, I have made a decision. If you are willing to publicly acclaim that I am your true father, I'll happily leave this property to you, in my will."

She is taken aback at this offer, but she realises the strings attached will have far-reaching consequences. "I know that you believe you're my real father and I can understand that there's a strong likeness between myself and my Aunt Millie, but of course I look like my own mother too and so it's hard for me to accept quite so easily."

"When is your birthday, Aurora?"

"It's 12th September 1851."

"Well you see your birth date coincides with about three months after your Aunt Millie left our employ and I'm convinced that you're my child, but I realise that you need time to think and so we'll say no more for now, but you must come to me, when you do finally accept the truth in what I'm telling you."

She has already fallen in love with Merry Meadows. Even the name sounds droll. She looks up at him, tempted to accept his proposition, but how can she hurt the two people who she has always thought were her real parents, in that way?

"I promise I will come to you, when I'm sure that what you're telling me is true."

"That is fair enough. I'll let you ponder on the matter until then."

The staff at Alvington realise after two hours that no one has seen Aurora since four o'clock and a frantic search of the estate begins to no avail. Mrs Abbott asks John Moore to go in the gig to visit Mr Fairway to see if Aurora is with Luke. Mr Fairway assures him that they have not seen her and Luke betrays nothing, but Mr Fairway suspects he knows more than he is letting on. After the groom has left he takes Luke into his office.

"I'm sure, Luke, that you don't realise the importance of keeping Aurora away from Nathan Meakins. You've probably been protected by your parents from hearing any gossip about him, of what a miserable specimen of mankind he really is and how he committed both rape and murder in Somerset, before he was transported to the Antipodes. However, more importantly, Lord Dryer has been reliably informed recently that he hasn't learnt his lesson and has continued raping and murdering in Australia. He has also allegedly robbed a consignment of gold from the miners over there, but we're struggling to find the evidence over here to prove this. If we could ascertain which bank he uses, we might stand a chance of getting the necessary proof."

Luke looks abashed; he has promised Aurora that he will keep her meeting with Meakins a secret, but perhaps he could help in some small way. "I've seen him entering the Wiltshire and Dorset Bank in the Borough before now."

Mr Fairway is pleased with this information "Have you, indeed? Well that might be very helpful. Thank you, my boy. I'll inform His Lordship at the earliest opportunity." He ushers the lad back into the parlour, "Come on lad, I think you've earned your supper."

Later, when Aurora finally arrives back home, having been dropped off at Watercombe Bridge and hurrying across the fields, she is shocked to find the staff searching frantically for her throughout the estate. She has taken the precaution of picking some wild flowers in the field near the bridge and is first alerted to the commotion when she comes across Emily calling her name, down near the stream, closer to her home. She rushes up to her, "Here I am, Emily. Whatever is wrong?"

"Oh Rora, we've all been so worried about you. Where have you been?"

She smiles to herself, secretly pleased to have been missed. "I've been out walking through the fields, enjoying the spring sunshine and picking wild flowers. Look!" She holds out her hastily picked bunch of cowslips, red campion and lady's smock.

"But it's past supper time! You'd better hurry home now, for Flora, Nanny Beth, Mrs Abbott and Grace are all very worried to have lost you and Gabriel has been crying."

"Oh dear, I didn't mean to worry anyone. I'm so sorry."

They head back to the house together to let everyone know that she is safe and sound.

CHAPTER TWENTY-TWO *(May 1866)*

WEDDING BELLS AND MERMAID TAILS

Ambrose Fairway has informed Joshua that Meakins uses the Wiltshire and Dorset Bank and he has in turn asked the judge to prepare the search warrant to go through Meakins' bank accounts, to ascertain the nature of his current funds and any large deposits that may have resulted from the Australian gold robbery. He is happy to put the matter out of his mind and enjoy the happy family event on Portland until they all return and then he will pursue the grounds for his arrest in earnest.

He has decided that, as promised, the family should all travel, together with Rosa and Beth, to Portland on the steam train to attend Ben and Becky's wedding. The damaged section of the rail track, after the December storm, has now been repaired. The tickets are booked in advance, and on the day preceding the ceremony John Moore conveys the family to the station in the landau with some of their luggage and Billy takes Rosa and Beth in the smaller carriage with the remainder. Rosa's children will stay on the farm during the day with their grandparents.

The weather is rather dismal and overcast, but the travellers in contrast are quite ebullient. Aurora and Gabriel are both excited to be travelling on the steam locomotive for the first time. Louisa is anxious for them to keep away from the edge of the platform and she holds tightly onto Gabriel in an effort to curb his enthusiasm, entreating her more sensible daughter to stand well back.

The train eventually arrives with a terrific rattle and rumble of the piston engine and rail track; and panting, puffing and belching of steam. Gabriel's eyes light up. "Wow! It's enormous!" The porter loads their luggage into the guard's van and Joshua helps the ladies and his son into the carriage. They are all able to sit together in one wood-panelled compartment to the exclusion of all others and Joshua closes the door.

Louisa breathes a sigh of relief. They are safely on board with all their wedding outfits securely consigned to the guard's van. The guardsman blows his whistle and the train chugs slowly on its way. Soon she is watching the countryside rushing by, with the smoky steam billowing and wafting past their window. Gabriel and Aurora are seated opposite each other, nearest the windows, looking out at the pastureland and farm stock, fascinated by the fact that everything appears in miniature – the distant buildings, people and animals – and saying how it reminds them of their old Noah's ark. Gabriel comments, "It's as if I could pick them up and play with them."

Louisa is feeling more calm now that Aurora knows the truth; ten months have passed since her declaration and things seem to have settled down. Nathan Meakins has not reared his ugly head and Aurora has neither mentioned the subject, nor been sleepwalking since. Determined to enjoy this happy family event, she relaxes and looks around her. She is impressed with the workmanship of the locomotive's interior. The upholstered bench seating is very comfortable and on either side of the carriage there is a framed picture of the seaside town of Weymouth set in the wood panelling above the seats between two bevelled mirrors. Behind her the framed view is of the sweeping bay, with its sandy beach and esplanade and opposite her it is of the harbour, but the moving panorama of the countryside is more enthralling. She sits dreamily watching as the landscape alters from neat farmland to rolling hills and the speed they are travelling is both exciting and scary.

This is the second time she has travelled by train from Penn Mill station. True to his word, Joshua took her and Rosa northbound up to the city of Bath to shop for the wedding costumes for themselves and the children. She and Rosa would never have experienced such a thing if she had not been fortunate enough to marry Joshua. She looks up at him lovingly and he smiles back at her and takes her hand in his. Rosa and Beth are both seated beside Aurora, and after Beth has gently chastised Gabriel for inquisitively playing with the window blinds, she happily chats with the children, whilst Rosa sits serenely by her side. She is so lucky to be blessed with such a wonderful family and such loyal friends and staff.

The time flies by, the moving vista is so engrossing. The train stops at Yetminster, Evershot, Maiden Newton, Dorchester, Weymouth, and finally on to Victoria Square on Portland. The miserable weather changes as soon as the train passes through the tunnel under Ridgeway Hill, when the sun emerges and everything suddenly glistens and sparkles reflecting her sunny mood. Aurora and Gabriel both cry out excitedly when they spot their first glimpse of the sea.

Joshua comments, "Our journey time is a quarter of what it would have been in the landau."

Louisa replies happily, "And it's lovely to be privileged to see a different view of our beautiful Dorsetshire countryside."

When they disembark at Victoria Square, Violet and Rebecca are there to greet them and there are hugs and kisses all round.

Louisa quietly takes Rebecca's hand and draws her to one side, "Congratulations, Becky. Joshua and I are so pleased for you, knowing how much you want a little one."

Rebecca giggles excitedly, "Thank you, Lou-Lou. It took long enough! But Ben and I are both over the moon."

"Of course you are." Louisa smiles, "August is a lovely time to be born, but you'll have the winter ahead of you. Poor little mite, let's hope we have a mild one."

"Don't you worry, Lou-Lou; we'll take such good care of him he'll be wrapped up in cotton wool."

"Him?"

"I know, we'll have to wait and see, but I just feel in my bones I'm carrying a little boy and I cannot bring myself to call my baby 'it'. I expect Auntie Sarah will have an opinion when I'm a bit further on and everyone else gets to hear the news!"

Joshua pays a porter to convey their luggage into the Royal Victoria Hotel and his mother and sister follow them; also keen to see the interior of the new and imposing building, only recently opened. Louisa watches him fondly as he deals with the concierge, sorting out the accommodation for them both; Beth and Rosa; and Aurora and Gabriel.

Once shown upstairs to their rooms they find they are very small compared to what they are all used to, but beautifully appointed with all they require to make their stay comfortable. Violet and Rebecca help Aurora and Gabriel to unpack their suitcases and fill their closet, whilst the others are soon organised and refreshed after their journey.

Joshua looks proudly at his family gathered in the

foyer of the hotel, "I'm just going to the Cove House Inn to sort things out with John Motyer and I'll catch you up shortly." He kisses Louisa warmly, whispering, "I'll try not to be too long."

Then, apart from Joshua, they all set off up to the Cove Cottages.

Violet takes Aurora by the hand and Gabriel saunters along beside his Aunt Rebecca, who is chattering merrily about all the arrangements for the following day. "We're to be wed in the Methodist Chapel where Ma and Pa were wed back in 1837."

Her mother, Violet, smiles, "That was almost thirty years ago! Where has the time gone?"

Rebecca laughs, "Well, most of the time you've been running Fortune's Corner and Pa's been busy in his boatyard."

Louisa joins in enthusiastically, "Joshua and I went to Bath on the steam train for our shopping trip and he purchased two lovely matching gowns for myself and Aurora. They're in a sort of bronze-coloured silk dupion, with double sleeve flounces of the same silk and an under flounce of cream lace at the elbows, draping prettily down to the wrists. The bodice has back lacing and, decorating the front down into the V shape at the waistline, there are four matching bows, decreasing in size from top to bottom."

Aurora joins in the conversation, "Mama's dress has a low, square neckline and to go with it, Papa has bought her a beautiful rose-gold necklace, set with tiger's eye and smoky brown quartz."

Louisa smiles contentedly, remembering happily how pleased Joshua was to be able to treat her with the jewellery. "We chose a more demure neckline for Aurora, which I think suits her better."

Aurora continues enthusiastically, "My dress has a high neckline with little lace collars to match the sleeves."

"They both look beautiful," says Rosa wistfully.

Rebecca puts her arm around Aurora, "They sound just perfect; I can't wait to see everyone all dressed up in their glad rags. We have only just, last night, finished stitching all the seed pearls on my gown. I hope you like it."

"I'm sure we will, Becky." Louisa looks at her sister-in-law and smiles warmly as they proceed up the hill in the sunshine.

Violet asks, "What's Gabriel going to wear?"

Louisa turns back to address Joshua's mother who is walking behind them, "He has a lightweight grey velvet jacket, with indigo moleskin breeches and waistcoat, which are both soft and comfortable for him, and a white silk shirt and golden necktie to tone in with our dresses."

They reach the row of Cove Cottages and walk along the lane to Violet and Rebecca's home. Violet unlocks the front door and they all go inside.

Whilst waiting for Joshua, Louisa helps the women to prepare some food. However, she is starting to feel uneasy without Joshua's support in the home of her in-laws, when eventually he turns up. "I finally managed to escape John's enthusiastic and friendly questions to come and join you all."

His mother smiles, "He's such a good friend, but like all landlords, he does like to gossip. Anyway, we've set out the tea things and your pa and Ben will be joining us shortly. Please don't wait for them; you must all be very hungry after your journey."

"Thank you Ma, this looks marvellous!"

The children are already filling their plates. Joshua indicates a seat for her, then he sits down beside her, passing her various platters and helping himself hungrily to his mother's home cooking.

"So, Becky, where are you going to live, once our Ben has made an honest woman of you?"

Rebecca smiles, "We've been really lucky; we're going to lease Mermaid Cottage from old Mrs Atwool, who has been a widow for some time now and has decided to move in with her daughter and family."

"That'll be really handy for Ben." Joshua looks impressed, but observing him, Louisa can detect a knowing smile. He turns to her, explaining, "'tis only a stone's throw from the boatyard."

Moments later Ben and Matthew arrive, crowding the small living room, and again there are hugs and kisses and congratulations all around.

The men are going to celebrate Ben's last night of freedom at the Cove House Inn, whilst Violet has organised for the ladies, including Aurora who is now fifteen, to have their hen party at Mermaid Cottage, where they intend to prepare the cottage for the wedding night. After the tea things have been cleared away, they leave Beth in charge of Gabriel and set off to the cottage, armed with Rebecca's personal belongings, including her treasured sewing box, made for her by her beau.

Violet surreptitiously takes with her a bottle of honeymoon mead for the young couple to enjoy on their wedding night. She watches everyone around her and feels especially proud of her two children now all grown up. Ben and Joshua carry Rebecca's dowry box between them. It is heavy with the things that she and Rebecca have sewn and collected over the years since their betrothal, and once the two boys have dropped it off, they kiss their ladies and rush off eagerly to join the stag party.

Violet could not be more pleased that Rebecca is at last carrying the child she has longed for and feared she may never be able to have. Her daughter has already made her mark by hanging her home-made curtains. Violet had managed to get a bolt of material in Weymouth at a bargain price and they had made them together. Now she looks at them wistfully, remembering how she and her own mother had made the curtains for Richard Dryer all those years ago. She shivers, her skin tingling as if he is touching her from the grave.

Rosa, Louisa and Aurora carry the freshly laundered bedding up the stairs and together they make up the double bed. Whilst they are busy with the bedding, Violet is helping Rebecca filling up the chest of drawers with her clothes.

Aurora asks Rebecca, "Have you something old, something new, something borrowed and something blue, Auntie Becky?"

Rebecca pauses and thinks for a moment… "I have something old, because the lace on my dress was made by my grandmother when she was a girl, and something new, is my gift from Ma and Pa, my gown, shoes and matching reticule. My other grandmother, on Ma's side, has given me a handkerchief she embroidered for me with tiny blue forget-me-nots, but I haven't actually had to borrow anything."

Louisa then says, "Well, I have with me, back at the hotel, my own mother's pearl-drop choker necklace, which you're very welcome to borrow, if you would like to."

"I think that would be a lovely idea. Thank you Louisa, I'll take good care of it."

"My ma wore it on her wedding day and I'm sure it will bring you good luck, for they've had the happiest of marriages. You may remember I wore it at the summer ball."

There is an uneasy silence and Violet watches with concern, as her daughter's expression changes to one of bitterness. Immediately Louisa puts her hand to her mouth, "I'm so sorry, Becky, I didn't mean to dredge up painful memories for you."

Then Becky smiles, "It's not your fault, Lou-Lou; I'd love to wear your necklace. No sad memories are going to mar our wedding day tomorrow, I promise you." She hugs her warmly. "Tomorrow we'll truly be sisters."

The moment of sadness is brushed hastily aside and they all continue with their tasks, but Violet is suspicious that something serious happened back then, at Joshua's summer ball, that her children are keeping from her. She pushes her suspicions to the back of her mind; nothing must spoil tomorrow for her family. It is going to be the happiest of all days.

Once the bed is made up and everything is packed away tidily, they all go back downstairs to unwind and enjoy some metheglin. After Rebecca has left the room, Violet carefully places the honeymoon mead on the bedside table with two wine glasses.

It is not long before Matthew's sister, Hannah, and Mrs Stone join them, bringing the ingredients for a punch. They are soon blending a good rum punch with water, some cane sugar and fruit juices. Whilst Aurora grates some nutmeg into the mixture, Violet is setting out some punch cups when her mother and some of Rebecca's old school friends arrive at around the same time, followed by Ben's mother and her sisters. Then Mollie turns up with some pies and sandwiches and they all sit around talking of past times, of their men-folk, their romances, and their children.

The men are all drinking and carousing at the Cove House, telling jokes and tall stories and teasing the prospective groom throughout the night. Joshua really enjoys spending this happy time with Ben. He has missed their closeness and comradeship, but eventually Matthew takes charge and ushers everyone home, "Come on, lads. Tomorrow's a big day and we don't want to let the ladies down, do we?"

They all stagger off in their different directions. Ben's uncles help him on his way back to Annie's, and Matthew and Joshua go off arm in arm. Violet's brothers set off with their own and Matthew's father up towards Brandy Row. Tomorrow is going to be another happy day of celebration.

During the ceremony the following day, several people are experiencing intrusive thoughts despite joining in with the singing and prayers. Violet is reminded of her own wedding to Matthew nearly thirty years earlier in this very same chapel, but then she also remembers her first wedding to Richard. Unhappily, she recalls the moment when Ikey Shaddick made his vindictive comments about Ben's parentage, and his sister Annie's relationship with her beloved Richard. She is annoyed that these thoughts should intrude on such a happy occasion, but she cannot resist looking across to her right, at Annie seated in the second pew on the groom's side. *What if the spiteful comments that wretched Ikey had made were true and the boys really are brothers?*

Annie notices Violet looking in her direction and she wonders if, like her, she is recalling how their two young children, Josh and Ben, had run off and were lost on the occasion of her marriage to Matthew. *Thank goodness they found them both safe and sound.* But no, there is no relief in her eyes; there is fear and Annie's guilty secret tears away at her.

Also looking at Violet is Annie's brother Bill, remembering Richard Dryer being shot by the smugglers, how Matthew had persuaded him to go and see Violet when she was acting strange, like a mad person, and how he was able to tell her that Richard had known in the end he had misjudged her, which seemed to give her such immense relief. *It was a good thing he did, back then, because it seemed to trigger the change in her.*

Seated nearer the back of the church, Rosa is observing the likeness between the groom and his best man; apart from their colouring, she can see even more clearly from their back view that they both have the same tall physique with good, broad shoulders and narrow hips, the same mannerisms and supple body movements. She remembers overhearing Meakins' accusations and can see the truth in them. *I wonder if His Lordship ever did tell his brother the truth.*

The ceremony, however, goes off without a hitch and as they exit the chapel, Ben looks very handsome in his smart charcoal-grey suit, top hat, highly polished shoes and romantic golden-coloured waistcoat and silken necktie. Smiling down at his beautiful bride, he takes Rebecca by the hand, as the villagers' crowd around them.

Violet and Matthew follow them down the chapel steps, both of them looking and feeling so proud of their lovely daughter, prettily dressed in her pale ivory, silk dupion wedding dress, cleverly cut with a contrasting darker-coloured stomacher panel to conceal her growing bump. Her gown is decorated with tiny golden sprigs of honeysuckle, embroidered in metallic golden thread, which gleams in the sunlight. It is complimented by a headband, decorated with artificial flowers of gold and bronze tumbling down and framing her elated face. All these things Violet had been able to purchase through her regular shop suppliers.

Then Joshua and Louisa come out of the church into the sunshine followed by Beth, Rosa and the children. Joshua puts his arm around young Gabriel and Louisa takes Aurora's hand. Their happy family makes a pretty picture all done up in their wedding clothes and Joshua waves to several villagers who are there to lend their support.

There are loud cheers and catcalls as Ben bends to kiss his new bride and then, firstly announcing her intentions, Rebecca turns her back on the crowd to throw her bouquet. One of her old school friends catches it and blushes madly as everyone claps. Then the procession sets off to visit the neighbours on the way back to Violet's cottage for the wedding breakfast and some bride cake.

Aurora feels alienated from the rest of the family now that she knows she was abandoned and adopted. Although she stood there outside the church, with her mother's hand affectionately clasping hers, their physical closeness seemed to emphasise the chasm that has appeared between them since her revelations. She cannot get the dreadful thoughts out of her head that she is really part of a different family and she no longer belongs in this one. She feels like an imposter playing a role to keep everyone happy and she is beginning to resent it.

By the time they are ready to toast the bride and groom at the end of the day, everyone is very inebriated. Matthew stands up to make the toast, but Joshua speaks quietly to him before he begins. "Before your speech, Pa, do you mind if I present them with my wedding gift?"

"Of course not, you go ahead."

Joshua goes with Louisa to extricate his sister from her conversation with Rosa. "Becky, would you and Ben mind joining us for a moment? Louisa and I have something to give you both."

Joshua hands Ben a package tied in ribbon and sealed with wax. "It's for you, to celebrate your union with my sister."

"Thank you, mate," he smiles at Joshua and turns to Louisa, "That's very kind of you both. I'm intrigued, whatever is it?"

His sister is standing impatiently beside him, her early pregnancy enhancing her beauty; with her glossy hair and flushed cheeks she is looking radiant in her wedding gown. "Open it then, Ben. That's the only way to find out."

Ben fumbles with the ribbon and Rebecca gently takes it from him, she dextrously unties the bow and passes the parcel back to her husband. Ben then pulls the wrapping apart to reveal some legal documents. He looks up at Joshua with a puzzled expression on his face.

Joshua explains, "It's the deeds to Mermaid Cottage. You and Becky are now the proud owners of your home for perpetuity, Ben."

Rebecca is thrilled. "I can't believe it! How did you manage that?" she asks him in amazement.

"When we were liaising over the wedding costumes with Ma, she happened to mention that you were planning to lease Mermaid Cottage and so I asked Ambrose to determine whether Mrs Atwool may be prepared to sell. He looked into it for me and sorted out all the legalities."

"It's too generous. How can we ever thank you enough?"

"It's *the least* I can do," says Joshua, smiling, but as he speaks he feels the weight of that comment. Then he catches the eye of Annie Shaddick and her look holds her pleas of the past, to remain silent.

Later, after Matthew has toasted the young couple, Joshua is serving up more punch when Annie takes him to one side and whispers, "I know you're uncomfortable Joshua, concealing from my son the truth about your relationship, but I swear if he knew you were both half-brothers he'd never forgive me for all the years of lying to him. I couldn't bear it if I lost his love and respect. It's the only thing that makes my life worthwhile."

"I hate being expected to collaborate in your make believe, Mrs Shaddick, but I love him as a brother and will never do anything to hurt him. I couldn't ask for a better husband for my sister and want nothing to mar their joy."

Annie Shaddick looks up at him with tears in her eyes and she squeezes his arm gratefully, "Thank you, son."

Aurora, who had gone into the scullery to wash some glasses, notices her father whispering to someone on the other side of the scullery door, which is slightly ajar. Her curiosity aroused, she listens to their conversation and is shocked and concerned at the revelation. *Surely Auntie Becky shouldn't be marrying Ben if they're brother and sister. It's not allowed and they'll get into trouble! How could Papa be complicit in this deception, when he's a Justice of the Peace? It's just more lies!*

She thought her father always did what was right and proper. He sits in judgement over others and yet here he is, not only hiding the truth of her own birth, but also hiding the truth from his own sister and brother. She is in a quandary, wanting to confront him, but scared of the consequences. She needs to sit quietly and think about this. She takes the clean glasses through to the parlour and pours herself a generous glass of punch. She sits beside the punchbowl listening to all the chattering around her. *Auntie Becky is already having Ben's baby. How could Papa allow this to happen?*

After about an hour of sulking, Aurora has already had three more glasses of punch when she attempts to stand up and stumbles against the small table, tipping the punchbowl to the floor. The contents splash all over Aunt Mollie's gown, but the sturdy bowl survives the fall. She slumps back into her seat, "Sorry, Auntie Mollie," she slurs. "I'm afraid I'm a bit dizzy."

Violet goes to see what has happened and then rushes to get a cloth from the scullery to dry Mollie's gown.

"Don't worry about me, Violet; I think maybe your granddaughter needs you more."

Aurora has rushed back out into the scullery to vomit into the sink.

Violet follows her, "Whatever's the matter child?"

"I think I've drunk too much punch, Grandma."

"Oh Aurora, I'd have thought we could trust you to be sensible; why did you have to choose today of all days to misbehave, with all our relations here to bear witness?"

"I was upset, Grandma. I heard Papa saying that Uncle Ben is really his brother… not his cousin and yet he's let him marry Auntie Becky and that's not right, because surely they're brother and sister. It's just more lies!"

Violet's blood runs cold. *Not that again! Why does that insinuation have to come out today of all days?* She tries to pacify Aurora, "No, no I'm sure you misheard, darling."

The door swings open and Ben stands there with his mouth open in shock, then he asks her distinctly, "What do you mean, Aurora… we're brother and sister?"

A deathly hush has fallen over the gathering and Violet can see, beyond the scullery door, the shocked faces of Matthew, Joshua, Rebecca and Ben's mother.

Her daughter goes a deathly white and swoons. Matthew catches her and sits her in one of the armchairs, whilst Grandma Allen passes the smelling salts.

Ben looks at Joshua, "What's she saying, Josh? Is this true?"

Joshua has a pained expression on his face as he answers, "Not exactly, but I do believe you ought to speak to your own mother about this. She's the only one present who knows the true facts."

Violet looks anxiously at Mrs Shaddick.

Ben turns to his mother, "Ma?"

Annie hesitates, pushing a loose strand of hair behind her left ear. She has no choice but to come clean now. She takes a deep breath, her voice broken with emotion, "It is true that you share the same father, Ben."

Ben gasps in shock, as a muttering of surprise ripples among all the guests, but Annie continues resolutely. "Richard Dryer was your real father, son... but he didn't want me, he wanted Violet." She goes towards him fearfully, looking up into his solemn face. "We were both pregnant at the same time... but he married Violet and so I had to find myself a husband. I married William Stone. He was always good to us, he loved us and he believed you were his own child, as did everyone else hereabouts. It suited me to keep it a secret... but then that devil Meakins, Joshua's arch-enemy, managed to get the truth out of me... by getting his steward to ply me with drink. He even tried to suggest there'd been some skulduggery over the inheritance. I know this wasn't true... because Joshua was the firstborn and Richard had legally married Violet."

She looks Violet in the eyes, "He truly loved you, Violet, but I was just a convenience... he never looked at me again, once you two got together."

Then she turns tearfully back to her son. "I thought I was protecting you from the truth, Ben, and I'm sorry it had to come out like this, after all these years."

Rebecca has recovered from her swoon and asks her in a tremulous voice, "Are you saying that we're brother and sister, Mrs Shaddick?"

"No child, your parents are Violet and Matthew, and Ben's parents are me and Richard, so you're not related and your marriage is legal, have no fear."

She looks at her son fearful both of his reaction to the revelation and his opinion of her behaviour. His expression is one of shock and bewilderment. "I'm so sorry, son." He turns away from her and her heart sinks.

He goes to Rebecca's side and bends to kiss the top of her head reassuringly and then looks back at his mother, "But you're quite sure that Josh and me… we're half-brothers?"

She sighs, this could not have come out at a worse possible moment, but she looks her son in the eye and tells him the truth, "Yes, son."

Amazingly, he grins at her and turning to Joshua he says, "I always knew we had a special bond, Josh." He goes over to Joshua and holding out his arms he gives him a bear hug.

Joshua looks like the weight of the world has been lifted from his shoulders.

Annie gives a huge sigh of relief and turns away from the gathering, tears running down her face.

Aurora vomits once more into the sink.

Violet appears to be resigned to the unpalatable facts, and Matthew puts his arm around her supportively. He is, however, shocked himself that, after all this time, he has been treating Ben like his own son and planning to leave his business to him, and now, when he is finally his legal son-in-law, he discovers the irony that in reality he is the son of his old rival.

He wonders what the preventive man might be thinking, if he is up there looking down on this scene, having now twice deceived him. *But maybe I have the last laugh; at least my life wasn't cut short in my prime – I have, in truth, had a fatherly influence on both Dryer's sons and I've had the pleasure and pride of watching them develop into two admirable, kind and courageous, upstanding young men in the community. I've been blessed with all I ever desired with a family to be proud of – what more could any man want?*

CHAPTER TWENTY-THREE *(May 1866)*

POETIC JUSTICE

For several days after their return home from Portland, Aurora still feels guilty for her behaviour at her Aunt Becky's wedding and unhappily she believes her father has not yet forgiven her for betraying his secret. However, the following Saturday she is given permission to accompany Nanny Beth to Montacute market.

It is a typical warm and sunny day in May and Billy drops them off in the square, saying he will be back at around noon. As well as the usual stalls, they can immediately hear lively music and they soon spot through the crowd an accordionist and some fiddlers playing whilst the village children dance around the maypole. The atmosphere is merry and bright and Aurora feels her despondency lifting, as she watches the young girls dancing with the brightly-coloured ribbons and dressed in a multitude of different pastel-tinted summer frocks and pinafores. The many stalls are set around the perimeter of the circle formed by the maypole and Aurora happily follows her nanny around.

Aurora listens to the cheery music whilst Beth enjoys looking for bargains and chatting with the stallholders. Suddenly her nanny is spotted by her old village friends and they surround her, excitedly giggling and asking her for all her news.

While Nanny Beth is distracted, Aurora is drawn to a stand selling all manner of ladies accessories; there is a variety of hatpins, buttonhooks, costume jewellery, trinket boxes and dressing-table sets. A tortoiseshell hair comb decorated with copper-coloured flowers is particularly eye-catching. She is about to ask the stallholder how much, when her hand is clasped firmly and she is pulled behind the stall and into the roadway outside the Phelips Arms. Her heart is thumping at the suddenness of the attack, but she is thrilled and surprised to see that her assailant is actually her father. He pushes her forward, whispering urgently, "Come quickly, before we're spotted."

She pulls back exclaiming, "But I cannot, I'm with my nanny!"

He ignores her protest, pushing her up into his gig, climbing swiftly up beside her, tossing a coin to the lad who had been minding the horse and flicking the reins hastily. Aurora turns back anxiously, to see if anyone has noticed, but from the height of the gig, she can see Nanny Beth is still chatting to her friends, whilst the music and dancing continues.

Her heart is racing as the gig hurtles along the narrow country lanes. The other road users look disapprovingly at them as they fly past. She is all at once elated that her father wishes to see her so much that he is actually willing to kidnap her, stimulated by the adventure, but fearful for the consequences.

Beth Puddy is delighted to see her old school friends and has completely forgotten about Aurora, until she is telling the girls about her trip on the steam train and the wedding on Portland. She is about to draw her charge into the conversation when she realises that Aurora is nowhere to be seen.

"Oh! My God! Where's Aurora!" Beth is panic-stricken. *What will Lord and Lady Dryer think of me if I'm unable to find her?*

She turns to her friends in alarm, "Please help

me to find Aurora, she's a pretty fifteen-year-old redhead and I was supposed to be looking after her." They spread out around the market square, but soon realise there is no sign of her.

Mabel Mead looks at Beth's worried face, "I'm sorry to have to say this, Beth, but either she is a wilful miss, who's hiding from us deliberately to worry you, or she's been abducted."

"No, she isn't a wilful child at all. I'm sure she wouldn't do it deliberately." *It has to be her father!* Her heart contracts with dread and she returns in panic to the point where she last saw her, to question the stallholders there. Mabel and some of her friends follow her.

One old lady, several stalls along tells her, "I do remember seeing a young redhead. She were taken by the hand and led away by a tall man. 'Ee bundled her up into a gig and then swiftly drove off. It was the urgency of 'is actions that made me notice 'im."

"Oh no! I feared as much!" She turns to her friends, "I must get word to her parents." *But Billy's not coming back for us until noon. Whatever will he do to her?* "I'm going to have to run all the way back to Alvington. I'm sorry, but I have to go, there's no time to lose. Bye!" She rushes off, leaving them looking from one to the other, concerned and mystified.

Nathan Meakins looks down at his daughter, "How would you like to be properly introduced to the rest of your real family at Summerville House?"

"I'd like that, but I can't be away long. My parents will be worried."

"*I'm* not worried, Aurora, and *I'm* your father."

"I know, but *you* know where I am. My adoptive parents don't, and last time they were all extremely concerned."

"Well, in that case, we must make haste."

Aurora hangs on grimly, as the carriage lurches from side to side through the town, but as the gig turns into the carriageway of Summerville House she is curious to see where her father grew up. It is a lovely honey-stoned mansion set in the river valley and she can see wading birds in the water meadows, beside the brook to her left.

Her father tethers the horse to the hitching post at the outer edge of the driveway and helps her down. A liveried man stands aside as her father walks straight in and she follows behind him obediently. His sister, Olivia, greets them as they enter the main hallway, almost as if she was expecting them. She holds out her hands to Aurora, "I'm extremely pleased to meet you, for the first time as my young niece, and a very warm welcome to Summerville."

Aurora allows her to take her hands and she says shyly, "Thank you, ma'am." She dips a curtsey.

Olivia releases her with a smile, "Please, come this way."

She follows her aunt and her father into a beautifully furnished drawing room, "I would like to introduce you to my husband, Alistair."

Alistair puts down his newspaper and stands up to greet them both. "Good morning and welcome." He shakes hands with each of them and then Agnes comes running in to meet Aurora.

Olivia berates the child, "Slow down, Senga, where are your manners?"

"I'm sorry, Mama, I was just eager to meet my cousin."

"Well, go and sit beside her on the sofa like a proper little lady, please." The child sits beside Aurora and her mother says, "That's better." Then she looks askance at Aurora's father, "At least this time we don't have to worry about being mauled by the dog!"

Aurora feels decidedly abashed, as her face flushes shamefully, but her aunt then goes on to offer them all some refreshments. The conversation is a little stilted, but her father tells Olivia and Alistair about his latest alterations to Merry Meadows and she sits and listens, whilst Agnes brings her various dolls and toys for her amusement.

Eventually her father asks her if she would like to be shown around the house and she says that she would like that, but she feels she ought to be returning home now. "I'm worried my parents will call out the constables if I'm not home soon."

Nathan Meakins is suddenly concerned that the girl might be right and the first place Dryer and the constables would come looking would be Summerville. He gets up and looks at his sister, "Aurora is right, we ought to be making tracks, but thank you for your kind hospitality and I'm sure we'll do this again sometime soon."

His sister and her husband both stand up and he thinks he can detect relief in their faces, as Alistair says, "You will be most welcome." His old steward then turns to Aurora, "Very nice to meet you, my dear."

Aurora gets up from the sofa and dipping in a curtsey she replies, "For me too, sir, thank you very much for the refreshments."

Olivia says, "Come on Senga, say goodbye to your cousin."

Agnes jumps up from the carpet where she has been dressing her dolls, "Goodbye Aurora, please come to see me again soon."

Aurora bends down to give her little cousin a big kiss. "I will," she says and turns towards the door.

Olivia sees them out.

As they set off back towards the Ivell to Dorchester road, Nathan Meakins has an idea. *It wouldn't have been safe to stay any longer at Olivia's and I can't very well take her back to my own home, for they'll soon be on my tracks there, but I could stop off at Catkin Mill where she could meet my other pals. There's always the place where William Bell and I used to hide our contraband and they'd never find her there.* He flicks the reins to make the horse go faster as they travel along Two Tower Lane. He is more anxious with every passing carriage, lest he be recognised, or challenged by anyone connected with Lord Dryer, but then they turn down the lanes leading to the mill and he believes himself to be safe.

Beth Puddy is in a fearful state of exhaustion and apprehension by the time she finally reaches Alvington. The perspiration is running down her face and her heart is thumping wildly from her unaccustomed running. Out of habit she uses the tradesmen's entrance and then she runs wildly through the building until she literally bumps into Mrs Abbott.

"Miss Puddy, please calm down. Whatever is the matter?"

Beth bursts into tears, "I've lost Aurora, Mrs Abbott. I'm so sorry, but she just disappeared and we searched and searched the whole market, but she was nowhere to be seen. The mistress will never forgive me for this. I'm so sorry!"

Mrs Abbott looks horrified, but to her relief she takes control, "Come with me, Beth. We have to tell Lord Dryer immediately." Beth guiltily follows her to Lord Dryer's study. The housekeeper knocks on the door and they hear his request for them to enter. She takes a deep breath and then shamefacedly she follows Mrs Abbott into the room. She stands beside the kindly housekeeper with her head bowed as Mrs Abbott tells him what has occurred.

Lord Dryer seems to blanch at the thought of losing the child. "Did you see anyone suspicious in the vicinity at the time, Beth?" he asks her patiently.

"No sir, I saw nothing to alarm me. I'm so sorry, my lord. One minute she was looking at the display on the stand beside me and I was talking to some old friends, but the next moment she was gone! It happened so quickly, my lord. My friends helped me search, but there was no sign of her. Then one of the stallholders described seeing a tall man leading her away by the hand and driving off with her in his carriage."

"My God! How long ago was this?"

"It must be about an hour now, sir. I'm sorry, but I had to run all the way back here to let you know, because Billy wasn't coming to collect us until noon."

He looks at her sternly, "Beth, it is the second time you've allowed that family access to Aurora and this is the result! We've warned you to be vigilant! Placing more importance on chatting with your friends is just not good enough! You will have it on your conscience if any harm should befall her."

"I'm so sorry, my lord. I've been praying all the way here that she'll be found safe and sound and unhurt."

"I haven't time for this, I can see that you're devastated and I do know how cunning that man can be, but we trusted you with her safety! Please go back to your duties and I will call out the constables."

Beth follows Mrs Abbott from the room in a distressed state. Her master's anger is completely understandable. How will she live with herself if Aurora is harmed in any way or even worse, if she is never found?

On arriving at the mill, Aurora is extremely reluctant to descend from the gig. "I'm sorry but I really do have to go home straight away. My nanny will have alerted my parents by now and they'll be very worried and angry with me, if I'm absent any longer."

"Come on, Aurora, how often do I get the chance to spend time with you? I promise we'll be no more than a jiffy. I'd like you to meet my friends." He grabs her hand and pulls her down firmly. Giving her no choice he leads her into the building.

In the saloon bar there are a few of her father's cronies drinking and playing poker and he takes her to be introduced to the barman. "Hey Frank, this is my daughter, Aurora. Can you fetch us some punch, please?"

"You kept that quiet, Nathan. Didn't think you had it in you."

"Well, I believe you'd be surprised about that, my friend." He turns to Aurora, "She's a pretty little thing, don't you agree?" There is pride in his eyes as he looks down at her, then he fingers a lock of her hair and she cringes; it seems most inappropriate.

The other man looks her up and down like she is a prize cow in the cattle market and her discomfiture increases. He pours out two glasses of rum punch and her father slides her glass towards her. She feels obliged to drink out of politeness.

The other men in the room are leering at her lustfully, one of them is licking his lips and she nervously looks away from them. It's then that she notices a woman dressed in what appears to be her underwear, sitting on an elderly man's knee in the corner, behind the door. The man's right hand is busily kneading her exposed breast, like Flora making dough, but his tongue is halfway down her throat. *Whatever is this place?*

341

She takes a large gulp of her drink. It is pleasant enough, but she really feels uneasy … *I must go home now*. "Please can we go now, Father?"

"Yes, of course we can." He throws the remainder of his drink down his neck. "But first I just want to show you something." He takes her hand and leads her out of the saloon bar and along a scarlet-coloured corridor. The wallpaper is Chinese in style, with pagodas, oriental figures, blossom trees and storks decorating it. They pass several closed doors, but her father encounters the owner as they go along and they pause, chatting in the narrow passageway.

Aurora is standing just outside a door that is ajar. She can hear strange, rhythmic grunting and bedsprings squeaking; her curiosity is aroused and she looks through the opening. She can just make out a naked man leaning over a scantily-clad woman, who is in a crawling position on her knees on the bed. The revolting sight of the man's hairy backside pushing backwards and forwards into the woman is repellent and shocking. She feels sick with anxiety. *Why has my father brought me here, of all places?*

Suddenly he grabs her hand again. The owner has gone on his way, "Come Aurora." He drags her unceremoniously up a spiral flight of stairs, until they have reached an attic storeroom. The place is dirty and dusty with grain scattered in the corners and spider webs everywhere.

"What is this place?"

"It's the grain store for the mill."

Aurora is confused and fearful, "Why have you brought me up here?"

"I just want you to wait here for me for a while." With that he rushes out and closes the door behind him, turning a key in the rusty lock.

He's locked me in! She panics, her heart racing, "Wait! Father! I have to go home! You can't leave me here in this horrid place!" She bangs on the door angrily, but all she can hear are hasty footsteps, rapidly descending the stairs. She paces the room fearfully. *How could my own father treat me this way? He really is a villain! My parents were right after all!*

Aurora looks around her in despair. The room is dimly lit by two high, narrow windows. There is a pile of sacks full of grain along one wall and some empty sacks in the corner. The large hopper, where the grain is milled, is opposite the wide wooden door on the outer wall. She decides to open this door to see what is beyond and thus she sees how high up she is and how there is no escape. There are some workmen in the yard far below and she is fearful they will spot her. She doesn't want the lustful men in the bar to discover her, alone and vulnerable. As she quietly backs away from the opening, she notices the rope-pulley system for hauling up the sacks of grain; maybe that could be the solution? But she is so high up she feels dizzy and she silently pulls the door closed again.

She slumps down on the grain sacks feeling confused and bewildered, her mind going over and over her situation. *Where has my father gone…? Why has he imprisoned me here …? What does he want from me…? Will anyone else come up here and find me…? What will my parents do when they find I'm missing? They'll never think of looking for me up here!*

Joshua is fearful that Louisa is about to faint when he tells her of Aurora's abduction, but, after guiding her gently into the nearest chair, he has no choice but to leave her in Rosa's capable hands while he rushes off to call out the constables. He needs them with him, lest he be tempted to kill the man. His main purpose has to be to return Aurora to safety as soon as possible. His hatred of Meakins has to take second place to their daughter's safety.

Their first place of call is Summerville House and he can see that Olivia Meakins is horrified when the police constables have the audacity to search every room in their house.

She is angry and thin-lipped as she shouts at them, "He doesn't live here anymore! Why would you think he might be here with Aurora anyway?"

"I have it on good authority that she has been abducted by him."

Olivia looks surprised, but rallies quickly, "Surely he has the right to see his own daughter?"

"He has not earned the right to steal her," Joshua replies angrily. However, he persists in questioning her, "When did you last see your brother?" he demands.

He can see by her worried expression that she now realises this is serious. "Earlier today… he brought her here to introduce her to her *aunt* and *uncle* and her little *cousin*, but they left about two hours ago."

Her pointed references to their family relationships are like arrows to his heart, but he braces himself to continue with his questions, "If he no longer lives here, where is his current address?"

"It is Merry Meadows, in Ryme Intrinseca."

Joshua speaks to Sergeant Gundry and they rally the men. "We need to make haste to his home in Ryme Intrinseca."

"Right you are, sir."

Olivia is again belligerent when she shows them out. "I told you he wasn't here," she says haughtily. "There was no need for your men to go marching through our home in their clodhoppers!"

Nathan Meakins caught the scent of the green ash whilst chatting to William Bell earlier and its draw is so strong that he has recklessly put aside all else to surrender to its magical charms. He is now lying in blissful oblivion on his favourite chaise longue in a semi-trance.

Up at the top of the building Aurora is fearful that he has forgotten all about her. The poor light seeping in from the two high windows is ebbing, as the day turns to night-time and she is terrified of spending the night in this cold, dirty place all alone. *There must be rats up here and they'll surely come out after dark!* Bunny from the farm had told her that rats will eat babies. She is afraid she will fall asleep and the rats and spiders will crawl all over her. She cannot stop trembling and her eyes are sore from weeping. She longs for the comfort of her own bed and the safety of her own home. *Why didn't I heed my parents' warnings?*

She puts her hands together and prays earnestly for deliverance.

Joshua and the constables have no luck at Merry Meadows. The staff inform them that their master has been gone since first light and they know not where. Regardless of their protests the constables search the property thoroughly, but they find nothing incriminating.

Joshua is feeling angry and frustrated. This man has lead them a merry dance for long enough. He had, only yesterday, obtained legally authorised permission to peruse the man's bank records and, as suspected by Hugh Davies, he *had* returned from Australia with a large deposit of gold.

He looks at Sergeant Gundry, "This is where the miners' money has ended up!"

"Yes, you're quite right, the man is unscrupulous! We can arrest him now for suspicion of armed robbery and abduction. He will surely be tried and sent back to see out his days in incarceration."

Joshua snorts derisively, "It should be the noose, but I doubt we'll ever be able to obtain sufficient evidence of him murdering anyone in Australia." He longs for the dark shadow cast by this man to be gone from their lives forever, for Aurora's sake.

Sergeant Gundry then says, "I'm afraid we're getting nowhere here. However, I think we should leave some men behind, in case of his return; but where else could he be?"

Joshua urgently considers this, then he suddenly remembers where they found him the last time they arrested him. "Catkin Mill! The only other place I know where he feels quite at home is the Black Panther Club. Come on, let's make tracks, we've wasted enough time."

Nathan Meakins is awoken by someone wailing and screaming somewhere along the corridor. *They must have had a bad trip!* He stretches languorously and then he remembers he has unfinished business upstairs. He swigs downs the remainder of his glass of absinthe and struggles to his feet from the low chaise. His head is still a bit woozy, but he has a pretty filly waiting for him who has no idea what he has in store for her!

He takes up a lantern and slowly climbs the stairs, wobbling from wall to wall until he finally reaches the door into the grain store. *Now where did I put the key?* He fumbles in his pocket until he finds it.

Aurora has been fearfully trembling and weeping, listening to the rats scurrying around her in the shadows. Eventually she hears footsteps slowly ascending the stairs and someone shuffling about outside the door. She is terrified. In the darkness she blindly rushes to the opposite corner, hoping to conceal herself under the pile of empty sacks. She feels for the sacking, lifts off a layer and plunges beneath the dirty, dusty bags. She holds her breath, fearful lest it be one of the horrid men from the bar. The key turns slowly in the lock. She draws the bags over her head and lies silently in the pitch black, terrified of what is to come.

A man enters the room, holding a lantern before him. The rats scurry away. She peeps out between the bags and is momentarily blinded by the light. She cannot see who it is, but as her eyes adjust she can just make out his hands, as he relocks the door and pockets the key. The man hangs the lantern on a ceiling hook in the corner of the room and then at last, he turns and the light reveals his features. She breathes a huge sigh of relief when she sees it is her father. Overwhelmed with indignation she throws off the sacking and jumps up, startling him. "Where have you been?"

He smiles at her annoyance, but there is something odd about his expression, "I'm sorry. Did you miss me?" he slurs.

She is no longer weeping, but aware her hair is matted with dust and grain husks, she is very cross and even more frustrated by his strange behaviour. She looks at him disdainfully and says irritably, "I'm not used to being treated this way. Why did you leave me up here in this filthy place?"

He raises his eyebrows nonchalantly and hiccups, "I had things to do downstairs, but I'm here now."

"I thought you were a gentleman! I trusted you

to take care of me!" she protests, "What if those horrid men from downstairs came up and found me, what then?" Her face is flushed with anger as she challenges him.

He laughs at her, "You always were a spirited little minx." He pulls her down beside him on the bulky grain-filled bags and says persuasively, "Come on Millie, I don't have time for histrionics. I think you need to loosen up a bit. Here, have a little nip of this." He removes the cap from his silver hip flask and placing one hand behind her head, he forces some of the liquid between her lips. She tastes the strongly flavoured aniseed of his favourite tipple and tries to push him away, but he is strong and pours more down her throat until she is spluttering and coughing. She manages to grab the flask and throw it across the room, the fluid spilling onto the floorboards and a couple of rats running for cover.

"There was no need for that!" He hiccups again. "Whatever's come over you, Millie? You were always so obliging? I think I deserve an apology for that and I want a little kiss?" He unexpectedly lunges towards her, pushing her back until she is lying flat on the lumpy sacks.

Panic wells within her. She cannot believe he is so drunk that he believes she is her mother! She attempts to push him off her, protesting angrily, "I'm not Millie! I'm her daughter and I want to go home!" But it is as if he has gone deaf.

He kisses her on her mouth, his tongue intruding and touching hers and then he tries to put his hand up her skirt, but she frantically fights him off.

"Don't be a tease Millie, you know you like it." He leans his chest against hers, heavily pinning her down and, whilst trying to push her legs apart with his knee, he is fumbling with his breeches. Thinking quickly, and in desperation, she manages to bring her knee up to catch him in his crotch and he hollers out in pain and rolls off her. His lustful thoughts are obviously banished, with the painful throbbing in his breeches, but he is now the one who is most angry and Aurora knows she's in danger. She cannot appear weak.

She jumps away from him, her heart racing. Then looking back down at him she says contemptuously, "You're drunk! You called me Millie! You know very well that I'm Aurora. I'm supposed to be your daughter and this is how you treat me!"

Meakins' drink-fuelled and drug-hazed eyes attempt to focus on her and it's as if a fog has lifted as he replies, scornfully, "What makes you think that I could care less about a daughter? All I want is vengeance against your father, the high and mighty Lord Dryer. You're just a pawn in the scheme of things."

His mocking words cut deep into her soul; she feels worthless and unwanted. *No one deserves a father such as this!* She is deeply hurt and her voice is shaky, as she pluckily responds, "My parents were right all along, you're a mean, vindictive man and I understand completely now, why they were trying to protect me from ever knowing about you." She watches him warily as he continues massaging his painful crotch area.

He looks up at her, "Well, they're not here to protect you now, are they?" He sounds triumphant, "Your precious parents don't know you've been sneaking around meeting me on the quiet. Perhaps you're more like me than you think."

"I thought I ought to decide for myself. I wanted to give you a chance, to prove you could be my father, but this is not at all what I expected!"

Suddenly he is on his feet attempting to grab her,

but she manages to sidestep him. He sniggers, sensing her fear, "I'm not interested in being your father, Aurora. I have two incentives here. One is to get back at Dryer and the other is because you remind me of Millie and she was always up for a bit of hanky-panky. We have all night and I assure you, I haven't finished with you yet."

He is still unsteady on his feet and he staggers to the pile of grain sacks once more. She watches him warily as he appears to doze. Perhaps, if she was able to get her hands on the key, she could escape from the attic and hide somewhere until daybreak. She waits anxiously until his breathing is regular, then she plucks up the courage to approach him stealthily. He is leaning over to one side, thankfully exposing the pocket where the key is hidden. She gingerly slides her small hand into his pocket and draws out the key, her heart racing for fear of him grabbing her, but she is successful, his breathing is still regular. She swiftly turns away from him and creeps towards the door. The key makes a grating sound in the rusty old lock and the click sounds loud in the silence of the attic.

She is about to open the door and make her escape when, with a shout of, "Hold your horses, missy," he is up on his feet and across the room in seconds, slamming the door shut and dragging her away, until they are both slumped back on the grain sacks.

Her heart sinks; no one knows where she is and who would ever imagine she would be imprisoned in this dreadful place. She tries to reason with him, "You can't keep me a prisoner here. What would your sister Olivia, or little Senga, think if they knew what you were doing? You asked me to publicly acknowledge that I am in truth your daughter. Surely you can see that, by keeping me captive here, you're unlikely ever to achieve that."

"I think we both know we're beyond that now."

In the silence that follows his words she can just make out the sound of footsteps running up the narrow stairway and her heart thumps for renewed fear of her father's pals joining them and the danger she is in. She retreats back into the shadows, climbing onto the pile of grain-filled sacks, drawing her legs up under her and, regardless of the rats and spiders, pushing herself back into the furthest corner, fear contracting her throat.

The door suddenly bursts open and uniformed men swarm in. Nathan Meakins furiously lunges towards her, attempting to take her hostage, but she manages to kick him away. Thankfully, he is grabbed by one of the men, spun around and punched forcefully in the face. Again and again the man keeps angrily punching her father like a man possessed, until eventually two burly constables manage to hold him at bay. He struggles furiously trying to get back at him, but he is held fast.

"All right, my lord, he's had enough. We have him now and she is safe." They immediately arrest and handcuff Nathan Meakins. "You are under arrest for abduction of this young lady here tonight and armed robbery in Australia…"

Whilst they are reading him his rights, Aurora sees with relief that the angry, breathless man who took on her mad father, like a delivering angel, is her true papa. She drags herself shakily off the lumpy sacks and falls thankfully into his arms, weeping with joy and relief. He has found her and saved her.

Nathan Meakins cannot believe that after all he has gone through Joshua Dryer has again outwitted him. His only thought now is of getting away somehow. He cannot face further years of incarceration;

besides, this time he fears it will be the hangman's noose. His capturers stand between him and the stairway, but there is the loading door and there is hope. With a sudden surge of adrenalin he springs to life pushing the nearest policeman aside and running at the door, kicking it open and wildly leaping into the black night. He is falling fast, his legs madly scrabbling, when suddenly by some mischance (or by some unseen hand), he is caught around the throat by a tight grip that is squeezing… squeezing the life out of him. His hands, cuffed as they are behind his back, prevent him from releasing the grip of death from around his neck and his bodyweight is tightening the noose. There is nothing he can do. He coughs, chokes, kicks wildly, his eyes feel as if they are going to explode as he struggles, there is pain roaring in his brain and down his spine… his head and lungs are bursting. His whole worthless life passes before him, as he defecates and floats forever into eternal unconsciousness.

Joshua and Aurora immediately run to the opening. The moon is hidden behind thick clouds and all is in dark shadow below them. One of the constables grabs the lantern, holding it out over the drop and they can see the body of Meakins in the throes of death, swinging at the end of the tangled rope-pulley.

"Poetic justice," whispers Joshua to no one in particular, as he pulls Aurora away from the horrific sight and gives her a loving, comforting hug.

THE EPILOGUE *(June – October 1866)*

Mr Hugh Davies Esq
The Brecon Valley Mining Company
C/O Bendigo Post Office
Sandhurst
Victoria
South Australia

My Dear Hugh,

I am writing to inform you that you were quite correct, in that Nathan Meakins absconded with a large amount of gold that he deposited in the Wiltshire and Dorset Bank in the Borough in Ivell. He used the money to purchase an estate in Dorsetshire and therefore the estate will unfortunately have to be sold, before I am able to reimburse yourself and the other miners in Australia, but apart from the delay, I can see no difficulties otherwise.

I am afraid things rather came to a head regarding our mutual friend, when he abducted my daughter Aurora and held her in the attic grain store at a local mill. Thankfully, my daughter was discovered and rescued that same night, when Meakins was finally tracked down and arrested on Saturday 26th May. However, unfortunately for him, he attempted to escape. He died in a strangely appropriate freak accident, when he was hanged by the neck in the mill's tangled rope-pulley. So, at long last, his lawless reign of bitterness is over and we can all resume normality once more.

As soon as I have a buyer for Merry Meadows I will be contacting you again, and once the sale has gone through I will be able to authorise money orders for each of the named miners in your documentation. I hope this good news finds you well and settled with your family in Bendigo Creek.

Best wishes,
Joshua Dryer

16th August 1866

Dear Josh, Lou-Lou, Rora and Gaby,

I am so pleased and proud to be able to tell you that Becky gave birth to a healthy baby boy on Tuesday 12th August. He weighed 8lb 2oz and has his mother's dark hair and at the moment he has blue eyes. We are calling him 'Jem', as it goes so well with Stone. Becky says he is 'our little gemstone'. They are both doing very well and Becky is the happiest I have ever seen her.

I have been repairing and repainting all the external woodwork on Mermaid Cottage and the shutters are now robust enough to protect us from any future storms. I cannot thank you enough for your kindness, Josh.

With fondest wishes,

From your loving brother, sister, and little nephew;
Ben, Becky and Jem.

23rd August 1866

Dear Ben and Becky,

Many congratulations on the birth of young Jem from us all at Alvington Manor. We all like his name very well and are looking forward to visiting you shortly.

At present I am much involved with the installation of our new piped water and sewerage systems in Ivell and I am pleased that, at long last, the plans have been agreed and work has commenced, digging up the main roads to lay the network of lead piping. Naturally this has caused some problems with the local traders and it is going to be a long job for the navvies, probably taking us into the next decade, but in the long run the residents of the town will, I am sure, be very thankful.

We are planning our visit to Portland for the 3rd September, when Becky and the little one will be more settled, and looking forward to seeing all the family and our little Jem Stone.

With love from us all,
Joshua, Louisa, Aurora and Gabriel

4th October 1866

Mr Hugh Davies Esq
The Brecon Valley Mining Company
C/O Bendigo Post Office
Sandhurst
Victoria
South Australia

My Dear Hugh,

The sale has gone through without a hitch for Merry Meadows and I am happy to inform you that the Wiltshire and Dorset Bank have today transferred funds into the relevant bank accounts in Australia for reimbursing yourself and your fellow miners. There was some profit from the sale and I understand the bank has included the equivalent interest that would have been earned in the interim for the miners; any surplus cash we will divide *among the domestic staff who unfortunately lost their positions. I am extremely pleased to be able to organise this for you and glad that my unprincipled countryman did not get away with his dastardly plan.*

I trust you and your family are now quite settled and they are all happy and enjoying their new lifestyle.

With best wishes,
Joshua Dryer

HISTORICAL FOOTNOTE

Transportation to the Antipodes spanned the years 1787 to 1868. However, convicts were sent to Van Diemen's Land only between the years 1812 to 1853. This did not quite fit in with my novel's timeline for I am a year out, but I trust you will permit me poetic licence. I could have chosen New South Wales to send my character, but the prequel was dealing mainly with witchcraft and the 'Demon' connotations associated with Van Diemen's Land was irresistible. I have tried to keep in step with historical facts and dates throughout the rest of the novel and I trust you will allow me this small inaccuracy.

You may have expected conditions on board the transportation vessel to be more appalling than those described for my characters. This would have been the case much earlier, in the eighteenth century, when the prisoners were kept below, restrained in chains and behind bars in cramped, unhygienic conditions. Discipline was brutal and punishment by flogging was frequent. Numerous prisoners did not survive the journey; weakened by lack of food, dysentery, scurvy and fever, they died of diseases such as typhoid and cholera. This was at a time when any food supplies remaining at the end of the voyage where allowed to be sold by the ship owners to increase their profits. However, by the mid nineteenth century bonuses were paid to ship charterers for the safe landing of each prisoner and with the surgeons no longer in the pay of the ship's master, it meant that the prisoners' well-being was their main concern. Thus conditions and the survival rate improved.

With Bingham Lake I am also using poetic licence, because the lake wasn't formed until the construction of the Sutton Bingham Reservoir in the 1950s, but I found it difficult to imagine this area without it!

APOLOGIES

I would also like to apologise for a different discrepancy that accidentally occurred in *Dawn to Deadly Nightshade*. I am always extolling the virtues of word processing and the cut and paste facility is a real boon to writers, however it can also be a pitfall and one in which I fell into with my second novel. I had decided in the wedding scene to change *The Entrance of the Queen of Sheba*, as the bride entered the church, which sounded rather pompous for my character, to *The Wedding March* by Mendelssohn (which was originally as the bride and groom left the church) and swap it with *The Trumpet Voluntary* for the end of the ceremony, but in doing so I mistakenly left behind the words 'by Mendelssohn' and so poor Jeremiah Clarke was robbed of the glory of composing *The Trumpet Voluntary*. To Jeremiah Clarke and all those musical people who found it to be a glaring error, please accept my sincere apologies. Also for some reason *Jesu Joy of Man's Desiring* became *Jesu Joy of Man's Desire* and I am not quite sure how that happened, or went without correction!

These are the only two errors of which I am aware, in my second novel. However, I trust *Legacy of Van Diemen's Land* will turn out to be error free, but I ask you to forgive me in advance should you discover any in this one, or for that matter in *Brandy Row*. I hope you enjoy all three stories and would love to hear your comments on my Facebook page: The Heart of Stone Saga.

ACKNOWLEDGEMENTS

Thank you to all my family and friends for their support, particularly my husband Barry, my sisters Bridget and Maddy, and my daughter Nicky who all read the manuscript and gave their encouragement and advice. Thank you also to all the staff at Matador for their hard work and professionalism.